PRAISE FOR

FIND YOU IN THE DARK

"A well-crafted crime novel that proves utterly absorbing . . . with vivid scenes and complex psychology, *Find You in the Dark* lingers long after the last page has been devoured. And Ripley proves a stellar addition to the Canadian crime novel scene. An addictive debut."

Toronto Star

"Engrossing. . . . This debut thriller by the pseudonymous Ripley (Journey Prize winner Naben Ruthnum) is highly recommended for fans of Lee Child and C. J. Box."

Library Journal

"A fast-paced book . . . akin to dark British crime TV dramas such as *Broadchurch* or *Luther*, satisfyingly sinister and unsettling in their explorations of the violent possibilities of humanity."

The Globe and Mail

"Ripley . . . has come up with a fresh angle to the serial murder game . . . clever and diabolical . . . This unusual debut thriller has a lot going for it."

Kirkus Reviews

"A fast-paced, morbidly addictive novel of chilling infatuation. Ripley's impressive debut is a rich and innovative thriller."

IAIN REID, bestselling author of *Foe* and *I'm Thinking of Ending Things*

"A wickedly smart thriller that manages to be both chilling and wry. The page-turning plot . . . is thickened by a great cast of characters and Nathan Ripley's fantastic eye for detail and dialogue. Just when you think you've got a grasp on it, the story twists to new and darker places."

AMY STUART, bestselling author of *Still Water* and *Still Mine*

"An unsettling exploration of obsession you won't soon forget . . . a first novel that fans of Patricia Highsmith's psychological thrillers and Thomas Harris's cat-and-mouse suspense will devour. I certainly did."

ANDREW PYPER, bestselling author of *The Only Child* and *The Demonologist*

"Crafty and dark, Nathan Ripley's novel toys with the lines between predator and prey, his sentences as careful and considered as the crimes he depicts . . . a truly exciting new voice in the thriller world."

ROZ NAY, bestselling author of *Our Little Secret*

"It's not always easy diving into the mind of an obsessive protagonist, but Martin Reese's fixation on finding dead bodies makes for one heck of an addictive thriller . . . an original, inventive take on what happens when you go looking where you shouldn't."

JENNIFER HILLIER, author of *Jar of Hearts* and *Wonderland*

FIND

YOU

IN THE

DARK

NATHAN RIPLEY

PUBLISHED BY SIMON & SCHUSTER

NEW YORK   LONDON   TORONTO   SYDNEY   NEW DELHI

SIMON &
SCHUSTER
CANADA

A Division of Simon & Schuster, Inc.
166 King Street East, Suite 300
Toronto, Ontario M5A 1J3

This Simon & Schuster Canada edition May 2019

SIMON & SCHUSTER CANADA and colophon are trademarks of Simon & Schuster, Inc.

For information about special discounts for bulk purchases, please contact Simon & Schuster Special Sales at 1-800-268-3216 or CustomerService@simonandschuster.ca.

Manufactured in the United States of America

10 9 8 7 6 5 4 3 2 1

Library and Archives Canada Cataloguing in Publication
Title: Find you in the dark / Nathan Ripley.
Names: Ripley, Nathan, author.
Description: Reprint. Originally published: New York; London; Toronto; Sydney; New Delhi: Simon & Schuster, 2018.
Identifiers: Canadiana 20190064773 | ISBN 9781982131876 (softcover)
Classification: LCC PS8635.I65 F56 2019 | DDC C813/.6—dc23

ISBN 978-1-9821-3187-6
ISBN 978-1-5011-7908-2 (mass)
ISBN 978-1-5011-7903-7 (pbk)
ISBN 978-1-5011-7907-5 (ebook)

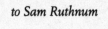

to Sam Ruthnum

BELLA GREENE LEFT HIS APARTMENT FOR WHAT SHE knew was going to be the last time. He didn't know that, would never believe his grip on Bella was so fragile after all the humiliations she'd gone through at his whim, but it was true. She wasn't going back.

She was outside his apartment building, which she'd left without making eye contact with the concierge. He had a Stalin mustache that was always flecked with brown cigarillo fragments and leered at her when she buzzed up alone, once asking her, "How much?" Bella had spat on his desk, a nice thick gob on the marble. He'd laughed at her and wiped it up.

"Tell him when you go up, see if he believes you," he'd said. Bella hadn't bothered.

There was a dry fountain outside the building, turned off some arbitrary day toward the end of summer. Bella walked by it, picking up speed as she got farther from the building. When she was nine, her mom had caught her picking through the change in a fountain for the silver coins.

She'd gotten a slap on the arm for that, in front of the other moms and Marianne, her best friend at the time, who betrayed her at the end of the fifth grade to hang out with Kelly Robinson, a tall girl whose parents had cable.

It was well past midnight, not much pedestrian traffic, but a slouching man coming out of a building identical to the one she'd just left smiled at her, and not just politely. Expectantly, like she had an offer for him.

"No," Bella said, walking past. This was the problem: she'd never gotten to the point of effectively taking back from these guys who constantly wanted to grab from her. Something. Anything. For a while she'd liked the free drinks, then the free drugs, then she found that the longer she stayed around the clearer it was that neither was free. Especially the drugs.

That slouching guy was still following her. It had been half a block, Bella thought. He might just have been walking to his car, but there were eyes on her. She knew that. Had a sense for it. The guy upstairs, he was her first successful use: thought he was getting something out of her, some sort of bizarro sex challenge, but she was just pretending his pathetic desires and fantasies were extreme, going along with them as long as she felt she had to. Bella had needed a place to stay and someone stupid to talk to while she got free of it, the last piece of her old life: the people, the tapering grip of heroin, then methadone, even booze. She hadn't had anything other than orange pekoe tea for three weeks. She'd shaken it—not just the stuff, but the life. She'd be in San Diego by the end of the week, out of Seattle and ready to invite her mom down for visits. Nice, normal, family visits, with none of the bullshit, the stealing. The lying.

Bella rolled the leaves of her silver bracelet on her arm and felt the eyes on her again, this time from her right. An alley, some sort of truck or big vehicle in the shadows. A man leaning on the fender.

"Keep looking," Bella called out, walking on, before stopping and turning to face the guy again. He leaned his torso back, out of reach of the light, and laughed a little. Bella walked toward the alley.

"You get off on scaring women? You that kind of creep?" She came a step closer to the guy—he was wide across the chest, tall, his face still hidden. She didn't expect him to be so fast. Guys that size never were.

There was a pain in her neck as he gripped her by the shoulder and his other hand whipped toward her throat, a feeling altogether unlike the punch she was expecting. Deeper than an insect sting, but the rush of injection afterward was profound, hot, almost calming. She'd never pierced that particular vein before.

Bella Greene didn't fall to the pavement: the man caught her and lifted her backward, into the dark.

1

CLEANING UP THE DIG SITE TOOK LONGER THAN
usual, leaving me little time to sleep. I grabbed two
hours in my tent and was on the highway to Seattle by four a.m., with
a thermos of coffee and some of those legal speed-drinks truckers use. I
would have been at the club an hour ago, if the traffic had cared about
getting my daughter from swim practice on time as much as I did.

I checked the rearview to make sure I'd ditched every piece of my
equipment, and that only camping gear was visible in the back. Nothing
was sticking through. My scrapbook was under, not on top of, the backseat where Kylie would throw her gym bag. Looking for traces of dirt or
worse on the fabric of the seats, I almost missed an old Camry turning
illegally across my lane. I tapped then slammed my brakes, accepting the
honks from behind me and kept going, finally pulling up at the curb.

"You're late," Kylie said, falling into the front seat and throwing her
gym bag overhand into the backseat, nicking my eyelid with the strap.
She waved out the open door at Danielle, or Ramona, or one of the other

fourteen-year-old girls on her team—after practice, they all looked eerily identical, with their wet hair gathered and tucked into wool hats and their collars pulled up. Sliding her schoolbag to rest at her feet, Kylie looked hard at me. Driving to the Seattle Athletic Club at five in the morning for half the week and five in the afternoon for the rest of it is only sane behavior under very specific conditions. Vanity couldn't have gotten me to do it. Love, probably not—not the wife-kind of love I had for Ellen, anyway. For Kylie, I did it, sometimes to my own surprise. I'd been late eight times in the past two years, and this was the ninth.

There was enough resemblance between us—the dark eyebrows, light blue eyes—and between her and Ellen—the narrow nose and the wide mouth, equally suited to smiling or abrupt dismissal—that getting stared down by Kylie was like being in trouble with my wife and confronting a disappointed reflection at the same time.

"Leave before anyone sees you, Dad. Screeching tires."

I pulled out at normal speed, but got the message. "Sorry. I drove right here from the campsite. Would have cleaned up at a truck stop if I knew I was going to embarrass you."

"Where were you again?"

"Place near Tacoma. Beautiful." I had indeed registered and paid in full for a slot at a campsite in Kent, near Tacoma, setting up a small tent there before setting off for my drive to California, just to have a paper trail if I got asked later, by Ellen or anyone else. Anytime I went on a dig it was a cash-only affair. Usually I "forgot" my phone charger, letting that GPS tracker we all carry fade to a dead-battery flicker by the time I was a few miles from the city. Other times, when I knew Ellen would be calling me, I disabled anything that would make me trackable. Twenty years of working in tech had left me with a skill or two, not just a bunch of money.

"You're late, and you stink," said Kylie.

"You stink, too."

"Chlorine isn't a stink. It's a scent."

"I smell of pines and fresh air and the glory of the outdoors, not the stuff they put in a pool to neutralize pee."

"You smell like unwashed old man, Dad." She was looking at her phone, and I was looking at the road, but I could feel her holding laughs in, just like I was. For the last year or so, this was what getting along had sounded like: an enjoyable exchange of insults, not much meant by either party. I'd never picked her up right after a trip to the field, and I was surprised how quickly one responsibility synched into the next. Next to the part I played in making Kylie, my digs are the best thing I've done with my life. Nothing that has happened since I started looking and finding has ever shaken me in that belief.

At the end of our block, I asked Kylie something I should have asked her back at the pool so I could prep.

"How's Mom? Things were good while I was away?"

"Noooope," Kylie said, popping in her fourth piece of the near-flavorless natural gum Ellen bought by the case in an attempt to keep aspartame and sugar out of the family's bloodstreams.

"Oh," I said. Ellen's car, a VW from last year, was approaching the house from the other side, the sun coming down behind it and beaming orange light through the back window to silhouette her head. I slowed down and let Ellen get into the garage long before I hit my blinker and turned in.

Ellen was waiting for us inside, a grocery bag in each hand and the leather strap of her purse in her mouth. While Kylie deliberately took her time getting her stuff together, I got out of the Jeep and walked over to Ellen, hopping up the two steps to the door that opened into our house, feeling the stiffness in my legs and arms from the strain of digging for hours and then sitting down for a long drive. I took both grocery bags from her and she keyed us inside.

"Am I in for another high-tension week?" I asked Ellen, being quiet even though Kylie was still sitting in the Jeep and likely would stay there until her mom and I were in the kitchen and she could safely bypass us both on her way to the upstairs shower.

"Oh, I didn't realize the point of all of this was to minimize impact on you, Martin. Real sorry." She smiled midway through telling me off and gave me a kiss.

Ellen wasn't good at maintaining the exasperated spouse stance, even if she'd had plenty of time to practice. She'd stopped being my girlfriend and started being my wife eighteen years ago.

"You stink," she said.

"Your wonderful daughter said the same thing."

"We got in a small fight on Saturday. Should have been a mini one but we were both tired and it got out of hand. She wanted to sleep at Jhoti's house after they went for dinner. The dinner was planned, the sleepover wasn't, so I said no."

"Firm no?" I started emptying out one of the paper bags item by item, avoiding the tomato sauce spatter and sticky milk-glass rings on the counter: the tidiness of the kitchen, in particular, tended to fall off when I was away in the woods. Ellen was watching me, so I just upended the bag and let the produce tumble out for sorting. I'm good at faking carefree.

"With sleepovers or late nights out, all my no's to her are firm, Mart, you know that. I didn't think I needed to bicker about it with her or you anymore. It's just the way it is."

"Yeah." I slit a small plastic bag of plums open with my thumbnail, which still had a rim of dirt under its white crescent, a leftover from disposing of the dig tools. I was always thoroughly gloved-up when I was doing the actual work, never leaving any of my skin free to flake over or touch my finds. The fruit tumbled into a wooden bowl on the counter, covering up a shrinking, aged lime. "But I think we'll all have to talk again about this, and soon. She's hitting fifteen in what—five weeks?" Before Ellen could answer, I added, "You were totally in the right, stick with the plan this weekend—not that you need me to confirm. What we need to talk about is if we can be more flexible on future plans for her, not last-minute changes. She's not a kid."

"I was less worried when she was a kid," Ellen said, without the half-smile that I guessed most parents would add. She could tamp her fears down, but the worry was always there, a pressing anxiety I could feel as a static pulse in the room when she didn't know where Kylie was. She was stocking the fridge, still wearing the wet waterproof shell that transformed her upper body into a rumpled cylinder, disguising the combination of elegant dress and ultrafitness she'd moved toward after Kylie was born. I hadn't given birth to any figure-destroying children, but was the proud, or at least unashamed, guardian of a healthy gut I bottle-fed with pilsner every evening.

I heard Kylie's feet on the stairs and took the chance to dodge out. "I don't know if that's true, but I get what you're saying. Going to unpack the Jeep," I said. "You two play polite until I get back so we can all fight together, okay?"

The camping stuff I stowed in various places in the garage. I always returned lighter than I had left, because I ditched the digging gear, probes, and metal detector in various dumpsters on the way back, after carefully treating everything with solvents, bleaches, and other corrosives fierce enough to chew through the paint on steel and definitely to destroy any genetic traces. Anything I camped in or sweated in and brought back never came anywhere near the actual site of a dig; my focus when I was at work out there was absolute, but the rush of being right, of finding what I was looking for, could get so powerful I had to have a strict procedure on every dig. That meant setting up camp at least three miles away from each site, digging from early afternoon into dusk, going more gently when I thought I was near enough to bring out the brushes. I'd never broken anything yet, and I was proud of that. It showed respect.

The garage was peaceful, as quiet as the air around me last night, when all I could hear was the silvery chop of my shovel cutting into the dirt above the bones I knew I was about to find. I rehearsed a few lines in my head for the call to the cops I'd be making later that night; I'd been running a few variants on the drive back, testing out what they sounded like in my own voice, a voice I could never let the police hear.

I folded and buckled the last bit of tenting and was left with just the ticking sound of our car engines, mine finally relaxing after the long haul from Northern California that had left me more tired than I could ever explain to Ellen. A syrupy can of Red Bull from the flats of canned goods on the shelves above my stowed camping gear would have to do the work of wiring me up. I opened up the back door of the Jeep and slid out the big, mid-2000s Apple PowerBook I used as my scrapbook, safely cased in a padded canvas slip.

Inside, I took the scrapbook to my enormous desk at the end of the hall and unlocked the bottom drawer. Slipping the scrapbook inside, I fought a deep compulsion to flip it open.

"Can you check if the City Light payment went through?" Ellen called, her voice curving around the hall from the kitchen, where she was probably sitting on the counter eating one of the plums, or rooting around in the little clothes basket she kept in there for quick postwork changes into comfort wear.

"Look on your phone," I called back, locking the drawer and testing it with a quick, light pull.

"I don't trust the stupid app. Just do it, okay? And when were you planning to throw this lime out?"

"That's your lime," I said. "I thought you were holding onto it. Any limes I buy I put in the fridge, which is where limes belong."

"Smartass," she called, then lapsed into silence, waiting for me to actually enter the room to go on with the conversation. I wasn't ready yet. Talking to Kylie could pull me back into the world rapidly after a dig, and it had, but I still needed a second of total peace to reset my brain to domestic mode, my internal parallel to Ellen's change of clothes. My desk faced a blank wall that I wouldn't allow any paintings or photos to invade. No distractions, just me and that huge block of oak with its four canyon-deep drawers. Only the bottom drawer stayed secure to keep my scrapbook from prying eyes. Not that there were any of those in the household, other than my own. Ellen wasn't into snooping. She was as trustworthy in our home as she was behind her desk at the credit union, and it didn't occur to Kylie that her dad's business could contain anything of interest. I shut my eyes, got where I needed to be, then stood.

"You seen my phone charger, the kitchen one?" I said, rounding the corner.

"It's in here, genius. The kitchen," Ellen said while I fumbled the plug off the counter and into the socket. "You going to be cooking?" I could feel the gaze and turned to it. She'd worked a regular eight-hour day but looked more tired than I was.

"I'm not, and neither are you." As my phone buzzed back to life I pressed it onto speaker and dialed the Szechuan place in the strip plaza a few blocks away, a place that mainly did takeout but delivered for us, because I tipped twenty bucks. "Salt and pepper squid, yeah, ginger beef—"

"Lemon chicken," Kylie almost screamed from the top of the banister, with a desperation that even got her mother to forget they were fighting for a moment and laugh.

"Lemon chicken," I said into the phone, pretty sure the guy on the other end had heard her anyway. Kylie thumped back into her room, and I turned to Ellen with a look on my face that must have been apologetic.

"What?"

"I'm going out tonight. Meeting Keith for a beer," I said.

"Cop Keith? So you're out camping for two days, you come back, and we lose you right away to the police?" This time there was a slight pout in her voice, but it was still miles away from real complaint.

"We'll have a good dinner and good talk, okay? And I have no plans of going anywhere for the rest of the week. Honestly, I'm pretty run down, but you know how Keith is. Feels like a bad idea to put off meeting him when he's in one of his urgent moods."

"I don't feel like fighting with you and Kylie at the same time, so I'm going to pretend I'm fine with it until I actually feel that way."

"I am sorry, Ellen, really."

Ellen only knew about Keith at all because she'd spotted us having coffee a few years ago, across town from her work. She'd taken a half-day off to look for new curtains, and instead came across her husband having a nice midafternoon date with a policeman. I'd invented an elaborate but tight lie about meeting Keith in a long lineup at the post office one day: I talked him through various personal issues sometimes, in exchange for exciting cop-life stories. Ellen seemed to like the idea of me having a pal I helped out, since my social time was mostly spent with her, Kylie, or alone at home. Or in the woods.

I slid-walked over to her in my socks—we'd only put in the slick hardwood floors four months earlier, and I didn't think I'd ever get sick of doing that *Risky Business* drift or rolling across the floor in my office chair when I got a beer or club soda from the fridge. When I reached Ellen, I pillowed my head on her shoulder and said, "Sorry." She patted the back of my head, then gently pushed her fingertips against my forehead. Ellen always kept her own nails short, dispensing with what she called "manicure-bitch bullshit," which she associated with a couple of loathed coworkers.

"Everyone will be in a much more forgiving mood if you take a shower. Immediately," she said.

"Okay." I took the stairs two at a time. Kylie's bedroom door was closed, and a Drake song that had grown on me despite deep resistance pulsed through loud enough to be heard in the bathroom. I hummed and showered off the dirt and sweat, then took out as much of the muscle tension as I could with the high-pressure showerhead. When I came out the music was off and Kylie was standing at the head of the stairway.

"If you ever sing along to anything I love again, I'm going to move out," she said.

"Be my guest. I'll donate your trust fund to a chimp sanctuary if you do."

"I love chimps."

"It's a deal, then, sure."

Ellen was going for her purse, the delivery guy at the door, by the time we got downstairs. I pulled the wallet out of the inside pocket of my jacket, hanging on the rack by the door, and paid him off. He looked relieved to see me, the customary giver of the extra twenty.

"I was going to pay," Ellen said when the door was closed.

"I know, I just got there first."

"I was going to give your stupid huge tip, too. I hate it when you're fiddly about money stuff, Martin." She'd pulled on a U of W sweater, one she'd owned since I met her in class back when we were both in college. She barely looked older than Kylie, adrift in the enormous garment. I could remember seeing that sweater for the first time, an October afternoon two decades ago, when I followed Ellen back to her apartment building from class after I found out who she was, who her sister was. The fabric was rich purple then, not the grayed-out blue it was now. I was a professional at following, back then—Ellen didn't see me, even when I was directly across the street, or right behind her, close enough to pluck the scrunchie out of her hair if I wanted to.

I did want to, but I controlled myself. And it paid off.

"Obviously you could have paid, I didn't mean—"

"Don't soothe me like a child, Mart." She sighed, a short one, seemed to reorient herself. She did this sometimes, a sort of thinking-in-real-time thing that ran counter to the calculated way I had to do everything. I admired it. "Forget it. We have to talk about some bigger things this week. Along with whatever you want to float about Kylie, I need to talk to you about my career. I was going to do it tonight but I guess that's not possible anymore." We could hear Kylie clattering plates in the other room. She liked to undo the takeout containers and use them as the serving plates, but knew that when her mom or I dished out the food we used proper bowls. She set the takeout-table up much more quickly than she'd perform any other kitchen task.

"Yes. Soon. Whenever you want, just when I can give you my full attention."

We sat down and started to eat, hard, the three of us. Kylie was refueling after a no doubt brutal swim practice, her coach screaming something about nationals and hustle no matter how far away they were. My heart rate was still up from the energy slugs and caffeine, and I needed the food to start flattening out again. Ellen chewed with quiet purpose, a little anger, and the suspense of the conversation we were about to have. I was going to start but Kylie did instead, with a little less elegance than I would have hoped.

"Mom still thinks I'm going to get murdered anytime I'm out of the house past ten."

"Oh," Ellen said, with an authentic pain that made Kylie wince, as her newly braces-free teeth nipped a piece of beef off her chopsticks. She'd been going for a fight, not an injury.

"Never say that again, Kylie. That would be past the line in any house, let alone this one," I said.

"You're right, Martin," Ellen said. She'd put down her sticks, and looked like she was reaching for Kylie's hand, then thought better of it and grabbed the bottle of Sriracha, making a red pool of the sauce at the edge of her plate. "I can't believe you, Kylie. Yes, I do worry more than a normal mom would. I ask you to understand that, Kylie. My anxiety creeps up. And it's not something pills can take care of. It's a real leftover from a real thing that happened."

"Tinsley," Kylie said. Ellen had wanted to name Kylie after the vanished sister, but I'd asked her not to. It would just make things worse, I'd said, back when we found out she was pregnant, a little after I started ReeseTech and began digging seriously.

"Yes, Tinsley," Ellen said. "Noises from the street talk to me when neither of you are here. Even when it's totally quiet. I think about my sister, how strong and bulletproof she seemed, and then I think about you, and how no matter how strong I think you are or you think you are, there are men out there who want exactly that. A strong girl to hurt and crush and kill. I wonder if you get that."

Kylie was quiet, so I winced for us both. I couldn't bring myself to interrupt, but I hunched over my noodles, shoveling them in and listening closely. Ellen had never spoken this graphically about Tinsley to our daughter, at least not when I was around. At her most serious, Ellen could talk to you and make it seem like she was talking to herself, like you'd intruded on a truth she hadn't intended to share.

"That fear I have when you're out, when we haven't planned where you are, when I don't know where you are, Kylie? It's a pretty legitimate way to feel, I think. Even if it was twenty years ago." Ellen looked at me and I nodded, then looked at Kylie.

Twenty years. She had it right: next week would be the anniversary of Tinsley Schultz's disappearance. I understood what Ellen lived with, the emotional intensity of her days and years after that vanishing. I still had my own leftovers to deal with when I saw a woman with a certain kind of hair or neck, or heard a laugh that had the right combination of unashamed enjoyment and elegance. I made a point of never looking for too long—I had to concentrate to make sure I never went back to the person I was in college, when I was following Ellen. But I kept every one of those impulses stored up for my digs.

"But we need to find a way that you can have a normal teenage life and that I can feel comfortable, is what your father is about to say, right, Martin?"

"I was gearing up for that. Look, can you two start eating so we can do this without knowing that the reward at the end is cold Chinese food?" This didn't get a laugh, but there was a hairline crack in the tension, and chopsticks started moving again.

"The thing we need, all of us, is to talk in advance, premeditate, stay in touch. No last-minute plans for you, Kylie, and you have to make sure your phone is charged up and you text your mom back as quickly as you text Ramona back."

"You can't talk, Dad. We never hear from you when you're out camping or whatever."

"No one's worried about me. We worry about you, okay?"

"Yeah."

"I'm not insane," said Ellen. "Your aunt was kidnapped and murdered."

"We don't know that," I said.

"I do. I know that. She would never have left us without saying why, and she would have come back to us by now. I just fucking worry about my daughter, okay?" For a second Ellen seemed to have forgotten that said daughter was at the table, because she never swore in front of Kylie.

"Mom. Mommy. I know. I just need to—we can organize it, I can make sure you know where I am when I'm not here. But someday I'll be at college and then someday maybe in another city, so we have to start to find a way to make us both feel good about this, alright?"

Annoyed that Kylie had found a better way to put this than I had, but proud enough to mask it, I ate while they talked, checking my watch. I had an hour and ten. I was meeting Keith to get more files, ones he'd been hyping up for days as being the best ones yet. He said that every time, but I couldn't resist being excited, anticipating what he'd have for me, who'd be inside those scanned pages. Ellen and Kylie were still talking when I left, about swimming, about a celebrity divorce, about an upcoming break from the rain, not about kidnapping and murder. Our greasy plates were still on the table, and my goodbyes were barely noticed.

I couldn't stay patient about looking at my scrapbook any longer, though. I had to go back to my desk before I left. Leaving my family talking, I moved down the hallway, quietly keyed the drawer open and slid the scrapbook out. It powered up in a few seconds, the old software rustling to life, aided by the processor and the rest of the new parts I'd swapped into the machine, and I clicked open the ancient version of iPhoto where I'd dumped yesterday's pictures before wiping my camera. I sat and rotated my chair so I could see both screen and kitchen doorway at once. It would just be a quick flip-through—I couldn't allow myself to lose my grip on time, not with Kylie and Ellen so close by.

The first shot was of my shovel, as it always was, the blade of this tool I'd only use once before laying it to a dishonorable dumpster rest like its predecessors. My left hand had been just outside of the frame of this photo, gloved, ready to start, to seek her out in the earth that had hidden her for decades.

Then: the dig site unspoiled, if dirty with highway trash, shots of the markers I'd laid out, of the evidence of a small mound only a few feet away from where I'd estimated it would be from the case files. I looked up at the kitchen door and counted out five seconds with my right index finger on my left wrist, a trick I had to slow my pulse. I flicked through the rest of the pictures quicker, wanting to get to the end before the voices in the kitchen slowed and I had to stow the scrapbook and leave. I made it through the digging, the carefully arranged dirt, until I finally hit the first bone: an ulna, the thin forearm bone of a woman in her early twenties. The next few pictures uncovered the rest of her, showing how carefully I'd taken the dirt off her yesterday evening.

2

I DROVE MY JEEP THROUGH THE NARROW, SLOPED
streets around my home before surrendering to the
traffic leading downtown. It wasn't quite rush hour thick, and I was
heading in the right direction, but progress was still slow. At least Seattle
drivers can handle rain; throw more than three days of snow at the roads,
and it begins to look like the least-fun bumper cars ride you can conceive
of. I was heading for a 7-Eleven near the Pemberton, where I'd be meeting Sergeant Keith Waring after I finished what I had to do.

I'd gone to California to find the bones of Winnie Mae Friedkin,
a hitchhiker who'd vanished in 1976. She'd been one of the many
(fourteen, give-or-take) victims of Horace Marks, the dull truck driver
who'd spent a year doing conventional pick-up-and-kills along the Pacific Coast Highway. If he had a refrigerated load, he picked up young
women in Cali, did what he did, then threw them in the back and
waited until reaching Washington State to get rid of them. Not exactly
a brilliant strategy, but spreading the distance between kill and burial

was a sure way of keeping some of those bodies in the ground forever.

Marks had supposedly forgotten most of the burial sites by the time he was arrested in a nearly botched operation that had eleven plain-clothes female cops nervously extending their thumbs along that high-way in 1977, trolling truck stops for rides from likely psychos, or just pretending to be lot lizards. Marks had picked up Officer Dana Brant just north of Newbury Park, and when he reached his strangling hands toward her, she took a Beretta out of her cowboy boot and shot him in the stomach. He's still in jail, and still suffers from major digestive issues.

I parked a couple blocks away from the 7-Eleven and started putting on my non-disguise. No facial putty, no wig. Just a toque, glasses, and a hooded rain slicker over the top of my perfectly adequate Barbour jacket. The cut of the jacket was too good: expensive stuff looks expensive, even on a closed-circuit camera. The cops didn't have the time to put much legwork into tracking the calls I made, but if they ever decided to dedi-cate hundreds of hours to scanning security footage at the stores that sold these phones, I wanted to be more or less covered.

I made a rainy dodge through alleys where a couple of bums were setting up lean-tos with their shopping carts and lengths of blue tarp, the construction-site discount versions of the expensive forensic plastics I used when I was out on my digs.

One called out "Change?" as I walked by. I passed him two loose dollar bills I had in the back pocket of my jeans. I couldn't say what he looked like, and he couldn't say what I looked like; he kept his eye on the cash and I kept mine straight ahead, walking in an unmemorable businessman stride through that dirty alley and then onto the suit-and-umbrella crowded pavement in front of the convenience store. I paid for a disposable cell, preloaded with the minimum number of minutes. I'd be using less than five. Maybe ten if pickup times at 911 were bad.

Winnie May was victim number eight, one of the five Horace Marks couldn't locate for the cops when they drove him up and down the highway in the months leading up to his trial. The files Keith provided showed that even an idiot like Marks enjoyed the concealing game; he liked having the girls out there, in the ground, a hidden monument to what he'd done. The only time he came close to dropping a hint about one of the girls he supposedly couldn't locate, it went right past Bobby Flowers, the lieutenant who was grilling Marks with decreasing patience. The transcript likely left out a few well-deserved beatings.

> I bought Winnie ice cream. She wanted a sundae, hot
> fudge, only that. Not a cone. I let her finish it
> before I did her.

Not much in the way of a clue, but that's the crucial thing about digging through old files. You have to look for things that cops, smart cops, missed at the time. There's always at least one or two keen guys in the department who look through the file, scanning for details, hoping to amp up their careers by spotting something everyone else missed. But they're looking for something important.

I'm looking for something so dull, so trivial and off-the-cuff, it escaped everyone's ears at the time, and all the scanning eyes that looked at this same file until the cops stop caring about a given victim, when the perp has been in jail for long enough that he's a memory, not a case. And the girl, the body in the ground, is remembered by barely anyone, just as a grainy picture on a true crime site. And by her parents, who won't forget her until they're dead as well.

Back in the car, I shed the extra gear and stuffed it in the backseat, then set up my scrapbook, cueing the voice program. I twisted the key in the ignition and started moving, starting the Jeep in a loop of downtown. I dialed the cell.

"911, what is your emergency?"

I didn't even breathe into the phone, just set it snugly on top of one of the speakers, pressed the spacebar, and kept driving. The automated, dull voice talked through the operator's questions, which I couldn't hear, but were no doubt still happening.

That is the exact location of Ms. Winnie Mae Friedkin, lately of San Francisco, victim eight of scumbag Horace Marks, currently resident of San Quentin. I found her the way I found the others: by doing your job. She was in a cluster of trees—beech, I believe—about two hundred feet behind what used to be a Dairy Queen in 1976, and is now an out-of-business outdoor equipment shop. Glennis Camping, a victim of the recession. She was only shallowly underground. My metal detector picked up her zipper, her rings, her St. Christopher medal. It was a quick and easy dig. Tell her mother so. What you didn't do to find her. Tell her mother that she can bury her daughter now, and it's no thanks to you. Goodbye.

I waited until the coordinates were read out and the message had stopped playing, then clicked the cell off and put it in one of the cupholders, still circling blocks and driving around downtown until the most paranoid frequency in my mind had calmed, was sure that not even the most cunning satellite could triangulate the short call the cops had just received.

I pulled up to the Pemberton, an almost-dive in the lobby of one of the cheaper downtown hotels. A place I'd met Keith once before, about two years back. I got a perfect parking space right out front, but had to think for a second about which direction to angle my tires on the steep uphill incline. I got out, rain wicking off my jacket where it had beaded on the plastic piece of shit in the backseat of the Jeep. I slipped my new temp cell phone into a rain gutter by the rear tire and walked on.

Keith would be in one of the dark back booths, so I made my way past the small crowd around the bartender. Keith got drunk somewhere or other every night, from what I'd seen, but I'd made sure he'd kept the Pemberton off his list of regular stops since our first meeting here. On the nights I met up with him, he left the station a little early so he could start drinking sooner, as I'd be picking up the tab. I'd followed him carefully before the first few times we met, flipping on those old surveillance skills. I made damn sure he wasn't trying to set me up before I started buying his files and putting them to use.

The Pemberton's big hook to early drinkers is the steam trays of free food brought down in the early evening, the kind of perk you're more likely to see in a strip club than a straight drinking establishment. It's been ages since I've been to the strippers on one of the regular weekend expeditions the ReeseTech guys would goad me, the boss, into joining. I recall the shows seeming more like grim anatomy lessons set to music than entertainment. I also remember the food being a good sight better than the sweating microwaved tacos that sat in a sad pyramid on the Pemberton's bar.

They keep the beer lines very clean, though, knowing enough to avoid tampering with their moneymaker. The crowd is dense on the frequent rainy nights, businessmen and construction workers bundled in together, waiting out a downpour they know won't end before they absolutely have to set out for home, but that will encourage them to have another drink.

Despite the packed booths and maze of occupied barstools in my way, it wasn't hard to spot Keith. Three hundred pounds of bulk with incongruous Paul Newman eyes embedded near the top. He was leaning back, watching for me, taking sips from his pint and eating a gherkin. "Always face the door," he'd said solemnly during our first meeting. "Keep an eye on them, because you know they're going to be keeping an eye on you." I still wasn't sure who "they" were, but I was soon entirely certain Keith was a complete idiot whose only worth was in the goods he had to sell me, and the cowardice that would always keep our secret safe.

"Have a seat, Mart," Keith said, grandly offering me the damp and torn upholstery of the banquette opposite. As long as one of us was facing the door, we were apparently both okay. "I've brought treats and treats for you. How was California?"

Before I could get an answer out, he was flagging down the waitress and ordering a pair of Dead Guy Ales. Despite our business here, it wasn't an ironic order. Keith lacked imagination, and Dead Guy tasted good.

"Haven't been to California since I retired," I said, suppressing my shock. "Silicon Valley douches wore me out. Ellen still goes down, though."

"It hurts me when you bullshit your friend Keith. I know a direct hit when I get one. The guys were talking about the latest pile of bones before I left, thinking it was maybe an old deposit of that trucker guy's. Guy who owns the lot came across the hole before you could make your little phone call. Probably just missed you by a couple hours." Keith waited to see if I would fill in Horace Marks's name. I filled my mouth with beer instead, and let him try his best grinning stare-down. The fact that I'd just missed being discovered by a couple of hours underlined what I'd been thinking for months: the next dig was going to be the last.

"Fair enough," Keith said. "I'll see if a certain someone has called in a certain find when I go in tomorrow. It'll be all the answer I need."

"What have you got for me, Keith? Anything? I'm pretty tired here."

"Husbanding-and-fathering is tough even when you're retired and filthy rich, right?"

"Yeah. Right, Keith." I could see him getting annoyed, and since I wanted to at least see what he was going to offer me, I added a smile. Keith probably liked having a captive audience almost as much as he liked the money I gave him.

"Why did you retire, anyway, Martin? Your hobby's not full-time stuff. Don't you miss being a dot-com superstar?"

"Your terminology's a little out of date, Keith, but I get what you mean. When Kylie was about eight, after a couple-month stretch where I'd been working minimum ninety-hour weeks, we took her on a trip to a cottage I used to own in Oregon. Kylie and Ellen and our nanny had been out a couple of times, but me, never. We were dozing on the beach by the lake, the three of us, then Ellen wakes up and starts screaming for Kylie. No one was around, it was a big property, and I started to panic, too, after a minute. Big flat beach, you could see everything for a mile on each side, but no Kylie. Then we heard her calling, and spotted her on this island in the middle of the lake. Must have been three football fields from shore. She'd just started swimming out there and kept going until she arrived, is what she said when we took our boat out and got her back. She just kept going.

"Anyway, I found out I didn't know anything about what my daughter could do or what she was like, and I figured I'd made enough money for forever if I sold up ReeseTech. I wanted to make sure her childhood was as little like mine as possible, so I did."

Nothing shut Keith up like sincerity. He'd looked progressively more uncomfortable as the story went on, and I could see the moment where he tuned out in order to search for an answer that could fit, either a brash brush-off or some kind of empathetic story of his own that would match. He settled on nodding, then unfolded the newspaper he had in front of him, revealing a USB key. I reached for it slowly, knowing he was going to put his sweaty, gravy-scented paw on top of it before I could get it. The hand came down.

"Why don't you just hack in to the database if you want this stuff so badly, Mart?"

"It wouldn't all be up there, now would it? That's why they pay you to scan and archive it." I had done the kind of hack Keith was talking about, in the late nineties, working from a Portland internet café and sweating as much as I ever had, downloading as much raw data as I dared before my backdoor portal was discovered. Security was laxer back then, and I'd never tried a law enforcement hack since. I preferred this method, anyway. It left less of a trail. Only the scanner and the wreck across from me knew what I'd received on CD-Rs and data keys over the past decade.

Keith lifted his hand up with a wink. I palmed the USB and put it into my wallet, removing a sheaf of bills I put under the newspaper. Keith would pick them up at the end of our liquid meal. These covert elements of our exchange, closer to corner drug-swaps than backroom espionage, were silly to me, but they let Keith feel important.

"Guess what's on there," he said.

"This is a funless game, Keith. Narrow it down, at least."

"It's a local. An hour-long interview session. Almost as long as your precious daughter-bonding story."

"Kerr? Greg Roberts? Lewis Harper?" I tried.

"You're just running down the list," the big man said, his pissed-off expression changing as the booze arrived. I sipped as he gulped. Keith was proof that many cops are just civil servants, waiting for their paychecks and weekends in the exact same way City Hall receptionists do. He'd been promoted in the earliest days of his career for making a huge cocaine bust; it had happened when he pulled over a scared half-Asian kid who was supposedly just up from Orange County on a pleasure jaunt. My guess was that a mixture of racism and jealousy over the youngster's late model BMW caused young patrol officer Waring to waylay him for driving twelve miles over the speed limit. The kid was crying by the time Keith reached his window, and the three pounds of coke in the trunk were cause for a few more years of weeping in a federal facility.

Keith got boosted to narcotics, then passed through the auto theft division and finally vice before everyone accepted that he didn't have a clue, was unlikely to gain a clue, and would lose the clues for everyone else if he continued to have access to crime scenes. By that time, his never-trim figure had inflated to a size that made him unfit for patrol duty, so he ended up spending most of his career in a box-crammed portable unit off to the side of the main precinct. It looked like the type of building you'd see on the grounds of an underfunded elementary school, but it was where Keith had lived his working life, as part of the two-person team digitally logging old evidence files. For eight hours a day, Keith and his partner digitized audio and video tapes, scanned countless pages of unevenly scrawled and typed material, then put it all in a database that eventually, possibly, someone might give a shit about. These were all closed cases, files that had gone untouched for a decade plus. Even when the department shrank the initiative, shedding his partner and moving Keith back into the precinct, he worked in the policing equivalent of the dead letter office, and that's exactly why he was useful to me.

"One real guess," he said. "Come on, what's on the key?"

"Your baby pictures. I don't know."

"Martin, you're no fucking fun, especially once your wallet's closed," Keith said. "It's Jason Shurn."

I set my beer down too hard and it sloshed onto the newspaper. "Shurn only gave two interviews, both to the cops. And he only talked about the discovered victims."

"Sure. But he did talk one last time, on the day he went off to ride the lightning. Or whatever cool term they have for lethal in—"

"Why hasn't anyone heard these? Why hasn't anything come of this?" I had to be careful not to whisper, because quiet voices carry farther than yelling in a room as full and as loud as that one was.

"Because he riddled his way through the answers like he was fucking Gollum. Wasn't a scrap of sense to be found in that audio, and anyway, the pressure to look for more possible victims was off. Feels like the whole interview process was more of a favor to his murdering self than anyone else, really."

I was quiet, and reached into my breast pocket to check on the USB bump in the joint of my wallet. Keith grinned at me. "You're all personal about this guy—so sweet. Do you and your wife talk about him at night or something, get you heated up?" He leaned back and swallowed an entire pickle, like a fish deep-throating a hookworm. He disgusted me and pissed me off, all at once.

"He did take your sister-in-law off the surface of the planet, right? Tinsley Schultz, the missing Shurn victim. Forever chased by the honorable weirdo knight champion who managed to marry her sister. Like that was a coincidence."

"Shut up, Keith."

"Yeah, yeah, sorry." Keith sulked with his face in the pint glass, then came up grinning. "Even besides this California find I'm pretty sure you made, you've been really active with that lil' spade of yours in the past few years. Ramping up the pace of your finds and your cute calls. Working up to something, maybe? It's almost your sis-in-law's twentieth anniversary of being bye-bye, you know that?"

"Congratulations on the math," I said, more than a bit surprised at Keith's accurate, if nasty, guessing. "Someone helping you with your homework?"

"You better hope not. I did this all by my lonesome, boss." Keith's smile got bigger, and he started fumbling on top of the booth seat next to him. He brought up a sheet of paper.

He hadn't brought me anything in print for ages, not since I'd told him I wanted to stick to off-line data. Minimize the physical trail. The paper was, of course, creased and a little damp at the corners, but Keith had probably done his sloppy best to keep it pristine. With a slow sense of ceremony, he passed it directly into my hands. Before I looked at it, I knew what it was going to be.

"Every file I've ever pulled for you, coordinated with the dates and times of the calls the department received about the skeletal remains of various victims being discovered all around Washington State. And outside of it." Keith leaned back in the booth, crossing his arms, a British television detective addressing the aristocrat he's just cornered with the murderous truth.

"Do you know how stupid it was to make this, Keith? Did you pull all the call times yourself or were you dumb enough to ask someone else to get the info?" I stopped talking then, knowing I was on the verge of screaming at him, of throwing my pint glass in his face.

"Contrary to what you think, tech-genius-millionaire-fuck, not all cops are stupid." Keith waited for this to land, but I didn't react, just looked back down at the paper. I didn't think all cops were stupid. Just him. The rest of them were mostly too tired and underfunded to do all of their jobs completely.

I scanned the sites and names on the sheet. Spokane, Hoquiam, Lakewood. Belinda Cross, Cara Collingham, Jenna Roth. I saw my shovel poking the earth around Cara's rib cage in Hoquiam, finding her place in that dense hillside thicket of trees while the smell of the Pacific, sharp and rich, melded with the soft smell of the earth Cara had been buried in for twenty-three years. My heart rate went up so high I thought I was going to pass out when I found her and touched her clavicle with latexed fingers. The excitement on the digs could start to overwhelm the calm, screaming through my lungs and chest and blanking out my mind entirely, until I shut my eyes and pressed fingers into the dirt, coming back to myself, to what I was doing. Cara Collingham's dad thanked the anonymous discoverer of his daughter's remains in the *Post-Intelligencer*: said he could sleep again. I made that happen, with Keith's files. Me, no one else.

"I typed it on a typewriter, not a computer," Keith said. "See? There's a bunch of old ones at the department, electric, half of them don't work. I know how picky you are about trails, so I pulled all the data by my lonesome, the times, places, and names, and wrote those on scraps of paper, and when I typed them out I got rid of the scraps. One copy for me, one copy for you."

"Why?"

"To make it clear, Mart, that we're in this together. And that I think it's about time I started getting some of the credit. The, uh, accolades."

A server walked by, and I found I'd lost my voice for a moment. I hailed him and gestured at our glasses, making a two-more motion. The dumbshow loosened my tongue. The noise of other drinkers behind us had become a looped racket of mocking chatter and laughing.

"You want to claim credit for all of this? All of these discoveries?"

"No one at the department wants to take a hard look at who does all of these calls. They piss cops off, Martin, with your shitty tone. But you're doing something real police don't have time for. That's got a value to it. I want a piece of that value, for my career. And I want to be on TV." Keith's grin broke into a giggle, a small slight sound coming from his bulk. Our beers arrived and he buried his mouth before the laugh could break through the last defense I had against rage and send me across the table to his throat.

"How would you explain selling police files to a citizen, without going to jail?"

"Thought of that," Keith said. "We say I did all the digs, told you about it recently, and you started to help. I think it makes a lot of sense—I'm a cop without an outlet for my, you know, justice instincts, you're a citizen with a family and a wife who's suffered a terrible loss. We could bring it all together for the anniversary. Of Tinsley Schultz going bye-bye."

"No."

"You know where she is, don't you, Martin? You know where Shurn put her."

If Keith hadn't started out with a threat, I would have pitied him then. His little Hardy Boys plan of how he could whitewash misusing police files, explain pulling a citizen in for extracurricular cop philanthropy, that *anyone* would believe he had any concern for families that had lost people they loved, families that just wanted the remains of their daughters, sisters, mothers back. But I didn't have any pity for him. I saved that for the people in the ground.

"Remember what you're paid for. By me and the department both. You're not a detective, Keith, so you can stow this plan right now. You're

Sergeant Secretary. You have the foresight and planning skills of a sandwich artist. There's no chance you telling anyone anything lands us anywhere but prison. Both of us. So just stick to this very nice arrangement we have, enjoy the money and think very hard about what you're going to say to me the next time we talk." I put money down to cover our drinks and left the paper file on the table.

"Wait," Keith said behind me. Then he said it louder, enough that one or two people turned around. In the interest of not being noticed, I walked back a step or two and did what Keith asked: waited.

"I know you, Martin Reese. You're a sweet family man, you're rich from a company brand no one quite remembers, but there's something rotten under it, and I know about it. You know exactly what I mean. Calls, games in the dirt, it's not public service. Not just public service, anyway. You do it because of what's wrong with you. I can prove it. The names Misty and Darla ring a bell?"

"So you fished out the breaking-and-entering charge I caught that went nowhere from what, twenty-five years ago? Yeah. I grew up broke and stole a few times to eat and buy smokes, and yeah, I targeted the rich kids I went to school with. Then I stopped. So that's it? We're done?" Keith didn't have anything else rehearsed, so he nodded. I walked out of the Pemberton into the licking, rainy cold and walked toward the Jeep.

I already had the Shurn dig planned for the coming weekend, as Keith had almost guessed. This lost interview I'd bought was icing, an ideal indicator that fate or time was running in my favor. Even Keith's nonsense threats couldn't distract me from that. He was another problem I could solve with the correct combination of dollars, apologies, and faked respect. Gripping the USB in my hand, I focused on the gorgeous luck of what I held, the confirmation it might hold of the contents of the site I was going to dig up. The body I was sure was Ellen's sister.

3

"WE GOT ONE OF YOUR PET PHONE CALLS, SANDY,"
Detective Chris Gabriel said, talking to Sandra Whittal over the divider between their desks.

"The name is never going to catch," Detective Whittal said. "I won't allow it. Let's play a game where you make sure you never use it again and I make sure not to shoot you."

"Come on. You can give me a nickname if you want."

"Dumbass? Shitdick?" Sandra added a few more increasingly brutal ones to the list, bluing in the air the way she'd learned from her siblings and sharpened with satellite radio morning shows. Hitting hard and fast had kept the other animals in her division from going too far since her six-month-old promotion. She was thirty-two and lacked the penis that functioned as a skeleton key to acceptance, but she had the competence and could properly talk shit, which went a long way. Chris held his hands up as though she'd drawn on him.

"Okay, okay. Anyway. Computer-voice caller. Pretty sure it's a genuine one, checks out with something that just went down in NorCal, a body found by sheer coincidence by a guy who owned the property. It had just been dug up, he says, because he was out there last week and it sure as hell wasn't lying out in the open then."

"Old one?"

"Yep. They haven't made a solid ID yet, but according to Mr. Roboto, it's Winnie Mae Friedkin. Do—"

"If you say 'Domo Arigato' I'm putting a bullet through the carpeted plywood bullshit we talk through and ending this forever."

"Fine." Chris got out from behind his desk and walked around to her desk. He wasn't fat, yet, and maybe never would be. He had that three-years-after-college-football padded muscle, and was about forty now, so he might keep that look forever. His last name, Gabriel, had been a lot more Italian sounding before his grandfather lopped off the last syllable, but his complexion told you where he was from. He waved a USB key at Sandra.

"I know you're technologically retarded, so here's the call, nice and tidy in one little file for you. I'm going home."

Sandra took the key. "Thanks."

"Come over in two hours if you want. Probably making something nice tonight."

"Maybe."

"I'll make it with seafood instead of beef if that's a little more than maybe."

"It's more than maybe, but it's not a for sure." Sandra wasn't dating Chris, and probably neither of them would consider anything more than uncomplicated sex with another cop, especially from their own division, but she said yes more often than not to his invitations. Lately he'd started talking quite a bit about his life outside of work. Ex-wife, family, an up-tick in mentions of his nine-year-old son, Michael, who stayed with him three nights a week. Normal, good guy stuff. It was throwing Sandra off a little, so she was sure to keep sharp in their verbal exchanges and to withhold most physical contact and affection that wasn't completely sexual in nature.

"Probably that shrimp pappardelle thing," Chris said.

"Yum. See you, maybe." Sandra Whittal put the USB into her personal laptop, violating department policy, then untangled her earbuds. She listened to the call through to the end: a precise coordinate, ready to be inserted into a GPS. This was repeated twice, in the computerized voice she had once associated with Stephen Hawking or generic PC voice programs, but that had become something else to her in the past few months, while she should have been focusing on the fresh homicides that had been placed on her desk. She'd solved those anyway, and figured she was owed this time. She clicked the audio file back to the beginning and listened to the voice again.

That is the exact location of Ms. Winnie Mae Friedkin, lately of San Francisco, victim eight of scumbag Horace Marks, currently resident of San Quentin.

There was something irritatingly British about the words the caller chose. It was one of many things that pissed Sandra off and skeeved her out, all at the same time. The room around her had almost emptied out. The guys on duty were next door, eating around the big interrogation table that subbed as a dining table on slow nights.

I found her the way I found the others: by doing your job.

This was as close as the caller got to a signature—on all of the recorded calls Sandra had excavated, there was some sort of finger-wagging admonishment of the police, of the FBI, of lazy law enforcement who were too busy preventing murders to roam the country looking for corpses. This, also, pissed Sandra off.

She was in cluster of trees—beech, I believe—about two hundred feet behind what used to be a Dairy Queen in 1976, and is now an out-of-business outdoor equipment shop. Glennis Camping, a victim of the recession. She was only shallowly underground. My metal detector picked up her zipper, her rings, her St. Christopher medal. It was a quick and easy dig. Tell her mother so. What you didn't do to find her. Tell her mother that she can bury her daughter now, and it's no thanks to you. Goodbye.

After the coordinates, the call ended with the rasp of plastic against metal, the sound of the phone against the surface of whatever spoke that voice, the voice orchestrated by the man finding these bodies, bringing them into the air, making a game of it. Saying it was all for the families. Anyone in the media who had picked up on the story over the years believed that, like the guy was some sort of postmortem Batman, setting the world right in a way the cops couldn't, or weren't willing to.

But his combination of showing off and secrecy—Sandra knew what that was. And it wasn't innocent. This caller hadn't killed any of the girls he called in, as the DNA and testimony and timings on all of his other finds could attest. Maybe he'd never killed anyone.

"Maybe," Sandra said, talking to no one in particular. No one would listen, anyway. She took out the earbuds and thought about what was in her fridge for a minute before walking out to her car and driving to Chris's apartment for dinner and what came afterward.

After sex, Sandra sometimes had to watch Chris as he did a set of chin-ups on the bar he had mounted in his bedroom doorway. It was a repeated, unnecessary bid to impress her, especially if his performance had been off in any way. She was glad he skipped his calisthenics tonight, choosing instead to lie half-slumbering in the bed as she pulled an old tablet from her purse and began playing the sound file of the call.

"Jesus," Chris said, pulling the covers over his chest. "You're playing that in my bedroom? At least put some clothes on."

"Shut up."

"I won't. It's weird. What you're doing is weird." Chris reached over and flapped the cover back on to the tablet, gently. The digitized voice of the caller continued on for half a second before cutting off in the middle of the word "underground."

Trying not to be annoyed, Sandra hooked on her bra and swung her legs out of the bed, rooting around in her purse for the spare pair of socks she usually carried with her in particularly rainy weather. Nothing worse than wet feet. She found them and put them on carefully, dressing more slowly than she usually would, to make sure Chris was aware she was leaving, not storming out.

"Going?" Chris asked.

"I want to work this."

"The call? You're not going to get anything out of that tape other than what you hear. A mobile signal, from a prepaid phone, sold at some chain convenience store in downtown Seattle, always just used for the one call. And he's too smart to drop any useful hints, no matter how many times you listen."

"Sure."

"Is that why you're fixated on the guy?" Chris asked while feeling around under the covers for his boxers. "You jealous of his sleuthing skills?"

"Fuck no," Sandra said, sitting on the edge of the bed. She handed Chris one of the tees he had lying on the floor, a Hole tour shirt from 1994. The frat boy touches in his decor were annoyingly charming. "I'm worried we probably have a cop or ex-cop or fired cop or failed cop trying to make us look like idiots. You should be worried, too."

"Some old man or armchair detective wants to help get bodies respectfully buried at family funerals. That's really not a problem for me."

"You're regurgitating his own take on what he does. Like he's the soul of angelic generosity, not a weird ghoul. Come on, Chris. He's not

going around looking for people who died hiking and haven't been recovered, or even living runaways. We've got plenty of both on our books.
He's specifically looking for serial killer victims, all women."

"Most serial victims are women, because that's who sick men want to
kill. This guy helps them get proper burials. Get closure for their parents.
Who cares if he's an arrogant dick about it?"

"That is some naïve shit for a cop to be saying, Chris," Sandra said,
keeping the shake of annoyance out of her voice with some effort. "The
caller's following up on a few guys in particular. Killers, I mean. Collect-
ing their work. Pretending it's a public service."

"It *is* a public service, Sandra. I know you don't want to hear it, but
I have a kid, and the idea of first, anything happening to Michael, and
second, of never knowing? You have no idea. This guy does."

"You've seen for yourself that 'closure' is pop-psych bullshit. How
many parents of vics keep calling you for years, wanting to talk about the
case? You get the sense they feel way better after the funeral?"

"So what's your working theory? He's a pervert, getting off on this?
The scenes are DNA clean."

"Meaning what?"

"Meaning no semen. If it's a sex thing, he's keeping it to himself."
Chris pushed the pillows behind him into a support as he sat up, pulling
the t-shirt on while keeping as much of his skin hidden as possible. Other
than the chin-ups thing, Chris was generally protective of his nudity,
especially when they got right into a work discussion after screwing. He
was excellent cop material, but he and Sandra were both aware of where
the next-level investigative talent in the room rested.

"I'm not going there yet. I'm not saying he's a freak," Sandra said,
doing a quick scan of the room to make sure everything she needed in
her bag was back in it. "Just that he's, as you say, arrogant, and knows
things he shouldn't. Like one of these neighborhood watch guys who
tunes into the police band and does pathetic fake patrols with a stun gun

or sidearm until he gets shot or kills someone. Only this guy sticks to bothering the dead, and us."

"I still don't see what's so bad about families getting to bury their kids, even if it is a few years late." Chris found his boxers after reaching around with his toes under the sheets for a few seconds. "Hold on," he said. "Neither of us have to be in early tomorrow. If you're going to go all game's afoot on me, we can at least do it over drinks somewhere."

Sandra waited for Chris to get the rest of his clothes on, using the time to transfer the call audio onto her phone. She took the audio from the rest of the calls while she was at it, pooling all of the caller's taunts, all of his irritating bull's-eyes, into one cordoned-off collection marked "Creep" in her music folder. If his poking around pisses a cop off this much, Sandra thought, he's lucky none of the guys who hid the women in the first place are around to take notice.

4

JASON SHURN. LIVE FROM WALLA WALLA STATE
Penitentiary. If I'd had the right laptop with me, I
would have plugged the USB in right in the car so I could start listening
on my ride home. But I was careful when I handled this sort of material;
the only device these drives and their data ever came into contact with
was my scrapbook. I drove down Broad Street like a power-mad ambu-
lance driver, not caring if I got pulled over. Hopefully the rain, which
was picking up, would create enough accidents to keep ticketing cops
busy. I'd eaten well at dinner and the beer was sitting fine, but there was
a gnawing in my stomach that had everything to do with the data key in
my wallet.

"Slow down," I told myself, feeling the slickness of the road under the
Jeep. I pushed my shoulders back, releasing myself from the car-chase posture that had me hunched over the wheel, relaxing into a normal speed. I
kept talking, slowly, convincing my heart rate to ease down and my mind
to avoid the fogged doubts at its borders, to focus on the weekend ahead.

"Keith's stupid list means nothing. I could call the cops myself tonight, tell them I'd found all those bodies over the years, that I made the calls. They'd pin a goddamn medal on me and I'd get fan emails."

I sounded so creepy saying these things to myself that I involuntarily looked out my driver's side into the streaked window of the Tahoe next to me. It was piloted by a red-haired guy who was also moving his lips, to music probably, progressive rock by the looks of him. He was watching the road the way I needed to be.

Maybe I would ditch the anonymity with my final call. I'd tell the cops exactly what Keith had done, let them decide whether to jail the man or just to archive his sad career with an early retirement ejection. And I'd stop digging for good. A last find: Tinsley Schultz, closure for Ellen, and then The End.

I hydroplaned for a scary second when I took my turn homeward too fast, but the expensive tires my mechanic had hard-sold me gripped the asphalt. That cylinder of data I had in my wallet might have the last fragment I needed, the part that would make me utterly sure Tinsley was where I thought she was. My phone buzzed in its dashboard holster, and I flicked the steering wheel button that channeled Kylie's voice through the speakers.

"Dad."

"Yeah?" I answered. Kylie sounded younger than her fourteen years, half-asleep. It was early for regular teenage bedtime, but she had morning practice, which would get both of us up before the sun tomorrow.

"I think I made Mom a lot more upset than I meant to."

"I think so too. You tell her that?"

"She's in the bath. Has been since you left, almost. We started to fight again."

I nodded, having half-expected this. "I should have stuck around." I didn't have a refereeing role in the house, but sometimes my simple, lumpish presence could extend peace that had already been established.

I turned into our street and slowed the car down, wanting to hang up before I hit the driveway.

"It's okay, Dad, I just feel like a total dick."

"I'll talk to her for you. Then you guys can talk in the afternoon. It'll be okay—you're not hurting her feelings, she's just worrying about you and making sure you're worried about yourself."

"Thanks. And I need something else, okay?"

"Yeah?"

"Take another shower when you get home, that reek was still definitely there." Kylie pushed out a laugh that was part yawn.

"You finished picking on me? Go to sleep."

The water heater at our house was big enough for a multi-unit apartment building, and I'd put it in because of Ellen's bath addiction. The bathtub was cavernous, almost like a room itself when you were in it. Ellen used it as an isolation tank, sealing out the job I kept telling her to quit. She didn't want to leave the credit union, because then she'd be dependent on my money, a situation she refused to be in so vocally it was almost insulting. I bought her gifts like the bathroom reno and tub as a sort of generous revenge, a way of forcing her to feel cared for.

Ellen was walking around in her robe on the landing when I got in, shuffling through something on her iPad. Work stuff, from the pained look on her face. Her legs were still wet, her face and neck glossy with almond oil, her hair rubbed with coconut oil, some of which clumped whitely together on the dark strands. When she got closer she smelled like a bakery, her elevated body temperature pushing the scents through.

"All clear?" she asked. I let myself drip rainwater onto the mat. "All clear" was our stock spousal greeting, loaded with meanings as disparate as "How's it going," "Are we still fighting," "Is my fly up" and "Is your period over." Tonight it just meant hello. A hello I didn't want to hear, because it meant I wouldn't be getting the privacy I badly needed.

"All clear. Keith's good, other than his cholesterol." And his fumbling attempt to blackmail me, that too.

"Tell me the number, it'll make me feel thin," Ellen said. She giggled and I made my way toward my desk. I sat down and unlocked the bottom drawer, pulling out my scrapbook. Stamped with the Reese Technologies logo, just like the forty others I'd purchased for my employees at the time, exhorting them to get rid of their old Toshibas so we could have a slick, uniform-looking office. I let some of the anti-Mac programmers hold on to their old units, as long as they kept the PowerBooks propped open on their desks as they did their work on whatever homemade assemblage they were attached to.

Since my retirement, this digital version of my scrapbook had replaced the hard copy I used in the early years of my hobby. I'd scanned then destroyed the old one with a minimum of ceremony, comfortable with having it preserved in this machine as a permanent piece of data. A record of each of my finds, and a detailed account of how I made each one. Winnie Mae Friedkin's death and uncovering lived in the two-hundred-plus digital shots made of her skeleton. The rest of her was for her mother and her surviving brother. A grave in a place they could visit, where they could remember whatever happiness Winnie Mae had in life before it was snuffed by a worthless beast in a truck.

Ellen was coming down the hall now, when I'd been hoping she'd loop over to the kitchen or living room and wait for me to be finished. Usually she didn't bother me when I was in this unofficial little study space, which had taken over from the more spacious home office I'd kept when I was still working remotely for ReeseTech. I liked doing my scrapbooking up here, in the open. As long as I was reasonably careful about it, doing my work here made it look even less like I had something to hide from Ellen and Kylie. Being expert at concealing all of this from them was a necessary part of what I did on the digs—a part of what I had to do to make my life, and our family, function.

"You and Kylie okay?" I asked. "She called me on my ride back."

"She's supposed to be asleep," Ellen said, her hand on my right shoulder. I touched the fingers as I lowered the screen of the scrapbook a bit.

"Well, she is by now. She's worried she made you feel awful."

"At least our daughter is perceptive after the fact, then, because she sure did."

I didn't answer, because I'd stopped listening. I was minutes away from hearing Jason Shurn's voice outside of canned courtroom audio. A discovery that couldn't approach the naked thrill of brushing dirt off a white skull that's been waiting for years, but, still, a discovery. I inserted the drive into the side of the scrapbook and started to transfer its contents. The USB gave up the last of its files and I turned around to face Ellen. Her hand was no longer on my shoulder and the skin on her face was a more threatening blush than the hot-water glow on the rest of her.

"Were you just passing along a message in a bottle from Kylie because she's too cool to talk to me and you're better at tuning out whatever I say?"

"Christ, Ellen, no, I've just got a million things on my mind."

"You're a camping-trip retiree, Martin. All you have to worry about is the people in this house and not accidentally bank-transferring four million dollars to Nigerian scammers. So listen to me when I'm talking."

I looked at the scrapbook screen: one of the audio files, a title only with numbers, was playing in iTunes. The volume was off. The track was forty-seven minutes and eighteen seconds long. I closed my scrapbook and sat on the desk, crossing my arms then uncrossing them immediately, to make it clear I was all acceptance and no defensiveness.

"Is this about, what, your job, or Kylie, or is it really about me being an absentminded jerk? Because guilty as charged. Kylie's doing what she's teenage-programmed to do, which is to push on your boundaries and pick me as her backup because I have less worries than you—"

"That—"

"Which, like I said at the dinner table, is because your life has given you genuine reasons to worry, especially about young women, especially about ones in your family. I completely get you on this, and you need to understand Kylie does, too, as well as she can. She understands but she still wants that extra hour, or extra mile, of freedom, and we have to give it to her. Build in text-message checks, make her wear a goddamn chip implant or convict bracelet, whatever it takes to make you as comfortable as possible—and me, too—and tell her she needs to stick to the rules if we're going to let her go."

"That's not going to be enough. I don't trust it to be enough. I don't trust the world to respect that she's playing safe."

"What it looks like to Kylie is that you don't trust her. And if she's going to be responsible, she's got to believe that we trust her to be responsible. That's the best weapon we can give her." I wanted to go on a little more but I could see that the "trust her" part had landed with Ellen, so I shut up. She stared at me for a second, making the decision on her own, the way she made every important decision. I could only say my piece, never hope for compromise.

"Responsible. Okay. Good weapon. And bear mace. Can you get her bear mace?"

"It's just called bear spray, and yeah, I'm sure I can do that." I turned and bent to put my scrapbook back in its drawer, and Ellen leaned over me. Her hair dripped onto the back of my neck and I shuddered and turned. She'd dropped her robe, and when I faced her she mashed her breasts into my face and laughed. "I had a hard week," she said, and moved toward the stairs, her fingertips hooking into my left hand with a touch so light it seemed more magnetic than physical. I left the scrapbook on the desk, resisting the urge to break away from Ellen to stow it, following her up to the bedroom because I knew it would get me downstairs quicker if I just did what she wanted.

"While your blood pressure's up anyway—and I'm glad you're okay,

of course, if that isn't obvious—I want to talk to you about something."
She lowered her voice a little as we crested the part of the staircase in
front of Kylie's door, even though Kylie usually slept with her earbuds
piping in white noise or the weird ambient electronic music one of her
swimming summer camp mentors had gotten her into last year.

"What?"

"Shh," Ellen said, until we were in the bedroom. I toed my socks off
and she turned off the overhead light, taking a shirt lying at the bottom
of the bedspread and throwing it over the too-bright bedside lamp I
kept meaning to swap the bulb out of. The light beamed red through her
blouse and pinked the walls until it hit the dark curtains and vanished.

"I know you've got this second youth thing going here," Ellen said,
sitting down and crossing her arms over her naked breasts. "I get that.
And you've been great with Kylie, almost the whole time, always putting her first so I could work and only had to step in when you went on
your little bachelor solo *Deliverance* trips. You did the responsible thing
for years, you've been responsible with the money you made, no goofing
with house flipping or casinos. And I'm grateful. Grateful for the home
that's built for me and for Kylie."

"It's not as if you haven't contributed as well," I said, taking off my
jeans and pulling my t-shirt half-off before letting it settle back down
over me. It was cool in here, and I knew I'd be back at the desk with my
scrapbook as soon as Ellen fell asleep. Better to stay as ready as possible
for my departure.

"Thank you for saying that, but it hasn't been on the same scale." She
got under the sheets and came close, putting her back against my side.

"I've been meaning to bring this up with you for a while," Ellen went
on. "I mean, I've talked to other people about it, and that's starting to
seem wrong. Since this is something that really should start with you."

"I'm getting worried now," I said, and it was true. I didn't want to
have to deal with a marital implosion when I was so close to finding

Tinsley and letting the news find its way back to her sister, to my wife, so she could finally be at peace. "Stop circling, Ellen. Finish the thought." I realized she was talking to me while looking away so she could be more direct.

"No, no, it's not bad. I just don't have anything, Mart," she said.

"That sounds pretty bad."

"Enough with the irony for a few minutes, okay? I'm not like you were when you had the company. I hate every day of what I do. The older Kylie gets, the closer she gets to you and the further she drifts from me."

"That's just teenager shit, Ellen, come on." She edged away from me minimally when I said this, then relaxed back.

"Yes, it's 'teenager shit' for Kylie, fine, but that equals years of my life where I don't have a center in what I do for work or in my home."

"Jesus, thanks," I said, trying to smile at Ellen's back but failing.

"Martin, come on. I'm talking about my fucking identity here, not how well we get along. It comes back to Tinsley again, to be a broken record."

"You don't need to apologize for that. I know she's always in the back of your mind. And it's coming up on twenty years. I've been thinking about her, too."

"Maybe that's why I've been giving Kylie an even harder time, I don't know. I think of Tinsley more than a few times a day. When I first took in that she was gone—that she was dead—I had the idea that I should live her life. I know that sounds silly."

"It's not, at all," I said, reaching my right hand down to squeeze Ellen's forearm, then pulling the weight of her over to me, resting her upper body against my chest. My arms were still aching, but I didn't let on.

"You get what I mean. I think about how I should stop working this stupid job where I make myself and others miserable by telling them how poor they are and always will be. I could do what Tinsley wanted to do. Live independently, do exactly what she wanted. That's what she did since she was a kid. Exactly what she wanted.

"Instead of two lives, though, hers and mine, I've got, at most, half of one. I'm the opposite of you. Still working, retired from the things I enjoy."

This last bit sounded rehearsed, too good to have been an improvised thought. So did the stuff about Tinsley. I briefly wondered who she'd been testing these ideas out on before getting to me. Not Kylie, certainly.

"I haven't made anything in months, my wardrobe is boring off-the-rack stuff I barely care about, I stopped doing any graphics stuff after that wedding invitation mess—I need to get back into what matters to me, but not just in a hobbyish way."

I was relieved when she veered away from Tinsley; I thought she was heading for a divorce announcement.

"I need you to be listening to this," Ellen said.

"I am! I mean, what can I do for you? You know I'm on your side about this stuff. Quit the cred union already, we don't need the money."

"I know. I mean, I've saved some up. I've been planning something for months, putting it in place, laying out cash. I'm going to quit tomorrow."

"That's great."

"But I need a tiny bit more cash to pull it off."

"Pull what off?"

"A store. Hear me out for a second."

The nothing-to-live-for, grim rundown of daily misery disappeared as she described what she wanted: a small, boutique clothing store.

"Personal, creative, you know, it pays for itself if you bring the right stock. Kylie can work the counter when she doesn't have practice. Learn how to talk to people, maybe learn to respect her mother again. To like her."

"Ellen, she does like you."

"She loves me, sure, but that's about all right now, except for occasional doses of hate."

We talked for another fifteen minutes, Ellen flicking off the lamp halfway through, which allowed me to close my eyes and trail my attention off. Back to Jason Shurn, back to bringing Tinsley Schultz into the light again. Being a loan officer, Ellen had a better idea of her business practicals anyway, and the money she wanted was a pretty small sum. I checked back in when she mentioned the number.

"Do you want to borrow it, or would this be a gift?"

"Neither," she said, with a glinting return of the anger that had struck off this conversation. "It's an investment, Martin, a sort of mutual faith thing. I want this to be official, with returns, all that stuff. I want to contribute to your life through what I'm doing with your money. Don't you get it?"

I told her I did, and she turned all the way around and held me. I had barely ever done any serious investing, letting my money fester in moderately high-interest savings accounts instead, playing stocks just for fun. The growth rate of money that just sat around was slow, true, but I'd been almost bulletproofed from the recession when it came. The money Ellen was asking for was a tiny fraction of what we had.

"I've been talking about it with Gary, actually. Pretty actively."

"ReeseTech Gary? My Gary?"

"Yes," she said, laughing. "You know what a total clotheshorse he is. You've made fun of it often enough." I'd never gotten properly vicious about Gary and my dislike of his scumbag behavior in the decaying days of the company, but I had swiped a few times at superficial stuff. I should have gone further.

"Yeah. Well, we ran into each other once on one of my coffee shop drifting-around days. Sort of fateful, I think, because that was when the idea of the store got really cemented, me sort of vaguely mentioning it then Gary jumping all over it. He's convinced it's a masterpiece of an idea for us to do."

"Us. As in, you and I?" I knew that wasn't what Gary meant. Insinuating creep.

"Well, that too, but he wants to chip in. Not much financially, but you know, he wants to give me his time and business insight, for free, so I'm not always bugging you." My wife's plans, flecked with ideas of Gary's, were now tumbling out of her with torrential force into the dark of our bedroom.

"I'm in for any amount you need from me, El," I said. I was thinking about exactly what it was that Jason Shurn said to Tinsley to get her to come with him, to leave the street and her life behind her when she got into his car and exited her potential future. Maybe he asked for her help. Maybe he offered her something—money, excitement. It wasn't anything her bones would be able to tell me.

"That's great. I'm actually—tomorrow, I'm meeting with Gary to talk it over," Ellen said. "I'm going to call the place 'Tinsley.'"

"That's a little—"

"You're not going to say morbid," Ellen said. I had been about to, actually.

"Sad, if you'd let me finish. Bittersweet."

"I want it to be a tribute. Plus, I'd feel too awful if a place with her name on it went out of business, so I'll have to try extra hard, right?" Ellen rolled off me and looked at me in the dark. I could see the brown of her eyes against her white face, the snow and wood contrast of a Japanese painting, pressed into the dark air behind her head.

"I love you," I said, so we could stop talking, at least for the night.

"I love you," said Ellen.

5

"SO HOW'S HE DOING IT?" SANDRA WHITTAL ASKED,
spearing two popcorn shrimp and letting them soak
in the cocktail sauce trench in the middle of her plastic serving basket.

"Doing what, exactly?" Chris Gabriel asked, looking at the booths
of families around him and wondering how he'd ended up sitting in an
Ivar's at the age of forty-one. "Do you know how insulting it is that you're
following up the fucking handmade pasta I served you with this deep-
fried sludge?"

"That was two hours and one sex ago. I'm hungry." Their server, a
young black girl with three blue braids striped through her bundle of
hair, overheard Sandra and smiled as she refilled their Diet Cokes.

"What I mean," Sandra said, "is how's he finding the bodies, obviously. That, and the question of why he's doing it, are the only things
that matter."

Chris was wearing the one pair of skinny jeans he'd ever purchased,
the last pair he ever would, and crossed his legs with difficulty before

answering. "Well, what are the basic elements of investigation he'd need? Same as with us. Time, for starters. Enough to properly concentrate on a single investigation."

"Exactly. Or else we'd get them ourselves. The bodies. The department doesn't have the manpower or the time to chase old burials."

"So he has no job or a nondemanding job," said Chris, picking up and eating one of the shrimp despite himself. "Maybe some psych case who makes his money from disability checks?"

"You called it a service?" Sandra asked.

"Yeah, I did. Ask Winnie Friedkin's parents if they agree, when they get to put her in a casket and bury that casket in a grave they can visit, instead of lying awake wondering where she is."

"Where she is is where she's been for years, Chris. Dead. That story ended when she got into Horace Marks's truck. What he did to her in his truck before she died, and the way he cut her up afterwards? Burial doesn't fix that." Sandra didn't notice the server had returned until she picked up the empty shrimp basket, looking blankly at the table, pretending she hadn't heard anything.

"Just talking about a TV show," said Chris. "One of those autopsy ones. Sorry." He smiled at the girl, whose nametag read "Nia," and she tried to smile back before walking off. "You just don't understand, Sandra. You don't get the emotional part of it from a parent's angle."

"Oh, I've understood this angle since you brought it up at your apartment, Chris. 'If anything happened to my son I'd just blah blah oh my sob sigh.' I get it. You strongly believe there's a zone of investigative knowledge that's sealed off to me because a baby never has and never will come out of my vagina." Sandra whirled the ice cubes in her glass and chewed on the straw.

"Jesus."

"You're the one who's not getting it, Chris, not me," Sandra said, finishing the last fragments of batter and rooting in her purse. Chris unfolded his wallet on the greasy table, but Sandra picked it up and frisbee'd it at his chest. He didn't protest, letting her pay in order to quicken their flight from this crime against seafood. Chris wanted to pick up the conversation on their way out but knew his partner hadn't finished her volley, that she was leeching some of the anger out of it to avoid saying something permanently hurtful. Halfway to the car, Sandra started to talk again.

"You're suggesting I'm not maternal enough to understand this guy's essential goodness. That he's digging up these bones as a heartfelt service to the families of victims. Okay. How about this. You're making the mistake of thinking this lowlife meltdown shares your decency, your way of thinking about your kid. That love. Let's say he does have kids. Let's say the messages he leaves us are the real deal in his conscious mind. I don't fucking believe that's the truth of what drives him, Chris. Not for a second."

"Why not?" Chris put his hand on the car door, but Sandra was holding the fob, not making a move to open up. "What's so unbelievable about that?"

"You're being naïve. He's not just some random mentally ill guy getting cash from the state. He's not a sweet dad who wants the best for mommies and daddies everywhere. He's an obsessive. Efficient, highly mobile, meticulous in covering up after himself. And he gets weird data, Chris. The next thing he'd need, after time, is information. He's a wannabe-cop with a chip on his shoulder, with ways of getting at our files. Contacts in the department, something like that. He could be a journalist. God knows there are enough unemployed, bitter, research-skill-heavy reporters out there. It's someone with inside information, stuff that wasn't released, officially."

"That seems to be about it. Time and access to information."

"The third thing is that he's crazy. Crazy somehow." Sandra bleeped the fob and then, unexpectedly, tossed Chris the keys and walked around to the passenger seat.

"You haven't said anything to prove that. A little weird, yes, but I don't see why we need to go further than that." Chris slid into the driver's seat. He didn't know where they were going next, and knew better than to force a destination on Sandra without consulting her. She liked to choose. "Nothing you've said makes me see this guy as something to worry about. I also don't know that you're right to discard the obvious possibility here."

"Which is?"

"Finder's not a guy with access to cop info, he *is* a cop. How about that?"

"Put it this way. You're a cop why?" Sandra put her hand over Chris's, preventing him from turning the key in the ignition.

"Because I was a bully in high school, according to my sister."

"Janet says that about you? That old hack idea?"

"Yep."

"Reason five hundred I'm never meeting your family. But really, why are you a cop?"

"I don't know, the usual reasons. Seemed like a good job, something I could do, would take up some mental space once I got past patrol, stuff like that. I can't remember that far back."

"People who become law enforcement don't tend to be the kind who hide their good instincts, is what I'm getting at. Even the worst cop, the kind who's just logging hours until retirement, wants his good work to be recognized. He understands it as good work, even if he's not going to be a full-on showoff about it."

"I'm surprised you're not using more gender-neutral terms, Detective," Chris said.

"People don't hide the good things they do. Especially arrogant people who brag about their goodness and ingenuity right alongside their good deeds, in little anonymous phone calls. The fact that this Finder guy, if that's what we're calling him, has been hiding who he is, and why exactly he's doing this 'Good Samaritan' work? It points to something.

He's such a fucking gloating showboat in those calls, telling us what we missed and pointing out how smart he is."

"Yeah?"

"It means he sees the major part of what he does as something to be hidden away. Something about himself he wants to keep obscure, because it's closely linked up to a deeply antisocial something-or-other about him. I think he's more interested in what got these girls dead than he is in getting their corpses back into family hands."

"Wait," Chris said. "What if he did call in a body long ago, publicly? Then just started to do it on his own, not wanting to make a big deal out of it."

"No," Sandra said. She was fumbling in her purse again, extracting a hardback reporter's notebook. "In the last twenty years, there have been seventeen accidental or maybe on-purpose discoveries of serial victims by civilians between NorCal and Prince George. All by different people, all of whom I've looked into over the past couple of years. No consistency. Nothing about them comes close to fitting a profile, and all their stories of discovery check out as accidents. Usually the bodies were discovered by groups, or couples. Normal people having an unusual day, calling the cops, and going back to being normal."

Chris reversed and pointed the car toward Fiddler's Inn, which had what he liked to drink and was close enough to his apartment to cajole Sandra into coming over afterward. "How much time have you been putting into this?" he asked, letting Sandra flip through her notebook a little more. He slowed down early for the roundabout at Thirty-Second and was about to ask again when Sandra finally spoke up.

"A few hours here and there for the past couple years. Nothing significant."

"Gotta ask again. Why are you doing this?"

"This is a long-term pattern that's escalating, Chris. That's why the calls have been coming in more often these past four years. If it's recognition he wants, he's going to start wanting it publicly, and I'm not sure what that means. My best hope is that he's going to drop the anonymity, march into a precinct with a femur and tell us he wants the key to the city and a parade for being a quiet hero for victims all these years."

"What's your worst hope?" Chris asked, pushing down on the gas so he could get to the bar and have a drink in hand as soon as possible after Sandra's answer.

"I haven't gone there yet," Sandra said, taking out her phone and pretending to flit through texts. "I just want to make sure we find out who this guy is. Quickly."

6

ELLEN SHUDDERED WHEN SHE HAD HER ORGASM
and I shuddered long after mine, as she was falling
asleep beside me.

"Tinsley," I said, so quietly it was barely more than a thought.

"Hm?" Ellen asked, her voice thickening as she passed beyond consciousness. She started snoring, adding volume, and rolled over again, drawing toward the other side of the bed. She generated a huge amount of heat during the night, and couldn't stand to have any body contact while she slept. This was fine by me. It had been a constant in our marriage, this habit of somehow sleeping separately even when we were in the same bed. Since she didn't really need her half of the violently expensive Canada goose down comforter I'd ordered online, she used it to delineate a soft border between us. The cloth wall had been there through good times and bad, and had initially consisted of a ratty Pier 1 quilt that had followed me from my student apartment. Ellen had always been willing to roll over the barrier and into my arms; sex was sex and sleeping was sleeping, and fair enough if she liked to do one of those alone.

"Just talking to myself," I said, quietly enough. She didn't say anything back. I left the bedroom. It was a little after one. I'd have to be up in four hours again to get Kylie to swim practice, but I could sleep after I got home. The light in Kylie's room, near the head of the stairs, was off, and we had a "no devices in the bedroom" rule for her, so her phone and laptop were on the little table outside the bathroom.

I still had the trucker speed-drinks and a sex adrenaline boost to go with the thrill of the new audio, and the three of them had me in front of my desk with my earbuds in and the volume jacked to pick up on the audio file where it had been cut off in its silent playback as I talked to Ellen.

The first file was nothing. Just preamble, cops talking and testing out the mike and reel-to-reel.

"Gonna get out of here before I get the reek of him on my clothes," a Southern-and-cop-accented voice said at one point.

"They wash them good before execution. So you get that nice rotisserie chicken smell when they cook 'em up," another cop voice answered, this one pure bright-eyed Washington.

"He's getting the injection, dummy. What fucking state you think we're in?" Southern answered.

I flicked to another file, this one thirty-two minutes and eleven seconds long.

A coaxing voice sounded after a moment of hiss. I recognized it right away: Ted Lennox, the psychologist who worked the case alongside Seattle PD.

"—the bodies, is all we mean. For the victims' families. I know you can understand that."

The hall around me, the wall in front of my desk, the glow from the scrapbook all vanished when the audio started, and I was in a blank metal room with a brilliant naked bulb bouncing harsh light off a steel table with an empty set of cuffs on it.

Silence. Then it came in.

> "*The souvenirs or the bodies?*" *said Jason Shurn.*
> "*The bodies, Jason.*"

The psychiatrist sounded tired. This must have been a clip from late in the interview. The files were disorganized, as they always were when Keith Waring threw them together. This one also had a minute of clicking silence at the end, one of Keith's trademark errors. I scavenged, clicking through the other files, looking for Jason Shurn's answer to the psych's question. I found it, ten tries in.

> "*The souvenirs are the bodies, not 'or' the bodies.*"
> "*What does that mean, Jason? Come on.*"
> "*It means itself and nothing else. The souvenirs are the bodies.*"
> "*In that case—*"

There was a scratching sound, as if someone had accidentally dragged a thumb across the microphone.

> "*—why have we found more scalps than corpses? There are two in excess, Jason. The, the freezer one—*"
> "*Oh, yes. Young red.*"

Jason was saying the words like they were the name of his favorite soda pop. Jenny Starks. My first find. I shook off the memory of that first, almost accidental, dig, and focused on the tape.

"Yes, that one, and then the one we spotted in the
overflow pipe."
"Ash blonde."

Tinsley Schultz had, of course, been an ash blonde. Ellen had started dying her hair after her sister vanished. Police spotted a scalp where Shurn had disposed of it, but the sanitation crew that forensics had enlisted to grapple it up had triggered a valve and shot the evidence away with thousands of gallons of runoff water. It was never recovered for testing, and never reported to the press. Cops tend to avoid advertising evidence-losing mistakes. I only knew about the lost scalp from a file I'd bought from Keith a few years back.

"Who were the women, Jason? And where are they?"

The psychiatrist—I was sure it was Ted Lennox now, I'd heard his voice on other tapes, and on episodes of A&E's *Biography*—became louder, as though he was leaning in. There was a long silence.

"If you want to know where both of them are, you'll have
to ask someone else. I only know where one of them is."

Another voice broke in. The investigating detective, no doubt.

"The fuck does that mean, Jason?"
"Turaluralura."

At this, my heart expanded in my chest, my lungs seeming small and flat. I was right about where Tinsley was buried. This was spoken proof, from her killer.

"What?"

There was sharp, quiet violence in the officer's voice.

> *"It's an Irish lullaby."*
> *"I'm Irish, fucker, and it still sounds like you're talking utter bullshit."*

It sounds that way, Officer, I thought. If you're not paying careful attention.

> *"Detective,"* said Dr. Lennox. *"Get out."*

That was the place to stop, to get back to proper procedures. I opened my eyes and vanished from the interrogation room, landing back in front of the scrapbook and the USB key that had just confirmed the X my research had marked over Tinsley's burial place.

I checked that all the rest of the audio files had transferred properly with a brief click and scan-through, then crushed the USB with a pair of needle-nose pliers. In the garage, I took out a small vial with a screw-on top that was tucked in with a few others and a lot of empty mason jars. I put the pieces of the USB in the vial and filled it with a glug of the muriatic acid I'd bought at a chemical supply store. The jar found its destiny in the kitchen garbage, nestled into a fist-sized wad of coffee grounds. I looked back up the stairs as I walked to my desk, thinking of just going to sleep then, dreaming of the luck of what I'd already found. But I wanted to hear more, so I settled back into my chair and put the earbuds back in.

You can get caught for doing absolutely nothing wrong. Rescuing those bones from an eternity in anonymous dirt, taking them out of a covered hole that couldn't properly be called a grave, only a hiding place: that's not wrong. But Ellen could never know.

That's what getting caught would mean, of course, and that's what the dream always is: the headlights of her VW illuminating my back on a dig, the glow bouncing off the streaks of black and silver metal still visible on my moving shovel under the patina of dirt and mud. The guilt on my face, the impossibility of explaining, the plain, dumb-sounding phrases pouring out of me. "It's so her family doesn't have to be haunted like you are. So there's no more Ellens waiting to find out where their Tinsleys are. That's why," I would say, in each dream, pointing to the small teeth in the small skull near the blade of my shovel.

"That's not really why." Ellen had the same single phrase to say in the dream, every time, looking at the anonymous bones in the grave and her husband standing over them, getting into her car just as I woke up. In some of the dreams, I'd put the bones there myself.

When I woke up this time, it was into the reality of a huge mistake. I wasn't in bed, but at my desk, slumped in my chair, the headphone jack of my scrapbook empty but the earbuds in my ears, the cord dangling free, knocked loose by a nightmare flail of my left hand as I slept. Jason Shurn's voice spoke at a middling volume into the hallway of my home. Every word sounded enormous, because I wasn't alone.

"Dad? Is that him? The other guy keeps saying 'Jason.' It *is* him," Kylie said. She'd convinced herself before I could answer. My lower back was pressed into a hot band of muscle, fat, and spine that I had difficulty straightening as I swiveled the chair to face her.

"Is it who?" I said, trying to buy another second of time, to suppress panic and push off the last dull wisps of sleep and dreams. I should have closed the scrapbook first. "How long you been here, kid?"

Kylie didn't have a chance to answer. The tape did our talking for us.

"And what about Tinsley Schultz? The 'ash blonde,' that's her, isn't it?" Ted Lennox asked, his voice coming out clear but low from the scrapbook speakers, into the darkness of the downstairs hallway. Kylie was in her sock feet, even though she was normally a slippers girl, and had on

gray leggings and a holey Brian Wilson shirt I'd gotten on a revival tour I went to with Ellen, a show we both cried at.

I slammed the scrapbook shut, immediately worrying I'd damaged it, almost laughing that I could think about hardware damage with Kylie there. Her socks shifted, making a little whiffling sound on the floor.

"Kylie, I get that this seems weird. But I need you to be really straight with me that you're not going to tell your mom one word of any of this."

"I don't think it's weird, Dad. I think about what happened to Tinsley, too."

"Yes. So does your mom, we just very consciously don't talk about it. That's why it would strike her as weird," I said, silently thanking Kylie for being more helpful than I could have hoped for. "And with it being twenty years—and talking about Tinsley with you tonight—I just couldn't sleep. That's all."

"I want you to tell me about Jason Shurn," Kylie said, in that determined voice she used when she was sure she was going to hear a "no" back. A pipe under the kitchen sink that hit a periodic guttural clearing note sounded, rumbling from its position just above the garbage can where the USB Keith had given me was dissolving into atomized gunk.

"What?"

"Shut up, Dad. Jason Shurn. I know that's him on the tape. The other guy said Tinsley's name, even! He messed with Mom's head for life, how could I not want to know everything about him? I've tried reading this bullshit on the internet in that slimy way they write about it, like the girls are video game characters that the killer defeats so he can be famous when he, like, decides to get caught. I want you to tell me about him without any of that crap."

"You know everything you need to already. Shurn was an evil man who's dead now."

"I want to know for the same reason that you do, and that Mom should. So I'm less afraid of things like him. So I know he's a shitty person, not a monster." Kylie was looking at me instead of her feet now, and I saw what was in her eyes, what I'd seen when she was eight and swam out to that island in the lake without Ellen and me knowing it. When we'd come for Kylie in our boat, she'd watched us with something like curiosity, something like capability, but mostly a capacity that was unknowable and entirely hers. I still wasn't sure what Kylie was capable of, and even in her sock feet and that big t-shirt with the dumb *Smile* logo, she was formidable.

"Jason Shurn is both a shitty human being *and* a monster. Was both."

"Then tell me about that."

I thought about the portion of truth I was going to have to offer my daughter, and the promise I was going to need to take from her first. That's what it was: I would be taking something from her by asking her to enter this lie with me, this part of my life Ellen could never touch or know.

"Okay. We'll talk about what little I know about this in the morning. But your mother can't hear any of it, you promise me that."

"I promise. Why not now?"

"Because we both have to be awake in three hours." What I really meant is that I had no idea what to tell Kylie about Jason Shurn, Tinsley Schultz, and especially myself. I knew plenty of places to start, but I didn't know where to end the story once I started talking. Kylie hearing the tape was a mistake I could fix.

I didn't know yet that I'd made deeper mistakes I wouldn't ever be able to put all the way right.

7

I SNAPPED AWAKE AT 4:54, BEFORE MY PHONE'S alarm, and swiped the buttons to keep it quiet. *If you want to know where both of them are, you'll have to ask someone else. I only know where one of them is.* I got Keith's point about the riddling nature of the tape, even after a few minutes of listening, but where Keith's dumbness shone through was his thinking that Shurn was impenetrable. The killer's way of talking was part of his disguise, just like his good looks were part of the window dressing that hid what he really was.

The Irish thing, Shurn's *tu-ra-lu-ra-lu-ra*, I had figured. Shurn knew where he'd put that body. So did I. The only edge he had on me there was that he knew whether the bones I was going to dig up belonged to Tinsley Schultz or not. Then again, Shurn was dead, so I had that on him.

I brushed my teeth and ran the tap, hearing Kylie on the other side of the wall, moving around to pull on her tracksuit.

"Start with the generalities," I told the mirror, having no one better to ask for parenting advice on what to do when your daughter comes upon you in the dead of night, listening to recordings of the man who murdered her aunt.

But it did seem like a fine place to start. With what kind of man Jason Shurn was, how he was a boring person who was able to exceed the rest of us in two ways only: a narcissism that let him murder others for his satisfaction, and the capacity to murder once and then keep on murdering. A serial killer's mind isn't impenetrable, even if those FBI connect-the-dots profiles never seem to nail down the guy's tics until after he's been caught or killed. That insane foreignness is just a comforting idea the nonmurdering public would like to nurture. A serial's thinking is just this side of ours, in the way that a two-year-old's logic is alien to a teenager. Within a few months of Kylie being verbal, I could tell she meant she wanted a banana and granola when she pointed at the yellow table in our sunroom and screamed "ner." There's always sense in it, somewhere, just as there is always sense in the patterns and impulses of the guys whose work I follow. *I only know where one of them is.* That pause in the tape before Shurn coming up with his "Irish lullaby" line was him planting a clue with its own embedded logic. Easier for me to say this, of course, because I'd figured out the answer to the riddle before I'd ever heard the riddle.

I met Kylie in the hallway just in front of the door to the garage. We were always quiet in the early mornings before practice, her alternating bites between a protein and a granola bar, me drinking coffee in the kitchen out of my Sub Pop travel mug. But this time she broke ritual as I was turning the knob, before we'd even looked each other in the eye.

"Can you call Coach and tell him I'm sick? Say 'cramps sick.' He won't ask. I want to have breakfast with you and talk without having to rush." Kylie hefted her schoolbag, thick with textbooks and a jostling water bottle, onto her back.

"Okay," I said. We left Ellen sleeping upstairs, to talk about her sister and the man who had murdered her.

"This is where they figure he picked her up." We were parked in front of El Corazón, on Eastlake. Kylie looked through the back window at the overpass and the dark tunnel behind us. The sun was still low, and there were cigarettes and other drinking-related garbage on the sidewalk between the doors of El Corazón and the Jeep. Kylie's right hand crept over to the lock, making sure it was engaged. She didn't want me to see her do it.

"What was it back then?"

"Same thing it is now. In the nineties it was called the Off Ramp. Those bands you and your friends don't care about—Nirvana, Pearl Jam—started out here, or at least played here back then. I don't think Tinsley liked any of them. Maybe Nirvana. From what your mom says, she was too punk for the rest."

"She was here watching a show? When he took her?"

"Let me tell you in order." What I left out was going to be as important as what I said. There was movement inside the venue; it probably hadn't been long since cash-out, if there'd been a show last night. "Last time I was here, maybe 2004, it had a different name. Graceland. There was no seat on the toilet in the men's room, I remember that."

"Gross."

"I went to a show alone because your mom refused to come. When I pressed her on it, told her we could easily get a babysitter, it was a Tuesday or whatever—she made it clear how serious she was about never coming anywhere near this place. That's when I actually put it together that it was here that Tinsley was last seen.

"Your mom was with her that night. She was younger than Tinsley— they were both too young to get in, but there was a guy who lived near UW who made great IDs, they were easier to fake back then. Don't even try that, by the way. They're going to be scan-embedded within a year."

"Okay, Dad, okay," Kylie said. I nodded, then turned the ignition to get heat back into the car. I figured our bodies would have been enough to fight off the gentle early autumn cold, but neither of us seemed to be generating much warmth.

"Your mom, from what I've been able to get her to tell me, and what I found out from talking to the police later, some nice detective named Dave—your mom went to the show because she knew Tinsley would be there that night, and she wanted to convince her to move in with her and stop the runaway thing she was doing before it was too late. When your mom turned up, Tinsley said no. I imagine it got to be a heated conversation."

"Like when Mom and I fight."

"Probably," I said. "But Tinsley was older, and less connected to her family than I hope you feel. So a little different."

The detective, whose entire name I remembered, of course, Dave Broadwell, had told me he remembered Ellen "screaming to us that she'd told her own sister to fuck off and die if she wanted to, like she'd killed her herself with some magic curse." But that was too private, too much of Ellen's own story, to tell Kylie.

"Mom would definitely yell at me if I—"

"Do you get why she's so protective now?"

"I always did get it, come on."

I turned the ignition key the rest of the way and we drove until we found a Starbucks. Kylie went in for an enormous black coffee for me and some sort of chocolate caffeine abomination for herself. I hummed *tu-ra-lu-ra-lu-ra* when she was in there. Soon I wouldn't be talking about Tinsley, I'd be finding her. Cars fired in and out of the parking lot around my Jeep like a time-lapse video as I waited for Kylie and the café filled up with students and quick-stopover commuters.

Holding our drinks, Kylie pushed the Starbucks door open with her right elbow and pivoted counterclockwise to avoid the people coming in, clearing them and the garbage can between her and the car with an athlete's confident knowledge of space and the exact reach of her limbs. I got the passenger side open for her, even though she could have managed it herself. She pulled the lid off her drink and put it on the dash in front of her right after I did the same with mine, an unconscious imitation that made me feel both proud and old. The sun was up, beams grasping the black paint of the Jeep, warming the outside as our drinks heated us. I got right back into Shurn.

"Jason Shurn probably was there that night. He was a dealer before he went to jail and after he got out. Cocaine."

"You can skip the gateway drug stuff, Dad."

"I can't. And that's not what I'm saying. If you really want to understand this, we need to go even further back." I started to lay it all out for her. The Jason Shurn story, soon talking to myself as much as I was talking to my daughter, laying out the historical map that was about to lead me and the tip of a shovel to the ground above Tinsley.

"Shurn was a lot of things before he came for Tinsley. Most of them bad. But he was a young entrepreneur."

"Like you."

"Nothing like me," I said, twitching enough for a lick of coffee to slosh out and run down my thumb. "He was a deviant from the beginning, even if it was partially his messed-up family's fault. His stepdad forced him to get two paper routes in junior high—one at five a.m., and one just after school. And once, when a homeowner on the route asked to stop delivery for a couple of weeks while they were on holiday, Shurn took the chance to supplement his income by breaking and entering."

"So that's how he started being a criminal."

"He kept stealing until he got caught." I skipped over the facts of young Jason's first arrest: his thieving skills escalated through the years, but he was eventually caught rifling through Mr. and Mrs. Leonard Trilby's dresser drawers by the live-in maid who hadn't been invited to accompany them on their annual trip to Maui. According to Shurn's juvenile record, the boy was "nude and tumescent when the maid entered the master bedroom, and ejaculated when he turned to face her." A two-week stay in a youth facility, which came with a package of psychological tests and examinations Shurn managed to outsmart, wasn't enough to take away the taste of transgression his early thieving had gotten him.

"He could have chosen to get better at that point, you know. Shurn could have turned his back on acting out that way, done anything to avoid becoming a monster. I had a rotten dad, too, I had phases when I was a kid, but I made sure I became the kind of person who deserved your mother and you."

"How do you know this stuff about him?" Kylie asked.

"It's all out there. You just have to be patient and get through that internet gossip bullshit you were talking about," I said. I was lying, of course. Most of what I'd told her, and that bit about the maid I'd skipped over, was still classified. I had all this information from Shurn's juvie file, another USB handoff from Keith. "This shouldn't even exist," Keith had said when he gave it to me. He'd made me eat a Cuban sandwich that time, which was admittedly delicious, but the sight of him chomping and drooling—at one point jetting pork juice over the length of the table to land on the manila folder—quickly slayed my appetite. "It was wiped, supposedly, once he turned eighteen and had a clean bill of mental health."

"So where did you find it?" I'd asked, pretending to be interested. Keith's half of the investigations he felt we shared was completely dull.

"Exactly where it would be if it hadn't been 'wiped,' bud. Sitting in a big ol' box. That's the magic of paper files. Sometimes they just find a way to stick around. More luck for you, huh?"

"Guess so," I said, wiping Keith's pig spray from my new acquisition. "You'll like this one. You'll like it plenty."

I shook the greasy memories of Keith and got back to the story, watching Kylie's eyes go a darker, cobalt blue as she pictured what I was telling her. Jason Shurn's next job also involved delivery: A grown-up, recidivist paper route. On his own at sixteen after he left juvie, he started running cocaine around town by bicycle. Mid-eighties dealers in Seattle had found that teenage cyclists were the safest method of getting their product distributed—the supply was kept mobile, and as the delivery boys stayed clean-cut and worked outside of school hours, they were closer in appearance to background characters in an *Archie* comic than ex-cons. This career choice didn't show up on Shurn's juvie record, because he'd stopped doing it after a couple of close shaves with the cops.

"If the drug stuff isn't on his record, or in like the articles, how do you know about it?" Kylie asked. "Is that the recording you were listening to?"

"No, that was just some YouTube documentary thing about serial killers. The drug thing was in some of the papers, I think."

"Oh," Kylie said. It was the first time I'd lied to her that morning, and she almost caught it. The drugs had come up in a court transcript from Shurn's trial, when his lawyer pulled an improbably stupid Hail Mary and called the serial murderer to the stand in an effort to show that his client didn't deserve the death penalty.

DEFENSE COUNSEL: *Did you feel trapped by your new*
   position? Enlisted by a sort of Fagin—

SHURN: *Fagin? What are you trying to say?*

JUDGE MCKENZIE: *The next person who laughs during*
   these proceedings will be ejected from the courtroom.
   Counsel will keep questions and language basic.

DEFENSE COUNSEL: *Yes, your honor. Jason, did you feel*
   as though your life was a trap?

SHURN: *No, those were good times. Good as I'd had,*
   ever. Money all the time, my own place. I skimmed
   coke to take to bars, met girls.

DEFENSE COUNSEL: *You were telling me, earlier—*

JUDGE MCKENZIE: *Avoid references to your attempts to coach your client, Mr. Marlon.*

DEFENSE COUNSEL: *Yes. Jason, why did you quit?*

SHURN: *Didn't want jail again. Thought I could make more money another way.*

DEFENSE COUNSEL: *By obtaining legitimate employment.*

SHURN: *Yeah. I started doing regular delivery work. Was an office courier. Also, my bosses found out I'd been hiding their product in places, graves mostly, building a stash for my own business. They agreed not to kill me if I gave it back and got out of their business.*

DEFENSE COUNSEL: *You didn't say anything like this earlier on.*

SHURN: *I guess not.*

JUDGE MCKENZIE: *Finished, counselor?*

DEFENSE COUNSEL: *Yes.*

A throwaway moment in the court transcripts. Really, all it illustrates is how much the judge disliked Shurn, and how little Shurn cared about saving himself from execution.

"Could they maybe have fixed him when he was a kid, if he'd had better doctors or if he hadn't met bad people in jail?" Kylie asked. She was chewing on the rim of her Starbucks cup, leaving little animal bite crescents in the waxed cardboard.

"No, I don't think so. Shurn got a fair chance in court when he was a kid and much more fairness than he deserved when he grew up. There was something rotten in him from the start."

"Why are you telling me all the drug stuff, then? What does it have to do with Tinsley?"

"A rush leads to a bigger rush for guys like him, I think. That's what the books say. And it's true for people who are sick like him, but not everyone. I smoked pot four times and it was boring every time, and that was it for me."

"Dad. Holy shit."

"Oh, come on. You—I don't want you to, and you shouldn't, and you definitely won't in high school, but people do stuff like that in college. And that's that. I didn't care for it but I understood why other people did. Guys like Jason Shurn, they want to keep pushing. But there's always a way to stop before people get hurt. That's where I lose sympathy, where my empathy taps out, and yours should, too. The moment Shurn decided to kill women, and the gap of time between then and before he started killing and decided to keep on killing? Even if he had to kill himself, he could have stopped. But he didn't, and that's what makes him evil. Evil, dead, human garbage."

I was almost out of breath from giving Kylie this supercharged dose of adulthood and frankness, and I didn't know when I'd decided to add that made-up part about pot, but I knew it was right. I was giving her something secret of my own to wedge that trust in deep, to make sure she'd never talk to Ellen about any of this.

"Okay. I think I understand."

"I hope you don't, Kylie. The deeper you get into understanding a person like him—I don't know. At least it keeps us scared of the people we should be scared of, right?"

"Right."

Shurn was too dumb or too ready to die to play safe in his testimony.

But his straight talk about stashing drugs in graves showed that he was capable of being direct when he was bored enough to stop playing around. It also demonstrated that his transgressive instincts had started to lean toward death-territory even during his cocaine days. He was always pushing toward death. First the women's, then his own. The bigger rush.

A few of the sleazier contemporary papers, while the killings were happening and then when he mentioned the stashing in court, suggested that Shurn had been a teenage necrophiliac. No one questioned the logistics of hiding contraband in a municipal graveyard—these are spaces that are regularly patrolled, which leaves anyone looking to hide something without much time either to hide or to recover goods. If Shurn was hiding things in a graveyard, it had to be disused, abandoned. There are plenty surrounding Seattle. My job had been to tie Shurn to a particular graveyard. As soon as that idea came to me, I knew there would be a body waiting for me if I could find the right tombstone. If.

I started the car and Kylie was quiet. "You okay?" I asked. "Gotta get you to class."

"I just don't know if I know anything more now than I did before," she said, changing her tone while she was still talking, from sulky to thoughtful. She pulled her backpack out of the backseat and shoved her hand around the outer pockets, emerging with a packet of saltines. She started eating them.

"You don't know anything concrete," I said, reversing us out of the parking lot and pushing into the stream of commuter traffic, where we came to an almost immediate standstill. "But know that I'm as confused as you are, and we're both sure of a couple of things. People do evil, messed-up things to other people who don't deserve it, and the rest of us stand around not understanding why."

"And that's kind of like what not ever knowing where Tinsley is buried is."

"No. That's not a symbol. It's just horrible." Traffic started moving and I accelerated, hearing Kylie's chewing distinctly until I flicked the radio on to give us some music to not-talk over.

The information I needed was in Shurn's juvie file. During a psych analysis, an old-school notepad and couch session when he was only thirteen years old, Shurn made a reference to his alcoholic stepfather being an ardent Irish American flag-waver, a champion of his people's claim to territorial fame in Washington State. My own dad had the alcoholism and unpleasantness thing down, but I'd never had to deal with him being a patriot of any sort, thankfully. He was either gone all night at the bars or looking for me with a fork he'd heated up on the stove. Shurn's voice came through differently in that transcript, stripped of the bravado that seeped into it after his killings. The psychiatrist, Dr. Milton Stephens, hadn't recorded his questions: only Shurn's answers.

> My stepdad just won't leave me be until he's really
> pass-out, can't-see-me drunk. I f***ing—sorry. I wait
> in my room most afternoons right after the paper route,
> just playing around with whatever I've got in there.
> Stuff, you know. I wait 'til I don't hear him
> talking anymore, because he always talks when he's
> drinking. Worst is when he starts singing.
> No, I like music. Real music, I mean, Stones, Zep.
> He sings that g****mn reedy pipe Danny Boy s*** he used
> to put on the stereo until he pawned it. Yeah, Celtic.
> If he starts up with that he's liable to pile into my
> room and drive me to the g****mn cemetery again to
> visit Dan O'****Reilly, guy he thinks is his great-
> great uncle.

Those weeks ago, when I read Shurn's juvie file in my scrapbook after taking a look at the full court transcript, that cemetery detail jumped out and played *tu-ra-lu-ra-lu-ra* as soon as I ran across it. That night, I made a seared duck breast with madras curry sauce for Ellen, quietly reveling in finding the link between the drug stash and Shurn's childhood cemetery visits, running her roughly a billion calories over the limit she was trying to stick to, making her eat the delicious thing because we were celebrating, dammit. Kylie was at a swim meet in Portland, staying in the hotel room directly next to the coach's, subject to text-message check-ins from mom every two hours.

"Celebrating what? That you'll love me fat or thin?" Ellen asked.

"No. Well, that too. Maybe," I said. She air-slapped me, her hand passing an inch in front of my nose so I could feel the breeze of it.

"Some stock deal I made two weeks ago went really, really well. We are slightly richer." This lie was composed of almost 100 percent truth; I had recently had a better quarter than usual with my modest investments. It's just that I didn't really care about the money. Not the way I cared about finding Tinsley.

Back in the Jeep, pulling up in front of the school, I realized it was time for me to put some sort of moral on it for Kylie, who had finished her saltines and was pushing her right thumb into the side of her kneecap, probing and shifting the hub of bone and staring straight ahead.

"Jason Shurn killed Tinsley because he cared more about what he wanted than he cared about other people being living human beings who aren't objects. That's what evil is. Okay, Kylie?" I asked.

"Why didn't he just tell us where he put her? The police. And Mom, I mean, and Grampa and Gramma before they died. He could have told them where she was."

I cut myself off there, but I could have told her where Shurn had put Tinsley right then. An Irish cemetery. Containing the remains of Sean Dunsany's forefathers, the Irish settlers whose steady issue over the generations had eventually produced Jason Shurn's alcoholic stepfather, a man whose only function seemed to have been the steady beating and mental torture of the boy that his dead wife had left him to care for.

"Shurn didn't tell anyone where Tinsley was buried because it was the last little bit of power he had. Being able to hurt people by saying nothing," I said. Kylie waved out the front window at one of her swim team pals, who was giving her a mystified, fake-annoyed why'd-you-skip-practice look.

"Yeah," Kylie said. "I think I get it. Um. There was no lunch in the fridge today, or did I miss it?"

"I forgot. You could have taken the leftover Chinese, though," I said, smiling as I leaned over to pull my wallet out of my back pocket. I gave Kylie a twenty and she left the car after squeezing my hand, a gesture meaning goodbye, and that we'd either pick up our conversation later, or never talk about any of this ever again.

8

SANDRA WHITTAL WALKED OUT OF THE STATION WHEN
she got Chris Gabriel's text, changing her walk to a
striding half-jog when she saw that the Greene woman was in front of
the station, pressing leaflets on every cop. Four patrol guys had come
in while Sandra was leaving the building and thrown her flyers into the
recycling bin by the desk sergeant, one of them—Rick Garner, a new kid
Sandra usually liked—seeing Whittal's eyes on him and losing his grin
fast. Bella Greene, missing for not that long but likely looking nothing
like the smiling high school portrait her mother had photocopied, smiled
out of the blue bin. Sandra and Chris didn't talk on their ride to the scene
they'd gotten hustled into taking a look at.

Chris Gabriel badged the woman on the porch of the care home,
then looked at his buzzing phone and excused himself. The lady who
nodded back at Chris was black, and surrounded by three heavily medi-
cated men in jogging pants and t-shirts. She wasn't wearing a uniform,
just a badly cut green t-shirt, dark slacks, and latex gloves. By the time

Sandra had her badge out as well, the woman had gone back inside, bypassing the buzzer at the entrance with a swipe of the key card that dangled from her waist.

Sandra looked at the men on the porch. They looked through or past her. The skinniest one was lounging, full-length, on the top stair. He had a face like that classical composer who'd done a couple of horror soundtracks: Philip Glass, Sandra remembered, from the DVD extras of a college ex-boyfriend's copy of *Candyman*. This Glass clone, and it really was a close resemblance, had the sides of his head shaved and hair longer and with more volume than Sandra's growing down out of the middle of his scalp. He yawned and looked at her.

"Who landed that Bella Greene thing again?" Sandra asked Chris, who was sitting on the hood of the car, still texting. He had on the expression of suppressed pain and rage he always did when he was texting his ex-wife.

"Greene? The hooker with the worried mom. Yeah. Nobody, yet." He nodded at the building. "This body's on the top floor, third."

"We'll take care of it once you finish up with your little conversation," Sandra said. "Sounds accidental anyway, from what the uniforms said. Pickett got the call on this, he's good. Good instincts. Doesn't step on things." Sandra walked to the side of the building, still within earshot of the car. A city-owned house on a gentrifying street where all the neighbors could sell for upward of a million dollars. A few more of the patients—residents, actually, even if they were being treated—of the care home were in the grass and cement alleyway there, leaning against the garbage can, or sitting at a wet card table under a piece of overhanging ribbed tin that looked like it had been pulled out of a makeshift housing settlement in a different, poorer country.

"None of us are on Bella Greene? We're not doing anything? Her mom was down at the station again today. Cornered Gutierrez outside. Someone should be looking for that girl. Been three days."

"Bella Greene's not a minor, and she's in the life. Those girls drift, you know it as well as I do, come on. I'm sure someone's asking around, maybe. Fuck," Chris added, but that word was directed at his phone, which he slipped into his overcoat pocket. A dent had appeared in Chris's forehead, a crease of annoyance that only solving the problem that had just come up would take care of. Sandra walked back toward the car and they spoke in quieter voices.

"Everyone's still out looking for that Todd Bisley kid. Even though he's most definitely dead with a bloodstream full of MDMA, at the bottom of some ravine at a bush party his friends are going to finally tell us about in a couple days."

"Bisley's seventeen, on the lacrosse team, with a rich dad," Chris said, getting off the hood of the car and into the driver's seat. "I gotta go. Take care of this thing, okay? Like you said, looks like an easy one."

"No fucking way I'm going in there alone," Sandra said, with more fear and anger than she knew she was actually feeling. It stopped Chris, who took his hands off the steering wheel.

"I have to get my kid, Sandra. Just from Caroll Elementary, like ten blocks away, then drive him to his mom's. He's throwing up. You can wait out here if you want, or we can meet up again when I'm done and come back. Come with me to the school if you want, even," Chris said.

"Hell, no," Sandra said.

"Knew that'd scare you more," Chris said, turning the ignition key. "What's the matter, anyway?"

"I just don't like these places."

"No one here likes the place, either. You'll be fine," Chris said, smiling for a second as he backed the car away, before his face got back to worrying about his son. Sandra turned around. The black woman with the key card was back on the porch, waiting, propping the door open. Sandra avoided a discarded plaid shirt on the walkway, before doing an athletic hop over skinny punk Philip Glass and landing on the porch.

Sandra's guide turned out not to be her guide. She gestured up the stairs then made a turn into the small staff room just right of the entry-way, where a couple of other support workers were eating lunches with forks off tinfoil: pungent, delicious-smelling stuff Sandra wanted to move closer to, instead of going deeper into the atmosphere of the facility. Be-yond was a small kitchen with a communicating window in the drywall, locks on the drawers where she figured the knives were kept. A short and very old woman, too old to be working, cooked discs of sausage in their own fat on the flat top grill, a huge stack of pancakes idling on a plate next to her.

Sandra turned back to the stairs and put a foot on the bottom step. Just keep doing that, she told herself. Soon she was halfway up the first flight. Everything in these shared areas was clean, but it still smelled. Dankly human, with the chemical edge of industrial cleaning agents. When Sandra reached the first landing, she was struck with the smell of the rooms. That's when it became too familiar.

Male sweat. Cum. Institutional food that could only be choked down on a liquid flow of ketchup, syrup, hot sauce, mustard. Like a dorm hall, but with a different pH balance. The hot linoleum curling under the full-blast radiators that lined the walls. And from inside the rooms, stares. Sandra walked past doorways and saw either the flats of feet in bed or eyes, watching her, the way he'd watched when she came to see him, every third Sunday until she told her mother she never wanted to come again.

"Detective Sandra Whittal. I used to visit my dad in a place like this," Sandra said when she reached the third floor and was waved over by a woman sitting in a small vinyl and aluminum chair in front of the only closed door in the building. The woman was about six years older than Sandra, wearing latex gloves like the rest of the staff, but with a nicely matched and medical-looking striped green top and pants that looked like slightly more formal scrubs.

"Oh," said the woman, indicating the beginning and end of her interest in the topic. Sandra badged her and the keys came out. The rooms locked from the inside, but this one also had a padlock and latch.

"Your name?" Sandra asked. She hadn't taken her notebook out yet, thinking she could probably get through this on memory alone, make notes back at the station.

"Emily James," the woman said. The dead body was on the bed, an unremarkable stretch of bones and skin lying on top of the mattress, wearing a bathrobe. Sandra went over to take a look and Emily James stayed near the door, unlocking the cage around the small smoke detector and switching it off. James took out a pack of Marlboro Reds and opened the room's window.

"Should I not be touching things?" she asked Sandra.

"Normally, no," Sandra said. "But I think you're okay." There was piss on the mattress, but that seemed to be all. Guy didn't eat much. Sandra had stopped thinking about her father as soon as she'd seen the body, taking comfort in her routine of sizing up the dull commonalities of a pill death.

"What's his name?"

"Rudy Clive Fox. He was the worst person in here," Emily James said.

Sandra looked up at the woman, staring into her eyes, seeing a confession in there.

"I'm the only white woman who works here. So he just called me cunt and bitch most of the day. The others got every racial thing you can imagine. They're used to it, sure, from the other guys, but most of our boys are just scattered dopes, patients, you know? They can't help it. Rudy was mean. He said chink and nigger and made up stories about their families and what was going to happen to their sons, talking like he needed it, like it was only spitting that evil that made him feel okay." Emily James looked younger when she smoked, something Sandra had noticed in other men and women who had brutal labor jobs, including her own mom: smoking relaxed their shoulders, pulled some of the wrinkles flat when the smoke was drawn in. Sandra didn't talk, worried that Miranda rights might tumble out of her mouth if she did.

"I didn't do it but I didn't stop it. I knew he was stealing pills from the other guys, knew he was hoarding his own. And I didn't do his bed check. Stopped last week when it started to be my turn to do this floor. So no one was up here for the hours when he was flat-lining, when I should have been in his room at least twice."

"Okay," Sandra said. Emily James looked like a taller version of Bella Greene's mother, especially now the smoke was done and the worry was back. "So you thought of this man as disposable, and allowed him to go through with a suicide plan."

"I didn't." James shouted the "I" but quieted down for the "didn't," the frank delivery of her story cracking now that the part she'd undoubtedly been running in her head since Rudy Clive Fox died was over. "I don't think of any of these men as disposable. You can't do this job if you start thinking of these guys as better-off-dead skin sacks."

"I know, Ms. James. My father was in one of these places," Sandra said. Emily James nodded, as though that didn't mean much in this context.

"I let him kill himself because I'd gotten to hate him and he was poisoning everything around here. He made everyone feel awful. I truly hated him. It wasn't that I didn't think he mattered. It's because he did matter, because he made every day bad for us, that's why I was good with him dying."

Sandra leaned back against a dresser, then leaned forward, thinking not about smudged evidence, but potential bedbugs.

"You tell anyone else about this?"

"No."

"Anyone have any way of knowing?"

"No."

"Don't tell anyone else. Ever. And I'll forget it. Okay?"

"Yeah," James said, confused. She'd practically had her wrists out for the cuffs. "But why?"

"Some people do the world a favor when they decide to leave it early. It's not necessarily my job or yours to stop that," Sandra said. "And if I say any more than that, this conversation is going to turn into something neither of us want it to."

Sandra thought about giving Emily James her card, but didn't. She left the room, climbing down the stairs fast and leaving through the front corridor faster, calling to give the coroner an all-clear for pickup while she was waiting at the end of the block for Chris Gabriel.

"I wouldn't have left if I'd remembered," Chris said when he opened the door. "About your dad."

"I should never have told you about him in the first place. You've been fishing around for an origin story ever since, like it's Spider-Man and he's Uncle Ben."

"Life has stories in it, too, Sandra. That's where stories come from, right?"

"Oh my god. How's your stupid son? Never mind, I don't care."

"Jesus."

"Sorry. Kind of. Let's get coffee."

9

WHEN I FIRST KNEW I WAS ON TINSLEY'S TRAIL, THAT there was a high chance she was exactly where I thought she was, I fooled myself into thinking I could go find her and then cover her right up again. No call to the cops, no somber reburial ceremony a couple weeks later with Ellen and Kylie at my side, no non-denominational guy in black saying some words while we finally gave Tinsley Schultz a resting place in the real world, not in the nightmare zone where Jason Shurn had left her.

I'd be found out, and not on my terms, if I called Tinsley in like the rest of them. An extra body in an ancient grave—that's the kind of thing even the laziest cop starts to ask questions about, no matter how old the crime is. It'd be a news story that would get the police looking extra hard for the person making those calls. Especially when there's a wealthy ex-CEO guy involved, even if he never made much of a tech-news imprint, just a lot of money when he cashed out. And especially when the serial is as infamous as Jason Shurn.

But of all the bodies I'd brought out of the dirt and into the light again, was I really going to let my own sister-in-law—flesh of the woman who'd brought me out of my own darkness and into a life with her and our daughter—was I really going to let her, of all of them, stay underground?

Of course not. It was all I could do to wait another week, a week of Ellen talking about the store in vague terms but letting me know, just hinting, that plans were further along than I thought. A week of taking Kylie to swim practice, picking her up from school, letting the peace in the household resume. Tinsley didn't come up, and Kylie didn't ask me any more questions about Jason Shurn. And I resisted the temptation of driving up on Friday, even when Ellen made it hard for me not to by mentioning the significance of the date.

"Twenty years," she said to me over coffee, after I'd come back from leaving Kylie at the pool and grabbing a couple extra hours of sleep for myself. My internal clock was still reeling from the adrenaline spikes and interrupted sleeps around the Winnie Mae Friedkin dig. I was getting old, and needed at least a week to get back on schedule.

"I know," I said. "You okay?"

"Yeah. No." Ellen shivered over her mug, her hair dry and pinned back and her office makeup on, a pore-blankening foundation, soft pink on her lips, and a thing with mascara that changed the way the zone between her hair and forehead looked in a way I couldn't quite understand. "Twenty years."

"You really should just not go in to work."

"Seems tacky to take a sick day in the middle of two weeks' notice. I'm supposed to help train the new guy, and he's really, really slow on the uptake. Byron something. Has the right degree and managed to escape without a single skill or useful instinct." Ellen was so efficient at work that her bosses took for granted that her job was easy—but the delicate mixture of financial and people skills, the judging, weighing, rejecting, the management of grief and failure—being a loan officer who actually gave a shit would be beyond me, and beyond most people. Not Ellen.

"Don't go in, okay?"

She didn't. She went up to bed again, assuring me she was okay but wanted to be alone, holed up with the records she and Tinsley used to listen to, away from any media or internet or texts talking about "Tinsley Schultz: 20 Years to the Day Since She Disappeared." (None of the papers, and nothing I could find online, did talk about Tinsley. I made that headline up. I wish someone had used it, but the papers forgot her two weeks after she disappeared, remembered her again when Shurn was arrested, and forgot her all over again when he was executed.)

It was hard not to leave that day for the dig, to close the shape of the ritual, taking Tinsley out of the ground on the anniversary of the day she was put into it. But I didn't. I made dinner and I told Kylie to grab a cab home. We watched a Liam Neeson movie as a family without any of us saying a single word about Tinsley.

It was the next morning that I decided to do it.

I showered and went downstairs, where Ellen was midworkout. "Going to Federal Way for a bit," I said to her. She was laboring on the elliptical we kept behind a curtain in the living room. It had a clear sightline to the TV, and she was watching an ancient rerun of *Oprah*. Judging by Oprah's weight and hairstyle, probably early nineties.

"What the hell is in Federal Way that you can't get here?" She could have been talking at me from the couch, the way her voice sounded; she was in exceptionally good shape. Cardio, toning, the lot. My shoulders and lower back were already aching in anticipation of the shoveling to come.

"There's a guy out there, owns a few goats. I met him at the farmer's market that time we got the pepper plant. He said he'd sell me raw goat cheese anytime I actually drove up to his farm—I'm not sure how legal or not it is. Supposed to taste way better. Plus, Kylie has that little swim meet at the school, and you've got your Gary meeting today, right? I figured you'd be busy with that."

"I am. Thought I might rope you into tagging along, though," Ellen said, ratcheting up the intensity of her workout. Her ponytail whipped her in the face. She shook her head and blew out of the corner of her mouth to put it back in place.

"You don't need me, and I sort of made an appointment," I said.

"Sort of, or you did?"

"I did." Now I knew she was annoyed, but the idea of putting off my last dig just to have a fight with Ellen was laughable.

"That's that, then. Okay, no fighting all around all day, let's try that. I'll have a great meeting and you'll have a great cheese-gather and then I assume you're going to make us a meal French peasants would have climbed the walls of this place and cut our heads off over." The elliptical did its patterned beeping thing and the whirring picked up. Ellen draped her towel over the readout so she didn't have to look at the numbers—watching the time click by so slowly made her want to quit.

I walked over to the machine, kissing the sweaty hair at her temple.

"Gross!" she said, laughing a bit, more automatically than happily. "Get your cheese. See you later." She closed her eyes and pumped her legs harder, ending the conversation by absorbing herself into her body.

After picking up my scrapbook from the desk and my keys from the counter, I headed for the garage, getting behind the wheel and driving into a light gray, low-clouded day, the kind where the sunlight that does come through is in the form of particles, not beams. They'll flit through holes in the clouds for long enough to make you blink when you're accelerating or shifting lanes, but it's still a good idea to take a Vitamin D pill or spend a few minutes staring into one of those eerie light machines, if that sort of thing boosts your mood. I wasn't ecstatic at the prospect of doing the day's work in the rain that looked to be inevitable in an hour or two, but at least the wetness would loosen the soil for my shovel, at the same time as it made each load heavier.

Just off the Orillia Road exit. That's between Seattle and Federal Way—I'd have to remember to pick up some goat cheese and to rewrap it in seedy-looking butcher paper on the ride home. The drive to the cemetery was quick, almost nonexistent, like the passage between two fictional places in a dream.

It always gets like this when I'm near a dig, near a body. Reality sort of blurs, piles up on itself, events get closer together, like someone flicked cruise control in my brain. It was a version of the feeling I'd get in high school, before I'd gotten control of everything. Back when I followed Darla Crane or Misty Laroche home, from the store near our school where kids congregated to get smokes, first watching Darla and Misty talk and drink blue Slurpees before they parted ways. I'd get that same feeling of compression in what I was seeing and feeling, time vanishing into rushing blood and lightheadedness while I hung back a block or two and followed one of the girls home, waiting in darkness across the road for hours until the lights in her house began to click off and I could enter the halls and rooms where she walked and was now sleeping, taking a keepsake and leaving. I had infinite patience then, just the way I had when I was watching my Ellen in her window at college, when she was only Tinsley's sister to me.

I resisted the urge to stop for directions; the old county map that registered Dan O'Reilly's cemetery didn't account for the asphalt scars that had changed the landscape in the years since the early twentieth century. I wondered if Jason Shurn's scalping job would be complete, or if there would still be a few wisps left.

The cemetery rose up in front of my headlights. I followed the Shurn of the past through the nonexistent gates, let the Jeep's tires roll over a few unmarked graves. The organized city of the dead in every cemetery doesn't care about the headstones or other markers that denote their placement to the living; they know where they are, and must believe they will stay put, no matter what happens aboveground. Of course, it doesn't always work out this way. Cemeteries get moved all the time, and the final resting place of a killing victim is all too often upset by the procedures of the police and the demands of family sentimentality.

I talk to myself in the last stages of a dig. I know it happens, and I stopped being embarrassed about it a long time ago. Someone needs to share in the excitement, even if it is just me. It was daylight in the cemetery, and despite the light rain it was as hot as autumn days get in the Pacific Northwest. T-shirt weather, as long as you're sure to keep a sweater tied around your waist.

I put on latex gloves and zipped into a normal-enough-looking forensic jacket specially designed to keep the wearer's cells from pepper-shaking all over the crime scene. Pointless precautions. No one ever came to this disused cemetery anymore. It had been hit hard by ghoulish metal-detector-wielding treasure hunters in the mid-seventies, then heavily patrolled for about a year after the Irish American Heritage Association had protested the desecration. Now, there were no visitors. The state of the grounds attested to the fact that maintenance, no matter how irregular, wasn't something the Heritage Association or anyone else took responsibility for. The scouting I'd done last month had resulted in zero sightings of visitors, and there were no tire tracks in the deep mud leading to the cemetery.

The sun cut in again hard through the half-naked branches. I had no shades on, but I liked it that way. Squinting brought me focus. "Dan O'Reilly," I said, running my eyes across all the gravestones. I was hopeful that Dan's would still be standing, hopeful because Shurn's stepfather seemed to have had no trouble finding it when he drunkenly drove his serial killer in the making out here on weekends. The graveyard was tiny, a space about the size of a basketball half-court at an elementary school, and about one out of every three graves had a marker. Herlihy. Cassidy. Carney. O'Brian.

"O'Reilly," I said, barely recognizing the excited hiss my voice had become. I whipped my right hand out, extending the collapsible shovel I had taken out of the backseat without being fully conscious of doing so. Just for a moment, I wished Kylie, and maybe even Ellen, could be here to see this.

I walked across the dead men beneath me and took a better look at the grave. Dan O'Reilly's name was etched into the moss-traced stone, which had been chipped away by time and vandals. Even the freshest marks on the marker, the ones that looked like they'd been put there by pocketknives that had attempted graffiti then given up the task, had been worn smooth by years of weather. Grass had grown over the grave itself, over the entire cemetery. Something about the growth over O'Reilly's grave held me back for a second, even in my rush; it looked scrappier and more bordered than the grass on the surrounding mounds.

"Doesn't matter," I said to my shovel as it entered the ready earth. "That much easier to fix it up when we're done."

Grave digging is serious business. Serious and hard. The cops use a backhoe, but it's still doable by hand, if you focus and work without letting your arms and shoulders tell you how tiring it is. I never notice while I'm actually on a dig, but the ache in my body the next day reminds me of the labor. This one could be especially tough. Could be Shurn had been extra careful and gone down the whole depth of the grave, all the way to Grandpa O'Reilly's rotting pinewood coffin. I cut the earth into rectangles and eased it off in portions, reining in my impatience during this most tender part of the task. The surface had to look perfectly unbroken when I put everything back. The other problem at the end of a dig like this is the question of where to hide the extra earth that's always left over after a grave gets filled in. The surrounding forest here would make that job easier, as long as I was careful in scattering the dirt around evenly enough to avoid leaving suspicious piles.

"Not that anyone'll see it," I said to the shovel, which had now gotten me three feet deep. The ground had been loose, not as hard-packed as old soil usually is. Old cemetery earth scoops easy, apparently. I widened the hole around me, moving more tenderly as I went deeper, gentle enough to avoid shattering bones that had lain undisturbed for such a long time. My focus became more than conscious, snuck through my entire body, made me more than myself, stronger than I could have thought possible. My pulse stayed low but blood rushed through me, draining out of my head and making me feel dizzy for a moment.

Four feet. The world around me darkened as another squadron of rain clouds passed over the sun. The reactions back in the city would be looks upward and grimaces, complaints about another damp day. I was already soaked with sweat. I unzipped the DNA-shielding jacket to let body heat escape and paused for a moment before zipping up again and continuing, looking down, looking at what mattered.

Five feet. This was the real caution zone; the bones were going to be close. I was sure by now. Sure that I was right about Shurn's deposit. To reinforce my thoughts, a plastic baggie that had no business being this deep in the dirt of a heritage graveyard poked out of the contents of my latest shovelful. One of young Shurn's discarded cocaine vessels. I knew it with the certainty of perfect intuition.

Six feet. I used the back of the shovel to smooth the dirt, then knelt and poked a gloved finger down into the earth, hoping to feel bone. Instead, wood. I was at the coffin. I dug more.

The coffin had rotted, for the most part; the wood I had felt was one of the surviving, reinforced edges. I finished the dig with my gloved hands, delicately pulling earth away, and found what I wanted to find. Almost.

A delicate skull, cracked near the left eye socket. The former ash blonde. The former, maybe, Tinsley Schultz. I was dry-mouthed and excited, as always. The sun was back out from behind the clouds, which had begun spitting wet pellets I could feel even in the grave. I straddled the two skeletons in the grave; Tinsley, as I couldn't stop thinking of her, had been rested upon the bones of Dan O'Reilly, his arms clasped around what had once been her breasts. I brushed the dirt off with care, making sure to keep the bones in the same position as they had been. Under the dirt for all these decades.

With a hand on either side of the grave, feeling bigger droplets of rain on my arms, I levered myself back aboveground, scrabbling up the sides of the grave shaft with the toes of my boots. I took a look around, even though I knew there could be no one around. If there was someone, what would I do? Explain that I'd dropped my watch down there, just seeing if I could snatch it up again?

From the back of the Jeep, I pulled out my camera and lights. I would need to anchor them to the grave, somehow, a contingency I hadn't thought of. Most of the hasty graves I dug up were much shallower than this, three feet, maybe four. I solved the problem by half-burying them in the walls of the shaft, embedding the lit eyes that would allow my camera to pick out Tinsley's final resting place with the proper accuracy, without the ugliness of a flash. I felt the urge to get a photo with my face next to hers, the family photo we'd never taken. I didn't, of course.

I zoomed, clicked. Every photo would pick out a feature of the corpse that I wouldn't notice in the moment, not in the state I was in. The photos were as essential a part of the experience as finding the body itself; I needed to be calm when I looked at them, I needed to have the ocular proof that I'd been here, that I'd done this. The lens took in her empty eye sockets, her perfect rows of teeth.

Zooming deep into her rib cage, past it even, into the bones of Mr. O'Reilly, I noticed something I hadn't when I had been standing in the grave. A glint, somewhere beneath the varyingly aged bones.

"Can't take anything," I reminded myself, even as I carefully laid the camera down a couple of feet from the hole in the ground. I climbed back into the grave, lowering myself with care, using the crude footholds

I'd made on the way up. With my fingers, I quested through the bones, shivering when I brushed past what must have been Tinsley's.

The glint was silver, or something silver-colored, and it was inexplicably bright after the length of time it would have spent under the ground. I checked my glove to see if any tears had opened up while I dug, then reached down to take hold of the silver. I pulled.

A fleshy arm and hand that were attached to the bracelet came up, and with them came the stench of meat going bad. The stink of a body when it's just starting to go off. When it hasn't been dead for long at all.

10

THE STILL MAN IN THE FOREST HAD BEEN WATCHING
Dan O'Reilly's grave for the past forty hours, ever
since he'd placed the slowly defrosting body of Bella Greene below the
other remains in the ground. She'd been in a deep freeze since he'd taken
her off the planet with a needle, ready to be on hand for his next move
with Martin Reese. And she'd done her part, perfectly, even with Martin
skipping ahead of schedule.

The man straightened up, uncoiling his long limbs, feeling his calves
tighten as they shifted out of rest and took on the weight of his tall, heavy
body. He watched Martin Reese running toward the vehicle parked in
the dirt road. Reese tossed in his digging gear—the man noted that panic
wasn't enough to make Reese completely lose his senses, as he carefully
ensured the dirty gear landed on a visible sheet of plastic. Reese pulled
away, driving past the man's own truck, which had been carefully concealed with camouflage tarps and an artful scatter of evergreen boughs.

The man walked toward his vehicle. The extremely expensive GPS bug he'd brought from his own private stock at the back of his store was magnetically bonded, with an additional black duct tape seal, to the underside of the Jeep speeding its way toward the highway. The man hoisted the tarp up, uncurtaining the passenger-side cab door and opening it. The list he'd purchased from the policeman lay on the seat. It included penned-in names, addresses, licenses, and serial numbers courtesy of the Seattle PD database, and a few paper-clipped photos he'd added himself. The pictures of Martin Reese were the most numerous, culled from newspapers and high-tech magazines. Once the man had found Keith Waring and coaxed a copied list of the sold files and call times from him, the answer had been clear. Who else could this caller, this disturber of graves and the past, be, but the man who'd been so obsessed with vanishings that he'd married Tinsley Schultz's sister?

Waiting for Reese at this site had been a slight risk. He seemed to enjoy doing things at a slow pace, not rushing his digs, reporting the bodies in order, forcing himself to space the finds out by time and likelihood of discovery. Keith Waring's presentation of the final Jason Shurn interview was the timely element that assured Martin Reese's hurried presence at this site—coming to the grave almost immediately would be irresistible to someone like Reese. The man removed another branch from his truck. He had purchased a copy of the Shurn recording a few days before Reese did. He'd known Martin Reese would eagerly buy a copy as well, and the surveillance he was running on Keith Waring (very easy, with the cop's dull and regimented habits) confirmed the meeting and sale.

The man walked back to the forest to gather his tenting materials, glad he would be back in his bed that night. When he threw the camping gear into the truck bed, he removed a shovel and his leather bag of solvents, and carried them toward the grave Martin Reese had filled in untidily. The man began to dig the whole works up again with strength and care.

11

THIS STARTED WHEN I FOUND MY FIRST BODY AT twenty-one years old, the same age Jason Shurn was when he started murdering Seattle college girls in the mid-1990s. By the time he was finished, the papers had his body count set at six, though there was evidence suggesting he'd killed more. Shurn was safely in prison, beginning the trial, conviction, and wait that would end in lethal injection, when I came across what must have been his last victim.

It wasn't pure chance that led me to that body, the final Shurn kill. It was a dropped clue. A throwaway comment he'd made to a reporter as he was being pushed toward the back door of the precinct by a flanking guard of cops, someone's windbreaker covering most of his face. Only his left cheek, a chin scabbed from being ground into the pavement during arrest, and half of his smile were visible. The question that had washed out of that sea of chattering reporters, was, of course, "Why did you do it?"

"Torland's didn't have any shifts. Got bored and started hiking instead," Shurn had said, from under his Gore-Tex cowl. The words barely came through on the news footage I saw at six, before the anchor cut in with his inane commentary. The reporters had listened to Shurn's response in a state as near to silence as they ever got, but immediately took it as a chilly joke and bombarded him with more moral puzzlers before the cops got him inside.

"The gravel plant," I said, sitting on pillows in front of my tiny television. I flicked it off a second later, when I heard Ellen's keys in the door of my shitty bachelor pad. I'd just given her that set of keys the week before, and she'd been coming over right after her last class every day since. I didn't mind.

"They caught him," I said, as Ellen shed her jacket and bag and settled into the floral couch I'd rescued from an alley.

"I know," she said. She started folding her body in on itself, gripping her shoulder blades with her fingertips as she locked herself off from hearing anything else.

"That's all I was going to say."

"Good." There had been more than a few theories about Tinsley Schultz being Shurn's first, the kill that kicked off the other six. I got up to make some tea for Ellen, hoping she'd uncoil from her defensive posture by the time I got back.

Ellen and I had only been going together for seven months. It had started a little oddly. Unexpectedly, for me, at least. When I'd heard that Tinsley Schultz's sister attended the same college as I did, I switched into a couple of her classes. Thorny poli-sci ones that I hated. I sat a few rows back from Ellen, staring at her ponytail, which was indistinguishable from the one her sister wore in the picture all the newspapers reprinted. I ventured as close as one row behind her, one seat over, once dropping my pen so I could brush the back of her sweater as I recovered it.

I watched Ellen around campus, too. Followed her home a couple of times, coming right up to the edge of a bad habit I'd tried hard to get rid of after the Darla and Misty months in high school. I watched the window of the apartment she shared with a constantly naked human kinetics student named Maria Sunestra. Ellen wiped down the chairs and couch every time Maria stepped out. I was able to see it all from the stakeout point I'd chosen, a cluster of pines on a slow-rising hill across from her building. Standing within those trees, I was invisible, even in daylight, the thick boughs shutting out the sky but allowing me a clear view of Tinsley Schultz's sister. I spread my coat out on fallen pine needles and watched her cook dinner, eat, watch television, read. I always put the binoculars down when Ellen entered her bedroom. I didn't allow myself to go too far.

Ellen was smart, and more importantly, she was and is watchful. She copped me somehow, noticing an average face that turned up more than an average amount of times. She followed me into the undergrad bar one day, asking me a question about term paper percentages, then another one about my t-shirt.

She was incredibly unafraid, considering what had happened to her sister. Just thought I was a shy guy with a crush, so that's what I decided to be. And really, she had no reason to be scared of me, I don't think. Even back then, before I had full control. And certainly not once we had started dating. She stopped having much to do with Jason Shurn, in my mind, no matter what might have happened to Tinsley. I didn't go back to that dark grouping of trees across from her apartment. I never watched her again, except when she was sitting across from me, or asleep in our bed.

With Shurn on the news and Ellen on the couch, I poured out two cups of Earl Grey and walked back to the living room. She had the TV on again, tuned to a rerun of *Cheers*. She took the mug in silence and I thought about what the killer had said to the reporters. Torland's. The gravel plant where Shurn had worked for a few weeks in the summer, before the general dislike the guys on the floor and the management had for him led to his passive firing. There were plenty of shifts, just none for him. But the other thing he'd said. Hiking. There was a thickly treed hill behind Torland's, a green North Seattle rise that had been an occasional camping spot decades ago, back before the plant had been built. The trails were mostly grown over now, since no one much wanted to hike near a belching plant and an abandoned train station. The way Shurn had put those two things together—hiking, Torland's—I was sure he was saying something. Something about his last kill.

"I'm going camping this weekend," I said, turning to Ellen. She'd unraveled a little, laughing at something arrogant Ted Danson said. "Wanna come?"

"It's raining."

"Just a little, right now. And it's supposed to be sunny for the rest of the weekend."

"It's still outside, which is a real step down from inside."

"You've got no patience for discomfort."

"Sure I do. It's not like I need to be cocooned in down pillows all day," Ellen said, grabbing at what little hair she had left after the Winona Ryder haircut she'd unwisely requested at the salon. Her hair looked nothing like Tinsley's anymore, cut or color, which was for the best. "I just don't see the point in putting up with needless, mindless discomfort. Not warm enough yet to be totally safe, either." She went on to make the argument more complex, drawing in terms from the philosophy courses she was taking and that I had no interest in.

"Been a lot more dangerous in the bars and along the highways lately," I pointed out. It was a dumb thing to say, and we were soon well into a fight. Small as the argument was, it was still pretty tense, one of those fights you have in an early twenties relationship that's passed the half-year mark and doesn't yet know what it's going to become. We ended up heading hard into the commitment lane. Part of Ellen's willingness to say yes to my proposal, which I made in the back of Elliot Bay Books, near the sci-fi, was based on how agreeable I'd become since the weekend I went out for that hike, alone.

In the rain, on the trail behind Torland's, a couple of hours after my fight with Ellen, I found Jenny Starks (Last Seen May 2 1997 / Please Call Us If You Have Any Information / We Want Our Daughter Back) while scouting for a place where I could stake my tent. On the way up, I'd started to give up on the stupid hint I'd taken from Shurn's interview, telling myself the trail I was walking would be teeming with cops if Shurn meant what I thought he meant. But I didn't figure on the more relaxed timetable the police have once a killer is safely nabbed.

I couldn't hike away my annoyance at Ellen's tensed-up impatience, how she was impossible to argue with once she arrived at a decision. The way that fight had escalated to the point where she felt cornered and forced to lock into a decision was my fault, though, even though I didn't know it back then. I retroactively give myself the pass young men have to be given: I didn't know when to shut up, and that's okay, because I sure do now. Ellen saw any disagreement after that defined point as an attack. Jenny Starks, in death, played a key role in teaching me how to keep secrets, how to keep my own counsel. A lesson every successfully married person has to learn at some point.

I was about three hundred yards up from the highway, and a little off the main, overgrown trail, when I made my discovery. I was beaming my flashlight around, looking for a relatively bare area where I could set up camp without having to hack a jungle out of the way.

Jenny's lower half was still shallowly underground, but the ground around her had been messily pawed at. I don't know exactly what had been at her face. Small creatures of some sort, maybe a coyote. And insects, of course. Shurn's last kill, and weeks of rain had pounded away at the loose dirt he'd laid over her. Jenny was a big girl, built like a Nordic athlete. She'd disappeared from a small town in the interior of British Columbia, and I'd only seen her "Missing" poster because I'd been visiting Vancouver the week before. Back then, the cops were much, much worse at the cross-border communication that would have led them to look for Jenny down here. Cop talk between Washington and Oregon was so minimal it wasn't until six months into the killings that someone thought to cross-reference the missing persons lists around the Pacific Northwest. And Canada was a whole other country. Bad luck for Jenny's parents, and Jenny herself had been beyond luck for a long time.

The hillside was pebbly and mossed around the ruined grave, and there were small objects scattered around the body. A leather wallet, worried into shreds, its plastic guts spread out. Conveniently, the driver's license was lying face-up, waiting for me. Her. I couldn't check the picture against the face, but what I did see identified itself as Shurn's handiwork, despite the careless nature of the body disposal. Her eyes were gone, and so was almost all of the facial skin. That was the animals' doing. But the deep, etched cut across the bone of what had once been a forehead, passing over the temples that had once bordered a working brain, was Shurn's work. He was a scalper. Everyone knew that much. It hadn't been in the news, or in any of the bits of tape we'd heard, but the rumor was strong, and the information that later emerged to those curious enough to seek it confirmed most of the darkest whispers that circulated on campus. Shurn had held on to a couple of the scalps for weeks, leaving them by the side of his bed. Jenny's hair was red in the wanted poster, but it was gone now. I went to my knees then, but not out of piety or fear: it was awe, it was excitement, it was fulfillment. I was right. I found her, where I thought she would be. The sheer rightness of it overwhelmed me, buried any doubts I had about what I had done.

I thought of picking up Jenny's ID, of driving it to the police station twenty miles down the highway. But when I looked around me and saw how perfectly enclosed this clearing was, fenced by obscuring trees and foliage, I had a better idea. There was a dense line of spruce blocking the half of the clearing where the body was laying. On the other side of the spruce, there was a flatter stretch of hard-packed earth that would be perfect for camping. I'd go back to town, apologize and beg Ellen to come out for a make-up camping trip on Saturday, and we'd set up our tent twenty-five feet away. I'd make sure Ellen didn't see the body until the following morning, when we could call it in together.

If I brought the ID in alone and led the police here, I thought I had a shot at being treated as some kind of suspect, even with Shurn in lock-up. He might deny this killing, for whatever reason. It was a risk I wouldn't have to take if Ellen found the body with me. Staying in that tent for an entire night, sleeping and all the rest, with that body so close. It might even help Ellen to shake her fears, pave over our tiny argument in the most dramatic of ways: she could discover that discomfort and fear could both be coped with, as long as you were in good company. Meaning myself, of course. I knew I wanted to marry her, and the thrill of finding Jenny together would be a unique bond, a confrontation with the unhappy world that lay outside our happy union. It might even help her come to terms with Tinsley's disappearance, somehow. I hiked back down to my car.

When I got back and saw Ellen sleeping in the living room, wearing the enormous Metallica t-shirt she'd asked me about when we first talked, I knew I couldn't go through with it. I thought of her in her old apartment, wiping down furniture after Maria left for the day, asserting control over her small part of the universe, what she had left after her sister vanished. I wanted to be part of the world she'd had to build again, the reasoned structure she had carefully placed over the chaos that had taken Tinsley away.

"Why you back?" she asked, groggy, her neck cricked from sleeping crammed against the couch arm.

"Because I'm an idiot," I said. "It's horrible out there, and I'm horrible for fighting and taking off like that. I'm sorry." I picked her up and carried her to bed, pretending it wasn't a strain (she was and is a light package, but I'm not exactly a powerhouse), and we had sex, then slept next to each other.

I couldn't reason out bringing Ellen up to see the body, not now that I'd seen her. All she'd be able to think of, after the terror, was her sister under that same knife. I knew that. I'd have to go back up and call the body in myself, assuming the cops didn't find it first.

There was no getting away from Ellen that weekend, so I went back to see Jenny again on Monday, during the hour when I was supposed to be presenting in my Shakespeare class. But she was gone. At the time, I thought some larger equivalent of the scavenging animals that had chewed her up had dragged her away.

When I dug up that Irish cemetery grave twenty years later and found a fresh body, I had my first real physical indication of how wrong I was. It wasn't a scavenger that had taken Jenny's body away in the night; it was a hunter. What began when I saw Jenny Starks in the hills started to end when I grabbed that newly dead wrist in the Irish cemetery.

12

DETECTIVE SANDRA WHITTAL'S IPHONE SPAT ITS RING,
the one she'd selected to cut through deep sleep, loud
music, and hangovers. Most of the ambient burbles that the phone came
with were more lulling than urgent, and Sandra preferred the violent
clang that pulled her off her yoga mat (a gift from her cousin that she
used for push-ups and crunches) and into the living room of her little
apartment, where she found the phone on top of a stack of Richard Stark
novels. She toed the power button on her stereo, silencing the Sabbath
record that had been sound-tracking her long day-off workout.

"Yeah," she said. Chris Gabriel was calling from his cell, not from a
department phone. "Sorry I didn't call last night."

"I had Mikey, anyway. Last-minute plan change. I thought you'd want
to know, and beyond that I also argued that you and I should land this:
Bella Greene. They're pretty sure it's her."

"Body?" Sandra walked into the bathroom, ready to jump into the
shower as soon as this call was over.

"Yeah. It's out in Federal Way. Besides Greene—it's weird. There's a tie-in with old cases, they think."

"What? Why?"

"There's more than one body. They're buried, and there's more than one body in the hole. Varying ages." Chris paused for a moment. "I'm thinking it may be relevant to that Finder guy we talked about last week."

"Give me a visual here, Gabriel, I have no idea what we're about to get a look at."

"Sorry. Bella Greene's body is in a gravesite in an old cemetery. She's not the only body in there. They've been buried across decades. One's a skeleton, one's a more recent skeleton, and then there's one more, a little more than a week buried. Bella Greene."

"Was there a call?"

"Literally just came in. Same computer voice, same bullshit."

Sandra skipped the shower, toweling off her sweat and pulling on her clothes. Chris's car was idling outside within four minutes of her leaving her apartment.

"Out there" was an old cemetery, disused for years. After listening to the Finder's call repeatedly in the car, Sandra had gotten the facts together from Chris on the drive up, taking considered bites at the bear claw he'd brought her and jotting a couple of notes in her pad. She had it braced against her knee, swearing when she wet a few pages with coffee when Chris rolled over a pothole.

"I'm warning you," Chris said, "forensics moved stuff around. Everything's photographed, but they got there when it was just FedWay cops, got an okay to start shifting."

"Ugh." Sandra hated having a scene touched. Ideally, the last thing that happened at one of her crime scenes was the homicide. "Fine. As long as every last goddamn thing was photographed, fine."

"Fuckin' heritage site, or should be," said one of the uniforms when

Sandra and Chris arrived. He was a mid-twenties kid who told them a little about his deep Irish American roots as he walked them to the grave. His slight swagger caused him to slip sideways in the mud a couple times. None of the cop cars had driven all the way up to the site, to keep any traces clear, but it didn't matter. The earth had turned into a soupy bog. Sandra's boots kept their seal but a few flecks of wetness licked in at the ankle, just where leather stopped and pants began. She'd forgotten her extra socks, but was too focused to be pissed off.

There was a forensic team doing detail work around the grave, looking hopeless even through their face masks. There were indications that two vehicles had been up there recently, one of which had left in a hurry, one of which had apparently been parked behind a screen of branches and perhaps some canvas covers that had been taken off-site. Four depressions in this area, suggesting that the vehicle had been there for some time. The tread marks, as far as they were visible, were for an extremely common tire. Nothing to go on.

Sandra walked a little closer, threading between collapsed tombstones and a few that had remained upright. The bodies had been taken out of their underground stack and tarped over. One, Dan O'Reilly, was a pile of bones. The other, a small-framed Jane Doe, was mostly intact. Then there was a third.

"Bella Greene," Sandra said.

"Can't be sure of that yet." Chris gestured at the body but didn't look. Sandra had noticed this on the cases they'd been detailed on together— Chris looked closely at first, memorizing the body and indignities it had suffered pre- and postmortem, but stuck with the charts after that, preferring to avoid even looking at photos. Since this wasn't even his case, the body didn't have to be stared at. But Sandra was staring.

"It's her. Look at the wrist." She grabbed Chris's own wrist and pointed, the forensics guys looking too. One, a short Indian guy who was closest to the body, gently picked the forearm up. The silver bracelet slid back, revealing an identically patterned tattoo: black leaves under the metal leaves that had slid up the emaciated flesh to rest in the crook of the body's elbow. "Greene's mother didn't mention the tattoo or bracelet when she filed the missing report, but she told the paper about it when they did that feature on her yesterday. The 'Vanishing Lives' thing."

"Good thing someone still reads newspapers."

"Stinks here," Sandra said. "Not corpse-stink."

"There's solvent all over the place," said the tech, laying the dead girl's wrist down then gracelessly levering himself into the pit the bodies had come from, poking at the dirt walls with a thin steel probe. "Paint thinner, bleach. Whole scene is doused, liberally, muddying up our shot at getting anything useful even worse than the—"

"Mud, right," Sandra said. She walked off a few paces, holding up her hand to alert Chris that she didn't want to be followed. She'd transferred the call Chris had played her into the sound bank of her cell, and she wanted to listen to it while she looked at this bizarre carnage. Anyone looking at her may have thought she was listening to her voicemails, but it was the hated voice of a computer program that cut through to her ears.

I think you've almost caught up to me, right? But I never gave you a good reason to take me seriously. There's one waiting for you, and I'll leave more soon. I'm tired of other people's memories. Time to make some of my own. Of our own.

Briefer than the rest. Maybe less elegance to the arrogance. And an odd sense, not quite precise, that he wasn't just talking to the cops. Addressing the media, too, maybe, encouraging the department to air this call. The digging-and-finding ritual of this creep, this intelligent beast, had escalated. The fun of looking for bones, replaced by the thrill of ending lives.

Sandra sat on a tombstone and looked at her colleagues, milling around the grave, pretending that what they were doing would have an effect on the outcome. But if this site were like the others, there'd be no new DNA, no easy physical shortcuts back to the guy. All she had were his fucking phone calls. This one, and the ones before it.

"Is this what you were saying you didn't want to think of just yet?" said Chris, seeing that Sandra had put her phone away.

"What?"

"When we were talking about what the caller was going to do next. The Finder. You said you hadn't let yourself think darker."

"Yeah."

"So?"

"So he's planting corpses of his own because he's worried he's going to run out of bodies to find. Not even that. The whole thing was a long-term pattern that was escalating, and that we ignored, because he was doing our cleanup work for us, roving outside of our budget to bring bones home to moms. He was escalating the whole fucking time. That's why the calls came in more often these past four years. The nasty messages for us weren't cutting it anymore. He needed more. Bella Greene was more," Sandra said. She had the nosebleed feeling of tears in her sinuses, and turned away from Chris Gabriel, forensics, and the dumbfuck Irish American flag-waving Federal Way cop to start walking back to the car. She'd taken her hood off while she listened to the call, and the rain had already soaked her hair. The cold dripped down her neck to the base of her spine, but she didn't allow herself to shiver.

13

I WAS PARKED OUTSIDE OF KYLIE'S SCHOOL, AFTER A
stop at ReeseTech to use the showers by the workout
room in the basement. No one had seen me. I hadn't spoken to anyone,
beyond a nod at the lobby secretary. Ellen wasn't home when I dropped
by to pick up my phone. I'd texted Kylie right away, asking her to meet
me across the street from her school, if she could get out of the swim
meet. She okayed me right away.

Kylie. That was the thought that exploded in my mind as soon as
I touched that skin that shouldn't have been in the grave, the arm of
someone who was living the week before. I knew it wasn't her, I knew
it wasn't my daughter. But for a moment, it felt like it. That I'd come to
find Tinsley and instead found her niece, my daughter. Because I'd been
digging where I shouldn't have.

I'd expected to see Kylie walking up from the smudged glass doors of
the sports complex. When the passenger door opened while I was staring
in the opposite direction, I screamed. Kylie yelped herself.

"Dad. What's the matter with you?"

"Where were you? Where have you been?"

"We only swam in the a.m. heats, it was like a weird not-competition thing. Basically a warm-up for the real thing in a couple of weeks in Spokane. Me and Soph left after and went to that accessory place by Nordstrom. It's like twenty minutes away. Near the place Mom rented for her store."

"She told you about that."

"Yeah. I know it was a surprise, she texted me last night that she told you. Were you surprised?"

"Yeah. Going to be a real pleasure to see Gary more," I said, not realizing there was no reason for Kylie to see the sarcasm in this.

"Why did you scream, though? Are you trying new meds or what?"

"No. Something scary happened to me earlier today. I just wanted to see you so I can get my bearings back."

"What happened? And how am I supposed to make you get your 'bearings back,' whatever that means?"

"Because talking to you means I can't afford to be a wreck." I could feel some of the tremble leaving my hands; the tremors that had been shooting through my legs since I left the cemetery were gone, as well. That grave had almost shaken me apart, and there was never a moment in my life when I needed to be more intact.

"You look weird and you're talking weirder."

"I went to some crazy guy's farm and he pulled a gun on me. Was completely drunk in the middle of the day and had no idea who I was—don't tell your mother any of this, again, and I know I've been saying that a lot lately."

I told Kylie the rest of my invented story about the cheese farmer with the shotgun and assured her I'd called the police, gaining more control of myself with every second of the lie, a story I could control entirely, pulling back from details any time I saw the beginnings of skepticism in Kylie's eyes. She sat in the passenger seat of the Jeep, so recently occupied by my sloppily stowed dig kit, with both solidity and total lightness, a person who was settled and who gave you the impression of being there only because she wanted to be, all at the same time. A person who was herself and alive, and not in the hole I'd just opened in the ground and in our lives.

"We saw each other a few hours ago, Dad. How close of a watch do I need to keep on you?" Kylie laughed.

I made her promise to cab home when the swim meet wrapped for real, and apologized for sounding like her mother. Kylie walked back into the school, melding with the crowd before she entered. Untouchable and not afraid.

Before getting behind the wheel of the Jeep up by the cemetery, I'd opened the passenger door and popped the glove compartment, taking out a cylinder of hand wipes and an old bottle of Ellen's nail polish remover. I poured the stinking, chemical liquid all over my hands, which still felt infested with the stench of that dead flesh I'd touched, even though I'd grabbed it through gloves. I prayed, to no one in particular, that the increasingly heavy rain would do the scene cleanup I hadn't been capable of. I'd filled in the grave, heaping dirt on top of what I'd found until it vanished, and I'd gone through some of my normal postdig rituals. Just way too fast. And with some steps missing, I was pretty sure.

After leaving Kylie, I took the Jeep to a service station and had it washed, eating an incredibly salty sandwich as they did an interior clean. While the guys did their work, I bought a prepaid TracFone with cash and sat on a bench in front of Cherry Street Coffee across the street, drinking a flavorless mint tea and preparing to dial Sergeant Keith Waring.

Keith's home phone rang. He had a landline, not a cell—he said it was to save money, but it was equally true there was no one in his life who ever wanted to get ahold of him in a hurry. He picked up on the third ring, his voice moving with his constant breathlessness.

"Waring."

"Keith. It's Martin, just wanting to check something."

"Over the phone?"

"Yeah. Just a customer-base question."

"Okay."

"Like we discussed. Many times before. I'm your only client, correct? We're exclusive."

"Hey, you know I wouldn't cheat on you, buddy," Keith said.

"That's good. Very good to know. Because I assume you know how heavily screwed we would both be if, you know, exposure happened."

"I'm not an idiot. Plus, even if I had—which I haven't—no one could Nancy Drew all that stuff together the way you do, right?"

"Right," I said. Waring was flattering me, but I'd had the same thought—the chances of someone aligning all those unlikely details from across the decades of Shurn files to arrive at that lonely Irish grave? Minimal. A professional detective, a cop, maybe, but I didn't think any amateurs other than me would be likely to find Tinsley's resting place. Not arrogance, just probability.

"Why do you ask?" Keith said. There was loneliness in his voice, now, a reluctance to let the conversation end. I wondered what the rest of his day looked like. Better than the morning I'd just had, definitely, but grisly and bleak in its own way.

"Just having a think, that's all. No reason. Forget it, I'll see you soon."

The photos would stay, I decided. They belonged in the scrapbook, with the rest, especially now that I'd damaged Jane Doe—Tinsley's—bones with my panicked scramble.

"All good?" asked a man wearing a Jesus badge, which I soon realized was his name tag.

"All good," I said, tipping him with four five-dollar bills and gesturing toward the other guys on his crew. On my ride home, Keith called the TracFone I'd forgotten to throw out.

"Why did you do it? What the fuck is wrong with you?" Keith was sputtering, his voice wet with panic. The cheap receiver crackled with his nervousness.

"What? What the fuck are you talking about?"

"I got a call from homicide. They want me to come in and pull a bunch of old files, trying to track down any mention of a bunch of bones they just found under a girl who got killed last week. It's going nuts down there. That body you called in, the new dead body? Bella Greene? What the fuck were you thinking? And what did you do to her, you sick—"

"I didn't do anything, Keith. I didn't call anything in." I attached the name "Bella Greene" to that slippery wrist and the stench that came with it. I tried to scan my mind for pictures of her from the news. "We can't talk about this now, Keith. Maybe not ever. Don't do anything and don't talk to anybody."

"It was one of your calls! The computer voice, everything, it was you."

"Do you really think I'd start being a fucking idiot about this at the precise moment something goes wrong, Keith?" He was quiet. "The Pemberton, eleven tonight. Calm down and shut up until then." I drove through an alley near the yacht club and tossed the phone hard against the open lid of a dumpster, hearing the plastic crack before it landed on the soft waste below.

14

CHRIS ASKED SANDRA IF SHE WANTED HIM THERE while she dealt with the mother. She waved him off, leaving him standing with the desk sergeant. The two men pretended to be talking as Sandra walked stocky, short-legged Sylvia Greene through the warren of offices and cubicles to a comfort area they had set up in the rear quadrant of the station, furnished to look something like a cross between a waiting room and a living room. The walk was long, as Sylvia Greene kept pausing, doing a fist clench and slight turn of her upper spine, as though she were gearing down from an argument. Rick Garner, one of the officers who'd thrown out her flyer a few days before, walked toward them as they entered the last corridor. Mrs. Greene was staring at the linoleum and didn't notice him.

Rick opened his mouth, and Sandra saw he had braces, something that must have made parts of the job hell for him, as far as getting teased went. Probably lied about it and said they were from getting his jaw smashed in a fight. As Garner's hand was coming up to touch Mrs.

Greene on the shoulder, he lost all his courage at once and walked past them instead.

Once they hit the room, Sandra let the woman collect herself. Sylvia Greene had wear in her face, the lines, puckering, and hollows that came from smokes, a decade or so of bad nutrition somewhere in her past, and probably a couple long tangles with substance abuse. But she was young to have a twenty-three-year-old daughter, maybe about forty. They took up seats in the strange room, sitting on soft, grandma's-house couches in a building of practical surfaces. Sylvia Greene had done the formal identification on her daughter's body in the morgue a couple of hours ago. It was late afternoon now, and Sandra wanted the sandwich in her purse. She left it there, let a little silence build, and Sylvia started talking.

"I asked this when they showed her to me, but I think there's a better chance you'll be honest with me."

"No one here would lie to you, Mrs. Greene."

"Soften things, though. They might do that." Bella Greene's mother, tendons rippling on her neck as she shifted the muscles of her face to stave off tears and crackles in her voice, looked hard at Sandra, who tilted her head a little, allowing that this might be true. "I asked them about any sex stuff that had been done to her."

"There was none," Sandra said immediately. "No evidence of anything like that. Or—torture." She'd been unable to find a softer word.

"So she was just killed."

"Yes. Drugged and then stabbed, just once, directly in the heart. Almost certainly no pain. She probably had no idea."

"Isn't that strange, in something like this?" Sylvia Greene said, pushing her hand deep into an inner pocket of her coat. Sandra decided that if the lady wanted to smoke, she'd let her. They'd take the battery out of the smoke detector if they had to. Sylvia pulled out a pack of gum, popping out two pieces. She didn't offer one to Sandra, just put both in her mouth and started chewing aggressively.

"I did think it was unusual, yes," said Sandra. "It seemed like a murder with purpose, not random or part of the usual kind of pattern behavior. Do you know of anyone who would want to kill her?"

"Where was she found?" asked Sylvia, going directly to the most important question.

"A location a little bit outside of town, in strange circumstances," Sandra said. Not the least of which was that the body had been frozen solid before it was buried, and had defrosted under the earth. That one was new to her.

"Which you're not going to tell me. They wouldn't tell me in the room, either." "Room" meant morgue. Relatives of the corpses almost always called it "the room" in these interviews.

"For the sake of catching the guy who did this to her, no, we're not letting anyone know that yet."

"Not even the mother of the dead whore on the slab." Sylvia looked at the floor as she said this, staring through the linoleum.

"Look," Sandra started, stopping when Sylvia put her hand up.

"I'm just glad you're handling this, not one of the men. You'll have a better idea of what I mean when I tell you she wasn't just street meat, from nowhere. Not that any of the girls you see are, but some of them just never had a chance. Bella had a chance. She fucked up her life, but she had a life to fuck up, you know?" Sylvia rubbed the inside of her left forearm.

"Yes. I know that."

"I don't care what anyone else thinks, just you. If you're the one who's going to be finding the thing who did this to her. And I'm going to be of very little help to you, I'm sorry. I've barely talked to Bella or seen her in three years." Sylvia Greene took out her gum and rolled it up in a receipt. Sandra pushed the paper cup of coffee she'd poured for herself over to Sylvia. It wasn't that the woman looked thirsty, it was that she looked like she wanted to bury her face for a second, chase back the saltwater pooling in her tear ducts while she pretended to sip. This was how cops tended to cry, at least at the station; at certain bars and in their homes, the flow was a little freer, but by their desks, the face-in-mug method was the way to go. Sylvia came up for air after a second, looking more collected.

"There's one guy Bella talked about. We ran into each other, near my office, I think really by accident. It had been so long since we talked that I led by giving her a fifty, wheedled her into getting Starbucks with me. She stayed for twenty minutes, getting twitchier and eyeing the door."

"Did she seem scared?"

"Scared she wasn't going to get a fix as soon as she wanted one, that's all. I could see her plowing through the dealer Rolodex in her head while I talked to her. But she did mention one guy. She was wearing this turquoise scarf I'd given her for grad, too. Can't believe she still had that thing."

"Who's the guy?" Sandra asked, trying to hope her way through all the improbabilities, trying to get this potential suspect to fit the profile she was cobbling together. Maybe the Finder also had grown a fixation with women who worked the streets, living parallels of the skeletons he'd uncovered over the years. Maybe he'd pushed that curiosity into his first kill. Maybe he'd buried that kill with an old kill of his own, of someone he'd known. Maybe. Maybe not.

"I'm telling you right now it's not him." Sylvia pushed a clump of her cheap haircut over her right ear, which had been hidden until now. It was shriveled and wavy at the top, thin and misshapen as a broken potato chip, with the shiny skin of a burn scar. A souvenir from Bella's father, or some later boyfriend. Sandra read the move as a wordless demonstration that Sylvia knew violence and men, and the places where the two intersected.

"His name," Sylvia said, "his dumb name is Keegan Fitzroy. Kinda sounds like a cop name from a cheesy old show, right? He's not a cop. He's a real piece of crap who owns a sports collectibles store on Third

Avenue. Must have family money, or something, because he lives in that new high-rise near the market. Bella said that a few times. Stressed it."

"Did you tell anyone about him when your daughter went missing?"

"Eight or nine cops," Sylvia said, staring at Sandra now. "I have the feeling no one followed up on it."

"I'm sorry. And how did this Fitzroy know your daughter?" Sandra wished that she had her coffee back, but it was too late. Not knowing what to do with her hands, she opened up her notebook and poked at it with her pen.

"Bella was never an actual prostitute. She didn't walk, or advertise, nothing like that." She hesitated, buried her face again in the cup. "I don't mean to say that proudly, like that was one way I didn't fail her, that she didn't fail herself. I'd rather she was a happy, safe sex worker with an apartment of her own and no track marks and with a pulse. But she didn't sell it straight up. She had rules, I guess. She only slept with dealers—this I found out when she was still in school—or had ongoing things with mostly old, mostly disgusting men. Men who kept her."

"Right."

"The few times I saw Bella in the last few years, it was different guys, but this time, in the Starbucks, she tried to sell me Keegan Fitzroy like he was the real thing. Some sort of real thing. So after she scurried off that day, I went into his store to check him out. Skinny with a *Grinch Who Stole Christmas* gut. Store's a bit of a mess, and so is he. A snob, too. I think he keeps the store just so he can show off to the losers who hang out there, scream at the occasional kid who comes in and leans on one of his glass cases."

"He doesn't necessarily sound like a direct hit, suspect-wise, but we'll check him out, Mrs. Greene."

"She was bruised, too. When I saw her. Bruised on her arms, and it didn't look needle-related. I know what junkie arms look like, by now," Sylvia said, pulling her upper lip into her mouth and chewing it.

There had been some light bruising on Bella's arms, according to the guys downstairs, but it didn't seem related to the murder itself. Looked like trace markings from a few days before death, not severe enough to be tied to a struggle. But Keegan Fitzroy was a little more interesting if he was into inflicting pain.

"You think Fitzroy had been abusing her?"

"Probably not. Jesus, I don't know. Just—"

"Don't worry about it. We'll talk to him."

"Yeah. Could you treat him a bit like shit, please?"

"Not officially," Sandra said, maintaining clear, frank eye contact. Sylvia Greene got out a small chuckle. Sandra was going to join in, but the laugh didn't last long enough.

Walking Sylvia back to her car in the parking lot, Sandra passed Chris, who was drinking a Coke and sitting on the hood of his car. He liked doing part of his reading and thinking out here, when it wasn't raining, at least. They didn't talk, but he looked up from his papers and gave Sandra a nod.

With Sylvia safely in her hatchback, Sandra walked back to Chris. She took a sip from his bottle while he laid it out for her.

"Forensics are what we thought. A fat zero. No fibers, no footprints, tire tracks uselessly generic, no hair or skin, and a drenching of this cocktail of bleach and about seven under-the-sink chemicals that would confuse even the sharpest testing. Then the rain. There's nothing out there. Even if we do get some kind of sample, it would be very helpful if we had the first goddamn clue of who we might be looking to test it against."

"I'm getting that feeling," Sandra said.

"That bad feeling?"

"Yeah. That we're going to have to wait for him to do something else before we get anywhere close to nailing him." Sandra took her notebook out of her inner pocket, the USB key full of the Finder's calls falling out when she did this. She picked it up from the damp cement. "And there is going to be something else, Chris. Someone else. This guy's been obsessed with dead women and with getting away with everything to do with murder short of the actual killing himself. Was a matter of time before he graduated."

Across the city, the man who had killed Bella Greene was staring at a screen, watching the moving blip that represented Martin Reese. Next to the screen was a detailed, foldable map of Seattle, which the man had marked with little stars in all the places Martin seemed to go most often. The beacon under Reese's car dutifully sent a coordinate every minute, and after cleaning the scene, the man had been able to return to this base and see exactly what Martin had done after running away from the grave. ReeseTech, probably for cleanup or an alibi. Then, and how touching it was, Kylie Reese's high school. Followed by a location downtown the man had later ascertained was a car wash. Then straight home, where that blip had stayed for hours, broadcasting the stationary cowardice of a boy who was scared of what he had gotten himself into, and who didn't know how to get himself out. Those domestic hours, Martin with his wife, interested the killer—he could start thinking of himself as a killer again—more than the predictable, amateur darting around Martin did outside of the home. A few days after killing Bella and laying her to rest in the freezer, he'd tailed Martin to his meeting with the fat cop, waiting outside the Pemberton and thinking about exactly how many people he was going to have to kill in order to keep the game going, to move it on to its next stage.

At least two.

15

THREE BODIES IN A GRAVE THAT SHOULD ONLY HAVE
had two. Put that way, doesn't sound so weird, does
it? Just one extra. A joke with no punch line, yet. After the car wash, I
bought a cheap Microsoft tablet with cash at Best Buy and used café
Wi-Fi to find out anything about Bella Greene, the dead woman whose
murder I'd just touched. The killing the cops would want to pin on me,
the one that had been pulled off by whoever was following me.

Whoever it was hadn't given my name to the cops in that message,
or this would all be over, and I'd be cuffed, or sitting on a steel bench in a
cell. Shurn's voice leaked back to me from the tape: *"If you want to know
where both of them are, you'll have to ask someone else. I only know where
one of them is."*

"A partner. Shurn killed with a partner who was never caught. You
never gave your boy away, Jason," I whispered. Dr. Ted Lennox hadn't
caught on in his Shurn interview before the creature was put to death,
and it had taken me a step too long as well. If that was it at all—maybe

Shurn was telling another one of his stupid riddles, fucking with people right up until the miserable end he deserved.

But if I wasn't being followed, if someone else had just known where the other body was and had happened to get there shortly before me to add another corpse—I stopped there, because it was just too stupid. Someone knew exactly where I was going, and that I had expected to dig up the bones of Tinsley Schultz exactly where they'd been left by Jason Shurn. Either someone had been with Jason when he buried the girl, or someone had made the same connections I had, at exactly the same time. This had everything to do with me, with someone trying to fuck with me and destroy me. Starting with Bella Greene's body, and continuing with that forgery of one of my calls to the cops.

Keith was too dumb and too scared to want to do any of this. Jason Shurn and Horace Marks and all the other men whose murders I'd brought into the open to be buried with human dignity were all dead or in jail.

I had a watcher, someone trailing me. Someone who knew where Shurn kept his bodies. What little the online news had to tell me on Bella Greene pointed to her being a total random, an easy-target streetwalker with only a mother to care about her. There was an interview with the mother, Sylvia, brief and prediscovery, all about how Bella could make it right with her next shot. In the picture, Mrs. Greene's chin was crunched into her neck as she pulled out a flyer with her daughter's image on it to hand to the reporter, or to a bystander. It got across exactly one thing: all she cared about in that moment was getting her daughter back. Well, at least she had that. There were a dozen more articles about the mother, but I couldn't make myself read them.

"I found her," I said to the picture of Sylvia Greene. If I had the time or if it was a sane mission to take on, I felt it would have been extremely worthwhile to make her understand that I was the opposite of the man or men who killed her daughter. That since I met Ellen, since Kylie came into our world, I had only ever helped people like Bella Greene, and their parents. But I knew how all of those skeletons, my work, could look to an outsider, to my wife, to the police. Especially after Bella.

I stowed the tablet inside an *Auto Trader* magazine and stuffed it under the front seat of the Jeep, making my way home with a wheel of artisanal goat cheese from the grocery store in the trunk. I was going to use it as the rueful, "shoulda done this in the first place" button on my crazy farmer story for Ellen. Turns out there was no need.

The front door was slightly open, which wouldn't have bothered me, usually. Ellen and I weren't always diligent about locking up when one of us was home and downstairs, only checking in for sure when we went up to bed. Ellen's fears didn't extend to a home invasion. But tonight, there was a car I didn't recognize in the driveway. A gray BMW, mud spatters on the doors.

I'd never been a gun person. So I took a screwdriver out of the glove compartment. I walked up the driveway slowly, having parked in the street instead of the garage. But when I saw Kylie's backpack lying in the hallway I booked it, rushing toward the door and running straight past the entry to spin and stand with my back to the staircase, giving me a view of both the kitchen and living room at once.

Ellen and Kylie were sitting on the gray couch under the front window, stunned. A slight man with his back to me turned, following my family's gaze, and started to laugh. They joined in, and I pocketed the screwdriver. It was Gary Leung.

"I guess we're on high alert here in Eastlake. Hear you came by the office today, boss," Gary said, walking over to shake my hand. It was warm and coated with sweat from gripping the screwdriver, and Gary made a show of wiping himself dry on his vividly white Acne t-shirt.

"Had to take a shower," I said. "Bad encounter with a farm-to-table experience that will ensure I stick to Whole Foods from now on. Hi, you," I added, talking over Gary's shoulder to Ellen, waving at Kylie.

"What happened?" Gary asked.

"Never mind, boring."

"Come on. You're with family, boss."

"Family plus you, friend," I said, and saw his eyes go dark even as his smile didn't dim a watt. He had psycho eyes, Gary did, a tell that any negotiator or high-level businessperson, especially a woman, could see a mile out. It was the reason I'd stopped taking him into meetings, even ones where he would have made me look good, racial-balance-wise. I didn't understand why Ellen didn't pick up on the slight wrongness that emanated from every other gesture or look Gary made—the way he smirked when he insulted you and thought you didn't notice, his boredom with absolutely any conversation that didn't directly involve his financial or sexual gain within five minutes.

"I get it, I get it, you're having an affair and just threw together a quick cover story to explain why you went to ReeseTech to wash the perfume and lipstick off," Gary said, as I shed my light jacket and hung it off the banister. There was a rim of dirt around the left cuff, a zone that must have been exposed between my glove and plastic coverall shell when I'd panicked during the grave fill-in. I'd have to dump the jacket. All of these clothes would have to go.

"My daughter's here," I said, in a whisper, right to Gary's face. Ellen didn't hear it but she saw me saying it.

"He's just making a bad joke, Mart, come on. Kylie knows well enough to ignore anything that comes out of Gary's mouth that isn't clothing, business, or tech-advice related."

"Yep," said Kylie. "And Dad's right, his farm story is boring. He slipped in goat shit while he was buying cheese, big whoop. He texted me about it like it was the end of the world."

"Kylie, don't say 'shit,'" Ellen said, her laugh counteracting the order. I looked at Kylie with something like wonder, quickly trying to bury the expression, wondering how I'd passed along these cover-up genetics to the person I was most honest with in the world. I nodded a little thank-you.

"It became clear to me that I'd never actually get you to come to one of our meetings, so I brought one here, okay, Mart?"

"Yeah, sure," I said. "The store."

"It's closer than you think, boss," said Gary. "We found the perfect space three months ago, started stocking—"

"Ellen?" I asked, cutting Gary off in just the way I knew pissed him off. Letting him get into the story first was the trick, just enough words out before shutting him up. I also wanted Ellen's version of what was happening, of course.

"We're having a soft open on Friday, Martin. Everything's set up, I wanted to surprise you with it, but it seemed crazy to make it a total surprise and have you turn up at a finished store. Tiny little storefront, but it's rectangular and goes way back, and we've designed it to look—"

"It looks great," Kylie said.

"You've seen it and knew about this, too, huh? Traitor," I said to Kylie. She crossed her legs and leaned way back on the couch, grinning.

"Am I really, Dad?"

"No. And Ellen, Gary, this is great. I'm excited, tell me everything," I said, crossing the short distance to Ellen and giving her a short, public-tame kiss. I took her left arm in my hand and gave it a squeeze, before I dropped it like I'd gotten an electric shock from her warm, slight limb.

I started to tremble, keeping the shake out of my upper body, but feeling it through my knees, thinking that it was just hours since I'd touched Bella Greene's dead arm. But there was nothing to be done. I sat down and smiled and asked to hear everything, waiting for my eleven o'clock meet with Keith Waring. Waiting for a knock on the door from the cops, or from whoever had put Bella Greene in that grave. Waiting for whatever was coming for me.

16

ON THE DRIVE DOWN, I SAW HER. JUST AS I CROSSED
over Fiftieth Street, on my way to a restaurant dumpster behind a Chinese place off Aurora that was reliably emptied every
second day and heaped so high with rotting food no bums bothered to
salvage it, I saw Tinsley Schultz.

Jean skirt, no tights. Too cold for that, but she had a thick pea coat
on. Hair the same color as Ellen's used to be. I slowed my car down and
willed her not to turn around as I parked.

We were at Forty-Fifth and Latona, the signs coming into focus as I
automatically parallel parked, ignoring a light rap I made against the Ter-
cel bumper in front of me. She walked past a café and thought better of
it, but didn't turn around—she walked backward three steps and pushed
the door, dodging inside for warmth.

I got out of the Jeep and stood there for a moment, watching the
door of the café. A little hipster-type joint with a nineties hangover, I
could tell from the outside. It had one of those Sharpie-graffitied walls,

tags going back decades, probably a musician or two in the scrawls that meant the owner couldn't bear to paint over it. And in there, ordering a tea, an Earl Grey with cream, same thing Ellen always grabbed to stave off the cold, was Tinsley. I crossed the street, walking away from the café, aiming for the lip of an alley where I could disappear.

I knew it wasn't Tinsley Schultz. Of course I knew. But for a few minutes of calm and thought, I was going to let myself believe that it was just after high school, that I'd never gone away for watching Darla and Misty, that no one I'd gone to high school with knew to call me a creep. I'd watch Tinsley the way Jason Shurn had watched her, waiting for the right moment to make her to disappear. I halted that for a moment, penciling in a shadow next to Shurn: the partner he must have watched Tinsley with, the one who knew where she was buried, knew well enough to leave the body of Bella Greene there for me to find.

Jason and his partner watched Tinsley, way back then, the way I'd watched Ellen before we met, planning something I'd never dared to say to myself or even think at a certain volume. The thoughts I'd had until Ellen had come to real life, approaching me and suppressing whatever it was inside me that wanted to do what Shurn and all the other men like him had done. Ellen had started and Kylie had finished pulling me back from that brink.

I could see the Tinsley girl through the front window of the café. Her hair bobbing down into the cup she'd ordered, the steam rising to hide her face from me and anyone else who might be watching. I closed my eyes and waited in the alley for a few minutes. Then I walked back to my car.

The Pemberton was near empty, except for a few alcoholic fixtures who took up space in the back booths, clicking away on laptops or just staring into their glasses. I'd parked two blocks away and threaded in and out of alleys to get here, staring at the backs of men's rain hoods, my eyes fixed on any exposed female wrist I could spot, looking for the leaf tattoo I'd pulled out of the grave. It was either fear or a wish that Bella

Greene would be walking around Seattle again, her resurrection erasing my problem. I poured liquor onto said problem as soon as I sat down, picking a booth across the room from the one I usually shared with Keith, paying the prematurely aged, wattle-necked server with bills that looked too fresh and crisp to be used in this room. The regulars I expected were there, along with a couple of guys sitting at the bar itself, facing away from my booth. I waited and tried to do as little as possible with my thoughts, making the steady up-down of the pint glass the main event.

Keith came in with his talcumed after-work and pre-shower odor, a mix of pancake batter and Old Spice. He was carrying a little lime-green file folder that was conspicuous in his sweaty hand, making him look like a dad rushing to drop off his kid's forgotten school project. I resisted my strong, movie-driven urge to ask him if he'd been followed. From the way his eyes scanned the room, looking for familiar cop faces, he may have had the same question for me. Keith settled into the banquette across from me, and I felt it in the floorboards we shared. I leaned forward and dug my nails into the soft puck of flesh above his kneecap.

"Who else did you sell those files to? Do you have a Craigslist ad or something, you dumb fuck?" I let go and pulled away, in case he should feel the urge to swing at me to conform to his idea of working-class manliness. Keith put a finger on my chest, brushing the foam at the top of my pint on his way, and pressed the digit in for a second while he tried to think of something threatening to say.

"I've been very discreet this whole time," Keith said. "And you can't say the same thing, can you? Making your stupid phone calls for, what, ten, fifteen years?" A server came by, skinny but with twenty years of brown liquor dragging down the flesh of his face, and took Keith's order. We were quiet for an extra second after he walked away.

"You know there's a cop who's had a hard-on for you for a few months. Because of your phone calls, boy. Her name's Sandra Whittal, miraculous piece of ass and way too young to be a detective. I'll let you guess how she got there. But she's no dummy, and she's hungry for you. And guess who happened to get this Greene case?"

"What do you mean, hard-on for me? There is no 'me.' I never did anything wrong." I took a big, masking gulp, covering fear and even a strange churning guilt, something that hadn't left me since I'd gripped that buried wrist.

"What, you're going to wrong-place-wrong-time me? There just happened to be a short-stack of corpses in an abandoned graveyard your shovel tumbled into?"

"You and I both know what I do, Keith. And you know I've never crossed any sort of border like that." The server set a drink down between us, was about to ask me if I wanted anything, but thought better of it when he saw Keith and me in a stare-down. He left.

"Before we go any further," Keith said, "I want you to know that when I mentioned Darla and Misty last time we met, I wasn't just going on the B&E charge." Keith pushed the green file folder over to me. "Like before, I made one copy for me and one for you. I just brought this so you'd know I'd know."

There was a gasping anger in me as I turned the few pages. Saw the mug shot of my young face, the cop legalese around my arrest, the transparently wrong psych reports from Dr. M. J. Trainor, a man I still remembered with a fairly significant degree of hate, but whom I'd been able to use very effectively. I'd read enough criminal psychology books to outsmart this fresh graduate, with his Wayne Gretzky mullet and leading questions, which he always asked while looking at my chin or a ceiling tile. I sold my recovery from what he called "budding recidivism" at a pace that matched the short length of my stay in the facility, the last institution I'd ever allow myself to be in. *Doc Trainor, you're kind of, kind of a miracle. I see things—well now I see I wasn't seeing anything, really, not until you led me there.* I hadn't thought of his face in years, the bashful arrogant smile he'd had at the last hearing, when he gave me a full clearance. I'd looked him up a few years ago. Ended up in a Thai prison for predictable offenses.

"These were destroyed. I had this taken care of."

"You don't have a record anymore, Marty, but that doesn't mean they carry all the paper out to the parking lot and have a bonfire. It's buried a little deeper, but I was still able to find it with some searching. I've had it for about five years, now, thanks to a little naughty breaking and entering, maybe, or maybe even just a phone call. It's the stuff that isn't in there that interests me most. So, you at what, sixteen? You were breaking into the houses of certain young ladies and spending a creepy time pacing the premises. Taking a souvenir or two, probably. That's not mentioned here."

"Shut up."

"What I'm wondering is how far you took it before the cops scooped you out of that tree. Had you been strangling their cats or anything like that? Isn't that what you people do?"

I looked down at the file. My only encounter with the courtroom part of the legal process, before I sank into my few months at juvie for my nighttime activities at Darla's and Misty's houses, had also been my first indication that I wasn't as dumb as my parents and teachers seemed to think. The judge I'd landed—an older woman named Volquez who my public defender told me had two teenage daughters of her own, in a tone that told me I was fucked—responded well to the few details I gave her about my home life and my concentration on the deluded, romantic fantasy ideals I'd had about Misty and Darla, about their wonderful homes and nice lives. I kept sex out of it entirely and summoned up a few tears, and that's why I got the light sentence I did.

I realized I was squeezing nail dents into the file. At the top left of each leaf of paper was a diagonal line, the photocopied impression of a staple.

"Where's the original?"

"Nestled in the part of the records department it always will be. You're on that line between fanboy investigator and genuine profundo-creep,

Martin. These pages prove it. Research is fun, you know. I learned a lot from watching you work."

"You didn't learn discretion, Keith. You didn't learn to be smart."

"So you were stalking girls that are around your daughter's friends' age now, huh? She'd probably be pretty grossed out to hear that."

"If you ever mention or imply anything about Kylie again I'll have you killed, or kill you myself. I will."

"I'm in a fucking panic, too, Martin, don't you get it? I should have known, looking at this shit, that you were going to go full-psycho on me soon enough. You were practicing for it in high school. You don't just, just blow out your knee and decide to quit being a night stalker pervert creep like some guy hanging up his football cleats. You finally killed some stupid bitch and planted her and now you've ruined my life, too, and we're both going to trial and jail and that's it for me," Keith said, his voice shaking, a mist starting to surface at the lower rim of each eye.

"Don't call the Greene woman a bitch. And of course I didn't kill her."

Keith laughed at this, shocking his teary eyes, releasing about fifty percent of his tension. "Don't call her a bitch, he says. Sitting down across from the fucking Angel of Death and getting PC language lessons. Fine. If not bitch, junkie. Apparently she wasn't a full-on whore."

"If you were going to blackmail me with this juvie record, Keith, you're a little too late, and a little too involved."

"I'm just letting you know that *I* know, Martin. I know what you are," Keith said, nuzzling his pint and taking what I realized was his first sip. I'd never seen him wait so long to drink before.

"Who did you sell the case files to? Who else other than me?"

"I'm not ready to talk about that yet," Keith said. The laugh had restored a little of his fake swagger, and I reminded myself that he was currently the only person with access to any of the information I needed. Him and whoever had filled that grave.

"What are you willing to talk about?"

"Well, the girl. Bella Greene," he said, whispering now. "Nothing—I keep my ears open, the guys talk around me—nothing was done to the body, other than the killing part. Fucking weird."

"Yeah," I said. Very strange. "Not even any pain stuff? Rope ties?"

"You can say 'ligature' around me, Mart, I have a TV too." Keith snorted some foam off the IPA and onto the table. "No, nothing. One clean stab in the heart, while she was drugged. Stung and done."

"So—"

"So the weirdest part of this whole thing is, she's in a grave with another vic, one that has something to do with your poking around. She a Shurn girl?" I hesitated, but Keith wasn't going to go on unless he got an answer. I nodded.

"Figured," he said. "You must have been over the moon to get those tapes when you did, right? Any clues you needed on them?"

"Just confirmation of what I already knew."

"You're such a pathetic show-off," Keith said, some snarl to it. "I listened to all those calls you made, on the way up here. This detective, Whittal—"

"Tell me what you know about her. Everything."

"In a minute, Martin. I pulled the USB off the detective's desk to dump the files onto my laptop and give them a listen again. No one noticed." This I doubted, but I let Keith continue.

"You know how arrogant it is, thinking you're smarter than cops? It just hasn't occurred to you that we're spending our time trying to prevent guys like you from doing the shit that gets the girls buried, right?"

"You personally aren't doing anything other than shuffling through filing cabinets, Keith." This got to him, even if it wasn't worse than the other insults I'd pushed his way in the past—maybe because this time, I wouldn't be following up my jibes with a wad of cash. Keith looked at the surface of the table for a minute, tinged the unclipped fingernails of his right hand against his pint glass, then took my wrist in his left hand

and squeezed, hard. So hard my knees moved together and clicked at the caps, so hard I felt my bladder spasm. Keith let me go when he saw the begging in my face.

"Just being at this table with you, I'm doing you a favor, Martin." He patted the red part of my forearm with his hand, before I slid it under the table. Keith made a shots gesture toward the bar and said "Jameson," then held up two fingers. I waited for the drinks to arrive, and sipped mine as he threw his back.

"A favor, Martin. We're doing each other a favor, one that keeps us both out of jail, or worse trouble. Right?"

"Right."

"So you're not going to insult me anymore."

"Sure. And you're going to be straight with me about the files. Because someone else out there has them. Or none of this would be happening." I drank from my pint and Keith matched me. There was a hole in the carpet near my left foot, some hardwood beneath it begging to be liberated in a reno, one that would probably happen in a few years when the lease here came up. I teased the corners of the hole with my boot while I waited for Keith, who made a show of considering his reply.

"Some stuff, okay," he said, relenting. "I have sold some stuff to other collectors, but very little that overlapped with your little field of interest. The particular serials you're into—they're footnotes, compared to some of the guys I have sitting in the cabinets back at the station. That's where I do most of my business. The bigs. But you? Barely anyone is interested in Shurn, Carl Hillstrom, those guys. You and—well, maybe that's all. Only other guy who asked about those files didn't even want to see them."

"What? What do you mean?"

"He didn't want to see the files themselves," Keith said. "He wanted to see who was buying them. He wanted my client list. A few notes on who was buying what."

I'd given up being startled by Keith's stupidity, which left me with my own to contemplate. The gulping moron across from me, who even now cared more about provoking me than he seemed to care about the trouble we were in—I'd married myself to his mistakes, just for the chance to look at more files, to find more burials. Keith undid the top button of the blue shirt he was wearing, revealing a black t-shirt underneath. He couldn't even dress himself like an adult, and I'd trusted him with my freedom and life.

"You weren't suspicious of someone asking for details of your illegal activities?"

"I ran him through every possible system I could, even dug up some buried juvie records on him, which confirmed the story he had. And the money. You think you pay big, goddamn. Guy had me thinking I'd finally be able to afford a boat and a few years of docking fees, business kept going that way."

The light racket of young people trying to keep their voices down came to us from the doorway. A few college-age kids, four women and a handsome male mascot, dressed in what a shitty magazine would call hipster style, a useless catchall that infuriated Ellen when she heard it. It covered the way she and Gary dressed, though, fitted and vintage with the occasional odd angle. These kids looked like younger facsimiles of my wife and her new business partner, except for the slave-labor cheapness of their pilling, shiny sweaters. I waited for them to do the inevitable: take in the bar and its customers, and pile out to go to the next place. They did.

"Keith, we need to get into some actual specifics. Who the hell was this guy, and what story did he give you?"

"I'm not sure if this is really the best setting for us to get into specifics, buddy. What I will tell you here, though, is that he said he'd been inside with Jason Shurn, as a kid. Wanted to follow up on that."

"He was in youth detention with Shurn. Someone approached you saying he was old pals with a known, executed serial killer, and just

wanted to check up on who else might be interested in said psychopath."
That shadow I'd pictured next to Jason Shurn out at the Irish grave got
a bit sharper as I spoke.

"You're making me sound like an idiot again, Martin. And I'm not an
idiot, or we'd be in a much bigger mess than we are now."

I looked at the Schlitz wall clock behind Keith's head, not really interested in the time, but intensely interested in not making eye contact with
him. It was 11:37. Ellen's meeting with Gary was probably over, unless it
was like the meetings Gary liked to take back in the ReeseTech days, which
ended with martini pitchers at one of the hotel bars he cruised for tourists.
I'd watched him chat up women countless times, some of the ReeseTech
programming geeks looking on in awe as he went from a couple drink orders to a room number written on a napkin. It wasn't impressive to me. He
was just good at choosing someone who might choose him back.

"If you want to talk about this more—and I think we should—let's go
to my apartment. I kept all the files there, anyway, stuff we might need.
I don't want to be seen with you here," Keith said. The evasiveness of the
way he was talking took me back to the Shurn tapes, Shurn whiling away
the last minutes he had before the needle delivered its payload into his
arm. The "someone else" Jason Shurn mentioned. This kid he'd been in
juvie with. Maybe, more than maybe, the guy who'd added Bella Greene
to that burial site before I'd gotten there.

"I don't want to be seen with you here either, Keith," I responded,
sighing. "Here or anywhere else." I unfurled bills and put them on the
table. At the very least, I could use this expedition to make concretely
sure Keith had no record of me left by the time I exited his home, that
I'd burned or wiped any evidence of my name from whatever primitive
records of his fuckups he kept. I had a feeling it was going to be limited to
a grease-stained notebook, maybe an Excel file. "Write the address down
for me and get a head start, I'll catch up. So it doesn't look like we're
going together. You're in what neighborhood?"

"Ballard."

"Fine. Look, this guy you gave the list to—you gave my name to—what did he look like?"

"I never met him. Just dropped the list at a garbage can near the police museum, pulled an envelope of cash out of another can down the street."

"Of course you did."

"I mean, I've seen his juvenile pictures, the kiddie mug shots."

"How can you be sure that's him?"

"Well, because he gave me the name, and he seemed to—" Doubt turned up on Keith's face after a few seconds, a good indication of how far he had to be led toward an obvious answer. "I guess I'm not sure it was him."

"Alright. Okay. If you're not going to give me the name here, at least tell me this. What did the person who called in the Bella Greene grave say? What was the call?"

Keith smiled and angled his several chins. "You sure it wasn't you made that call? Real sure?"

"I didn't."

"He said—" Keith pulled on his coat and made a few other adjustments that allowed for a dramatic pause, then started speaking in what was actually a pretty good impression of the inflections of the computer program I used to make my calls. " '*I think you've almost caught up to me, right? But I never gave you a good reason to take me seriously. There's one waiting for you, and I'll leave more soon. I'm tired of other people's memories. Time to make some of my own. Of our own.*' Then he read out a GPS coordinate, took the cops right to Bella Greene."

I watched Keith leave the bar and counted off five minutes on the Schlitz clock. Sent Ellen a text that I'd be going late at the bars, not to wait up. And, before I got up and left, worried for a second that I was going to be on that list of new memories this guy was making. List of new bodies.

17

"WOULD BE FUN TO HUMILIATE HIM IN FRONT OF HIS weird sports memorabilia pals," Chris said. "I always hated those people. Grabbing fouls away from kids in the stands at the Kingdome."

"Kingdome?" Sandra was driving this time, managing the thin downtown traffic easily. They'd eaten at a cheapish steakhouse near the precinct, pushing the clock so they could be reasonably sure that Keegan Fitzroy would be home. "Gone almost twenty years ago, Chris. What kind of baseball fan are you?"

"Yeah, Safeco, whatever. Awful name for a stadium. And I don't watch sports outside of Michael's league games, you know that." Chris might have talked more, but he needed his tongue to poke at a thread of rib-eye gristle embedded in his molars.

"Maybe you told me once, that doesn't mean I remember." They pulled up out front of the high-rise where Fitzroy lived, and Chris got out with his badge to have a word with the concierge, gesturing at their parked car. Sandra got out when it was clear they didn't have to move it.

"Gave me a fob of my very own," said Chris, wiggling the keychain attachment that allowed them access to the elevator. "1014." The lobby was slick in a boring cloned-condo way, green tile and brushed steel.

"I'd rather live in a fishing shack than a trap like this," Sandra said, while they waited a little too long for the elevator.

"Fishing shack's very doable, on your salary. This place, not so much. So there's no way this is our guy?"

"No. I looked at him this afternoon. Zero record, and he's too young for the earlier calls we got, I think. They started in '99, with the scrambled tape-recorder voice, before he started using the computer one. In 1999 Keegan Fitzroy was in high school out in Connecticut." The elevator came, and Chris checked his hair in the chrome reflection as they rode up, patting down a couple of flyaways with a licked hand.

"He could still have killed Bella," Chris said. "Don't get so attached to your Finder and this killer being the same guy. Not yet."

"Of course I'm worried," Fitzroy said, about twelve minutes into the informal interrogation. "Not lawyer-worried, but I just said 'escalating sex games' and this guy almost grabbed his cuffs. 'Games,' ma'am, is the important part of the sentence."

"'Detective' works better than 'ma'am,' but I take your point." Sandra hated interviewing guys who talked like this, grating sub-Tarantino patter. It would have been worse if she'd come alone. Chris, on the couch doing his bored menace thing, kept proceedings unfriendly and gave Fitzroy less freedom to improv his hard-boiled lines. Fitzroy, who mostly fit Sylvia Greene's description, skinny with a disproportionate and half-spherical potbelly, sank into a teak chair and sighed. His face was older than the rest of him, puffy pebbled leather contradicting his teen stick-limbs. Sandra was the only one standing.

"You buy all this with baseball cards?" Chris asked.

"Maybe a little of it. But it's a combo of family money and flipped houses. The memorabilia store is my retirement project, you know? As long as I don't lose too much on it too many months in a row, I'll keep it running. Officer. Sir."

Sandra shot Chris a look, brief and hooded, making sure he wasn't going to disrupt her line of questions with more of his interjections.

"These sex games. Could you tell us about them?"

"First thing I can tell you is that nothing I ever did to her would leave so much as a bruise, let alone put her in a grave. Consensual, psychological sex games." Fitzroy pushed his hair back, trying to look slick and blasé but only revealing the thinness of his carefully layered crop. "I don't know how specific you want me to be."

"Pretty specific," Sandra said, leaning against the side of the chair next to her. "How about you summarize what you've told us so far, then take us right up to the night she disappeared? 'Games' included."

"She came into the store two days in a row, about five months ago. With the way she looked, both out of my customer demographic and not exactly being the tidiest of young ladies, of course I was afraid she was going to steal something." Fitzroy shifted and tried to make himself comfortable by crossing and uncrossing his legs. The detectives waited for him to figure out that his posture wasn't what was making him uncomfortable, and he went on.

"She didn't ask me to take anything out of the cases—I would have said no—and I noticed that other than the clothes and some patches of skin, she looked pretty good. A little meth hollowness in her cheeks, but even that looked kind of supermodel in the right light. Low light." Fitzroy grinned, and Sandra wished she could believe he was guilty.

"So when I saw she wasn't going to steal anything, I started talking to her. Asked her if she collected. She said no, but an ex of hers, blah blah. I asked her out for dinner after close, but I was curious about more than her life story, obviously. I bought condoms before meeting up."

"Skip ahead," Sandra said. "The games."

"First I want to tell you what I did for her. I got her new clothes, I let her stay here some nights. Spending cash, too."

"Drug money," said Chris.

"I gave her the money to do whatever she wanted with it. And the sex, that was, I want to make it clear, pretty normal for the most part." He paused here, and Sandra could see him recasting his sentences. He'd probably told his sordid fuck-stories a dozen times to his friends and the customers at his little store, amping up his performance and using Bella as a plot element.

"Basic role-play," Keegan Fitzroy said.

"Like Dungeons and Dragons?" Chris asked.

"Detective Gabriel," Sandra said, not looking at him. Chris shut up.

"One thing was I'd pretend to be a cop," Fitzroy said, "and that I'd busted Bella for soliciting, or for possession, and she had to get out of it. Mostly it was scenarios like that."

"Did she enjoy them?" Sandra asked.

"Not sure. Hard to tell. She was a good actor, you know? Or maybe she wasn't. She looked upset, during, but she was supposed to." Fitzroy shrugged, his hands pointing to the ceiling. "But there was consent, all over the place, I made sure she said yes to anything before I did it to her."

"The 'escalating' part of the games, Mr. Fitzroy. That's what I want to know about."

"It's something we only did twice. Same fantasy world stuff, but we brought other people in, I guess. A fake pimp/prostitute scenario. Bella had never actually tricked, you know? She'd never done the standing on the corner thing. Always found guys like me instead." Keegan Fitzroy was starting to look ashamed, finally, but not enough.

"So I wanted her to do it. For me. Not with me watching or anything, but, you know, she had to bring back proof. We only ran it twice. Once the week before I last saw her, and once when I last saw her."

Sandra finally did sit down. Not to be comfortable, but to be able to look at Fitzroy in the face, to pull his eyes level with hers by staring intensely at his glistening forehead.

"When you last saw her. Which was when?"

"You know," Fitzroy said.

"Are you telling me, Mr. Fitzroy, that you saw Bella on the night she disappeared? She was over here?"

"Well, even you said you couldn't pinpoint the night when she went missing. But maybe, yes."

"You sent her out to act this prostitute fantasy, and she didn't come back at all that night. You didn't find that unusual." Sandra held up her left hand, not for Keegan Fitzroy, but to hold off Chris, whom she could feel heating up behind her, that rage he used so effectively in certain unofficial interrogations building up and vibrating in his big fists. Chris never hit the suspects, but he was extremely good at making them believe he was about to. That'd be no good for Fitzroy, who looked the type to grab onto any lawsuit that presented itself, especially when his personal freedom might be in jeopardy.

"It wasn't typical of her not to come back when we were supposed to spend the night. She at least would have called me. I bought her a phone, you know."

"Generous," Sandra said. She'd closed her notebook. "So you weren't at all disturbed that she didn't return?"

"The first time we did the fantasy, I told her to get picked up and insist on doing the guy in his car. I wanted her to come back with the money she'd gotten off him. And the condom."

"The condom?"

"Not as a fetish thing, just so she had proof she played it safe. I was already taking enough of a risk, what with the needles."

"You motherfucker," Chris said.

"Wait in the car," Sandra told him. "Detective Gabriel, go to the car."

She didn't turn around, but Chris got up and left after a minute's charged hesitation.

"The second time I wanted her to get picked up and go to the guy's place, or a motel. To bring back something from him. A ring, or something from his house. Take something of value, bring it back to me."

"You wanted to make her into a prostitute and a thief."

"Just in a game way," Fitzroy said. The act was crumbling, and she could see a tremble of snot in his right nostril. The tears were about to be born. "I didn't want her to get hurt. And as far as I know—"

"As far as you know? You do know. She's dead. Where did you send her to pick up?"

"I wanted her to stay away from the main drags. To pick up a business guy, nearby. I just sent her walking out."

"That's not very useful to me."

"It's all I've got," Fitzroy said. Sandra wanted to dig the heel of her shoe into the dent just next to his kneecap, to punch the back of his head when he bent from the pain, but she suspected he was the type to have cameras mounted and running around the apartment. For security, and for sex. He started crying anyway, curling away from her stare.

"I didn't do anything to her. I didn't kill her, that's for goddamn sure."

"You didn't kill her, no. But you know what you did, right?" Sandra got up then and left, ignoring the questions he was sputtering out behind her, adding only a "Don't leave town, please. That's just a request." When she got to the lobby, she flashed her badge at the concierge again and told him she needed to requisition the security footage hard drive. Anything from the lobby and building exterior. The concierge, a balding, thickly mustached man who smelled of cinnamon, nodded importantly, making the note and telling her that the security company would get it to her the next day.

Sandra checked the placement of the security cams on her walk back to the car, noting that their range would pretty much certainly fall short of showing them anything beyond Bella leaving the building.

Chris was in the passenger seat, reclined about halfway and listening to a Dio song that was mysteriously on the radio.

"Sorry," he said as she sat down.

"I was halfway kicking you out so I could beat him down without you having to witness it and then lie about it later."

"I'd love you for that, you know," Chris said. The way he looked at her for a moment, Sandra worried that he loved her anyway.

"He didn't kill her. But we know what she was doing getting into the guy's car, and we know it happened around here somewhere."

"And that's it."

"That's it." Sandra turned up the music. The louder it was, the easier she found it to say the next, painful, sentence. "We do know what kind of shithead we're looking for, though. Like Fitzroy up there, but less crass. Less aware of the kind of pig, or monster, he is. Those dead girls are—they're like live women are to Fitzroy. Placeholders for fantasy. Things he can fixate on."

"Yeah," said Chris. He looked uncomfortable, the way he usually did when Sandra got a certain kind of thoughtful. She made him notice that there were things about her mind that had nothing to do with the way he did police work, or the way he lived.

"We won't find him like this. Not with forensics, not with witnesses. I know it. We have to look for him on those tapes, Chris. On the tapes, in the pictures of the graves. In his head is where we'll find the guy, not by talking to shitbags like Fitzroy."

"And in your head, Sandra. That's where the finding happens, right?" Sandra didn't answer, starting the car instead.

18

I CHECKED MY PHONE ON THE WAY OUT OF THE
Pemberton: Ellen had texted me a couple times, without urgency.

*Bring back 1%. bank transfer Kylie tourney fee, can't find
the org acct number in my email. Going to bed early.*

I didn't know what "org acct" she was talking about, but the dullness of the tasks gave me a rewind second of comfort, put me back into last week, before I'd ever wrapped my hand around Bella's dead wrist.

I walked out and saw Keith's car, still parked outside the Pemberton, just across the street. I was angry he hadn't left yet, but remembered the desk cop's sausage fist closing around my wrist, so kept it restrained as I walked across the damp, sloped street to ask him why the hell he hadn't taken off yet. When I got a little closer, I saw Keith sitting in the passenger seat. A couple steps more and I saw the hypodermic needle sticking

out of the side of his neck, and the black staring eye of a gun barrel pointing at me from the back window on the driver's side.

I'd never had a gun pointed at me before, but I'd seen the moment
enough in the movies to be surprised by my own reaction, which seemed
to take place outside of me. I walked toward the car and the gun it contained at the pace I'd been keeping up until then, somehow knowing that
doing anything else would get me dead.

"That's good. That's very good, Martin," I heard from the backseat. I didn't
stoop to see the speaker, but I did see the blue windbreaker sleeve that the
gun and the hand holding it were growing out of. Royal blue, the same color
jacket one of the guys sitting on stools at the bar had been wearing. Sitting
close enough to hear us, probably, but that didn't explain what was happening.

"You have Officer Keith's address, correct?" asked the voice in the car.
"We have to be quick about this, and the less you think about it, the better.
We're going to go out there, the three of us, you in your car followed by
the two of us in this car. I'll be behind the wheel while Keith finishes his
nap. You have two minutes to get to your Jeep, drive back to this street, and
start driving to Keith's palace in Ballard. I know where it is already, but I'd
like us to travel nice and close. Park across the street, and I'll park underground. We'll meet in the lobby. I've checked the building and surrounding
streets for CC cameras—not much around. I was even extra-careful and
dolloped birdshit on a pole-mounted one at the convenience store you'll
pass at the end of his block. We'll be fine. Unless, that is. Unless you don't
listen. You call or text anyone, especially any police, I kill Keith and leave a
nice note explaining your connection to all of these buried women."

The voice coming out of the backseat wasn't as deep as the thickness
of visible arm and chest suggested. I leaned down a little, as much as I
could without making the move too perceptible, and saw his neck, and
above it, the bottom rim of a face mask: latex, the color of pale skin.

"All those women from years ago. Yes. And Bella Greene. This note
also explains where and how you killed Bella Greene, and what parts

of your garage and home her DNA can be found in. I scattered some around while you were out. The night before you came out for your dig. There are at least seven other compelling bits of evidence in the Reese household. Maybe even a couple at your office. A search warrant would unravel you, friend. To put it simply, the best thing you can do right now is to get in your car and start doing exactly what I say. And give me your phone, actually. Don't want any last-minute second-guessing from you."

I handed him the phone. And then found I couldn't move at all, until the man leaned out of the window and looked at me through his featureless mask, an oval that was blank except for two unevenly cut holes, revealing green eyes and some surrounding, living red flesh. There was another slit just below his nose, revealing nothing, just letting air in and out. He said another two words that pushed me back on the sidewalk and got me walking.

I was already in my car and driving, Keith's headlights in my rearview, when my conscious mind caught up to what the man had said. "Ellen. Kylie."

The drive was an automated haze, a slick and thoughtless highway cruise. I parked across the street from Keith's apartment building, a slumping three-story. I was lucky that the powerful bulb above the address was functioning, considering how broken down the stucco and other visible outgrowths of the walls were. A length of hose, its presence mysterious after the weeks of steady rain, lay across the brief front lawn that was between the street and the lobby's front door. I waited a few seconds, and pretty soon Keith's car pulled up alongside mine. There'd been a little bit of traffic on the way over, a few vehicles getting between us. I'd prayed that the man didn't think I was trying to lose him. Prayed to what or who, I didn't know. Maybe to the guy in the driver's seat of the vehicle that was easing alongside my Jeep.

Keith's unconscious face was dewed with sweat, a couple of fresh beads trickling past his right eyebrow, telling me he was alive. Beyond the smooth surface of Keith's flesh was the other man, whom I still couldn't exactly see. When he spoke, the features on the mask didn't move, because the mouth hadn't been properly opened. The lips were joined together by a sliver of white latex.

"Nice going so far, friend," he said. "Don't mind the face. I'm sorry I didn't attach it properly, but it gets really hot if I can't easily pull it on and off, let some air in. Before we go any further—and we're going quite a bit further, I promise—let's correct a little imbalance here. I know your name is Martin, and a whole lot of other things about you." The man pulled out Keith's green file folder, my juvie record inside it, and extended his long arm to pass it to me. He had to lean quite a ways, as well, until I could grab the thing with my fingertips and put it in my lap. The man continued his lean, staring at me.

"You know nothing about me, so you should at least get a name." The eyes behind the latex mask were in shadow, but I noticed them flit to the mirror constantly, looking to see if anyone had pulled into the street behind us.

"I don't want to know your name. I don't want to know anything about you. I want to go home and just forget this. Okay?"

"Jason—Jason Shurn, your friend and mine—used to call me 'the Ragman.' Stupid nickname at the time, but I sort of grew into it. Started to like it. I haven't used it in years, but I'd like you to take it up. Now follow me. Awful as this dump is, Keith has underground parking, and there are even extra spaces down there for your tidy urban rover. Fun's this way."

"Garages have cameras. CC."

"I told you, I scoped the place," the Ragman said. "Just a couple of dummy lenses wired into nothing. Boxes to scare smash-and-grabbers. You're not the only fan of being prepared. Now shut up and follow."

The Ragman—thinking the name did make me feel a little more secure, like I'd been given a scrap of knowledge I could use later, if there was a later—pulled away and I followed, swinging behind him into an alley and down the steep drive that led to Keith's parking. The barred gate rattled up as Keith's car paused in front of it, and the hand—huge, white, ungloved—of the Ragman pointed to the first visible parking space, which was marked Guest One. I pulled in as Keith's car vanished around a corner, and the gate lowered behind both of us.

"Now the risky part," called the Ragman's voice, bouncing with a plate reverb semi-echo from the dripping cement walls of the garage. "We have to get ourselves into an elevator and down a hallway without alerting a single solitary soul." I walked toward the voice, and saw the Ragman leaning against the driver's side of the car. He'd zipped the windbreaker up all the way, obscuring the bottom edge of the mask, and I could see the bulge of the gun butt poking out just above his waistline when he stretched. Spine extended, the man was tall, but not a giant.

"Are we taking him?" I asked. I walked around the car so I was standing next to the passenger seat, looking across the car at the Ragman.

"I don't know about you, but I'm not ready to quietly lift and carry 340 pounds," said the Ragman. He laughed behind the mask, a quick *haha* that sounded less than genuine. The sort of laugh I'd gotten used to using in business meetings, or sometimes with Ellen, keeping the conversation light when a serious negotiation was underway.

"So we just leave him here?" As if I'd poked him, Keith started to shift in his seat, and I backed away from the car. His head lolled toward the window, the tongue flapping out like a Saint Bernard's, breath making a reassuring fog.

The Ragman made an arm gesture that invited me to look around. There was barely any lighting in the garage, and around Keith's parking spot, there was practically none. Behind me was a cement wall, and the spot next to the driver's side was being used as storage, heaped with bicycles and boxes that sagged with moisture. I could see the Ragman's chest and torso because of his height, but I had to crane and stare to make out Keith. If the passenger seat were reclined all the way, only an exceptionally curious passerby would be able to see the man.

"We leave him. As long as we're sure he's napping." The Ragman reached into his jacket, too far up to be looking for the gun butt, and pulled out a capped syringe. He pushed it toward me with gloved fingertips. From another pocket, he took out a pair of forensic gloves, still in their package. I stared at both items resting on the roof of the car.

"We've got to start getting out of each other's lives, Martin. Here's step one. While he sleeps, we go upstairs and clean out any evidence of anything illicit Keith was doing with the police files that were stupidly entrusted to him. You never know who might go poking around up there after us. I don't trust him to do a proper job himself. Do you?"

"No," I said. "But we could wake him up the rest of the way, get him to walk up there with us. Show us around."

"I'm not really asking anymore. If you don't want to do it this way, then I'm going to shoot Keith and then you. After I clean the apartment, I'll go for a drive in your Jeep and kill Ellen. She's meeting with her—with that Gary guy just now, right? Maybe him, too, why not. And if Kylie's not a sound sleeper, I'll make sure she becomes one. Just with a bullet or a rope or my hands around her skinny neck, though, don't worry. I don't have any of Jason's rotten little habits. I like things clean and fluid-free."

I used the ice that was pooling in my gut and behind my eyes to steady my hands as I put on the gloves and picked up the needle. Ellen. Kylie. Ragman watching me from the dark as I dug up Bella's body. Waiting for Keith and me outside the bar. These things together held more menace than the gun tucked into his pants, a threat that carried past the violent simplicity of a bullet passing into my flesh. At least that was something direct. Something I could easily understand, in a way that I couldn't conceive of losing reality, losing Kylie, Ellen. The vital parts of my life, the ones outside the breathing and guts and blood a bullet would stop.

I opened Keith's door with my newly gloved fingertips, the white latex giving me some distance from what I was doing, turning my hands into ghostly appendages attached to my wrists. Keith immediately started sagging out, and I braced his padded thickness with my knee against the door. The Ragman laughed, then rounded the car to help me. I was aware of his gun prodding my own hip bone as he pushed Keith's head back and exposed the throat and veins. The Ragman took out a cell phone to illuminate the target area of skin.

"That big one right there," the Ragman said, unbuttoning the top of Keith's shirt with nimble movements of his right thumb and forefinger. A vein just above the collarbone presented itself to the syringe. Keeping my hand steady by making it distant, using the same control as I had in the last moments of a dig, when the first white bones showed through under my shovel blade, I uncapped the needle and emptied the fluid into Keith. In a few seconds, the snuffling noises and shifting stopped. He was as inert as he had been when I'd first seen him in the car. I pulled it out, carefully, recapping the point and handing it to the man whose gun was pressing into my side.

The Ragman reclined Keith's seat, which gave way rapidly under his weight. He kicked the passenger door shut and we backed away from the vehicle. In the half-dark, it was just a parked car, not worth approaching or looking into. Keith was invisible.

"Let's get to that elevator and hope there's no one in there," said the Ragman. He piloted, walking slowly, knowing I would follow. The elevator was empty until the Ragman entered it, holding the door for me. It was tight in there with both of us, his breathing thick behind that mask. He pressed 3 and we were slowly winched up, the ancient cable making a thin screech as we passed each floor. The ride was long enough for me to ask one question, and the back part of my brain chose it for me.

"The skeleton in the grave. Who was it?"

"You want me to say Tinsley Schultz?" the Ragman answered. "You'll find out sometime soon. Probably." The doors dinged open to an empty hallway.

"Keith's 307. Just left." Keys he must have liberated from Keith's jacket pocket were soon in the lock of that door, and we entered into a narrow hallway lined with dirty shoes and decorated with an Ikea rug I'd seen in a dozen other rooms. I went in first.

"Now what?" I pushed forward into the apartment, keeping my shoes on. The Ragman passed me, pulling out a couple of wooden kitchen chairs. He set them up facing each other, pointing at one. I watched him for a second.

"Martin, don't start thinking now. You'll ruin everything and your brain will end up on Keith's wall in the next ten seconds." The Ragman pulled the gun out of his pants and I flinched. He set it on the kitchen table, next to a fat manila envelope sitting there, and pointed at the same chair. I sat and he flicked the lights on.

Keith's apartment wasn't surprising in any way. A little tidier than expected, maybe. From the way the Ragman moved in here, finding chairs and switches in the dark, I got the impression that his scouting of Keith's building had involved the interior of this room as well.

The Ragman sat down across from me. I looked into the human eyes, their dead latex surroundings. The mask had no eyebrows. The eyes were plain green, friendly, with a deviant fleck of extra pigment next to the iris of the left one. I was stunned to feel my heart rate slowing, a bit of calm settling in. I could actually see this man now, reassure myself that I didn't know him from anywhere else in my life. Wide in the chest, a stomach that jutted a little, shoulders with useful bulk. He was wearing black jeans, and the thighs in them looked to have some power in them, too; the whole of him spoke of utility strength, the kind earned in hard labor, not in an executive gym. It was a farm worker's body, a construction guy's. Or a prisoner's.

"What are we doing here?" I asked. "What do you want?"

The Ragman laughed, the movement of his chin making the sealed mouth of the mask ripple unpleasantly. "What I want-*ed*, past tense, was not to have my private business poked around in. Jason's, either."

"Shurn."

"Yes."

"You knew him."

"I just told you that. Look, we've barely even gotten started here, so I'm not going to sit around explaining everything to you yet. Sit still for a second."

The Ragman pulled out his cell phone and started taking photos of me, backing off, getting the posters and furniture in the shots. "Tell the camera where you are, Martin," he said. I had to guess he'd clicked over to video. He put his other hand, absently, on the gun butt, tapping the barrel against the table. I obeyed, telling the camera I was at Keith Waring's apartment in Ballard. The Ragman set the phone down after another few moments of placing me in Keith's apartment, taking in the sparse landmarks of the place alongside of my face on the digital screen he was staring at. He pushed the gun he was holding against an envelope on the table.

"I'm going to be taking this with me, but you should take a look inside, first."

I pulled the envelope over. Two thick stacks of twenty-dollar bills, and a file folder, about twenty pages in it. The cash looked to be about double the payment I usually gave Keith.

"The file's for you," the Ragman said, pushing it over to me. I opened it. It was on Carl Hillstrom, the guy who'd written badly spelled letters to the cops in the late nineties while he vanished hitchhikers around the Pacific Northwest. It wasn't part of the file on him that I'd previously bought from Keith. This was an interview fragment I hadn't seen before, and I started scanning it despite myself. The Ragman reached over to me and closed the folder.

"Later, Martin. I gave that cash to Keith a few weeks ago, in exchange for all the hard copies he had of files and information on buyers of these files. I can't be absolutely sure he was telling the truth, but I'm quite sure.

He seemed relieved to get the stuff out of his apartment, really. He never had the stones or stupidity to write about any of this digitally, either. Or friends to tell it to. That I made sure of. Been through all of his devices. Our names aren't anywhere to be found.

"This," the Ragman said, tapping the phone, "is the only link remaining between you, Keith, and myself. And it won't have much to do with me if I end up dropping it in a mailbox for the police. You'll have to do all the explaining if that happens."

The Ragman got up and I flinched, squeaking the chair back a half-inch. The apartment was small, that little hallway, living room, and the kitchen I was sitting in. An odor of sleep and sweat came from the open door of the bedroom and adjoining bathroom to my left, the place where Keith slept and shit. There was a Led Zeppelin poster on the wall behind where the Ragman had been sitting, and a Picasso print that looked like it had been moving from place to place with Keith since high school. Each corner was speckled with thumbtack holes.

"So why are we here now?" I asked.

"We're not here," the Ragman said, gesturing with the phone. "You're here. Some anonymous accomplice, too, the man holding the camera, but he might as well be on a grassy knoll for all the reality he'll have for the cops." The Ragman picked up the envelope on the table and left Keith's keys in its place, then started to walk toward the door. "Wait here for a while. And really, don't worry, I've been in and out of this place at least twenty times while Keith was at work. Picked clean. With his phone gone, there's nothing to tie me to him. Anything else, witnesses, connections, that's your problem, though. I only take care of physical evidence."

"How did you know it was me?" I asked. The Ragman laughed.

"I knew some of the finds you made were impossible without police knowledge. And I can smell cop as well as I can smell someone like you, just from the stories. When I heard about the calls, I knew someone just like you, just like Jason, was out there, using files to sniff around. All I had to do to find you was to find Keith and the smartest guy he sold to. Were you fishing for praise?" He didn't wait for me to answer, and I didn't have one for him.

"Take a look at that file and find your way to where it says next Sunday." The Ragman pointed to the thin folder. I'd never dug up any of Hillstrom's victims.

"Well, don't read it in front of me, you'll make me blush. Come Sunday, I'll let you know how you can get off the hook for Bella and Keith. You're going to have to do right by me and Jason."

"I'm not on the hook for Keith. What hook?"

The Ragman waited for a second by the door, putting the gun back in his pants. He opened the hallway closet and felt around for a box on the crowded top shelf. A pair of never-worn New Balance sneakers tumbled down, and the Ragman pulled out the box they'd been purchased in a second after. He showed me the contents: more cash. A lot more cash.

"Keith liquidated his bank accounts just after the Bella Greene call came through. I was following him when he went into the bank. Knew then, knew for a fact, that neither you nor I could trust him to be quiet." The Ragman placed the envelope of cash from the kitchen table in the box, then tucked it under his arm. "I'm not the thieving kind, but if all this cash gets left behind, the cops will be even more curious about where Keith might have ended up. You are going to come on Sunday, right? Alone, without having told anyone? I can't tell you how many checks I have in place, Martin. You don't turn up, I burn your life down. Your wife dies. Your daughter dies. You tell anyone or come with anyone, same thing. I may even do it all anyway. And no one will find any of you, ever. If you do exactly what I say, you get to keep the life you have."

"What are you going to do to Keith?"

"Nothing. You've already done it. You shot Sergeant Keith Waring up with enough nasty stuff to kill a couple of men, even ones his size, Martin. Welcome to killing."

19

SANDRA SAT ON TOP OF HER DESK IN HOMICIDE,
making a last call before going home. She'd stayed
late after coming back from Keegan Fitzroy's place, checking in with the
uniforms and undercovers she had patrolling the usual prostitute strips.
Sandra didn't think the next victim would be taken from one of the typical hunting grounds, but she wasn't about to leave those girls completely
unprotected based on her strong hunch. There'd been nothing on the
CC tapes from Fitzroy's building except footage of Bella Greene walking
out, and tapes from surrounding buildings hadn't been able to zero in on
what they wanted to see: the pickup. All they had was Bella leaving the
building, Bella walking a strip of sidewalk half a block from the entry.
Then she was out of frame, a little before slipping out of the world.

The constantly active station became a little less busy as the night
went on. A check-in with forensics had nothing to add on the skeleton
they'd found with Bella, beyond the gender and age they'd started with.
The boys and girls downstairs were running the info against every bit

of genetic and descriptive information they had on early twenties girls who'd vanished in the mid-nineties. A list of names and pathetic yearbook photos, alongside dental and DNA information.

There was an evening of concentrated work on Bella Greene's case ahead of Sandra, but it was at home after a quick call, not here in the station. In front of screen and notepad, maybe with Chris in the next room to yell ideas at, if he didn't have work of his own to take home. Sandra didn't let him sit in her kitchen when she had it set up as a miniaturized investigation ops room; the chaos of files and loose papers had to share space with the grindings of her brain and physical thinking, which often resulted in sheets stapled to the wall in patterns only she could read. When Sandra was unpacking the Murdoch double-murder, the one instrumental in getting her promoted to detective crazy early, she'd even tacked a few photos to the floor, structuring her information as piles of words emerging from those visuals. There was probably a way to do this on a computer, maybe even an easy way, but she was afraid it would change the way she thought.

"This is Whittal. Has anyone else made the same call requests I have?"

"What? Requests?" The voice that came across the line was bored, with a slight accent; Sandra might have been talking to someone in a call center across the world, not Mo from the second floor.

"Requests to pull the calls. The computer ones, about the bodies."

"Oh. Usual media requested the latest one."

"No one asked for them as a package, then," Sandra asked, doing her best impression of patience. "The ones from the past few years."

"No, not really. Archives came by to ask if I had them quickly at hand, but I just told him to stop by your desk and ask you. Quicker for everyone." Mo meant it was less trouble for him.

"Archives? What the hell is archives?"

"Who. The big guy, has a desk down by you guys. Keith."

"Keith Waring?" The man in the corner was what some of the guys had referred to as a "furniture-cop," and he'd stopped occurring to Sandra as anything other than a direction to nod politely in when she walked past his desk. He never checked her out for over five seconds at a time, which she appreciated, but she couldn't recall ever having had a conversation with him.

"Yeah, Waring."

"What was it for?"

"Jesus, we didn't have a long back-and-forth. It was a ten-second phone call," Mo said, clearly wishing this call had been that short as well.

"I'll take it up with him," Sandra said, not about to do anything of the sort. She stood up at her desk, looking across the room to the little area where Keith sat, unboxing and scanning documents all day, taking the occasional photograph, labeling old files for shredding and disposal. Focusing hard, she pulled up a couple of memories, fleeting ones. He ate pungent hero sandwiches for lunch, wrapped in wax paper he'd furl down in pace with his bites. Once she'd asked him where he got them, and he chewed for a while before saying, "From home." Never interacted with other cops, and his job didn't really call for him to. Just moving papers around.

"You ready?" Chris asked, standing in front of his own desk and doing a back bend, confusing his bunched vertebrae with the elongated and weirdly graceful motion, which looked all wrong in this room. His lack of mustache and fat made him stand out from the other detectives on the squad, and he caught a fair amount of shit for it. Sandra didn't think any of their wives would complain about their husbands looking more like Chris.

"Ready for what? Assuming, are we?" She meant this playfully, but with her mind still processing Keith Waring's interest in the calls, she forgot to make her tone friendly, to swing up on the last syllable.

"All I meant was 'are you ready to head home for the day.' Individually, in your own car, as the strong independent person you are, etcetera."

Chris tugged on the lanyard of keys he wore on his gym days. Sandra took in the rest of his workout gear, proof he had no intention of trying to take her home.

"Sorry," Sandra said. "I'm still fantasizing about beating knobs into Keegan Fitzroy's head with his autographed Roger Maris bat."

"We'll stop by Ski Mask Emporium on the way over," Chris said, walking over and leaning against the wall of her abbreviated cubicle, extending a hand and putting it on her knee. She let him do it, because there was no one immediately around and because she had snapped at him. Plus, it felt alright.

"I wish it was as easy as caving in that loser's skull. Won't help anyone, though."

"We just have to find the right skull, Sandra. It's not Keegan Fitzroy's. I've been beating the bushes since we left his place, cruising Bella's associates, short list that it is. Not solid citizens, but decent people, mostly. Users and small-time pushers. If this was a straight impatient passion-kill, maybe I could see a suspect there, but this kind of ritual, this clean of a cover-up on the physical evidence? The call wasn't just made to throw us, that's clear."

"Don't do this much without checking in with me and keeping me updated, Chris. It pisses me off."

"Just grunt work. And please remember, we're partners, and I wouldn't talk to you that way." Chris smiled afterward, the way he did when he was properly angry. Sandra put her hands up and bowed her head, accepting the charge of being shitty.

"Sorry. Come here, one sec." Sandra got up and motioned to Chris to follow her, and they walked over to the corner desk she'd just been talking about on the phone with Mo. Waring's desk, the surface of it, was bare, but it was bounded by short pillars of bankers boxes, each stuffed full of file folders commemorating investigations of larceny, forgery, death. Sandra poked at one with her foot.

"This guy," she said. "You know him?"

"Officer Inertia. Sure."

"He requested all the calls. Mo just told me. He wanted all the computer calls."

"Yeah. He got them off your desk in that memory stick, just after lunch. While you were wrapped up with Sylvia Greene, just before I saw you out—"

"You let a third party—you, don't tell me you gave him *permission*—you let someone who had nothing to do with this investigation take relevant data off my fucking workstation and make off with it?"

"Only after checking to see the calls were the only thing on the stick. I watched him dump them into a folder and then took it right back. Figured you wouldn't have left anything out in the open if it was, you know, delicate."

"Jesus, Chris—" Sandra took down the volume when she heard a door across the room drift open on keening hinges. "This is a police station. I don't feel the necessity to squirrel away anything pertinent when I leave my desk for a few minutes."

"Exactly. It's a police station, and he's police, working on archival material. Most of those calls are years, months old. It made enough sense he'd want to have them gathered together."

"Why? Why does that make sense? This is an element of an active investigation."

"A historical element, and that's what he deals with," said Chris. "It didn't even occur to me that Keith asked on his own initiative. The lieutenant probably told him to throw together a Shurn file with any possible related materials, based on what we found today."

"Daley wouldn't dream of making calls in my investigation without making them clear to me first, or at least notifying me immediately afterward. So no, that isn't what happened."

Chris sighed instead of sending back another volley. "I fucked up, then. In an extremely minor way, though, I hope you'll agree."

"You understand, don't you, that this guy has access to literally everything he'd need to find these bodies?"

"No, he doesn't," Chris said. "He doesn't have the brains to find his nose when he's blowing it, as you may have noticed from the snot traces in his stubble, and there's also no way he'd keep his mouth shut about having done something right as a cop."

Chris tapped on the desk, picked up the one framed picture on its surface: Keith himself, getting a handshake and his sergeant stripes. A long time ago.

"He's an accidental burden of promotion and union politics. There's a reason a sharp detective like you has never taken notice of him, Sandra. He's not equipped for the job, let alone this covert shit. Have a little respect for my judgment." Chris's tone was sharp, but there was something pleading in his eyes that asked Sandra to confirm he was right, or at least that he wasn't absolutely wrong. With what could have been mercy, or just extreme tiredness—Sandra was too tired to parse it—she nodded.

"We'll see. Whatever. I'll get on his ass about it tomorrow." Sandra pushed papers off her desk in a canvas shopping bag, and left with a quick goodbye to Chris, leaving any friendly backspin out of her voice. On purpose, this time.

20

IT HAD FELT ODD, IN KEITH WARING'S APARTMENT,
for the Ragman to call himself the Ragman, but he'd
gotten used to it, the way he'd gotten used to talking to Martin in the
same fake-folksy tone he used on customers at his store. Since starting
up again with killing, he'd begun thinking of himself as the Ragman,
often, the syllables in his head bringing Jason Shurn's presence back into
the spaces where the Ragman lived and worked. Shurn's hot breath, his
capacity for absolute focus. The mistakes he'd make, the admiration he'd
look at the Ragman with when the mistakes were resolved. Jason's hand
on a blade, listening to the Ragman's instructions. The blade touching
flesh at the juncture of forehead and hairline, a drugged woman stirring
under it, her turning head beginning the incision by its own light force.

The only important discussions he had these days were with himself,
so a self-referent was necessary. Martin probably had that same problem,
if it could be called a problem: having no one to share the most satisfying
part of his life with. A state that forced a turn inward, caused you to look

back to the past, to have conversations with versions of yourself, with your memories.

The Ragman had outgrown his birth name years ago. Thumbing through the xeroxed documents in the file folder pulled from one of Keith Waring's pathetic hiding stashes (this one below the vegetable crisper in his fridge), he found this name, the one on the business cards from Acme Urban Surveillance. The name of the store had been Jason Shurn's idea, one he'd come up with before the killings, the arrest. They'd pooled their cash to order stock for the store, had planned to run it together. It was a miracle and Jason's insistence on always using cash had prevented the police from tying the two of them together. The Ragman knew Jason never would have talked, even if they hadn't killed him.

After watching Martin Reese slowly drive away from Keith's building, the Ragman had chauffeured the body to North Seattle, to his own home. He lived on the linked grounds of the three homes on the single lot he'd slowly taken over as his neighbors had moved away over the years. The neighbors he never spoke to thought he was being smart: becoming a slumlord himself. Really, he just wanted space, peace, storage. Keith's car was parked in one of the garages of these houses, a corrosive solution eating at the paint and metal of the car. When the body was unrecognizable, the Ragman would drive it to the bottle factory that had been slated for demolition by a now bankrupt developer, adding the vehicle to the growing piles of industrial garbage that had been unofficially dumped on the grounds over the past five years.

There'd be almost nothing left of Keith's body, if the chemicals worked the way they had in the Ragman's animal experiments. It was currently in three barrels, next to the dissolving car. The tarp the Ragman had lain out to section Keith on was also being eaten away by the solution in the barrel, which would liquefy the cop within three or four days. The man's body didn't deserve preservation, to become hidden and monumental; he'd been a functional kill, a prelude, the before-beginning of the Ragman's entanglement with Martin Reese. Not like the women the Ragman and Jason had put away, had buried with a care and ritual he could remember in detail.

The geography of this part of the world, a territory dictated not by state borders but by the reach of the Ragman's old career in ending lives, was landmarked for him and him alone by the graves that marked his accomplishments. Had been since Jason died. And someone, for years, had been hauling up these anchors in his life. The graves had been found much faster than they ever would have if the world had been carrying on its prying and revealing activities at a regular pace, reaching into the Ragman's stored memories with rooting dog snouts, clumsy hiking boots, urban development, and metal detectors. The solidity of what he'd done, of what he could assure himself was permanently there, had vanished, and it was all thanks to one of those men on the list he'd purchased from dissolving Keith. Martin Reese. Martin, who didn't have the integrity to do what he'd always wanted to do, who instead had to intrude on the works of stronger men.

The Ragman carried a box of Keith's papers toward the barrel that stood in the middle of the untended lawn between the three homes he owned, two of which would certainly have been condemned if a city official ever made his way out here. He poured a half-quart of gasoline into its ringing metal interior, then threw the box in and followed that up with a book of lit matches. The flames erupted upward in a column, straight for a moment and then weakening into a wind-bent, flickering menace of heat that consumed another trace of the Ragman's identity, along with some worthless, polybagged comic books and a set of inexplicably recent love letters Keith had been hiding in that box. These letters were printouts of emails, smudged and folded so often they'd gone cloth-soft at the creases. The Ragman had read two of them, out of curiosity: they were from a woman in Winnipeg, Canada, apparently, one enthralled by Keith's invented stories of cop prowess and danger.

Breathing the smoke of vanishing evidence, the Ragman thought of curious, digging Reese, who was trying to peel the Ragman out of his place in the earth. He was confident Martin would find his way to the right place in the forest on Sunday. If not, he could always just pick him up at home. Visit Ellen first. There had to be punishments if Martin couldn't hold up his end. The Ragman took out his phone and wiped the photos and videos he'd taken of Martin, that extra leverage that had put such selfish fear in the man's eyes. This wasn't a game the Ragman intended to play with digital evidence—it would all be quite real.

The light in the garage where Keith's car was parked was still on, the Ragman noted. Would have to be switched off after these papers were burned. The Ragman paid his power bills promptly and regularly checked the wiring in all of his homes, even the two he barely entered, giving the city no reason to check on him. This was an example of the caution that a man like the Ragman insisted upon, and knew to be necessary if he was going to continue doing what he needed to do.

Jason Shurn had been attracted to that caution, but had at first been inclined to take it too far. "I don't think we should, just yet," had been his consistent refrain on the first few nights they'd taken the dark sedan out into the strip of prostitutes along the Pacific Coast Highway that they had initially planned to start culling. Night after night they drove the thirteen-block strip, alternating positions behind the wheel, until their caution became dangerous; the Ragman noticed women were beginning to retreat from the curb when they saw the sedan. They thought it was a patrol car, perhaps. The next day, the women began to curse them, throwing pebbles and pennies at their car, telling them to pay for something or get the fuck out. Jason and the Ragman had become recognizable, which was fatal to their intentions.

Jason had broken out of his tendency toward overcautiousness by doing something the Ragman would never have allowed himself. He made a random kill. The Ragman had been awakened by a quiet but relentless knocking at the door of the apartment he'd occupied in the university district at the time. Jason stood outside, shaking. He was clean, but may as well have been soaked in blood for the look of guilt and panic on his face.

"The one I've been following. I did it."

"Need help?" asked the Ragman, knowing what the answer would be. When he received a nod, he gestured Shurn over to the couch and asked for details on what had happened.

He'd cried then, which the Ragman always remembered when he saw or heard footage of the persona Jason had adopted after the successful kills. They'd performed all of them together, all except that first one. It wasn't just Jason Shurn's loyalty to the Ragman that had kept him from reporting his partner to the police after his arrest; it was vanity. He was proud of something for the first time in his life, and wanted to keep the sense of accomplishment to himself.

The Ragman had cleaned and hidden that first kill of Jason's, the last "crime of passion" the Ragman allowed him once he took over managing his career. As with most passion-kills, the bagged corpse the Ragman stowed in a Tacoma pond, weighted down with cement parking blocks, was a victim who was too close to the perpetrator. Melanie Jones was a young woman who worked in the dispatch office at Jason's delivery job. She was a twenty-three-year-old brunette with an upper back that was slightly curved from too many hours of word processing, but with a pair of excellent muscular legs that set a physical template for all of Jason's later targets. Luckily, Melanie had a busy romantic life, so after a few weeks of her being disappeared, pressure had come down on the three lovers she'd had at the time. A mentally ill budding poet had been pegged as the murderer, but lack of evidence and a body had kept him out of jail. The crisis had been enough to ruin his life, however, which ended in suicide six months after Jason strangled Melanie in the alley behind Rick's City Couriers.

The case was never officially closed, but as the records the Ragman had attained from Waring showed, the investigation was barely touched after that poet hanged himself. A few cursory search parties looked for the body at common dumping grounds in the city limits, and a couple of areas near the shore were dredged, but no one ever got close to Melanie, who was presumably still resting in her thick, anchored cocoon of plastic.

Jason had been easy to groom once the Melanie Jones debt had been established and his appetites had stopped being repressible. Even if his subsequent kills were not crimes of passion in the traditional sense, Jason certainly went about his work with appetite, with many of the thesaurus companions of passion, so why not call the later kills passionate?

The Ragman had seen seeds of elevated deviance in the boy when they'd shared a few months of juvenile incarceration in the mid-eighties. The young Jason Shurn was a slender, unhealthy looking boy, always covered in a light sweat, like the dope-sick kids in the detox ward that branched off juvie. Shurn never touched the stuff. He just exuded bad health. There was also something else, the something else that led the Ragman to seek him out in the exercise facility all the boys referred to as "The Yard," anticipating the outdoor iron-pumping courts featured in the adult facilities most of them would one day occupy.

"Want to spot me?" the seventeen-year-old Ragman asked Shurn, who at that time had the habit of lounging against one of the walls, shuffling and sending covert messages from his dead eyes, like a juvenile hustler waiting for a pedophile to cruise by in a rusty Cadillac.

"Wanna fuck off?" the boy asked. "You got, what, 180 on, plus the bar? That's pretty much two of me. Ask one of the black guys or something."

The Ragman vaguely approved of the boy's avoidance of ugly racial slurs, which only served to spur pointless fights that got all the boys into lockdown for the night, and potentially for a few more days.

"I prefer to avoid talking to more people than necessary," the Ragman told Shurn. "Don't really need the spot that badly."

"On account of liking your attitude, I'll at least stand near you so I can yell for help if you drop that fucking thing on your neck." The Ragman could repair the way the kid talked, given time.

"Thanks." The Ragman lay down on the bench and did a few quick sets. The boy looked off to the side while the Ragman soundlessly pumped the weight, but the Ragman could feel the boy's left eye flicking toward the bulk on the bench with admiration and hopeless envy.

"What's your name?" the Ragman asked, rising to a sitting position, careful to avoid sounding out of breath.

"Jason," said the boy. There was a moment where the thrum and clank of equipment and profane conversation around the two young men seemed to fade, to become as unreal as the world outside the prison felt after a couple of months on the inside. It was oddly like a moment of love at first sight, a moment Shurn and the Ragman had seen simulated countless times in the movies. This close approximation of that feeling was enough to form the foundational relationship of their adult lives.

"Jason Shurn, if you need to know," the boy finished, spoiling the moment with his fake hood sneer. He looked a bit ashamed afterward, but a not-quite-seventeen-year-old-boy can't be expected to bask in a glow of tender feeling for long.

The Ragman stood up, his massive height and overdeveloped muscles establishing a superiority that would rule the bond between the two inside and outside of the jail. As soon as his shadow fell across Jason and he saw the look of awe in the kid's face, he knew he was on his way to deposing all of the authority figures Jason had ever struggled against: the juvie psychiatrist, the guards, any old bosses the kid might have had, maybe even Dad. Jason started calling him "Ragman" because of the meticulous way he wiped down the exercise gear before and after lifting, ignoring the impatient inmates around him. The name stuck inside the walls, and started to have another meaning when he and Jason started their work. Not all that different of a meaning, though—it was still all about keeping things clean, about leaving nothing behind.

Those days of devotion to the gym were long behind the Ragman now. He picked up a piece of rebar and stirred the flaming contents of the barrel in front of him, freeing any papers that might have sheltered themselves. His arms were still hard, as iron-hard as the bar he was wielding, but there was now a soft coating of banal American fat over the muscles that had once made his chest project ominously and his torso narrow into a threatening triangle above his crotch. A hunk of ashing paper drifted past the Ragman's ear, and he swatted it out of the sky and back into the barrel. The only muscle he exercised regularly was his memory, that storehouse of everything he had accomplished. The accomplishments that had started with Jason Shurn.

In the months following their release from the juvenile facility, the Ragman continued to think of Jason Shurn as his orphan, his adopted boy. The trick had been to make his own authority something Jason would come to love, to accept unresistingly, to give in to as easily as the weights the Ragman tested his muscles against every day. It had worked.

The Ragman stayed straight for years after doing that stretch in juvie for his first and last assault on his mother, who was now too terrified to contact him ever again, a handy solution to the problem of her consistent nagging. He had gone to her house just once after his release, to ask for some start-up money for his new life. She had stood on the front steps of her half of the pathetic duplex she shared with a series of identically useless boyfriends, staring at the utter foreignness in front of her, the boy who had once been her son. She smashed a mosquito on the doorsill before it could fly into the house, and the vigorous motion made her breasts shake under the paisley housedress she was wearing, the one she referred to as her "barefoot-and-pregnant lounger." The Ragman felt a lick of hate in the ticklish part of his throat where it always started, an irritation similar to the effect of inhaling burnt chili pepper smoke.

"Prison wasn't so bad," the Ragman added. "Going back wouldn't be so bad, I don't think." He kept his language terse, trimmed, close to the tough-guy talk that was everywhere within the walls of the prison.

Speaking in his usual voice would scare her, but it couldn't do any harm to make her think he'd changed for the worse behind bars.

His mother went inside for the money she kept stuffed in one of the cookbooks on the lightly populated shelf in the living room. She put it in the Ragman's hand. He got back into the car that was waiting for him, with Jason behind the wheel.

The flames from Keith Waring's burning papers were subsiding. The Ragman sent a long arc of urine onto the dying fire, his penis shriveling slightly in the cold air as the departing piss shot for the stars and landed on smoldering evidence. He walked back up to the central house after turning off the lights in the garage that housed Keith Waring's dissolving car and body, moving his thoughts on from Shurn to Carl Hillstrom, the man he'd worked with a few times after Jason. Hillstrom hadn't been as trustworthy, since he was never as much the Ragman's creation as Shurn. But the Ragman wasn't ready to stop after Shurn was arrested. He'd piloted the dumb drifter through his brief series of murders, forced to take on an increasingly active role when he realized how stupid Hillstrom was. In a certain way, it made the control he had over the man that much more tactile, that much more real. Carl Hillstrom had to be instructed every step of the way, especially with the Jenkins girl. The kill no one had ever found, or traced back to Hillstrom. They'd done that one expertly, creating an atmosphere of such incredible fear from the beginning that the girl was too scared to panic.

The Ragman was in the backseat of Hillstrom's four-door Buick Skylark, which they had modified to fold down. It was a cramped and rushed way to do things, but the Ragman could crawl into the trunk in the time between Hillstrom spotting a prospect and her getting into the car. On that day, a summer one when the air itself seemed to be sweating, they had seen the girl hitchhiking when they crested an incline on the highway. Her distant frame was the exact shape and size of those girls Hillstrom liked, and her limbs were naked, the clothing she was wearing a short swath of darker color on a pink torso. The Ragman had lowered the seat and issued his first instruction before closing himself into the darkness of the trunk.

"If she tries to get in back, tell her you're not a damn chauffeur and to come on up front. Use that same voice I just used and remember to smile when you do it, or she'll just go."

"Alright, alright," said Hillstrom. The Ragman noticed a pimple surrounded by a whorl of coarse hairs on the man's neck before he popped the seat back into place. Jason had been much handsomer, a better lure in these situations.

The car was already slowing and a pair of clacking shoes could be heard approaching. It was possible the girl was wearing a pair of short high heels; ridiculous footwear for a hitchhiker, but Hillstrom would like that. As the Ragman had expected, the girl tugged on the back handle. Hillstrom barked out the dialogue he had been assigned, no doubt punctuating his delivery with a smile that would have made Lon Chaney uncomfortable. The Ragman heard the silence, sensed the hesitation outside of the car. Then the sound of the passenger seat handle being pulled came, and the girl settled into the front seat. This gap between this correct instinct and the socialized reluctance to cause a scene consistently gave rise to the sweetest suspense the Ragman knew; he'd sensed it on all of his hunts with Jason, and the Hillstrom kills were no different. They knew they shouldn't, but they always, always came.

"Why you wearing a toque?" was Hillstrom's first salvo from the front seat, which was actually pretty good small talk for him. He still had a gruff and nervous voice, as though he were asking a man at the neighboring urinal for a certain type of favor.

"I guess it is kind of warm for it, but I just like having one on," said the girl, with a certain kind of lowing accent that the Ragman couldn't quite place until he realized it reminded him of Carl's voice. A Canadian.

"You said 'toque,'" the girl went on. "Thought Americans didn't say that."

"I don't know," said Carl. "I'm from Edmonton, kinda north of it, anyways, so I guess I just—"

"I'm from Calgary! Like, outside of it, too, closer to Canmore, but basically we're neighbors." She laughed, sounding less nervous and plainly homesick. The Ragman regularly scanned the Missing posters tacked outside of the grocery store he frequented; he thought he recognized Cindy Jenkins from the darkness of the trunk even before she announced her name.

"Cindy," she said, after Hillstrom had offered the stupid fake name he insisted on using, just in case the girl he was speaking to was to escape. He asked if she was hungry and the Ragman heard the crinkling of plastic as a bag of beef jerky was pulled from the recessed gap beneath the driver's seat. An early suggestion of Hillstrom's had been to drug the food they gave the girls, but the Ragman had explained that Hillstrom wouldn't enjoy the later activities if the girls were inert. Carl Hillstrom preferred the girls to be active, which eliminated one of the primary complications of hunting with Jason Shurn. Necrophilia had been Jason's downfall; if he hadn't continued to go back to those burial sites and tamper with them, to take souvenirs and stash them around his house, dull-witted Hillstrom would never have entered the picture, because the Ragman and Jason would still be together.

Hillstrom grunted when he handed Cindy the bag of dried beef. He grunted a lot, really, it being his major mode of expression when the Ragman had first come across him at the adult video store where Hillstrom worked the counter between midnight and eight a.m. The Ragman often came into that place at around six in the morning, before he started his own workday, curious to see who would come in to pluck worn VHS tapes of women and men bent into sweating, unreal, utterly unsexual positions, plunging into orifice after orifice. He was a casual renter, himself, seeing if the choreographed struggles on-screen could stimulate him in the way Jason Shurn's masterful handling of their victims had. It was never the case, unfortunately. But watching the men in the store could be wonderful. So many of them *looked* like pornography aficionados: wearing heavy coats in the summer, bristled with exactly three days of stubble, and with the half-closed eyelids of perpetual masturbators. The Ragman often shouldered these men roughly when he passed them in the narrow aisles of the video store, forcing the smaller men to be aware of his bulk, of the space he filled. The Ragman realized how directionless he was without Jason when his regular visits to the video store accelerated to the point where even the dull and silent clerk noticed him.

"Aren't you gonna rent anything?" were Carl Hillstrom's first words to the Ragman. The Ragman had felt sharp heat all over his body, prickles that went beyond goose bumps, a projection of pure rage both below and above his skin. This was what he had been waiting for. An invitation to the dance. This was the same feeling he'd gotten before he'd broken his mother's arm, the incident that had sent him to juvie and to Jason Shurn. He couldn't even remember what she had said to anger him, now; she'd always been too stupid to be the mother of someone like him, and she was angry about it all the time, picking at him as petty revenge. The hot rage blanked out the moments before and after the moment he grabbed her arm and twisted; all the Ragman remembered was turning to her, watching her mouth as it screamed, and the hot coating of thickening liquid on his hands as he stared down at the white splinters of bone sticking through the ruined flesh on his mother's upper arm. Two years wasn't such a bad sentence for what he had done.

This time, listening to the words uttered to him from behind the counter at the video store, the Ragman let the rage linger for longer, let it stay with him so he wouldn't make a mistake. He'd learned how to do this in juvie, learned how to control himself entirely. He turned to the man at the counter, who grunted.

"You don't have anything that interests me," the Ragman said.

"Then why you keep coming here? Looking for new tapes? We don't get new stock except on Tuesdays, and not even every Tuesday." The Ragman felt his anger leak away at this. The grunting man was only curious, in the way dull minds can be when they are prodded into thought by a repeated happening they can't explain.

"That's useful, thanks," he told the man behind the counter. "Maybe I do come in too much."

"Doesn't bother me. You're looking for something special, maybe I can help. The fag stuff is in that room behind the curtain."

The Ragman laughed. "Thanks, but no."

"Doesn't bother me."

"Me neither, but no, that's not for me."

The man gave the Ragman a look that, for the first time, spoke of some deeper consciousness, something below the dullness of his intellectual capacities. It wasn't intelligence, but it was depth of a sort. Perhaps the same depth he'd spotted in Jason Shurn.

"Then what is for you? What do you like?"

"What do you have?" the Ragman asked. Hillstrom lifted the flap on the counter and came to the other side in a slow, unthreatening set of movements, like an old woman doing a three-point turn at the end of her own cul-de-sac. He locked the door of the video store without flipping the BACK-IN-FIVE sign into its active position.

"Anyone makes a noise up front and I'll hear it back there." Hillstrom gestured at the red curtained room. The Ragman turned his head.

"Not the gay stuff," Hillstrom explained. "I keep some stuff of mine back there."

It was in this back room, which was really a closet behind the dead-stock boxes at the back of those columns of sweaty men pistoning in congress, that the Ragman found Jason Shurn's successor.

"You can't actually rent any of this, but I can maybe lend some to you. Or we can watch it together. At my place. Really tough to get hold of. These five are from Holland, and the rest is all Mexican."

"Let's go to your place. When's your shift over?"

The VHS cases weren't decorated with gaudy photographs. They were black, which was an accurate representation of the scenes they contained. As the dawn came and Hillstrom's daytime replacement came in, the Ragman followed Hillstrom to a tiny room in Capitol Hill, and they watched all of the tapes. Each film was brief. Most of them were shot dimly, almost in total darkness, and all of them ended in death. In addition to the six tapes Hillstrom had first taken out, there was one that was neither Dutch nor Mexican. Hillstrom extracted it from under a loose board beneath the mop bucket in his closet. The video was Canadian, and starred the man sitting next to the Ragman on the basement couch in front of the television, in an apartment nearly as bare as a monastery cell.

"She screamed a lot, and it was real loud," said Hillstrom. "I forgot to press the right buttons to turn on the stupid microphone. But it was real loud."

"At least you have the video," the Ragman said.

"Yeah. You see why I keep this one hidden though, right?"

"Souvenirs are a bad idea, no matter how careful you are, Carl."

"But I have to remember. Look back and know I did it."

"I understand. But I have a question for you." The Ragman shifted over on the couch, accidentally putting his elbow onto the arm in a damp stain of beer and semen.

"Okay."

"Don't you want to do it again?"

The jostling of a dirt road alerted the Ragman to the fact that Hillstrom had taken the necessary turn off the highway. He and Cindy were chatting away like friends at a high school reunion when the Ragman pulled the release panel on the inside of the trunk and sent the seat panel folding forward. He rolled out and took in Cindy's face, which was already contorted by fear. He remembered what it looked like in repose from the

Missing poster at the grocery store, and it was almost nothing like this scream-mask, which soon came complete with audio. Hillstrom punched her once, hard, in the side of the head, but even when the other side of her head came bouncing off the window, she came back at Hillstrom with nails and fists. The Ragman didn't do anything but watch, though, holding on to the back of the passenger seat as Hillstrom pushed down on her windpipe with an overhand grip of his right hand while he continued to steer with his left. The Ragman watched, and watched more, watching until the end, at which point he started giving the instructions the boy still needed to hear every time they did this.

When the cops had combed Hillstrom's Skylark for fiber and fluids, they had surely come up with some of the Ragman's. Maybe they had even tested them, thought the Ragman, opening a can of Diet Coke and lying on his bed. There was nothing to test against, though, because the Ragman had no liquids or swabbings on file at any agency. This DNA stuff was such a pain, now, and he was glad to be almost finished with everything. Killing Bella Greene had been quite enough to show him that he had no natural taste for doing it on his own. The real thrill had been going back to those burial sites, putting those memories he'd filed away back into use, even doing some detective work to track down the burial sites he'd let Shurn pick out on his own.

"And finding Martin Reese, that's been the real pleasure," he said, spilling a bit of the Diet Coke on his shirt as he tried to drink it from a lying-down position. He'd become such a slob in the past few years. In the unimportant ways, that is. When it came to the things that mattered, he was as careful as always. "As careful as Martin tries to be," the Ragman said, spilling more as he laughed and the can balanced in his loose grip shifted on his belly.

There was no denying it. He was bored. Enough following, enough waiting. He wanted to do it all again. Jason. Carl. Martin. He could make this work.

21

SANDRA WHITTAL CLICKED ON THE BELLA GREENE file again, starting the audio. The sun had been down for a long time, but she only noticed how dark her kitchen had become, how hard it was to make out her notes, when the voice spoke out.

> I think you've almost caught up to me, right? But I never gave you a good reason to take me seriously. There's one waiting for you, and I'll leave more soon. I'm tired of other people's memories. Time to make some of my own. Of our own.

"It's different," Sandra said, tilting her chair right to get within swatting reach of the wall switch. In the new halogen brightness, she stared at a picture of Bella Greene, alive, young, before the junk in her veins, before the shot of poison that killed her, before the dirt and skeletons were heaped on top of her. Sandra had propped the vic photo up on a bag of

Intelligentsia coffee on the kitchen counter. She looped the MP3 of the call and paced, talking to the photo, talking to herself.

"That last part. The 'Of our own.' That's new. As new as him killing someone. Up until now, he's just been talking to us, fucking with the cops, telling us how we flopped on our jobs, failed you." Sandra's *you* was Bella, and all the victims before her, the ones he'd dug up.

"So who's the caller's 'our,' his 'us'? Not victims. Not cops. Who?" There was still no ID on the other body in the grave, the skeleton buried just above Bella. A lot of potentials had been eliminated already, but there was no ID. A girl, early twenties or late teens, cause of death as yet undetermined, buried sometime in the early nineties. Naked up top, a pair of dissolved blue jeans down below. Levi's, as generic as could be. Pockets empty, some teeth hammered out of the skull (hopefully postmortem) and nowhere to be found, so dental records were proving tough.

The voice kept looping, and Sandra kept talking. She moved the photo of Bella aside and opened the bag of coffee, absently carrying a scoop over to her stovetop maker and starting a brew. "So, Finder, you're sick of just looking? Tired of the cops not taking an interest in you, not chanting praise for your godlike insight to the papers and TV?"

For some reason, she couldn't stop thinking of that dead man in the care home, Rudy Clive Fox. And Emily James, the nurse who'd gotten so tired of caring for him that she'd performed the opposite of her role. Fox couldn't defeat his nature, but that nurse, that woman, she could change her actions in a way that didn't defy her nature: she could allow Fox, this poisonous element in her life and in the life of everyone else in that home, to die, and still think of herself as herself, of her nature as unchanged. And it wouldn't happen again.

That's why I let her go, Sandra thought. But just what the fuck does that have to do with Bella Greene and this monster?

Sandra stopped just before pushing the button on the coffeemaker, realizing she didn't want any, and realizing something else. "Every other call, you show off a little then talk public service. This one, you confess a killing and dare us to catch you. No heroic lining. No avenging the injustices of the past and comforting parents." She pushed the on button anyway and the water started to burble. This call represented a total shift in how this man thought of himself, a shift she couldn't quite believe—he could make the trip from digger to killer, that she believed, but he couldn't just leap from thinking of himself as an instrument of justice to an instrument of the selfish, gleeful killing work he'd been telling the police for decades he was out to undo.

"People just don't stop lying to themselves that quickly. And if they do they don't blab it into the nearest disposable phone."

Sandra had asked Lieutenant Daley to confirm a guess for her earlier that day: the department had minimized mentioning the connected calls to the press and asked them to cooperate in keeping the calls unlinked for years, not wanting to encourage scavenger-hunting serial killer obsessives. Daley had a shaved head and eyebrows almost as thick as his mustache, gray hair on a gray face, smoke rust in his throat despite quitting six years back, and a strong liking for the way Sandra Whittal conducted herself in the field and in not taking any shit from his detectives. She didn't want him to find out about her and Chris.

"These freaks," Daley said, just after Bella Greene's mother had left and Sandra checked in to update the lieutenant on the lack of facts so far. "There's a spectrum of them. Our digging guy, the one who's making the calls, he's near the top end, still a few steps below actual killers."

"He was until this. Bella."

"Yeah. Well, below him are a whole bunch of other obsessives, guys who order paintings from Gacy and Charles Manson CDs, then below that are the ones who write porno-detailed true crime books, then the ones who hack out less fucked-up books, write for less fucked-up websites, all the way down to your mom and dad, watching *CSI* reruns five nights a week." Sandra's parents were hard-core Jehovah's Witnesses, something she hadn't told anyone but Chris, and they were about as into television as they were into Christmas presents. She wasn't about to interrupt the lieutenant's roll by explaining this to him.

"So you didn't want to put any blood in the water," Sandra said.

"It wasn't my call, I didn't have the stripes yet, but yeah, no one wanted a bunch of upper-spectrum murderhounds boy-scouting around the woods and parking lots with shovels and pickaxes, looking for dead bodies. One's enough. One's even kind of useful. Made a few families feel a little better, burying their girls properly. A few reports have gotten out there, the calls we've gotten, but nothing that put the whole story together."

"To hear most of those guys out there in the division, this guy's a real citizen, helping us out," Sandra said.

"Sure. He's something we don't want more than one of at a time, anyway," said the lieutenant. "Especially now."

"I want to keep a couple of patrol units and two plainclothes monitoring every patch working girls are using. Focusing between Seattle Center and Westlake, okay?"

"That's a lot of bodies, Sandra."

"Spare some live ones to prevent a dead one. It's good press, Lieutenant. We'll let the papers know."

"You'd let them know if I didn't give you the manpower, too, I'm sure." Daley didn't smile, but he did that mustache-ripple that almost meant the same thing. Sandra had left his office and headed for home not long after that. The units were commissioned, but there were ten times as many vulnerable women waiting to be collected from the internet, from phone numbers on escort cards left in little piles in motel lobbies, from bus stops.

Ignoring a text, Sandra propped up a different picture of Bella Greene as she drank the coffee. The body in the grave, the skeleton above her. Two bodies. On the wall above the counter were other prints, thumb-tacked in a circle, a whiteboard in the middle. It was still blank. Each photo was a different site the guy, the Finder, had called in over the past fifteen-odd years, across the death zone of the Pacific Northwest.

"They're tidy, though," Sandra said, poking the various sites with an eraser. The most recent one, just before Bella—the girl in Northern California, Winnie Mae Friedkin, behind the disused Dairy Queen—even before forensics had set up tenting, it looked like a film set. Thinking back to the six or seven bodies he'd called in before that, and the one back in the nineties Sandra had just looked up at the station that day—they all had that careful arrangement, that just-so dangle of bone, neatly cleared space around the burial sites. Not just to clear footprints, but to set the scene.

"You take photos, I bet," Sandra said. There was just enough of each skeleton revealed for some artful shots. Souvenirs. The initial state they'd found the Bella Greene grave in, though—no. Forensics had done most of the uncovering. The skeleton had been exposed a little, including some recent damage to the tibia that was probably the digger's fault, but Bella's skin had barely been visible. And looking at the photos, Sandra was increasingly sure the rain wouldn't have been enough to shift dirt like this. The result was certainly not a souvenir-caliber photo pose. And that broken bone, for such a typically careful digger? A little less certainly, but maybe—

"You were surprised to find Bella Greene there. Or, what, you wanted it to look like you were surprised? And then you douse the scene, clean it up professional-style, and call to tell us exactly where the bodies are."

Sandra's apartment buzzer went off. The TV in the living room was on, tuned to the CC cam at her apartment's front door, and she saw Chris's postgym outfitted body (loose jeans, ancient Everlast shirt) shifting from foot to foot by the front door. The apology shuffle. There was a paper bag in his right hand that Sandra's stomach responded to, and she buzzed him in.

"Just wanted to—" he said when Sandra opened the door. She took the bag from him and got her teeth deep into a chicken leg, then nodded toward the kitchen.

"Look," she said, "we'll talk to Keith Waring tomorrow about the audio files, find out what he wanted them for."

"You're not—you don't suspect him of doing any of this, do you? The guy's—"

"He's not a match for any of the wetwork or the investigative work involved in what went on with these dead women, no," said Sandra. "But I want every piece of stray possibility nailed down and explained. There's no real need for him to take those calls, and he's never shown interest in any other investigation, so why now?"

"I'm surprised you're not making calls right now if you think Keith Waring's a part of this."

Sandra eyed Chris, decided to trust him not to get annoyed.

"As soon as I left you at the station house I called Zadie and got her to do a sort of unofficial check on Keith Waring's vacation and sick days ranging back about ten years. He barely takes any, and when he has, they don't sync up anywhere close to when Finder calls have been made or digs done, the ones in Oregon or California. So he can't be our guy, but he could still be connected."

"I guess you didn't trust my instincts all the way."

"I don't even trust my instincts all the way," Sandra lied. "For now, look at this."

"What?"

"This." Sandra pointed at the photo, and Chris came closer. He was a professional when it came to studying footage of scenes, precisely because he preferred working from pictures to working from the reality of the scene. "Bella Greene and the Jane Doe skeleton."

"So what?" asked Chris. He opened one of the containers from the paper bag and started eating coleslaw with his bare hands, wincing when vinegar got into a cut on one of his fingers.

Sandra traced the area around the grave. "It's sloppy. As well as the scene was cleaned up chemically, it looks—I mean to the eye, aesthetically—it looks like shit."

"It's two dead girls and one dead ancient Irish pile of bones in a hole of dirt, Sandra, it's not going to look pretty."

"You're thinking like you, and that's not very helpful, is it? This guy"—Sandra indicated the years of past sites, the called-in corpses from the past decade—"this guy leaves us the sites looking *right*, to him, look-ing tidy. Photo-ready, is what I'm saying. I'm sure he takes photos of the sites before he calls them in. Doesn't take any souvenirs from the body, that much we know for sure, and a guy like him I know, I absolutely know, has to keep some record of what he's done. So it's photos. And this, Bella and the Doe, this is not album-worthy. This isn't one for the trophy case. It's sloppy. It's not his style at all. He even broke one of the bones, Chris. That's not his style."

"Killing wasn't his style until now," Chris said, getting cutlery and plates from the cupboard, clearing some files to lay a civilized table among the charnel house photos and gruesome text. "Murdering some-one for the first time is much more of a stylistic riff than leaving a clut-tered grave behind. You're piling a stretch on another stretch."

"Not according to this guy's pattern, to what he wants to get out of this. Working up to killing makes perfect sense," Sandra said, wiping chicken grease on her thigh, wincing when she saw the dark streak of oil on what was actually a pretty good pair of jeans. She picked up Bella Greene's picture. "He was going to start killing at some point, start slot-ting bodies into graves of his own, taking photos for his sick-fuck files, and keep on leaving us messages. But Bella's pose—with the site so clean of forensic anything, of anything to directly incriminate him—we know the guy wasn't panicking. We know he gave himself time to coolly erase himself from the scene. So there's no explanation for why the grave looks. Like. This." Sandra thumped the grave photo with finality.

"Sure there is," Chris said, pushing a laden plate of fried chicken, biscuits, and too many sides over to Sandra.

"What?" Sandra asked.

"Beats me, it's your case. But there must be an explanation, because that's what the grave ended up looking like. Someone did that."

"Yeah. Someone did," Sandra said.

"What's that tone supposed to mean?"

"Maybe the guy who's been calling isn't the same guy who did this. I just don't see why a guy who's been so careful covering his tracks when he didn't actually kill anyone would be both sloppy and brazenly provocative when he actually does kill someone. And it's a clear indication that whoever is involved in this isn't a cop, another strike against even a cop as deskbound as Keith Waring being our target."

"Yeah," said Chris. "A cop wants to murder a girl? We all know a million ways to get away with that, starting with picking a stranger, staying away from kids with rich parents, picking prostitutes or runaways. Girls just like Bella. All you have to do is not give anyone a phone call about it, bury the body deep, and never tell anyone, and you're free and clear."

Sandra stared at him, a drumstick halfway to her mouth.

"I don't write the rules of society, that's just how it works, sorry as we might be about it. If it is another guy who killed Bella, no cop smart enough to cover his physical tracks like that would be dumb enough to invite capture by tying himself in with some white-whale creep who's been on the department radar for years."

"That's where the message comes in," Sandra said. "The last one. *'Time to make some of my own. Of our own,'* he ends with. The caller used to just taunt us, the cops. That taunt—that's not for the cops, and it's barely a taunt. It's, what—"

"An invitation?"

"Yeah. That call wasn't just for us, it was for the Finder, the guy who's been looking for the bodies all these years. He didn't kill Bella Greene, maybe, but he's tied up in this deep."

"So our Finder guy didn't make the call, you're saying? That's a deep stretch, Whittal. You just said he's been warming up to kill someone all these years he's been digging."

"He has, but this isn't a stretch if you actually look and listen. The call's different. The crime's different, too. The site, the ritual, everything is different, and that just doesn't make sense: if this was what he's been building up to all these years, the Finder would make this his most perfect take on a dig, not this sloppy, show-offy, dangerous mess. And the call was just wrong. Against his nature, Chris. I can't buy him thinking of himself as a completely different person, as a murderer who's only out to kill and taunt."

"Alright," Chris said, trying to keep the skepticism out of his voice, respecting Sandra's hard stare at the picture behind him, the workings of that great cop brain in her skull. "So who would want to summon him up? Barely anyone knows that these calls exist, that this guy exists."

"The Finder, by calling in those bodies, he pissed somebody off. Digging up those girls all these years pissed somebody off."

"Get to it."

"The person most likely to be angry about an old body being dug up is the person who put it there in the first place," Sandra said. She gestured at the photos of the old burial sites with the stripped chicken bone in her hand, using it like a conductor's baton.

"All of the bodies at sites that were called in have been tied to existing serials. Jailed or dead ones."

"Except the latest one, Chris. That skeleton with Bella. We don't know who put that there, and we don't know how anyone would know to look for it there. And who knows if we were right about the perps on the other murders? Half the accused are dead by now. We can't exactly ask them."

"So you're supposing that there's someone who killed the other dead girl in the Bella Greene grave, back in the nineties, along with some other women—and he's pissed at this Finder guy for digging up his handiwork, even though there's no DNA ties to anyone on the bodies."

"Correct. Nice summation, Gabriel."

"Another thing. How would this second guy of yours, the one who made the call about Bella, figure that our Finder was going to hear the 911 call? Anyone who's watched more than four cop movies would know we'd be locking that material away from the press until we had this thing solved."

"Well, that," said Sandra, lying down on the couch and wiping her fingers on her sweater, "is exactly what we're going to ask Keith Waring in the morning. Why exactly he wanted all those calls, and who else he might have played them for."

22

I WOKE UP ON THE COUCH, WHERE I'D SLEPT FOR A
couple of reasons. The one I'd give Ellen was that I
came in late and didn't want to wake her or Kylie. The real one was
that I hadn't wanted her to know exactly how late I'd come in, after my
painstaking deep-clean of any evidence that might have been in Keith
Waring's apartment. And the other real one was that I couldn't stand to
be near her living body so soon after pushing the plunger on that needle,
ending Keith's life.

"He could have been lying," I muttered, my mouth thick with morning scum, the sunrise light from the bay window pushing into my slitted
eyes. There were glasses on the coffee table in front of me, two, melted
ice and bourbon in them. Ellen's lipstick around the rim of one, Gary's
dry and tidy lip prints all over the other, probably. I tipped that one off
the table with an extended toe, and it shattered on the flagstones in front
of our fireplace.

I knew intuitively that the Ragman wasn't a man who would lie to me. Not about murder. I'd killed Keith by filling his vein with that poison: he was dead, and I was a murderer. Both facts, both forever. I walked through a miniature courtroom scenario, ignoring all the other circumstances, picturing sympathetic nods from a jury when I told them that I just didn't know, that there was no way I could have known, that I was coerced. And having no good answer to the next question, whether I was glad Keith was dead. If it made my life easier.

Because Keith's absence was a relief, even if I never wanted a role in getting him gone. If the Ragman could go away, too, if he could just evaporate, all of this would be solved, expunged and gone forever. No more fresh bodies in graves.

"You see the news?" Ellen asked. There was a shake in her voice, and I propped myself up to see her standing on the bottom stair, iPad in hand.

"I just woke up. Hungover. Kylie up?"

"No. Did you check the news this morning?" Her voice was flat, zombied. I got up and took the iPad from her hand. A little capsule article, zoomed large. *Bodies found. Federal Way. Police source suggests Jason Shurn.*

"Tinsley," Ellen said. She wasn't the fainting kind, but she sat down heavily on the step behind her.

"No," I said. "No way to know that. They would have called you if they knew."

"They wouldn't, Martin. No cop has had my phone number for years. They had Mom and Dad's, anyway. By the time I was moved out they'd stopped looking for her. And why shouldn't they?" Her voice got flatter with every word, and her head started to droop. I gently pushed her over a little and sat on the step next to her.

"I can take care of this," is what I came up with. "I'll talk to the police."

"Yeah," she said, dully. "Can you call Keith? I mean, can you call him now?" The name stung me coming out of Ellen's mouth; I wanted to ask her never to say "Keith" again, but I wouldn't be able to tell her the reason.

"No," I said. "He won't be any use on this. It's just a stupid story in the paper, probably thirty percent accurate at best. Someone maybe found some bones somewhere. There's no reason to tie your sister into this. None at all."

"There is, Martin." Ellen sagged into my shoulder. She surprised me by making a honking sound, an almost inhuman cry that announced tears coming out of her in a shaking, wet revelation of rage and powerless hurt. I wrapped her up, felt the shoulder of my sweat-stained shirt, the same garment I'd been wearing when I killed Keith, soak through with tears until all I could feel was Ellen on my skin.

"Mommy?" I turned up to the head of the stairs and Kylie was watching us, looking about eight years old, that almost-adult assurance evaporated by seeing her mother in a state she'd never seen her in before. I felt Ellen brace up in my arms, draw some sort of stiffening energy from deep inside herself, all while I was making reassuring eye contact with Kylie, nodding.

"It's okay," Ellen said, her voice normalizing by halfway through the phrase as she peeled off my arm. "Here, come here," she went on, and I relayed off the step to hand my position over to Kylie, who took over the tight clench Ellen needed. I watched Ellen's spine lengthen as she pulled into the hug, her shoulder blades flattening under the thin cotton of the sleeveless gray shirt she'd slept in. Committing to reassuring Kylie meant making herself herself again: just like I couldn't be terrified around our daughter, Ellen couldn't be shattered.

"It's your aunt, again," Ellen said.

"You don't need to be apologetic, Mom, what is it?"

"There were some remains found up in the woods somewhere, kid," I said. "Tiny chance it might be Tinsley."

"It's—we were just talking about this, Dad. This is crazy," Kylie said, still holding Ellen. "At the dinner table, I mean," she added, flicking her eyes over at me and then back to her mother.

"That happens sometimes in life. Stuff piles up."

"That's great, Dad, really wise. 'Stuff piles up.'" Miraculously, this pulled laughter out of Ellen, and the women broke their hug a little to laugh at me.

"If there's a shred of a chance it's Tinsley, they'll know. I'm going to go find out right from the cops, okay? Ellen, you've got to ignore this until then. Concentrate on store stuff."

"I should have given the place a different name if I was going to use it as a distraction," Ellen said, almost wry. She got off the step and stretched, facing away from me. "Sorry, kid."

"You wouldn't make me say sorry for crying, Mom."

"Give us a second, okay?" I said to Kylie. She nodded and left.

"Do some work today, Ellen. Just something to get this slightly away from the middle of your brain."

"Yeah," Ellen said, her eyes telling me that wasn't possible, that she would be thinking about Tinsley all day. "I'll go down to the store after I eat and shower."

"Take Kylie, maybe. You talk to her and you won't be able to go too nuts over this."

"She has schoolwork."

"Take her anyway. This is more important than algebra. And don't walk near the fireplace, I broke a glass there in the dark coming home. Sorry."

"Never mind. And I won't go nuts, I have Gary. He's too shallow for me to be upset around," Ellen said, trying a smile. I tried harder back and didn't succeed. Going to the couch, I slipped the file folder the Ragman had given me out from under the cushion, tucking it under my shirt while Ellen went to the kitchen. I picked up her iPad and flicked the screen past the grave article, onto the arts section, giving Ellen that much more of a chance to avoid dwelling. Wouldn't work, of course, but I did it anyway.

I heaped my clothes and the file on the bathroom floor while I showered off last night's accumulated fumes, the beer from the Pemberton, the mothballs and sweat of Keith's apartment. The needle slipping into his neck, my finger pressing down. I reenacted the motion in the steaming air of the bathroom, watching my thumb slide toward my index finger, the lightness of the motion required to end a life. It hadn't been satisfying, in any way, I knew that. And I certainly hadn't felt any sort of control. Kylie rapped at the door once but I yelled "Use downstairs" and spent another five minutes under the stream.

I was going to tell Ellen she should sack out for a nap before going to the store, take a pill if need be, but she was gone by the time I exited the bathroom. She'd sent a text:

With gary at store til 4, later, good luck.

Good luck with the cops, that was. I dialed the station, talking through the various recorded and human barriers put up against the idly curious, weirdos, and nuts, finally getting to a sergeant who took me seriously about Tinsley. Kylie came down halfway through one of the calls, dressed in a purple sweater and black skirt, at least one of which she'd stolen from her mother. She was eating a banana and cereal in the kitchen, and I could feel her listening to every word.

Walking to my desk, I spent the time on hold scanning the Carl Hillstrom file the Ragman had given me onto a USB, then dumping the images into my scrapbook. I hand-shredded the sheets of paper and the file folder into a plastic bag while I talked to Sergeant Robert Peake, who gave me what facts he knew about the case and told me to come to the station in two hours.

"Ask for Detective Whittal," Peake said. "Sandra Whittal." He had a deep, TV-cop voice, maybe an imitation he'd started doing on patrol that he'd stuck with ever since. "It's not normal procedure, since she's in charge of the whole shebang, but apparently she wants to speak directly to anyone who might have anything to do with any of the deceased."

"You can't tell me anything?" I asked. Whittal was the name Keith had used, the one who'd been stuck on my calls long before Bella turned up. I walked to the bathroom with my little bag of shredded paper and ran it under the tap in the sink, mixing it into a rich mash I separated into chunks and flushed down the toilet.

"All I know, personally, is what was in the paper. And that's probably mostly bullshit, sir. But I'm not at that precinct. Whittal will sort this all out for you, I'm sure. She has a great reputation already."

"Already?" I walked into the kitchen, where Kylie was sitting at the kitchen table, scrolling through her phone and pretending not to listen.

"Fairly new promotion to Homicide. But lots of closed cases." Peake was being a gossip, but for good reason; my name wasn't well known outside of tech circles, but I had donated quite a bit to civic and police organizations over the years, in addition to my private donations to Keith Waring. Front-facing public relations police officers like Peake kept up with donor lists. Shame he had no information that was of any value to me.

"Sandra Whittal," I said. Keith hadn't said much about her investigative abilities, but he'd been plenty scared, which meant more than any stupid comment he'd made about her looks and youth. Being dead didn't make the dumb shit he said when he was alive any more profound.

"Yes, sir. I hope you find out what you need to in short order."

"Thanks, Sergeant."

I talked to Kylie after I hung up.

"You heard some of that, I imagine."

"Yep," she said, getting up and stretching, doing a toe-touching stretch that made me feel queasy, old, and fat at the same time.

"Don't do that right after you eat, you're going to throw up."

"Yeah, yeah. Should I come to the station with you, for moral support?"

"This isn't going to be pleasant or cool or interesting, kid."

"Okay," Kylie said, after a teetering second where it looked like she was going to argue.

"And thanks for being amazing with your mom," I added, hugging her hard, tears spiking the edges of my eyes. "I'm jealous you can make her feel that much better just by being in the room, you know? I can't do that."

"Shut up," Kylie said, but quietly, in a tone that didn't suit the words.

Before I headed out, a last piece of business: the device under my car, the Ragman's leash. I opened the door to the garage and hit the lights, then stood staring at the cement next to my vehicle for a solid forty seconds. The stain I'd noticed by my back tire the other day. Dark, almost black, evenly round on one side, a ridged, spreading cylinder on the other end. It was probably oil but I couldn't help picturing the Ragman in this garage. Upending a can, a jar, a something full of Bella Greene's blood, letting it seep into the cement my wife and I stood on when we got into our cars. I walked closer and stared into it, looking for red edges outside of the dark center. I shuddered back and sat down hard, as though a spider had landed on my hand. While I was down there, I lay on my back and wormed under the car, looking for the other thing the Ragman had told me about.

The tracking device was a long rectangular box, with a broken red LED light protruding from one corner. The Ragman, mask off, his features dark under my car at night. In this garage, while I slept. He'd shattered the tiny light with a sharp tap of something or other. He wouldn't want to give any indication anything was here, while he followed me around.

I detached the magnetic box with a screwdriver, and wasn't too surprised to find a note lodged between it and the undercarriage. I unfolded it. Laser-printed, Times New Roman italics. Unsigned. Not that it needed a signature.

Martin, you're clever, but a little less smart than me. So you reading this means we've already met. Just wanted to say it's been fun so far, and I'll see you soon. Don't bother looking around for other bugs or cameras or anything—that part of our relationship is over. We both know exactly what the other is capable of, right? And we're in too deep for me to spy on you. That would be a real violation of what we're doing here.

I put the note under the machine, and left both on a shelf behind my digging gear. He—the Ragman—knew, whether he was watching me or not, that I wasn't going to act against him before Sunday. I was too scared. I couldn't go against him. Not yet. I didn't have a single option that didn't end with me in jail, with Ellen and Kylie dead, with the end of everything I loved.

"See you Sunday," I said, climbing into the Jeep and easing down the driveway, going slower than I normally would. I didn't want to get to the police station too quickly. In my head I heard Dr. Ted Lennox's voice, the one I'd heard on tapes I'd bought from Keith or streamed on the internet and even in the odd true crime special. I flicked on the turn signal and the question came to me again, in Lennox's voice:

"Why weren't you satisfied by killing the police officer?"

"I didn't want to. I didn't want to kill him."

I heard myself through tape hiss and echo, the sound of my imaginary answer slipping into the smug tones of Jason Shurn's recording, punctuated by the light rain tapping on my windshield.

"You wanted to kill someone, though. You always wanted to."

I plugged my phone into the stereo and flipped to a movie podcast, wanting jokes about Stallone's *Judge Dredd* to silence the doctor's voice and my answers. The next answer, the one I was afraid of, came anyway. In my voice or Jason Shurn's, it didn't matter.

I've only ever wanted to kill someone I needed to kill, Doctor. That I wanted to kill so badly nothing else would do but to have them dead in my hands. I wanted to know I was killing them, and I wanted them to know it, too. I didn't want it to be an accident, or someone else's trick. That's why killing Keith meant less than nothing to me.

23

CHRIS GABRIEL, TOTING THE BANKERS BOX FULL OF crumpled papers that served as his desk-side recycling bin, stopped by Sandra's desk. She was staring deep into her screensaver, her fingers tapping the desk near the keyboard, but not touching it. Chris paused, partly not to interrupt her, partly trying to come up with a good joke to use when he snapped her back into the room. He gave up.

"When the desk buzzes, you gotta answer, Sandra. Martin Reese is here to see you."

"What?" Sandra had heard Chris, but asked anyway while she pulled herself out of the grave scene she was staring at in her mind. The unposed bodies.

"Martin Reese. Dot-com jackass, married to the sister of an almost-definite but never-found Jason Shurn victim. Tiffany, Tina, something weird. More of an Asian girl name than a white one. Saw the story on the burial site in the paper this morning."

"Tinsley is the name. Tinsley Schultz. We screened the remains against her file yesterday. Great. Always a delight to deal with wealthy citizens who think they've got a piece of a murder." Sandra got up and cat-stretched, catching a few necks swivel her way before she put her arms down.

"You wanted to talk to everyone potentially relevant, so it's your fault. He wants to know—"

"I know what he wants to know. Whether his sister-in-law is our Jane Doe." Sandra dialed the desk sergeant and started clicking around in the Bella Greene file she'd built, forgetting Chris was there until he wasn't. The sparse data they had on the other bones in the grave popped up, along with a couple of JPEGs of the jumble at the gravesite. Either Martin Reese was a quick walker, or the desk sergeant had waved him in before Sandra confirmed; he was standing in the place Chris had occupied moments earlier when Sandra turned around.

She had a chance to take him in while he stared at the pictures on her monitor. About six feet tall, maybe a little shorter without the Blundstones he was wearing below his expensive, but old, jeans. Good looking in that black Irish way she'd never been a sucker for, but most of her friends had; blue eyes that could likely do Santa Claus–kind when they needed to, but right now were in an attitude of cold focus, a shoot-out stare-down that had probably served him well in business meetings. Mid, maybe late forties. If you didn't think he was cute, he'd be nondescript, another half-fit Pacific Northwest guy in a jacket too nice to be properly waterproof. Sandra clicked the two photos closed on the desktop.

"Sorry," Reese said, as though he'd been caught in an accidental glimpse of her through a half-open door.

"Not at all, the apologies are mine. I didn't realize you'd get back here so quickly."

"I walk quick when I'm nervous." Reese gave her a lopsided grin, Han-Solo-meets-Tom-Cruise. "I feel like I'm not even supposed to be here. Are basic citizens allowed back here?"

"You're here and there's no problem, sir. I'm Detective Whittal. So you saw the papers this morning."

"My wife saw them first. She'd be down here herself, but, you know. It's a little much for her, even still."

"Of course." Sandra pointed over Reese's shoulder, indicating one of the empty interrogation rooms. "Let's get in there and lay this out," she said, grabbing her laptop from her purse and pulling up the same files she had on the desktop as they walked. She didn't want to have this little conference with the rest of the homicide department looking on.

Reese obediently followed her pointing finger, walking the few feet down to the corridor and entering while Sandra held the door open. Before she walked in behind him, she called out to Gutierrez, one of the few other detectives in the room whom she genuinely liked.

"Miguel, has Keith Waring been in yet?"

"Not that I've seen, but I've been out in the world most of the morning," Gutierrez said. He was carrying his blazer over his right arm, picking at his teeth with a dime. There was a large green stain on the jacket. "Fucking kid paintballed me when I was coming back from—"

"I got a thing, Miguel, give me a minute." Sandra dodged into the room and let the door glide shut, leaving Gutierrez's profanity and what was probably an excellent story on the other side. She gripped her laptop a little tighter when she saw the expression on Martin Reese's face. Stricken.

"You alright?"

"Just dwelling, sorry. Cell buzzed, probably Ellen calling me. Our daughter's really upset by all this, too, she can't help but pick up the tension in the house."

"Of course. How old?"

"Fourteen," Reese said, that stricken look fading out and some animation coming back. "You have one at home?"

"Definitely not," Sandra answered reflectively, then chased her repulsion with a smile. "Sorry, that sounded hostile—I don't have a child yet, no. Tough with the job."

"And what you see every day, bringing it home to a baby."

"Sure," Sandra said, aware that Reese was either going to ask for a story or get back to the point very quickly.

"Can you tell me, just, can you tell me now if that's Tinsley in the grave?"

"I can tell you definitively it isn't," Sandra said. She saw a little wave of disappointment on Reese's face. The eyes went blank and he let his mouth open for a second, then snapped it shut while he processed. This matched up well with the typical reactions from relatives of long-vanished people: they want the knowledge, eventually, the certain word that she's not just lost, she's gone.

"But I was so sure," Reese said, quietly. Sandra let him have a second, not for his own comfort, but to see what he would say next.

"How do you know?" Reese asked. He leaned toward the table, and Sandra reflexively twitched backward; usually, she'd sit in the chair at the side of the room when having a noninterrogatory discussion in here, but this time she'd unthinkingly sat across from her guest.

"We know because of height and dental. The bones of the girl, the woman in the grave who wasn't Bella Greene—they match up, time-wise, with the disappearance of Tinsley Schultz and about four other unsolveds, but none of them are a match. Running those numbers was the first thing we did after the discovery. Height rules most of them out. Our Jane Doe was tall, almost six feet."

"Yeah," Reese nodded. "Okay. Tinsley wasn't. Not even as tall as Ellen." He pushed back from the table, squeaking the chair, then took a post in the corner of the room. "What else can you tell me? My wife is going to grill me, you understand. My daughter, too."

"I know. It's not easy to get over a vanishing." Sandra was still deeply annoyed at whichever forensics geek or Federal Way cop leaked the details of the body find to the papers. For a second, as she began to recite the facts to Reese, she was sure the media's source was the tough-talking douche uniform who'd walked Chris and her to the scene. "I can't tell you too much, of course. Beyond what's in the papers. We received a call that there was a site of interest in a disused cemetery in Federal Way. Upon investigation, we found a partially dug-up site, containing one set of very old bones that were supposed to be there, the skeleton that we're talking about, and the remains of the recently vanished Bella Greene."

"Are these sex murders?"

"That, I can't tell you, Mr. Reese. I'm sorry. But, since it's not Tinsley down there, you don't especially need to worry about that."

"I'm not only concerned because it's my—because maybe it was her. I live here, you know. Our daughter lives here."

There, Sandra thought. The wealthy entitlement machine lurches into gear.

"I'm sure she wouldn't fit the victim profile here, Mr. Reese."

"You can't be sure of that. And how many killings are we talking? It's beyond the Greene girl and that skeleton?"

"We're not even sure the same person killed both, sir."

"Someone's just doing you a favor, digging up bodies and telling you where they are?"

"If someone was doing that, it seems odd he'd plant a fresh body before making the call."

"It does. Doesn't seem like something a reasonable person would do, at all," Reese said. He'd taken out his wallet, started playing with the cards in it. "But the guy's clearly a stone psycho, right?"

"Something like that. You can tell your wife it's not her sister. You can tell her and your daughter they don't have to worry about whoever is out there, doing this. He's targeting vulnerable women, ones who spend most of their time on the street."

"I wonder about that," Reese said. "Why they only stick to the one kind of girl? And how exactly you can be sure this one will?"

"Compulsion, sometimes. Other times, this one included, probably, convenience. He wants easy victims. Again, this is speculation on my part, but I can say with some confidence that your wife wouldn't have anything to worry about from this guy."

"Okay," Reese said, stowing his wallet. "Again, sorry to ask." He moved toward the door, and was about to start on his goodbyes when Sandra asked him a question.

"Did you know Tinsley Schultz?"

"Of course not," he replied, almost wincing afterward. "I mean, Tinsley disappeared when Ellen was so young. I guess we met right afterwards, but no, I never met Tinsley."

"You knew about the disappearance before you met her?"

"Everyone knew."

"Is it something that—do you mind if I ask how long Tinsley had been vanished before you met Ellen?"

"Less than two years. We met at college."

"While Jason Shurn was still free, probably," Sandra said. She'd learned early on, while she was still on patrol, dealing with domestics and trying to get the truth out of terrified wives, that there was another shade of hunch, of instinct, in the field. It had to do with questioning— when to pressure someone, and with what kind of inquiries, even when you had no idea exactly why you were doing it. She couldn't say exactly why she was curious about Martin Reese, but she was. It had something to do with the particular tone he'd been talking to her in, the questions she could tell he wanted to ask, but didn't.

"Shurn was caught while we were dating. I did this same thing back then, came down to the station to talk to the cops, in her place. They were a little less nice than you are being, since we weren't married, yet." Martin turned the doorknob, facing away from Sandra, with hesitance, as though he suspected it might be locked. The door popped open and Sandra followed him out.

"What came first, Mr. Reese? Your taking notice of the Tinsley Schultz disappearance, or your relationship with your wife?" Martin still had his back to her, but he turned at this.

"Are you—what are you implying, here?"

"Nothing. It's just that women who are associated with crimes, especially the kind that affected Tinsley, with a lunatic like Shurn in the wings . . . they achieve a weird kind of celebrity. I was wondering if you'd heard about who your wife was before you met her."

"Like I said, everybody knew," Reese said. "Everyone knew about the disgusting tragedy she was living with. I'm not sure what else you need from me, and I'm very grateful for the first half of this conversation, but I think I'm going to get on with my day now."

Sandra leaned against the edge of her cubicle as she watched Reese walk away. He paused, once, stooping down as though he was tying his shoe. He was down there for a few seconds, and Sandra couldn't pinpoint what he might be doing. The boots he was wearing didn't have any laces. He got up and left without turning back to face her. Sandra walked a few steps closer, to where Reese had stopped. Sandra looked at the sole photo on top of Keith's desk: Sergeant Waring getting those stripes he soon proved he didn't deserve.

24

I FUMBLED WITH A NONEXISTENT SCUFF ON MY boots for a few agonizing seconds, having followed a dumb instinct to check out the underside of Keith's desk when I walked past it, spotting that grinning photo of him in the clutter up top. Beneath a desk was just the place where a tech-phobic, not very bright guy like Keith would hide secondary records. They could be taped to the bottom of one of the drawers, but I couldn't very well start yanking those out with that cop's eyes boring into my spine.

All I clocked beneath Keith's desk with the darting right-eye glance I managed was a liberal studding of old gum. No paper. Nothing. I started to feel a little more sure even he hadn't been dull enough to hide records of illegal evidence sales in the police station itself. I saw the ass-dent in his chair as I stood up and strode out of the room. Keith would never be back to refresh it. I waved at the desk sergeant and got to my Jeep in guest parking, pulling out of the lot before I allowed myself to start thinking about the unexpected grilling I'd gotten from Sandra Whittal.

"Hundreds of idiot police in this country, and I can't get one," I said. I almost wished the Ragman had left a bug in here, something I could talk to other than myself. The fact that the detective had asked me anything, anything at all, was *bad*. Very bad. And why was a real cop curious about why Keith Waring was late to work? Also bad.

The buzz of a text from Ellen—*Come to store* with a downtown address—brought me back to Tinsley, the fact that it wasn't her in the grave. Someone else, some other victim. An undocumented Shurn kill.

"Or yours, Ragman. Maybe they're both yours," I said, lingering at a stoplight as it started to rain and my windshield teared up in front of me. A honk or eleven from behind roused me, propelled me back into the flow of traffic. It took me about twenty minutes to make it the few blocks from the police station to Ellen's store, because I'd forgotten the construction on Stewart Street. Maybe the cop had seen my reaction to Keith's name. Maybe she was looking into that right now. I had to tell Ellen not to let anyone know about my friendship with the dead sergeant, before anyone found out he was dead. For the first time I could remember, I was going to have to ask her to lie for me.

"Should have made her go down herself," I said, parallel parking ten storefronts ahead of the address Ellen had given me. But I'd wanted to go to the station, I knew that. I wanted to look the investigator in the face, even if I couldn't talk to her and tell her about the Ragman, about what he'd made me do. I wanted to know who I was up against, other than Ragman.

The address was halfway down the 1600 block of Sixth, near the old location of a record store I used to go to in college. When I came up to the window, I had a second of disconnect. Ellen was in there, behind the counter, but I seemed to have stepped a few weeks forward in time, seeing the store in the future, somehow. It was too complete, too decorated and stocked. In the foreground, blocking Ellen from sight as he moved on to the next letter, a window sign guy was carefully laying down the last decal that made up the name of Ellen's store: with the "Y," *tinsley* was basically complete, inside and out.

Gary Leung appeared just behind the window guy, saying something I couldn't hear—knowing Gary, it was probably something unnecessary about what kind of job the guy was doing. Encouraging and condescending the whole time. He saw me and smiled, but instead of waving me in, came outside to meet me.

"Surprise surprise, boss."

"How did you guys get set up this fast?"

"It was a slow grind, Mart. Not fast at all. Ellen just kept it to herself, and I—well, I didn't do most of the work, but a lot of the scouting and ordering, yes. Hard not to break it to you when you came to the office the other day, but I figured it was up to Ellen, of course. Your investment was for the last polish. What do you think?" Gary took me by the elbow and I jerked my arm away, realizing a second too late how aggressive it was.

"Sorry, Gary. Packed morning, I'm jumpy. Surprise after surprise."

"I know. I saw the news thing, about the girl. Ellen didn't mention it, but I could tell something was up." He gestured toward the door, offering the entrance to me gracefully, without any of his usual joking or schtick.

"Yeah. Well, it wasn't her," I said, then walked into a part of my wife's life she had barely told me about.

The phone went a little loose in Ellen's hand when she turned and saw me, her business mask slipping off a little. She'd been denying loans and applying polite pressure in the credit union for years, staring into desperate begging eyes, so she had a certain confirmed coldness. But it cracked for a moment, and I let it stay that way, maybe a little sadistically, before repeating what I'd just said to Gary. "It's not her." I mouthed it first, then said it out loud. She kept on going with her conversation, something about insuring a shipment from France. While I waited for her to finish, I watched Gary walk around the store in a proprietary way, the same way he'd walked around ReeseTech. Like he owned the fucking place. Which I guess he partially did, in this case.

Watching his back, the flex in his shoulder blades as he peacocked around, I couldn't see the partnership lasting with someone as strong and decisive as Ellen. There were talons in Gary's sense of competition, and the one look I'd gotten at his real face, below the usual set of expressions he deployed in the office, had stayed with me. "They don't want you as acting CEO, and I'm not going to insist," was the sentence that unveiled him, a day or so before I pulled the trigger on the final sale of ReeseTech. A second of pure rage between his aging hipster haircut and the crisp blue plaid of the shirt he was wearing, in the ReeseTech elevator. The buyers had passed on having Gary at the helm because of a secret meeting he'd booked with them, a gambit in which he bad-mouthed everything I'd done in my last couple years running the company, told them about ideas that he'd proposed and that I'd passed on. Rick Patel, the head of the conglomerate of smaller companies buying ReeseTech out as a unifying brand, had come to me right away. Out of pity, and because I knew Gary would hear that it was me who had saved him, and he would hate it, I'd asked Rick to keep Gary on. He stayed with the company in a reduced position, heading a small team of old-timers, not leaving despite the massive bonus and crate of stock options he'd received. "I just like coding," he'd said then. He'd ridden along with the company through the recession and now into the new tech boom, his bitter stubbornness paying off, if my ballooning stocks were any indication of how well the company was doing.

Tinsley the store was an oblong box, the same shape as the record shop I used to frequent on the block, but without rows of music-filled bins consuming the space. It was spare, like a gallery, the cement floor painted white and headless mannequins wearing various *Blade Runner* outfits people would hopefully be willing to pay three months' rent for. Gary tucked a price tag into a slim-fit wool hoodie (cowled sweater, it was probably called in lookbook-language) and pretended he wasn't about to eavesdrop on Ellen and me. She tapped my shoulder.

"It wasn't her," I said again. "They don't know who it was, but not her." Ellen looked different than she had before I'd walked into the shower that morning. Clothes from the *tinsley* stock she'd ordered in. Vividly red lipstick, not the peach shade she'd had on when her mouth was trembling with the worries she couldn't voice.

"Poor girl," Ellen said. She sighed. "I would still like—I really want to know who it was, just so I can be sure—"

"Really, Ellen." I spoke quietly, and pushed her a little toward the back of the store, the unpopulated racks and shelves away from Gary's probing ears. "The heights are completely different. Everything. Physically, it's impossible that it's Tinsley. The detective—she's a woman—was very compassionate, professional, on-it. It's not her." I'd improvised the compassionate bit, but the professional and on-it part was unfortunately true.

Ellen sighed out the rest of her tension, except the part that would never leave her.

"Good," she said. "I don't know how I could have handled opening this place with that—with knowing that. It would be like a curse." She gathered a few hangers from the floor in front of her and started putting them on the rack. "Switching gears totally. What do you think of the store?"

I looked around again, even though I'd already taken the room in.

"I'm a little surprised, really. Kinda pissed off, but it's beautiful, and you should be proud."

"Pissed off?" Ellen said.

"Yeah, well. I don't want to be petty about it, Ellen, but—"

"Then don't start using my name in that scolding tone, Martin. I wanted to do this by myself. I'm embarrassed about having asked you for that money, even, but I had to. I wanted something of my own, like I told you. Kylie and me thought you'd be kind of thrilled, you know, seeing it all alive like this."

"Yes, but did you have to go behind my back? This must have taken so much time, concentration, effort—I know what setting up a business is like. This was in the works for longer than you said. Also not the classiest move to make Kylie lie to me."

"Go behind your back? Lie to you? Do you have any idea when you last asked *me* a question about my life? You have no fucking interest in what I do with my days, Martin. I dropped a thousand hints, I even had piles of dresses and sweaters shipped to the house. I left papers lying around. I gave you every opportunity to notice and ask me what was going on, and nothing. On anything that isn't about our Kylie, you've been miles away for months. For years."

I looked over my shoulder. Gary and the guy putting up the sign were staring at us, peripherally, and hastily started to talk when they caught my look.

"So you've been confiding in this lunkhead instead? Gary's the guy you choose to let in on your life?" I caught myself, for two reasons: Ellen had bunched up her fists and rippled her eyebrows in a way that I don't think I'd seen in twenty years of fights. The other reason was Bella Greene in the grave. Keith in the car. This Whittal cop. The notion of picking a fight with Ellen was hilarious, suddenly—a smile almost ambushed me, but I caught it.

"Wait," I said, holding my hands up. Her forehead loosened a little, the wrinkles smoothing out. "That's not fair to you. Not even fair to Gary."

"No, you're right. It's very unfair."

"I'm upset, is all. Stressful morning for the both of us. I'm just— you're right. I have been so tuned out of what you've been doing, and there's no excuse. I'm sorry. I'm grateful you let me invest, and it really does look fucking amazing in here. Don't let anything I said dampen that. I'm an idiot."

"You're really not leaving me with anything to yell at you about." Ellen pointed toward the curtained off back of the shop, and we walked past the two narrow changing rooms to sit in the small stockroom, which was full of Rubbermaid containers and fastidiously flattened and bound cardboard boxes. It hadn't been repainted in here. Bright pastels, like a juice stand in the mall. Ellen shut the door. I pushed down lightly on a stack of beige sweaters.

"What is this, cotton?"

"Wool," Ellen said. She came close and kissed me, and at the same time, flicked me sharply once on the tip of my dick. I flinched back.

"You're a sweet man, Martin, and I knew I was signing up for your head in the clouds bullshit on a here-and-there basis from when we first started dating. You're absent, a lot, whether it's in the house and you're staring a million miles away while I'm talking to you, or on yet another camping expedition." She was still close to me, her chest pressing into mine. Probably not the best time to tell her I was leaving again this coming Sunday.

"Whatever it is that goes on in that brain of yours, Mart, whatever you need to keep happy, that's fine. You've been an amazing earner and we've got a great kid and we all love each other very much: that's how it looks outside, and most of the time, that's actually how I feel. Just don't start thinking you have too big a claim on what I think and what I do, all of sudden. Okay?" We sat down on top of a couple of the containers, stayed quiet like that for a couple of minutes while I tried to figure out how to shift gears into asking Ellen for a favor.

"Okay," I said. "Speaking of what goes on with me, there is something a little off. Keith. Our meeting last night was—weird."

"Weird?"

"I think he's into something. Drugs. Might have even stolen some dope from the evidence room."

"Martin."

"He didn't come out and say it, but he did hint. I'm starting to regret ever having known the guy at all." I leaned against the wall, toeing a stack of deep indigo jeans while I tried to look troubled and faraway, and a little noble. "It's just that I thought I could help him be less troubled. I don't know. To keep this all as out-of-our-lives as can be, just don't tell anyone I had a cop friend named Keith Waring, if they ask. Just say you don't know, that I've never mentioned it, you don't know all of my friends. Be vague. Being vague isn't lying."

"Who would ask?"

"The police. If they find my contact on him. Just tell them to ask me, that you don't know who I hang out with, but don't see why I'd be palling around with a cop. Say so and stick to it. There's no reason for anyone to disbelieve you."

"You're not going to turn him in?"

"I'm not even sure if he's done anything. I'll sound crazy and be letting down a friend, all at once. Not going to do that."

"Just stop spending time with him, at least."

"I promise I'll never see him again, okay?"

"This is really the last thing I need, Martin. More to worry about. You know that soft open's really soon, right? I invited anyone I thought might buy something or tell people."

"Forget this Keith thing, it's nothing. Literally all you have to do is forget him."

"I can do that. Gary's been bothering press and the blogs for the last couple weeks about the opening. It's really going to work, I think." Ellen's own ability to switch modes, something we had in common, came into play when she talked business. I'd only ever known her worries about Kylie, or Tinsley, to break her capacity for focus.

"No problem. I mean, that's amazing. I thought soft open meant a bunch of boxes and empty space and friends and family. Kylie gets to come, right?"

"Of course."

I left, hugging Ellen goodbye and sparing a friendly wave for Gary as I walked out. It was time to get back home, to my scrapbook, to my scans of the Carl Hillstrom file the Ragman had left me.

I pushed through the shoppers on the street outside, garnering a "Jesus, buddy" as I shove-walked my way to the curb. The Jeep was waiting where I'd parked it. The sun found a slit in the huge cloud bank on the horizon, and sent a beam straight into my eyes when I sat in the driver's seat. I lowered the sun visor, and felt the thing behind it as I pulled the visor down. Felt it before it dropped.

It was a feather earring, old, once turquoise and now mostly the color of dried blood. There were a few red hairs tied around it, stuck fast with the blood and time. Hairs from Jenny Starks's missing scalp, the scalp that had been found by the Shurn case investigators. The earring fell onto my lap, like an exotic butterfly that had been poisoned in a killing jar. I'd seen it in on Jenny Starks's Missing posters, one of which I'd found a digital scan of to include in my scrapbook.

For a moment, I even thought I remembered seeing the earring on the ground next to Jenny, up in the woods where I had found her, twenty years earlier. I contemplated it before folding it into a day-old *Seattle Times* I had sitting on the passenger seat, wrapping the whole package into a loose roll. I looked at the visor again. Something had been written on it, in ballpoint pen. *"See you Sunday, killer."* I didn't know if the Ragman had left the earring here while I'd been in the Pemberton with Keith, or if he'd been following me around today. He was probably capable of doing that, tracking device or no. I hoped he had been following me—at least I would have given him a nervous few minutes while he waited to see if I'd come out of the police station, or if I'd confessed everything. Everything I knew, that is, which seemed like less with each passing minute.

I stared at the handwriting, which was as neat as could be expected from a cheap pen on vinyl. Maybe a handwriting expert would have been able to tell me all sorts of things about the Ragman. His childhood, his taste in magazines, where he liked to spend his summers. How I could get him to leave me alone.

I pushed the visor up, felt around for my sunglasses, but ended up braving the glare of the drive with only a squint.

25

USING A PAIR OF NEEDLE-NOSE PLIERS THAT WAS
knocking around in the Jeep's glove compartment
under ballpoint pens and receipts, I picked up the bloody earring when I
parked in our garage, and put it into a mason jar. I filled the container with
bleach, then put the lid on and wrapped the whole thing in butcher paper.
Not that Ellen ever looked in there. The bleach would eat away at any trace
biological information left by my hands, my car, the Ragman, or the girl
who'd worn this while she died, years ago. I slid the container into the deep
freeze with steady ceremony, burying it under six packages of venison.

At my desk, I slid my scrapbook out of its drawer and plugged my
headphones into the appropriate port, in case I needed to cross-reference
the Hillstrom interview with audio material. I couldn't risk Kylie busting
in on me listening to tapes, not again.

I settled into the deepest focus I was capable of and began reading the
scanned pages. There was an undiscovered Carl Hillstrom victim, who'd
never been found or convincingly tied to the killer. That much was clear

immediately. I was insulted by the brevity of the document the Ragman had given me—only three pages of interview, a real zoom-in on exactly what I needed to know to find the site. It was another interview with Ted Lennox on the mike, perhaps interrogating Carl Hillstrom in the same room where'd he'd had that last chat with Jason Shurn, some years before. Even an amateur could have sniffed out the fundamental clue, halfway down the second page.

> TL: Listen to me, Carl. You've been good to these
>   families up until now. Two of these girls are buried
>   where they belong, in cemeteries. I believe you when
>   you say that you can't remember where you put Erin.
>
> CH: You don't believe me. You don't.
>
> TL: I do, Carl. What I want to know is if there's
>   anyone else to tell me about. Any other girls. You
>   know you're in here for good. We both know that. So
>   you can tell me. Is there any other girl?
>
> CH: No more names. But maybe I can tell you a place to
>   look.

And Hillstrom starts spilling, in the room. For a moment I wondered whether the Ragman had written this interview himself, because it read like a goddamn treasure map, Hillstrom giving distances and landmarks. How *couldn't* the cops have found this girl, with this much to go on? But Lennox's voice, his exasperation and his weaselly clever patience, was just too nailed for this chat to have been fiction. Unless the Ragman was a Pulitzer-caliber dialogue writer, the transcript was real.

Hillstrom was long dead, killed on a day when he'd accidentally been issued a yard pass. He hadn't been able to resist the chance to mix with other humans again. The prisoners had recognized him for the animal he was in seconds, starting to beat on him even before they remembered where they'd seen that face and its blocky Super Mario mustache. They hammered a barbell grip into his brain through the roof of his mouth.

Two known victims had been discovered in the course of Hillstrom's interviews when he was first arrested. That had been after a videotape was turned in by his landlord. Because he was impressively behind in rent, and barely turning up at his place anymore, the landlord had evicted him and begun a thorough cleaning of the filthy apartment. A loose floorboard had been discovered during repairs, and under that board was a snuff film. The girl in the video was never concretely identified, but was assumed to be one of the three prostitutes Hillstrom was eventually tied to in court. Apparently her face was already obscured by blood in the first frame of the poorly shot film.

Hillstrom had been cooperative, telling officers exactly where the two burial sites he could remember were, using landmarks: a certain-shaped boulder, a grouping of trees. They found the women buried deep, in cleverly obscure forested locations around highways leading out of Seattle. In the interrogations, Hillstrom had been spooky-precise in his recall of the burial spots: thirty-five feet from this tree, about seventy feet from the trail, and so on. When the data from the search crews came in, Hillstrom was nearly always spot-on. The "Erin" Ted Lennox mentioned, Erin Muckler, Hillstrom called "the practice one," and stuck to his story about being too drunk the night he'd gotten rid of her to remember much of anything.

And here he was, giving another location in the transcript, of someone new.

CH: *Up on Mount Rainier.*

Hillstrom laid out some specifics, which turnoff, which parking lot. Then he dropped the figures.

CH: *You walk down the trail. Third marker. Go about 50*
   before veering left. Then keep going straight through
   the brush, about 40. There'll be a clearing.

There was a little more of the transcript there, Ted Lennox wheedling to get an identity out of Hillstrom, but there was no more concrete information. My eyes were aching from gazing at the scans on the scrapbook screen. I hadn't turned on any lights in the house, and now that the sun had properly set, the scrapbook was the only light source on this entire floor of the house, except for the tree-screen leakage of the streetlamps through the big bay window in the living room. I got up to flick on lights and pace, glad Ellen wasn't home yet to disrupt my thoughts. After about seven minutes of pacing, flicking switches on and off, and rattling every cataloged thought on Carl Hillstrom I had in my brain, I figured out why they hadn't found the burial site of victim four.

Hillstrom had been born (yes, of course, to a prostitute and an absent father) in Edmonton, Alberta, and lived there for fifteen years (mutilating animals and being antisocial, yes, continuing to act out a stereotype he wasn't aware of) before the move to Tacoma. That span in Canada covered most of his schooling, which meant he'd learned his math on the metric system. The numbers he'd dropped in the interview with Lennox—50, 40—weren't feet. They were meters. Hillstrom had slipped backward, using the metric measures he'd learned in school—by accident, I think, because he wasn't clever enough to come up with such a precise deception. I took out my phone instead of trying to do the calculation on my own: 3.28 feet in a meter, 50 meters is 164 feet, 40 meters is 131 feet. A long ways off from where the cops had looked when they'd followed up on this interview.

Hillstrom was too dumb to be manipulative. That had always been clear. He was a smart killer and concealer, but that had never matched up with the way he presented himself in court, or how he came across in non-search-related transcripts. That he'd gotten away with three murders, let alone four, was miraculous.

"Hillstrom was a junior partner," I said, just as I heard Ellen pulling into the garage, the wheels of her car rolling up alongside the stain left by Bella Greene's blood. The Ragman's touch explained the smart burials of the Hillstrom girls. It explained the murders themselves. A guy dumb enough to leave a snuff movie in an apartment he's behind in the rent on? Probably not smart enough to get away with murder, alone. But with the Ragman? A Ragman who'd lost his first killing partner, Jason Shurn?

I caught a shiver in my right hand, the kind of shake an old man gets, or an alcoholic when he's waking up. It looked a little like it was being jostled by a small, irresistible, and invisible force. I pushed my thumb toward my index finger, imagining the needle there. The needle that had killed Keith. Could be the Ragman tricked Shurn and Hillstrom into their first kills.

"But you guys didn't need the encouragement, did you?" I said, then closed my scrapbook.

26

ON FRIDAY AFTERNOON, AN HOUR BEFORE HE WAS
supposed to officially close up shop, the Ragman updated the website for Acme Urban Surveillance with a banner notice:
"Away for Two Weeks. Any Order that Has Not Shipped Will Be Delayed—
We Value Privacy Over Speed." For the door, a briefer hand-markered
message, which read *"Back in Business on the 15th. Sorry."*

As he was posting it, Mike Guzman, who ran the convenience store
next to Acme, was having a smoke. Guzman watched him tape up the
sign from the inside, then walked out to check on it.

"Going outta town, Frank?" Guzman asked. The Ragman twitched
and looked at the ground for a moment.

"Yeah. Business is always a little soft this month, anyway, picks up
again mid-December. Same for you?"

"With me it's always bad," Guzman said, laughing. He was wearing a
tight yellow shirt with red stripes, the uniform he always wore to work,
even though he owned the store. The Ragman couldn't understand that;

picking an embarrassing outfit for yourself to wear every day, at the place you worked hard to buy. A forty-year-old man choosing to dress as a 1980s McDonald's employee every day for the rest of his working life.

"Recession, right?" the Ragman said with a forced wink, then pointed to the stack of boxes just behind the door of Acme. "Got to get those to the post office. Keep an eye on the place for me, will you?"

"You got it all alarmed up. And more cameras than you need."

"Right. Still, extra eyes don't hurt." The conversation ended, thankfully, and the Ragman loaded his car, locked up, and drove off. He wasn't sure if he'd ever be coming back to the store, and was fairly sure he didn't care.

In surveillance, it's the eyes the watched can't see that matter most, especially when they can feel the gaze when no one's watching. Martin Reese knew that, now, the Ragman thought.

The tracker on Martin's Jeep had been deactivated, and by now he must have found the earring the Ragman had faked up to look like the one that had been lying next to Jenny Starks in the woods, years ago. He'd used blood from a package of short ribs, and aged the feather earring in weak tea and dirt. If Martin had been paying proper attention, he'd have been suspicious of the token appearing at all. The Ragman didn't hold on to memories; he buried them. Even if Martin did suspect it was a fake, though, it would have done its job: shown him that eyes were always on him.

"Martin Reese," the Ragman muttered, and smiled. Martin Reese, Jason Shurn, Carl Hillstrom. The names had a pleasing concordance, and Martin even looked a bit like Jason, if Jason had grown up to be a real man, a worthy partner for this kind of work. If Jason hadn't failed them both.

After the post office, the Ragman drove to ReeseTech. The light of the sun, filtered by clouds and his tinted windshield, caught the light pink of the solution in the syringe the Ragman placed on the passenger seat as he parked. Across from the building, in a surveillance camera blind-spot he'd scouted weeks ago, he watched men and women filter out of the place where Martin Reese used to spend his days, when he wasn't out digging up the Ragman's past. He waited for the right person to come out.

27

COURTESY OF REALITY'S INSANE HUMOR, I WAS AT a Friday night party. Half-hosting the *tinsley* launch with Ellen, every "I barely knew what was going on until I got here to-night myself!" was greeted with laughter and indulgent eye-rolling from the sixty-odd people who were milling around the space. Doing my best not to answer every "So what have you been up to?" with "Accidentally murdering cops in parking garages."

The room was packed, the AC not keeping up with the body heat. If it weren't for the obvious wealth of everyone there, other than the fashion writers, shoplifting would have been a concern. Gary, in a black-on-black suit that would have made a less skinny man look like a Vegas magician, was greasing his way through the crowd with an indulgent laugh.

"Martin, did you see that pile of belts in the back, the green ones in the stockroom? Kind of ridged?" Ellen was using her best kindergarten teacher voice on me, and I would have gotten annoyed if she wasn't both worried and entirely in her glory. The potential belt customer, a woman I'd seen on real estate signs in our neighborhood and several better ones, pretended she wasn't listening, but emphatically was.

"Sure. I can find them."

"Thanks. Sorry to errand-boy you," Ellen said. She pushed three fingernails through her hair, a stress gesture that was particular to her business self, coming out only at the credit union, never in our family fights. Seeing her do that in *tinsley* made me absolutely certain, at that moment, that the store was going to succeed.

"Let me help, Dad," Kylie said, speaking from just over my left shoulder. The friend who was supposed to come with her, Lisa or Liza or something, had ditched at the last minute for a date. That had left Kylie wandering the narrow margins of the party, unable to find a corner that wasn't occupied by a display or an unbearably rich and boring person. Kylie had refused her mother's offer to wear some of the *tinsley* stock and was instead in her go-to special occasion dress, a green and black thing without sleeves that made her look a bit older than she was, but not in a way that made me worry.

"Aren't you having fun milling?" I asked Kylie, finding my way into my first genuine smile in a long time.

"I'm the social hit of the season, Dad, just want to help you out." Ellen had tuned us out and was in deep conference with the real estate lady. Kylie and I made our way through the corridor of bodies to the stock room. The belts were in a pile just to the left of the door, and I grabbed one.

"Wait," Kylie said. "Don't go back out yet. Close the door." I did.

"Not that bad out there, come on."

"It's what I expected," Kylie said, flapping her right hand at me like she was dismissing a servant. "Mom's doing great. That whole rack of those ugly red shirts is already gone, did you see?"

"No, but I know the ones you're talking about."

"It's you, Dad. You're not okay. You're not at all okay, and I don't understand why. That 'v' thing between your eyebrows is, like, as deep as an ax wound."

"It's just stress," I said, disarmed again by how clearly Kylie saw me, even through the noise and flash of a party like this one. "Not used to playing the hapless but supportive hubby at a big event."

"Dad. If Mom wasn't so busy she would have noticed something was really wrong, too. You lucked out having this crisis now. Just please let me help, okay?"

I don't think I'd come closer to completely shaking apart and handing over the hell of the last few days as a problem for someone else to solve, as when my fourteen-year-old kid was staring me down in that room full of gourmet cloth. There was something in her determination, her unwillingness to take anything but the real answer in that moment, that made me think maybe she could find a way out I hadn't thought of. A way for us to put Bella Greene back in that grave, resurrect Keith Waring, to keep the Ragman from ever bothering us again. Then I laughed, without any humor, while Kylie just watched me.

"I just don't know what to tell you, Kylie. You're right, I have a ton of stuff on my mind—nothing to do with your mom or you, everything's fine—but it's nothing you can fix. Even talking about it wouldn't help. But I love you and I love you more for noticing and caring and trying to help. Okay?"

"Fuck you, Dad," Kylie said, and left the little stockroom. Stormed out, more accurately. I took one of the belts and followed her, stopping to drop the piece off with Ellen, who took my arm.

"This is Julie Walker. She just sold the Bezanson house up the way from us, remember? She's bought and sold half of Eastlake."

"The nice half," Julie Walker said, with a combo Frank Gorshin/Vivien Leigh laugh.

"She wants to talk you into getting us a cottage again," Ellen said.

"Oh, don't make me sound like such a snake," Julie said. "I don't even have a stake in any of them, I'm strictly urban-property and a little— well, look, tell me how I can buy every one of these belts you have, so no one else in the city has one?"

"You have no idea how possible that could be," Ellen said. "The designer died last month and this is the absolute last run of this piece, they say."

Ellen had already let go of my arm but Kylie was out of the store already, likely pacing the sidewalk across from *tinsley*, waiting for me to come and find her. Gary waved me over from a small group of middle-aged guys I vaguely recognized, probably from appearances in the same Seattle tech scene stories my picture used to turn up in. I went over to do my night's job, to talk normally, charmingly, to get people to spend and tell other people to spend.

When I walked outside of *tinsley*, not more than fifteen minutes later, I couldn't see Kylie. I called her name, crossed the street, even checked the alley to see if she'd bummed a cigarette to smoke rebelliously so I could catch her and we could have an honest fight, as she'd done once last summer when she had really wanted to talk to me about quitting swimming. I couldn't find her. I called her name a couple of times.

"Kylie. Kylie." It was on the second "Kylie" that I felt a fear worse than anything I'd felt in the grave where I found Bella Greene, or in the garage when I shot Keith Waring up full of poison. I kept calling until I was screaming her name.

28

EARLY THE NEXT MORNING, ELLEN WAS IN OUR BED-
room, with two pills in her and a private nurse outside
the door. It didn't take long for the adrenalized force of her tension to
cut through the muffling syrup of the prescription pills, and she pushed
past the nurse, who followed her into the living room where I was sitting
across from Detective Sandra Whittal. Whittal wouldn't sit when I first
asked her to, but after fifteen minutes of talking, she relented and was
sitting on the arm of the couch across from me.

The nurse was a beefy Hispanic kid with a weirdly Canadian accent
who went by Tex. Probably he'd used childhood TV to get away from
sounding like his parents and had somehow ended up with this. I found
myself observing this bullshit and hating myself for it at the same time,
then thinking deeper into it, just so I could get a millisecond of mental
rest from thinking about Kylie and where she was. Who she was with.
And how little I really knew about the Ragman, other than that he'd
certainly kill Kylie if I told the cops about his existence.

I gestured the nurse back to his post, getting up to make room for Ellen in the deep leather chair where I'd sunk, trying to look more shocked and more clueless than I was. Ellen's hair was tied back and her face was pale and streaked with makeup she hadn't washed off. It looked like scraps of greasepaint on a soldier's corpse.

It had taken about four seconds of talking to Whittal to remember again why Keith had sounded so shit-scared of her and why I'd felt the same on my visit to the precinct.

"We can't assume anyone has her, not exactly yet," Detective Whittal repeated, for Ellen's benefit.

"Someone does," Ellen said. "She would never do this. She would have called hours ago, texted, done something. We looked all night. All night."

"She doesn't have her phone," I said. The phone had been deposited in a garbage can two blocks away from *tinsley*, wrapped in a sandwich bag that reeked vaguely of chorizo sausage. The cops had brought it up to me this morning, asked me if I remembered Kylie having it on her as she left the store last night. I didn't, but felt sick looking at the touchscreen slicked with grease, glad they hadn't shown this artifact to Ellen. I could easily picture it in the Ragman's gloved hands as he ate a sausage on a bun in his van, waiting for Kylie to walk the necessary number of steps away from the store for him to come in with his needles and grasping arm.

"I don't care that she doesn't have her phone, Martin, she knows our fucking numbers, she knows 911, she would have *called*, okay?"

"I'll be frank," Whittal said, which made me wonder what she'd been so far. "I do think someone has Kylie. I think it has everything to do with the anniversary of your sister's vanishing."

"And with that body you found?"

"Martin," Ellen said, a lacerating gasp with syllables.

"That's stretching it, slightly, but maybe. But I don't think there's any need to think Kylie's been harmed," said Whittal. "I think we would have gotten a call about that, some sort of tease. He's glommed on to your family because of your sister, Mrs. Reese. That's what I think. What we're dealing with, essentially, if I have our guy right, is an obsessive coward who has a fantasy around other people's murders. Ones he didn't have the courage to commit himself."

"Is that so?" I asked, a little annoyed, despite myself. I yanked my ego out of the conversation before it could make me say anything. Kylie was in the Ragman's world, and I was going to get her out. But if I was going to bring her back to the life she'd been plucked out of, I had to pretend to the police that they could help me, that I was a hapless idiot who needed them. Whittal looked at me with flat eyes, devoid of the compassion that glinted in them when she talked to Ellen. I couldn't tell which one was the act: the cold investigator or the concerned human being.

"The FBI will probably be in on this soon enough, and I imagine they'll tell you something similar, Mr. and Mrs. Reese. But I want this solved and Kylie back with you before they even have a chance to run their evaluations and size things up. I'm talking hours here, not days."

Ellen and Whittal did most of the talking after that, detailing Kylie's social patterns over the past year, including a boyfriend I didn't know anything about. I didn't tell Detective Whittal about the morning drive I'd taken with my daughter just a few days ago, when I'd told her all about Jason Shurn and monsters just like the Ragman.

"I'm sorry," I said, loud enough for both my wife and the cop to stop talking and turn to me. "I fucking failed, or she'd be here. I'm sorry."

"Martin, shouldn't you—" Ellen trailed off. I understood she was going to tell Whittal about Sergeant Keith Waring if I didn't. So I did. Being slack enough to let Ellen see me with him all those months ago had been one of the bigger mistakes in this disaster.

"I should say, Detective, even if it does seem silly, that I'm friends with a cop. And he's been acting strangely recently, the last few months.

I just don't think he has anything to do with this, you know?" Whittal's notepad was out and her lips moving before I finished my last sentence. I'd sparked something I hadn't expected, and then I understood. Understood what Whittal was thinking, what I had to say now: exactly what the Ragman had set me up to say. Of course. Keith.

"His name's Keith Waring. We just met in a post office line, around Christmas a few years ago, and he seemed to be an interesting guy with great cop stories. I thought hey, I should make friends out of my normal social circle, being retired and all."

"Waring. God," Whittal said, her professionalism fracturing for a second. I think she almost smiled. "Do you have many other friends, Mr. Reese?" she asked. Her hunting instinct made her more impatient and human than her compassion for vanished Kylie had.

"Not a ton of close ones, which could be why I put up with Keith when he started to get weirder. I told him last time we hung out that I didn't really want to keep going with these meetings, and he got sullen, threatening. This was at a bar, so there were people around, but I still felt a little scared." I certainly felt scared telling the story to Whittal: while Keith wasn't around to talk, she'd know what he'd done on the force, might guess why anyone might spend time with him. Access.

"Did Keith Waring tell you what he did for the department, Mr. Reese?"

"He lied, made me think he was still working the streets in Vice, or Homicide. It changed week to week. Eventually he let on that he just did paperwork." Scrapbook work.

"Why was your last meeting so unpleasant?"

"He kept on mentioning matters from the past. Including Tinsley. Stuff he said he knew and no one else did."

"Martin," Ellen said. "You didn't say anything about this right away?"

"You don't know Keith," I said. "He's too—he's not strong enough, not smart enough to have anything to do with taking Kylie."

"Did he know you had a daughter? Had they ever met?" Ellen asked. "Martin, he's a cop. He probably knows where the security cameras are near the store, or he could find out—that's how he found that blind spot where he took her." The police had viewed footage from two businesses near *tinsley*: Kylie walks by a frozen yogurt place but never makes the walk past the upscale housewares store two storefronts past it. Somewhere in that tiny space of sidewalk, the Ragman had taken away the most important part of my life.

"Ellen, stop. Keith never met Kylie. Maybe he saw her in my car once, but they'd never met."

"It's him," Ellen said. "It's him, isn't it?" She was asking Whittal, not me. I felt a cool wash of fear around my lungs and heart, as though the Ragman were in the room with us, instead of manipulating this scene perfectly from afar, from wherever he was with Kylie.

The Ragman had locked in Keith as the suspect no one would ever find. The man he'd made me kill was the one I had to finger if I was going to stay free and get Kylie back. It was a perfect plan, as far as I could see: setting up the police officer they'd never find as the caller and killer in one. Buying the Ragman and me both some time. Time for him to finish with me.

"It's obviously not him, Ellen," I said, just as I was supposed to. "He's at the police station every goddamn day, not out kidnapping girls."

"I can tell you this much," Detective Whittal said, answering Ellen and ignoring me. "Sergeant Waring hasn't been at work. And he worked on archiving cases like your sister's."

"He was obsessed with her, you're saying? With my sister?"

"I'm not saying that, no. Not yet, not at all."

"Oh my god," I said. It seemed like my turn. "So you're—so Keith talked to me to be close to Ellen, to Tinsley? He's some sort of ghoul?"

"We'll need to speak with Sergeant Waring, Mr. Reese. And I have to talk to you in greater detail, once I've found him," Whittal said, flipping her notebook shut and starting to text on her phone. Ellen looked at me with what I hoped was a haze from the pills, but could have been a disappointment so vivid neither of us could confront it. I left the room and walked into the garage, leaning against my Jeep, unfurling the slip of paper I'd found taped under the driver's side door handle the night before, after I'd finished running around the block, screaming Kylie's name. The note hadn't left my pants pocket since. Typed, printed, clipped precisely into a perfect square.

Dear Martin, I'm glad you're still working away on the Hillstrom papers I gave you. But here's another ripple! See, a normal someone would have gone to the police right after leaving Keith's apartment, you know. Jeopardized his own freedom to keep himself and his family safe from the hovering psychotic, right?

But I just wanted to see what YOU would do. And you didn't call the police in, did you? You never will tell them about US. Our Sunday appointment's still on (see you soon!!), and I wanted an extra special reminder of the terrible mess you've gotten your family in by poking around in other people's business. If you're good from now on, Kylie will be fine. I can't make any promises about you.

R.

I had to believe him. That he wasn't going to hurt Kylie. And I believed she could survive whatever she was going through, mentally.

I held these things to be true because I had to. Kylie had to be alive. If there was a chance that she was dead, if I admitted that possibility, I knew I was going to start screaming, and that I would never be able to stop.

Four walls, a ceiling, a floor, a metal toilet built into the wall with the tank cover welded shut, a flush button the only moving part. Opposite from the toilet, a mail slot, built into one of the walls, not the door. Because there was no door. But there was a deep freeze, the kind hunters use, expensive and big enough for the packaged remains of two or three kills. When Kylie Reese opened it, curling her fingers under the top-loading door and pushing up with her arms still weak and absent-feeling from the drug that had coursed through her body, the only thing inside was the cold. There was no plug in the wall, and getting on her hands and knees, Kylie saw a short cord extending into the floor. The light in the room was fluorescent, angry bright, making the white walls glow.

She'd woken up a half hour before, lying still in fear after whipping her head up and finding herself in a room with no door. She touched the invisible spot on her neck where she'd felt a sting after leaving *tinsley* and walking half the block toward the convenience store on the corner.

The Ragman watched Kylie through one of the four tiny, invisible cameras in the room, checking to make sure she woke up within the window of time the dose he'd shot into her outside of her mother's shiny new store allowed. He had a needle full of adrenaline loaded and ready to go if she was slow to wake. He wanted her alive for printed stills to be sent to Martin. She wasn't ready for the freezer yet.

Inside the room, the muscles in Kylie's thighs and shoulders un-kinked as she rotated and stretched next to the freezer, as best she could in her green and black dress. She wouldn't be taking her clothes off in this place, not with the lights on, not with that slot across from her ready to admit any gaze.

"Are you going to answer if I say anything?" she called, her voice cracking from a dry throat and the fear she was trying to keep down. A second later the mail slot admitted a small, lunchbox-sized box of apple juice, the kind with a straw strapped across like a little bandolier. Kylie walked over and checked the seal, then thought that would be a pretty dumb way to kill her. Her hand shook trying to get the straw out of its wrapping, and she kept trying, pretending to be calm, until its point pierced the plastic.

She walked over to the toilet after a few seconds of poking at the mail slot, seeing if she could get the box back through it. It was strictly one-way. But the tank had something to tell her: there was a note lying on top of it, typed and printed on normal paper, like a school newsletter, but without a masthead and in italics. A personal touch.

I'm not going to hurt you. I'm not going to touch you. As long as your
dad plays nice. Or else. You pay his tab.

"My dad will do or pay whatever you want," Kylie called to the walls, looking into the corners for a camera she could pray to. "He'll do anything. You don't understand how scared my mom is going to be, and him. They'll do anything you want."

The Ragman, watching the monitor but also able to hear Kylie through the walls, had to keep his laughter down at the "how scared my mom is going to be" part. He let Kylie keep talking, and left to take a nap in the camp bed he had set up in the garage. For the past couple of weeks, he'd been shutting down parts of the home, emptying them of his personal history and loading in newspaper and other easy flammables.

Kylie kept talking to the camera she was sure was up there for a few more minutes. When the words starting coming out automatically, she spent most of the time thinking of what she could do to hurt the man who'd put her in here if he ever opened the hidden door that led into this room. Because she was sure that when he did open up, it would be to come in and kill her.

29

"KEITH WARING ISN'T THE FINDER, BUT HE'S THE GUY who killed Bella Greene and made that last call," Sandra said when Chris pulled up to pick her up. "Hovering about ninety percent sure. We're going to his house, *now*."

"I called in for the address as soon as you texted. Some shithole apartment building in Ballard. You'd think Keith could do better than that, no dependents and a salary all to himself for barely doing anything." They were already moving east, hooking into a turn at a stop sign and picking up speed as Chris made a bet on what the best route back downtown would be.

"I think he was doing a *lot*," Sandra said. "All these years. He's been getting deeper into these files, reading about our Horace Marks and our Jason Shurns, and he got jealous of our Finder, who had the smarts he doesn't. Took it one step further and forged a friendship with someone connected to the Tinsley Schultz vanishing, Martin Reese—probably has a bunch more of these connections around. If the digs in the past checked out against Keith's time off, I'd think he was the Finder. But he's not. He's jealous of the Finder and wants to one-up him by killing." Sandra was riding on a deduction exultance wave, putting the story together as she said it, strongly believing parts of it. She wasn't sure which parts.

"What if that isn't it? If Keith's not our guy?"

"Then we think about it some more, Chris. Right now we're finding out if Waring is an obsessed weirdo who took Kylie Reese off the street and has her holed up somewhere. What do you know about him, socially? Anything?"

Chris reached down blind, switching lanes, and pulled up a coffee cup. He took a gulp then spat out the piece of discarded gum that had been hiding in the black fluid.

"I think that was mine," Sandra said.

"Socially I know almost nothing about him. He tries to joke around with us sometimes. The rest of the guys, I mean. He's clearly terrified of you. But there's something unnatural about it. Like he's a step behind, waiting for us to approve of each joke or set him up to tell a story. Socially he's not all there. Girlfriends, no mention, really. Boyfriends either. He did tell me he wrote back and forth with this one woman in Oregon, maybe Vancouver, trying to pass her off as an ex he was rekindling with. It was clearly an internet thing. I got out of that conversation pretty quick, soon as the coffee was brewed."

"I thought for a second that he and Reese, the dad, possibly had a thing," Sandra said. "A sex thing, because it just seemed so bizarre they'd be friends."

"Jesus."

"This makes more sense. Keith glommed on to him because he was connected to Tinsley Schultz. The obsession built and now it's at the point where Keith Waring takes Kylie Reese. She looks a lot like Tinsley Schultz, you know. He's got some idea of reenacting what happened twenty years back." Sandra let the theory out as they sped to Keith's apartment, not noticing Chris's growing silence.

"You almost hope you're right, don't you?" Chris said.

"What? Of course I do."

"I mean, what if the kid's dead, Sandra?"

"She's not fucking dead and no I do not want to be right that badly. Can't you stop analyzing me for a minute and just talk about the case? Can I kindly ask you to do that?" A wall of traffic stopped them halfway across the bridge, cutting the momentum of the argument, too.

"I can talk to you about the facts of the case. Remember facts?" Chris said. "There was nothing on the security cam footage we got. Three cameras hit the spot in front of the store, but there are two dark zones where there's no coverage. Kylie steps into one, holding her phone and texting on it, at nine twenty-seven. Then that's that. No way is it a coincidence, either—those gaps between camera coverage are just too narrow. Whoever grabbed the Reese girl must have hacked or otherwise gained access to every security feed on the block to determine the ideal place for a grab. No coverage in the area where her phone was dropped, either."

"Seems impossible. Middle of downtown, not a single street camera?"

"It's the only block within a square half-mile that has no coverage. Not an accidental dumping ground."

"Martin Reese looked like he was holding back on something," Sandra said, and Chris sighed. "What?"

"Nothing, go on." Traffic started moving again, and Chris relented and hit the siren, starting to weave in and out of lanes.

"He didn't mention Waring until his wife told him to, and even then, he seemed to only be giving up some of what he knew."

"He must be some sort of conspiracy vampire pervert, too, then, right?"

"That's not what I'm saying. Maybe the guy who took Kylie—Keith or not—got a message to him. Reese said he'd 'failed her' up there, could have meant that specifically, like he saw her being taken and didn't get to her in time. Reese could have been contacted and told explicitly that anything he passed on to the cops gets his daughter's throat slit."

"Injected," Chris said, turning into the parking lot of the coffee place he favored in this part of town, not so close to the university that the students bled over en masse with their laptops.

"Injected?"

"If it's the same guy who got Bella Greene, he's a needle guy, not a throat-slitter. Right?"

"Right. Which is why we're going to knock on Keith Waring's door. Or knock it down. I'll get someone from forensics to meet with us out there."

Sandra pressed dial, and within a minute, was screaming at whoever wasn't getting her what she needed in the time she needed it. Later, she was sitting at the kitchen table in Keith Waring's sad bachelor apartment, a place that was remarkable in only one aspect: how clean it was. Not necessarily tidy, but clean. Especially the living room, hallway, and kitchen. The small, recessed bedroom was a maelstrom of tissues, potato chip bags, bank statements, and gun magazines. It smelled in there, too, a more concentrated version of what wafted by her desk at work when Keith passed her to go to the bathroom.

Al Mingus, Sandra's preferred forensic tech, had come once she'd gotten a warrant. The pressure of the potential Kylie Reese connection made it an easy sell.

No one had reported Keith missing, but when Sandra filed the report and urged a press announcement that afternoon, she was able to convince the lieutenant that there was no one *to* report him missing. Whatever kind of cop he was—deskbound, maybe corrupt—he was still police, and it was up to his workplace to report him missing, and to do the necessary investigating.

"It's more than just clean here," Mingus said, doing another sweep with the black light. He was tall, and this kind of work had him bending and stooping frequently, his joints making snaps to soundtrack the job. "Looking at the state of that bedroom, and having sat across from Keith at the burrito place a few times, no way should every surface look like this out here. Still a bit of solvent stink coming from the laminate out here and the linoleum in the kitchen, too."

"This isn't just you feeding on my paranoia, as the guys at the station are guaranteed going to say?" Sandra asked.

"Nope. Doesn't really prove anything, but this looks like a place that was cleaned up by someone who knows what he's doing, either from experience or from deep research. There's barely evidence of Keith Waring himself in this room, let alone anyone else who might have been here with him."

"Then Waring did it, the clean. He's a cop, he has the expertise."

"Did you ever talk to the guy?" asked Chris, from his slight leaning perch by the kitchen table. "I can buy him being a pervert and a stalker, but not a brilliant murder-and-cleanup genius. Even with the cop knowledge that a dolt like him could be expected to pick up, he just isn't up to it. Keith isn't our guy."

"Shut up."

"A pro did clean this place out though," said Mingus. "I'd bet on that. Reason to suspect foul play, especially if we combo it with him not turning up to work. Tracked his phone?"

"We're on it," Sandra said, knowing, though, that it wouldn't be of much use. If a creep could clean this place up, he could get rid of a phone. "Chris, can you get back to the station and toss his desk again? I already did it lightly, but look for any files, any data, any mention at all of Jason Shurn, Horace Marks, any of the killers our guy has called in bodies of. And of Tinsley Schultz, anyone Reese-related, obviously."

"Yeah. Anything else I should have an eye out for? Besides, you know, the completely obvious things you just spelled out for me?"

"Look for anything that will help us find where he took Ellen Reese's daughter," Sandra said. That shut Chris up, and he left.

An hour later, Sandra dropped Mingus off and went for lunch, eating a bowl of ramen as she processed, checking in with the plainclothes detail she'd set up to make sure no street girls had been assaulted or gone missing. If Kylie Reese, an upper-class teenager on the state swim team, was this psycho's follow-up to Bella Greene, a destitute addict, there was perhaps little point in keeping an eye on any one group. Sandra hadn't found a pattern, if there was one. And if there was no pattern, no one was safe.

30

BY SUNDAY I'D THOUGHT OF A HUNDRED REASONS
to turn up early for my appointment with the Rag-
man, but I hadn't done it. Hadn't made the drive, because of what dis-
obedience could mean for Kylie.

Keith Waring's picture had hit the news and the papers on Saturday,
as a "Person of Interest," related to Kylie's disappearance. The reports
made it clear that he should be considered not as the suspect, but as
someone connected to the case who needed to be spoken to.

Ellen concentrated on postering and news campaigns for Kylie. We
paid off the nurse when it was clear Ellen wasn't going to be doing the
bedridden panic zombie role that was assigned to her by the movies.

"Every second we're not out looking for her is a second we're giving
up on her, you get it? Nobody knows what the fuck they're doing here,
the cops, you, nobody, or Kylie would be back right now," she said to me
when I'd asked her to take a nap between interviews, or to listen to what
the cops were advising her to say or not say.

Gary was running the store entirely, which I'd had to thank him for, as much as it pained me. Reporters and tourists were turning up with cameras and questions, and I'd personally seen him scream them out of the store.

The phantom sensation of pushing that needle plunger down and pulling the life out of Keith's body hadn't completely left my fingertips, even when I was dreaming. I thought of a different needle with a different dose of the same drug in Kylie's neck, at least twice a minute. The Ragman's hands on her arm, pulling her into his world. Breaking any of his rules seemed impossible at this point. So I checked and double-checked my calculations from the Hillstrom file all Saturday, like a good boy, doing the homework I'd gotten so good at. I knew, knew with the old certainty I'd had on my best digs, where that body was. And Sunday finally came.

Carl Hillstrom hadn't hidden this girl in the deep forest, which was a relief, especially since I knew who I'd be meeting at the site. I didn't feel comfortable in the depths of the wild, and neither did any of the guys I'd followed over the years. They had to be close enough to their cars, close enough to the city they hunted in. Far enough into the trees to feel like no one is around, but near enough to everyone to remember there was still a world around that had been changed by the removal of a life.

I went into our bedroom, which had become Ellen's miniature control center over the past two days, the TV blaring and two laptops open. She was between phone calls, staring at the wall above the headboard, standing in her housecoat with dried spit at the corner of her mouth, chewing a pen.

"Ellen."

"I've got searchers out, Martin. Volunteers. The cops told me not to but I think it's going to help, just a couple of groups of six canvassing downtown with her picture. It's still so close to when she vanished. People remember when it's been so little time, you know?"

"I know."

"We didn't look for Tinsley quickly enough. Not that it would have made a difference." Ellen giggled at this, and for the first time, I thought she genuinely might break before I had a chance to get our daughter back.

"Ellen. This isn't Tinsley."

"You should leave the house for a bit, Martin. You're not helping and I feel like you're not properly here, even. Look for your friend Keith, why don't you?"

"If I don't look like I'm crumbling into a panic it's because I'm doing what you're doing, Ellen. Pretending I'm not going crazy over her being gone, every second." I gripped Ellen's arms in both my hands, and she let me hold on to her, but wouldn't look me in the face. Her arms hung there, the muscles slack, the bones inside them still as slats of scrap wood.

"You're really good at staying calm, Martin," she said. "You can make it seem like you don't care at all."

"I can't fix this with us right now, Ellen. But don't ever say I don't care about her. Don't say something I'll never be able to forget. I'm trying to get Kylie back my own way."

"And what way is that?" Ellen asked, pulling back from me and sitting on the bed again, checking her phone for updates. For a furious second, I was at the edge of telling her exactly what happened, and how deviating from the Ragman's orders by a single syllable or move would land our daughter in a grave. But I was too scared for Kylie to tell my wife what she deserved to know. And too scared for myself.

"I'm going to look for Keith, okay? Like you said. Checking out some old hangouts he had, things he mentioned. But the cops can't know. Any detail makes it onto a police scanner, and he'll hear it. I'll text you where I'll be staying if I don't come back tonight." Ellen stared at me for a few cynical seconds.

"You talk like this is some tree house game for boys," she said. Her phone rang and she spoke into it, dismissing me.

Before getting in the Jeep, I texted Ellen the address of the motel I was going to use as my base camp, with a few quick words—

Keith mentioned a place he liked to stay near
this place. Going to see. Love you.

I left my iPhone on the kitchen counter, following old procedure. Didn't want another portable GPS beacon on me, especially with Sandra Whittal and the rest of the SPD gang poking around my family. The tent and outdoor stuff were stowed in the back of my vehicle, the digging and forensic gear below it. I wished for a gun. The eyes I felt on me every moment I wasn't in the house, cop eyes and Ragman eyes—they kept me away from gun stores, or from a sketchy back-alley arms deal I'd have no idea how to enter into anyhow. There was a hunting knife in a sheath on my calf, pressing uncomfortably into the elastic of my socks.

The cop car parked across from our house was empty, but I still waved as I passed by in the Jeep, senselessly. I hoped Kylie had eaten lunch, that there were blankets where she was. It was getting chilly. I took the long way, checking my mirror a few times, before getting onto the highway.

In the forest, with Hillstrom's woman, I could become myself again. I had a duty, the same duty I'd taken on years ago: to uncover what was hidden, to bring up what was put away. I could make the Ragman understand that, maybe. Or just, somehow, make him leave me alone and give us our daughter back.

Hillstrom's last, publicly unknown victim. I was pretty sure I knew who she was, and I was about to find out. One thing about hidden corpses: after the rotting's finished, they'll keep forever. I still have a tendency to rush as soon as I zone-in on these trips, and this time I told myself to be careful, to fix my awareness on the drive, with a stop at the Marpole Motel on my way to the Hillstrom site.

I checked into the motel, a little fleabag minus the fleas that was crowded in the peak of summer and desperately cheap in the fall and winter, in a quick five-minute transaction where I warned them that I'd probably be staying overnight, but that I'd be back by checkout time. The place seemed to be run by just one Hispanic man, who was pulling up the flooring around the front desk when I came in. I gave him a cash deposit before he could ask for a credit card.

"My accounts got hacked on Friday," I said. "On the road, it's been a pain to get the bank to actually take care of anything. They don't care about anything until it's their own money, right?"

The man, sawdust dusting the black hairs on his narrow arms, flicked through the bills in the envelope I'd handed him and nodded. "No problem," he said, then checked me in.

I took a look at the room itself. One bed, with an uncomfortable autumn-looking bedspread. An apology on the wall for the lack of Wi-Fi. Instead of a mint on the pillow, salmon candy. I dropped a sweater on the bed and mussed the sheets a little bit, then got back on the road.

On the Mount Rainier trails, my pack, heavy with the tools I'd be needing, nestled close to my body, keeping me standing up straight as I carried its weight through the woods. The parking lot had been close to empty, with just a couple of Park Service cars and four or five pickup trucks keeping my vehicle company. The rain that had started pounding down made me feel safe, extra assured there would be few people out in the forest with me that day. It would be closer to dry under the canopy, once I'd left the trail at the correct point. I had forty minutes of daylight left, and a bit of dusk after that.

Around me was the kind of forest that could be interchangeably used in helicopter footage for Enjoy British Columbia or Beautiful Oregon commercials. Tourists don't care about the niceties of arboreal differentiation, except for the nature weirdos or birders. What I always noticed most was the air, not for its cold freshness, but its clarity: it added to the vividness of a dig, being distant from the smoke and breath of a city, with the trees exhaling oxygen into my natural, hunter's high.

A pine branch slapped into my face while I was preoccupied and I realized I'd lost track of how long I'd gone from the third trail marker, the one Hillstrom used as a landmark. I cursed, and went back, flicking on the Stanley Distance Measurer I'd brought, and starting to gauge the distances I'd be walking. I kept going, fifty meters, trusting the odd precision of Carl Hillstrom in his previous jailhouse confessions. Forty meters through the brush on my left would be a clearing. In that clearing would be Carl Hillstrom's victim. A bit of extra research had led me to believe she was another missing Canadian girl: Cindy Jenkins. The date of her vanishing and the hitchhiking path her family and the cops had put together after a few months of her being gone put her squarely within Hillstrom's hunting grounds and active months. And the Ragman was out at the site already, maybe. Our appointment was for seven p.m.: two hours away.

Maybe he'd even brought Kylie, scared, blindfolded, silent. Safe.

Before entering the thick of the brush, I adjusted my gloves and pulled on the vinyl boot covers I'd brought with me. These flattened my print pattern into nothingness, at the expense of any sense of grip on the forest floor. They slid on comfortably, security blankets for my feet. I adjusted my pack and pushed branches aside with my flashlight before plunging in.

The dark came. I hadn't counted on the storm clouds piggybacking the canopy cover, blocking out this much light. The gaps between the pines were comfortable enough to navigate, but I didn't want to risk a branch directly to the eye, so I kept my right forearm in front of my face, advancing in this ridiculous Dracula pose while clocking my paces. I almost flicked on the flashlight, but was resistant to using anything that might catch a stray ranger's eye. Hillstrom hadn't needed to use any lights, and he was never an outdoorsman.

Research told me that Hillstrom had a habit of wearing overalls when he came out to the woods. Usually it was the same unwashed set, with no shirt or underwear underneath. It was sweaty work, hauling those bodies around, and he found that having a coat on was both too hot and too cumbersome when he set the girls down to do what he had come to do. He hid the overalls in the same under-the-boards cubbyhole in his apartment where the snuff video was found. There was a sorority house's worth of blood samples in the fabric, according to a true crime book from 2001. All bullshit, possibly. I couldn't see the Ragman letting Carl Hillstrom reuse a killing suit, instead of disposing of it right away.

"Fuck!" I yelled when I stumbled over a rock and came down hard on my extended forearm and elbow. The word echoed for a moment, but the forest seemed even quieter when the sound died away. I had an impression that a sound in the deep background, which had been with me as I walked, stopped when I paused. I stayed still for a moment more but heard nothing. The wind picked up just as the rain stopped, moving the clouds and letting moonlight leak in.

The ground was slippery under my vinyl treads, but the heaviness of the pack kept me steady. Darkness had eliminated the shades of green and brown I'd seen underfoot on the trail—it was all black below me, black mud, black leaves. Thirty-seven meters in by the Stanley, I pushed past a thick-branched bush and reached the clearing.

It was a beautiful spot. Not just its isolation, which seemed complete, but its plain natural beauty. The moonlight was bright enough in the high, smogless air to illuminate every raindrop. The clearing looked like it was being scattered with unstrung, white Christmas lights. I opened my pack and started laying down the plates from my stepping kit, which would give me a clear plastic path to and from the burial site. Reduced the chances of my spilling any stray DNA, which was always a possibility, no matter how well your body was condomed up. I was laying out the last plate when I saw something ahead of me in the darkness.

Someone lying on the ground, in a slight depression.

I froze up, my body colder than the frigid air around me, before calling out softly, "hey." It was too small to be the Ragman. It wasn't the Jenkins skeleton. It still had flesh.

"No. No. Kylie. Kylie. No." I started talking, chanting almost, while I left the stepping-plate path and walked over to the unmoving shape on the ground. I kept my pace slow, steady, locking the absolute impossibility that my daughter was dead into reality with each firm step.

It was a girl's body. The legs came into sight first, and they could have been Kylie's. They were bare, and the torso was covered by a long, dark, man's sweater. I couldn't tell what color the hair was. Her face was down, pressing into the dirt.

No.

I walked a few steps farther, risked putting my fingers on the skin of her right arm. It was cool, but not yet cold. I turned the body over and almost screamed with relief. It wasn't Kylie.

The front of the dead woman's sweater was torn, showing a tattoo of an eagle just below and between her breasts. It took me almost a minute to finish dragging my eyes up past her smooth neck—there'd be a pinprick on the vein if I could look closely enough, the sting that brought her to this— to see her face. The receptionist. ReeseTech. I'd only seen her the one time, right after digging up Bella Greene. I wouldn't have recognized her if the Ragman hadn't clipped her ReeseTech ID tag to her bangs.

Then came the full version of the vague sound I'd sensed behind me in the forest. Booted footsteps on twigs. The hard, running stomps reached my plastic track, and I looked up at a form that was taller than I remembered as he smashed his flashlight into the side of my head. I tumbled forward a few feet, and wasn't out by the time I hit the ground.

My face was inches away from the dead woman's wrist, as I felt the knee in my spine and the needle in my neck. The way Keith had felt it, the way this girl had, too. The way Kylie had. I couldn't think of the receptionist's name, even though I'd just seen it on the tag. I should at least know her name. Then the needle slipped out of my neck and I wasn't seeing anything anymore.

31

REACHING THE BOTTOM OF THE BOWL IN THE RAMEN

place near the station, chasing the last few noodles, Sandra Whittal indulged the powerful pang of doubt she'd ignored as she was inhaling the meal. *You could be wrong about everything* was her constant credo when it came to investigation, especially when she started to find the path she thought was the right one.

Kylie Reese's picture was on the news constantly now—a rotating selection of nine or ten pictures, actually, ranging from her posed school shot to casual snaps of her sitting with friends on couches or outside sports complexes, the faces of everyone else in the shots digitally blurred out. They get to be blurred, while Kylie gets to vanish altogether, Sandra thought.

People were talking about this disappearance, too, acting as though Martin Reese was tech royalty, that Kylie Reese was Princess Microsoft, not just a scared girl like the ones who vanished and were ignored every month. If you can fill a woman's absence with money, her disappearance

246 | NATHAN RIPLEY

gets more real to the public, Lieutenant Daley had explained to a bunch of drunk, celebrating homicide cops after Maloney closed a teen-on-teen private school murder last year. They'd laughed and toasted like Daley had made an out-of-place, smoking-jacket-witty comment, but Daley hadn't smiled. He'd just had another drink. Sandra got to the last noodle and scrap of pork by tipping the bowl up to her face.

Sandra pushed her chair in and left money on the table, ignoring the buzz of her cell. Another FBI ring, almost definitely. They'd stuck to phone calls, so far, a field agent named Alter announcing their arrival was imminent. The missed call was indeed from him. Sandra needed this to be wrapped before anyone else could arrive. With Kylie alive. With Keith Waring cuffed or with a bullet in him. While she was stowing the phone, she got a text from Chris telling her to get back to the station, double-quick.

He was lounging at the coffee machine when she entered, talking to Gutierrez.

"G. just closed that bathtub drowning," Chris said, poking him in the arm as Sandra approached. She tipped an imaginary hat at him, remembering for a millisecond what it had been like to wear one of the stupid things on patrol, how it had been one minor element among the major ones that had her ambition fixed on getting into plainclothes, getting to be a detective.

"Great. And how are we doing?"

Chris hesitated, drawing out a small silence Gutierrez almost spoke into, wanting to retell the story of his collar. Sandra cut off that possibility with a quick, cold look, and Chris continued. "Don't get too excited. Two things. One, Martin Reese has a juvenile record. Backtracking over every call and email Waring has sent for the past couple of years, we found a call he made to have the record dug out of sealed materials a few months back."

"What's the record? What did he do?" Sandra asked.

"Tell you in a minute."

"Shit on your suspense, Chris, tell me now." Chris held up his right hand, impassive, and went on.

"First, we've got a missing person report. Less than twenty-four hours, but the woman who reported it was insistent enough on the absence being atypical that it got booted up to our ears. Happened, looks like, about three hours after Kylie Reese was taken off the street."

"Who is it?"

Chris grimaced.

"You're going to be way too happy about this."

32

WHEN I OPENED MY EYES, THE DEAD GIRL WAS nowhere to be seen. I hadn't been knocked out since junior high football, but I remembered the cloudy ache of waking, the way it was different from coming out of sleep—you felt like no time had passed at all. But time, and space, had shifted around me while I was out in the forest.

I wasn't in the center of the clearing anymore. It was extremely dark, so much so that I could only make out the huge trunks that surrounded me, denser pillars of blackness in the air around me. Distant sounds came from what had to be the direction of the clearing, but I wasn't able to move. My legs were freezing, because the Ragman had taken off my pants and used them to tie my arms to the tree I'd been propped against. My boxers were stuffed into my mouth, held there by a strong tape that pulled on the bristles of the two-day growth on my cheeks. My cock was in full retreat, trying to curl up into my body, away from the cold and fear. I was just as scared as it was.

The noises from the clearing were of digging, dragging, scraping. At one point I heard a repeated plastic clatter, and realized that he was stacking the plates from my stepping kit. Sounds of ruffling fabric told me he was replacing them in my backpack. Then he started walking toward me.

I could taste the sweat from my hour-long hike in the fabric of the boxers, which was soaked with spit. I must have been hypersalivating after I passed out. The booted footsteps were slow, irregular, as if the walker was avoiding fallen logs and branches on his way. When the Ragman finally appeared, he was still easier to hear than to see.

"Hello, Martin."

I started to choke on my disgusting gag. The saliva was too much for the fabric to absorb by now, and was frothing around noxiously in my mouth. I was choking in earnest when the Ragman leaned in quickly, like someone had axed him at the knees, and pulled the tape off. I spat out the boxers and half a cup of drool and panted for a while, wondering how I could feel relief when I was still in so much trouble.

The Ragman laughed, then cut it off quickly. He wouldn't have brought me up here just to kill me, I thought. I thought it as hard as I could.

"I won't scream," I said, in my best hostage negotiator voice. Absurdly, I thought of the approach I usually took to calming down Ellen when I'd messed up—that same tone of voice, the repeated apologies, and finally the offer of some form of restitution. The tall man hadn't moved for a few seconds, and I could sense that he was thinking. I wanted to stop those thoughts.

"You can if you want to," he said. "Makes no difference to me."

"Just kill me," I said. "Can't you do that?"

"What?"

"Kill me and let her go. Let Kylie go, just please god let her be safe. I understand that you've beaten me and that I could never—I can't be what you are. I just want my daughter to be alive and I want to be dead. Please."

"That's just not right, Martin. More importantly, begging's not fun. You're the one who started this game, so don't make it my job to finish it properly."

The Ragman moved toward me and circled the tree, pausing behind it. I felt him stoop. A shape appeared in my peripheral vision on the right, then edged in front of my eyes. It was the butt of a huge knife, a hunting blade with finger holes in the handle, some Frankenstein-mix of a street fighter's blade and a deer-skinning knife. The Ragman remained silent as he cut the pair of jeans that bound me to the trunk with the blade in his left hand.

I was being marched into the clearing. The Ragman steered from behind with the butt end of the knife handle, prodding me this way and that to keep me from plowing into a tree. The air was freezing on my naked legs, numbing them to the nicks and flicks of the branches we were brushing past.

The clearing was about five hundred paces from where I'd been tied up. The moonlight was back on us, without any canopy to pierce. I paused, and the Ragman flipped the knife around and prodded me forward, poking a tiny, shallow hole in the skin above the middle of my spine. In the middle of the field I could see my bag, neatly repacked, and the body of the woman from ReeseTech. I couldn't see her face anymore. The Ragman had put her sweater over it.

When we got closer, I could see the name tag lying on the ground next to her right hand. The Ragman kicked me in the back of the knees, pushed my head toward the laminated panel, until the picture and the name filled my eye. Rochelle Stokes. The name attached another level of reality to what had happened, especially next to the logo I'd designed and tweaked as I built my company and bank account. The corpse of someone real. Closer to alive than she was to the bones, or to the body of Bella Greene. And closer to my life than anyone I'd ever taken out of the ground.

I moaned. I couldn't help it. I couldn't get any other sound out, and I couldn't be silent, as the Ragman pulled me along and set me on my knees in front of the grave he'd been digging.

Another body. In that open pit, four feet down, was the one I'd come for. The Canadian runaway Hillstrom had killed.

"Know who that is?" the Ragman asked.

"Cindy Jenkins."

"Good boy. Very good research boy, Martin."

Even her skeleton looked Canadian, I thought, feeling mercifully out of touch with my immediate reality as I took her in for the first time. For a moment, I almost forgot Kylie, forgot the Ragman behind me. It almost felt like another dig, where I could vanish into the intense thrill of discovery. The bones were minor, humble, sweet. There was a huge gouge in the right temple, which was odd for one of Carl's victims. He had always been a strangler. Cindy had put up more fight than the other girls.

"She's the only one I had to help out with. Started running when we opened the car door, after playing unconscious. Very clever, a real survivor. Absolutely paper-thin skull, though."

The Ragman rammed his knee into the base of my spine, half a foot below the small cut he'd made. I fell, screaming, just short of tumbling into the grave. I turned to face him and saw that he was wearing a blue balaclava. He pinched my nose, kneeled on my gut, and put something in my mouth. A pill. I swallowed out of fear, out of an instinct to obey. He got off me and I lay there, waiting for whatever was going to happen to happen. Waiting to die. The Ragman pointed at the fresher of the two corpses. I walked over to it, and he nodded, so I stooped and gathered her into my arms. I looked back again, and when he nodded, I dropped Rochelle into the hole, the icy weight of her striking the bones and shreds of cloth that lay in the grave she was going to share. The Ragman had used my shovel to dig, and she fell on that, too. It must have gone deep into the cold flesh of her back, because blood began to well out, dark, glowing black in the light of the moon.

We both looked into the hole and waited for him to speak, until I realized that he didn't know what to say.

"Why didn't you make me kill her?" I was saying and asking at the same time, less afraid when I reached the end of the question mark than I was when I started. I stared into Rochelle's dead eyes, still not sure enough to turn and face the Ragman. He stayed quiet and I kept talking.

"You meant to make me kill her, didn't you? Something went wrong."

"I meant to do exactly what's happening right now," said the voice behind me, but it wasn't quite the Ragman's. It had a shake in it. A small, slight shake.

"I had a three-point plan for taking care of Kylie first, then you and the wife in your own garage. I was all ready to deploy if you didn't turn up in another forty-five," the Ragman went on, sounding more like himself. "But you made it after all." I turned around then. He'd peeled up the underside of his balaclava a little, and I felt the vulnerability of my nakedness, beyond just the cold.

"You gave her the dose you meant to give me. You fucked up the needles," I said. The drugs in me made me move my lips. The drugs and the rush of feeling some of the fear leave me. "Didn't notice in time to bring her back with adrenaline, either."

The Ragman took up a position across the grave from me and squatted, watching. He peeled the rest of his balaclava off and laid it down on the ground beside me. Showing me his face in cold blue light from the moon. I stood there with my dick out, the grave between us, feeling my heart rate speed up, feeling warm. I looked back into the hole. Rochelle's eyes looked back at mine, with nothing in the gaze but old data, an unreadable record of her finished life.

"I never made doses for Jason, or for Carl, when they were doing their kills," the Ragman said. "I just had to plan, watch, and then make sure everything was cleaned up nicely. For you, I was making it a little easier. I didn't 'fuck up' the needles. I made a concession to how weak you are."

I moved my hands to cover up my nakedness. The Ragman laughed.

"Let me get dressed."

"No. And look me in the face. Look at me." I did. He had a shaved head, the pale skin on top sweating, beads he wiped up with a pass of his right glove. The face was as featureless as could be, the oval template of a police composite sketch before a description had been given to fill it in. Average nose, thin lips, green eyes with no glasses. The eyebrows, maybe sandy brown, but the moonlight didn't illuminate so much as push light near his face, barely letting me see what I hadn't wanted to look at to begin with.

"You can't do anything about it, Martin. What you see, what I tell you. Anything you tell the cops is going to lead to a few bad chats for me, maybe a quick suicide. And definitely, most definitely, your sweet daughter in the worst way you can imagine.

"I think you'll believe me when I tell you I don't care about what happens to me, Martin. But you care. And you're so sweet about Kylie it makes me blush, absolutely." The Ragman poked a pebble out of the tread of his boot and threw it at me. It bounced off my forehead.

I knew what he was about to do, but I couldn't think of how I could stop him.

"My name's Frank Connell. I own Acme Urban Surveillance, just off Garden Avenue. Bought it with my savings and bricks of cocaine cash Jason Shurn had hidden at my house. We were going to buy it together, until he went rogue and started keeping souvenirs."

"Ruined all your work of hiding the bodies."

"He got too excited." The Ragman pointed down into the grave.

"Rochelle parks just beside the ReeseTech lot, in the plaza with the coffee shop you all go to. I parked next to her car and punched her once in the side of the head from my rear passenger window when she went to open up her car door. I was a little tired from picking up Kylie from your wife's little party earlier in the evening, you know. So there was a small error."

"No. You were the excited one this time," I said. "Not Jason. You." In that moment, I forgot to be scared. I looked at him and saw the same shiver, the same weakness, that had landed Jason Shurn and Carl Hillstrom in prison.

The Ragman reached across the grave, moving quicker than seemed possible to my drug-blurred brain, and all of the fear came right back. I screamed as he pulled me forward and I fell into the grave, my naked chest landing full force on Rochelle's, one of Cindy Jenkins's bones breaking off under my wrist and giving me a deep cut. I started to stand but the Ragman put a boot on my shoulder and pushed me back down. I could feel my skin warming up Rochelle Stokes's dead flesh. I shut my eyes.

"You feel how skinny she is," the Ragman said. "Under a hundred pounds, probably. Anything can kill someone that small. Say, how much does your daughter weigh? Because I've been giving her shots, too. Don't tell me when I make mistakes, Martin, or I'll correct them all at once. Starting with Kylie, then you, then Ellen. Then I'll go back and sit behind the counter at Acme for another twenty years, and pretend you never existed. And it's too late to be selfless now and tell the cops all about me, you know that. The instant I hear a whisper of cop, I make sure Kylie dies. You believe me, don't you?"

The Ragman reached into the grave and hauled me up by the back of my neck, dangling me as I gurgled. He pulled his knife back out and made a long, ragged cut along my chest, below my nipples, around where Rochelle had her tattoo. Hot blood, my blood, dripped out and down, pouring down my stomach, legs, neck, dripping over both bodies below me.

"Give them both a good coating, Martin." The blood was coming thickly out of me. I was on the verge of fainting when he lowered me into the grave, almost gently, and the cold touch of Rochelle's flesh underfoot forced me awake. The Ragman—it felt ridiculous to think of him as Frank—pushed a bundle of canvas to the lip of the pit. A duffel bag, an enormous one.

"Put both of them in here." Struggling, trying to remember that Rochelle only weighed a hundred pounds as I levered her up, rubbing even more of my blood against her shoulder blades, crying out once when I caught her open right eye seeming to look right at me, I got her over the edge. Into the bag. Then I pulled up the bones of Cindy Jenkins, the intact ones and the broken, in a task that seemed to take hours. I filled the bag.

"I have a new deal for you," said the Ragman, grabbing the bag as soon as he saw I was attempting to zip it shut. "I'll trade you this bag and your living daughter for a fresh body. Your own kill. By yourself. I'll be in touch." He walked away, striding quickly, the steps soon inaudible as the cold and blood loss took me into the dark.

33

SANDRA WHITTAL KNOCKED AT THE DOOR OF THE
Reese house, alone. Chris Gabriel was down at
ReeseTech, doing interviews. Stuff she trusted him to take care of. This
one she had to handle herself. Asking a woman exactly how fucked up
her husband is is a delicate matter.

Ellen Reese opened the door quickly, ready to scream at a reporter.
The words died in her mouth. Sandra saw the tiredness under the anxiety and rage, the yellow baked-in weariness in Ellen's eyes, a sure sign
she hadn't slept for more than an hour or two since her daughter had
disappeared. Ellen pulled at the collar of her gray sweatshirt and put
a bit of it in her mouth, chewing nervously and then waving Sandra
inside.

"Mrs. Reese."

"You have anything for us? I have teams out looking, and I called the
swim coach in Oregon that she worked with two summers ago, she spent
weeks there. I just want to make sure that everyone possible has Kylie on

their radar," Ellen said. The eyes didn't change, flat, inexpressive, but the voice was TV-ready. Not manic, but alert.

"That's good, Ellen. We're doing the same through other channels. Can you tell me where your husband is?"

"No. He's out looking for Keith Waring, somewhere."

"What about last night?"

"Last night? What was that, Saturday?"

"Yes, Saturday."

"He was here. Being pretty useless. We might have fought, I don't know. But he was at his desk there, the end of the hall, all night." Pointing to the desk seemed to trigger more of Ellen Reese's normal-behavior instincts. "Sit in the living room, okay? You any closer to finding Waring?"

"Closer all the time," Sandra said, walking toward the gray couch she'd sat on, hours after Kylie first went missing. Martin Reese hadn't said too much, then. She was realizing how little he said most of the time, unless you asked him a direct question. "So your husband is out looking for Waring, you say?"

"That's what he said. Something about his old hangout."

"He should be telling us all of this. We need you both to work with us."

"Keith Waring is police. My husband is afraid that his information will get back to Keith, and I think he's right to be. You want coffee? I have instant, and an old pot from this morning."

"I'll take a cup from the morning batch," Sandra said, but Ellen wasn't listening anymore. She sank into the chair across from where Sandra was sitting, and hours of missed sleep were upon her almost immediately: her eyelids dropped into a blink that lasted too long, a slip into unconsciousness. Sandra got up quietly and walked to the kitchen. Let her sleep for five minutes. She might be a little more useful after she's startled into waking.

There was an iPhone on the counter, not the latest model. Ellen Reese had been holding hers when Sandra had come in, so this must be Martin Reese's. Pouring some black sludge from the expensive coffeepot in the enormous Reese kitchen, Sandra quickly went over the dialogue she'd had with Chris just before getting here.

"We have to unsettle her. Get her doubting him. Harmless if there's nothing going on, incredibly useful if there is something up. Get the wife and we'll get him," she'd told Chris, as they walked to their cars in the station parking lot, ignoring a couple of reporters and telling a more persistent third one to fuck off.

"What have we got?" Chris asked. "Really, Sandra. What do we have here?"

"We don't have Keith Waring. We know Martin Reese has an ancient peeping record, that Waring was probably using it to blackmail Reese, and that Reese, for some reason, hasn't told us this."

"He's scared," Chris said. They'd reached their cars, and Chris kept his hand on the door handle. Sandra walked around her own driver's side and continued to talk to him over the roof. "If Waring has his kid, the last thing Reese wants to do is let Keith find out he's blabbing to the cops. Maybe they're even communicating, somehow." It was starting to rain, but they kept talking, both getting into their vehicles and rolling down the windows.

"There's another possibility. And I'm thinking this because I don't know if Waring was capable of doing those digs by himself."

"Guy with his build," Chris said. "Yeah."

"Digging is hard work. Subtlety is hard work, too. What if Waring was doing this with a partner? He's obviously tangled up in this because of those files. But he was never off the job when the digs were happening, when the calls were made—he was at his desk, right behind us. But maybe someone else tapped him as a source of data, bought files off him, and did their own Nancy Drew searches for dead bodies. A person who is fundamentally fucked-up. A serial killer hobbyist. Obsessive. At the point that Bella Greene dies and ends up in that grave, a few things could have happened. Either this other creep decides he wants to kill for real, or Keith Waring decides he wants to escalate their weird partnership."

"Yeah. And what's your favorite option? How about some names?" Chris now had a notepad on his steering wheel and was writing, fast, almost as though he were transcribing everything Sandra said. Her brain was the collating and sorting kind, capturing and laying out every relevant detail in order. Chris only understood the full pattern of his cases once he'd actually solved them.

"Wait. Bella Greene's burial site. It wasn't staged right. It was forensically clean, but an aesthetic mess. Our Finder, our guy, takes photo souvenirs. Like a real serial, he needs something from the scene, a memento, to make what he does real. And, you know, it's the digital age. No need to keep scalps around the house anymore. He takes photos. But the Bella Greene site wasn't like his. It wasn't Kodak-friendly."

"You told me this already in your apartment."

"I wasn't sure then. I'm sure now. Someone else, someone who hasn't been doing the digs for the most part, did that one. Killed Bella, and hid her in a place he knew the Finder would look. Maybe that guy, the person who killed Bella Greene, was Keith Waring. And the Finder is Martin Reese."

Chris let his notepad slide into his lap.

"You didn't say anything like this yesterday when we talked to Reese."

"Yesterday I didn't know about Reese's juvenile record. Today I think Keith is pissed at Martin Reese and is using Kylie against him."

"Either that or he's dead and whoever killed him has Kylie Reese," said Chris.

"What?"

"Sandra, you do this every time, and usually you're right. You zero in. But there's other possibilities out there. I don't think Keith Waring comes close to the mental level needed to do any of these crimes. Let alone the technical know-how to find a blind spot in CC cameras downtown, and the physical confidence and strength to grab a high school athlete off the street quick enough to not be noticed. So what if you're right, and someone's buying files off Keith, and that's the person who killed him, made him vanish, and did all this other shit?"

"Someone who had something to do with those bodies pulled up over the years, you mean," Sandra said. "A killer we don't know about, one Martin Reese pissed off with his finds."

"Fuck no, Sandra, that is not what I meant. At all. This is insane," Chris said. "Martin Reese is a tech douche bore, not a fucking serial killer obsessive. No one is more boring and less complex than a guy who works in tech, except maybe a rich guy who's retired from tech. These guesses are an incredible reach—you can't build a case on what you don't know."

"You can build a suspect on it. And what I do have is a man who married the sister of a likely Jason Shurn victim. Who was 'friends' with a vanished records guys from our department. Who had his daughter kidnapped. Who just had a young female employee vanish from his company at a time when a serial is dumping fresh corpses in old graves. He's the only common link, Chris."

"The Reese family is being victimized," Chris said, but sounded less convinced than he had been earlier. Catching a text from his ex-wife, he begged off and left, putting a period on what would have become a circular argument with Sandra. She'd driven up to the Reese house so quickly and with her thoughts so entirely on the case that she seemed to have teleported onto the doorstep when Ellen Reese opened up.

Sandra tried to finish her cup of coffee in the Reese kitchen, but it wouldn't go down. She picked a bottle of Woodford Reserve off the counter near the secondary bar sink on that enormous length of marble, sweetening and cooling the aging brew in her cup with the bourbon. She took a sip then made the rest vanish in a deep, eyes-shut gulp before walking into the living room to gently shake Ellen awake. The woman's eyes flew open, alert, and her arms came halfway to her face in a defensive pose before she registered Sandra standing in front of her.

"Did you just want to get a good stare in, or do you have any questions?" Ellen said. She'd gone paler in sleep, and she rubbed the back of her neck while looking straight ahead, not up at Sandra. A bit of color returned to her face, just above her eyebrows. The cheeks stayed white.

"I'm wondering about your husband, Ellen. Don't you ever wonder about him?"

"What the fuck does that mean, Detective?"

"Since we're putting together a timeline that goes back years, I'm trying to get a little background on every person we've come into contact with who has anything to do with potential victims over the past twenty years. You know, to see if there's a tie between your sister and someone who had anything to do with what's happened with Kylie."

"It's Seattle. There are hundreds of people here who knew or worked with or drank with one of the screwed-up murderers in this part of the world."

"That's exactly right. It's very possible that the person we're looking for—who has something to do with Bella Greene's murder, with your daughter's vanishing—was obsessed with your sister." Sandra never lied, but she sometimes focused on specific areas of potential truth during these informal chats.

Ellen got out of her chair and walked to the mantel, where she moved a small clock aside. She took the pack of Marlboro Reds and the Dunhill lighter she'd revealed and lit up without opening a window, which Sandra was sure hadn't happened in this room very many times over the past decade.

"I'm not usually this rude," Ellen said, "but you can't wear that shirt anymore. The cuffs are frayed and discolored. And the sleeves of your jacket are about an inch too short, so we can see them much too well." Ellen kept her eyes away from Sandra's, staring at those cuffs until Sandra lowered her arms to her sides.

"A receptionist from ReeseTech went missing last night," Sandra said.

"Just after work. While your husband was sitting in your hallway, you say. We hit the panic button on it sooner than we usually would for a disappearance, just like we did for your daughter. Circumstances being what they are."

"Sorry about making fun of your shirt, but it can be a credibility thing. I used to work in a credit union. Things like that make a difference when you're sussing out a client."

"Are you listening to me, Mrs. Reese? Two disappearances in two days. Your daughter, and your husband's receptionist."

"He hasn't worked at ReeseTech, properly, for years. You should know that. And just because a psycho—the psycho your department hired, Keith Waring—took an obsessive interest in my family, and is now on some rampage, does *not* mean that you're helping matters by implicating my husband in this. He was here last night. He was with me when Kylie was taken. So were dozens of the richest and most credible people in the city, all of whom saw him panicking when he saw his daughter was gone."

"I'm not here to imply anything, Ellen. Mrs. Reese. I'm here to ask."

"I don't know what kind of sick sequence of thought could have brought you anywhere close to asking me these questions. You think my husband is guilty of anything other than the bad judgment of indulging Keith Waring's friendship? Say so or screw off, Officer."

"Simply put, your sister disappeared at around the same time as that skeleton we found out in the cemetery was put there. Even though it's not Tinsley, the timing of the death is the only thing we could have to connect it to what's been going on. Especially as it involves members of Tinsley Schultz's family. We're thinking that maybe it's someone who had something to do with your sister's vanishing."

"So Martin killed my sister and then married me? That's your theory?"

"No," Sandra said, with as much sincerity as she could find.

"If you're so determined to make a link, what about the body that was actually found with the skeleton? Where's the connection there?"

"No connection, necessarily. A random homicide. Maybe meant to throw off the investigation."

"The actual recent murder victim is the only dead body with no meaning. Gotcha. God. No wonder you people never found Tinsley. That killing is random, and nothing else is. Just the actual girl who actually just got killed, she's totally unrelated. Right."

"Are you aware your husband had a record as a juvenile offender, Ellen?" Sandra had been saving this, and she was rewarded with a tiny fracture in Ellen Reese's banker's expression, a little rictus of confusion below the left eye that was quickly smoothed out.

"It's not a secret-filled marriage. I'm aware kids do stupid things, yes."

"I'm only trying to fill in a picture of what's going on in the larger scheme of the case, Ellen. I'm not trying to corner you, or poke at you."

"If that's right, can you leave now? I'd like to get back to looking for my daughter."

"So you're aware that as a teenager, your husband broke into the homes of girls he went to high school with, who he'd likely been surveilling, and that he stole items from them and took them back to his own home."

"You finished?" Ellen didn't wait for an answer, but she'd given one in her widening eyes and concentrated look down at her knees. Sandra saw it.

"You didn't know. Just tell me, Ellen, it's fine. You know now. This is important to us looking for Kylie, it's relevant. And you shouldn't feel embarrassed about not knowing everything about your partner. Nobody ever does."

"Embarrassed? You think that's the operative emotion here, you stupid bitch?" Ellen got off her chair and walked out of the living room, not turning around again, just opening the front door and leaving it that way as she ran up the stairs.

Sandra left, not quite able to figure out if she regretted any of this visit.

34

THE COLD HAD NUMBED MY CUTS. THEY PUCKERED around the edges, on the wet and dirty skin of my chest. It almost occurred to me to worry about infection, in the few seconds before I was completely conscious again, aware of what I actually had to be concerned about. I looked at the earth walls around me and stood up halfway, leaning back when I got dizzy, shutting my eyes against the flow of blood and returning consciousness. The moon was vivid, turning the field around me gray, trees black, my skin white except for the filth and dark lines left by the Ragman's knife.

"Frank's knife," I thought. He'd armed me with his name, just to show how sure he was that I was bound to him, trapped by him. Just whispering that name to a cop would end Kylie's life. About ten feet away from the lip of the grave made for the body that the Ragman had taken away with him, my clothes and gear were lying in a tidy pile. The jeans were useless, almost, but still had enough structure and stitch left intact that they could be worn.

My blood moving around made me aware of how cold I was again, the tingling of reawakening flesh blending into the numbness of freezing skin. It was much colder up here in the mountains than it was in the city. If I hadn't woken up when I had, I might have gone hypothermic, able to forget everything that had happened and would happen as I lay in the dirt and kept sleeping. Instead, I pulled myself the rest of the way out of the ground and walked over to my clothes, stiffly putting them on, being gentle only when it came to drawing my white undershirt over the long, thin cut on my chest. Sticky, dark blood coated my neck and face, behind my ears, the dripping trail of what the Ragman had poured over the girl's body. Rochelle Stokes, who'd been unlucky enough to get a job at ReeseTech. Gary had probably been on the hiring panel—she was just his type. Small and alt. Now gone, just a body, a life extinguished to become a monster's weapon.

I started to clean the site, then realized I'd need whatever energy I had just to fill the grave in and make it vanish into the surrounding dirt and grass. Picking the shovel out of the hole, I made the first tentative pokes at the pile of earth I needed to get back in there, learning how I could move my arms and body without starting the flow of blood from my cut again. Short, stiff movements. I was working for what seemed like an hour, breathing hard, feeling my body warm and become usable again. All the while I thought of what I'd have to do for the Ragman, what I'd need to dispel him forever. When the digging became hypnotic, repetitive, I unfocused my eyes and saw Jason Shurn pacing back and forth in front of me.

He was handsome, still, kept young and alive by the cooperation of my imagination and hallucination. He was wearing the clothes he'd been arrested in: Lee jeans, a gray Dickies jacket, brown work boots with their tongues flapped out over the laces. His hair was greasy, or wet, which looked about the same in the moonlight.

"There's no beating Frank," Shurn said. "And I don't know why you'd want to, kid. He took you out of the cub scout world and into real combat, you know? He opened the whole fuckin' world to you." He walked over and sat, dangling his legs into the hole I was filling. I watched his boots start to submerge as I ladled another load of earth in.

"I haven't lost enough blood to have this conversation," I said. The Ragman's pill had kept my blood flowing, kept me from staying unconscious, but it had done something to my mind.

"I don't like you thinking of him as a 'monster,' Marty. That woman down there, that Rochelle, you put her there just as much as he did. Pretend to feel sorry for Rochelle if you want, but I think you're just sorry for yourself. You couldn't give a shit about any of these dead women, except maybe wifey and daughter."

"You don't know anything about me. You know nothing."

"You're just talking to yourself, pal, don't worry. Makes sense with what you've been going through. Your fantasies coming to life."

"They're not my fantasies. I haven't fantasized about having my life ruined. I was helping families, helping them get past what animals like you did to them. You, not me." Shurn's boots had vanished into the dirt, and the next shovelful covered about halfway up his shin. The legs didn't move, but Shurn did lean back a little, making sure no pebbles caught him in the eyes.

"Nobody buys that. You *are* me, Marty. You even have the same dance partner now, and Frank's the best anyone could hope for, believe me. Everyone's going to know exactly what you are unless you follow Frank's rules real close.

"The cops have always thought you're a roving pervert, a psycho in the making. See how quickly that lady detective saw the real you when you went down to ask about Tinsley? You should have begged off and sent the wife down to the precinct, or at least taken her with you. Lone wolf creep like you in there, looking into the eyes of natural police like that lady? You flipped every instinct switch she had. Miracle she hasn't arrested you for your lil' girl's vanishing already. That cop sees you, knows you, the same way we recognize each other. The way Ragman knew you were the guy messing with our track record. You've got the stink on you, son, and now you've finally drawn blood. Dead cop, dead girl, whatever happens to your daughter on your head—"

"I didn't kill any girl."

"But God, have you ever wanted to, for so long, right? Secretary Rochelle would have kept living her life just fine—fun nights in bars, watching TV, meeting someone she liked, settling into a nice house, some kids, a business of her own—if it hadn't been for your hobby, or am I wrong?" I considered swinging the shovel at his head, but kept burying him. Layering and padding the earth. I jumped up and down on it across the length of the half-filled grave, compacting the dirt, doing my best to make sure the filled hole wouldn't plump up into a small mound.

"I didn't kill any girl," I said. "Your friend, your Ragman, Frank, killed her. He fucked up and killed her."

"Ragman Frank. You make him sound like an old blues song, Martin. He's not quaint, you know that by now. The Ragman is the real truth. And you're going to have another kill of your own soon enough. That's the only way to follow the rules and stop this. To get Kylie back in the swimming pool instead of in a hole just like that one. You heard the man. The Ragman. He'll clean it all up, guaranteed, if you just give him what he wants. One kill, the two of you."

"I can't do it." I kept shoveling, not sure if I was saying words or just thinking them.

"You already have, buddy." Jason Shurn, now covered to the knees, and flickering a little in my vision, yawned, impatient to get back to oblivion. "You killed the cop, real easy. This would be just the same, maybe more satisfying, even. You could do whatever you wanted to whatever girl you choose. You know, follow through on what you wanted to do to Tinsley Schultz, killer. What you wanted to do to her sister before you went all conservative sweetheart and tamped down your fire.

"Think on it. You could pick any woman you want from off the street, follow her, watch her, take her to Frank, and make whatever you wanted come true and trust him to vanish everything that's left of her out of the world."

I looked away from the vision and focused on the filled grave, working to camouflage it, to make it look just the way it had before the Ragman and I came up here to disrupt what had been lying still for more than a decade. Doing my best in the light I had.

"I'm not going to kill any girl," I said. "I'm going to kill him." There was no answer. Because there was no one there.

I had to end the Ragman, Frank Connell. No one was going to help me. If I did it his way, the police would come for me, by which time he'd be hanging from a beam in his house while I filled a cell for the rest of my life, and Ellen lived out a ruined existence on the outside, spending my money to get far away from the city, from the monster the courts would tell her she'd slept next to for two decades. I had to kill him.

"I'd kill him and the world to get Kylie back." The grave I was working on was finished. Erased. I looked at the field around me, seeing no Jason Shurn to answer me, just the blank loneliness of the outdoors. I slept until dawn, and a little more, curled up in the cold dirt. I picked up the shovel, the rest of my gear, and started to walk back to the Jeep.

I flicked on cruise control, in the car and in my brain. I couldn't chance getting pulled over—I was still coming to grips with being alive and committing the everyday act of manipulating the wheel, the miniature puppeteering tugs up and down that kept me following the lazy curves of the highway. Roads not very busy. I had hours before checkout time at the Marpole Motel, which was about thirty miles and a lifetime away from the concealed hole I was leaving behind on the mountain. The sign, which mysteriously depicted a geyser erupting between two pine trees—maybe they were playing up the outdoor hot tub—rose in front of me a couple of minutes after I pulled off at the right exit. Clean the cuts, then go to sleep, I told myself, fumbling in my wallet to find the key card. There was no one outside the motel, the only car there a beige Chevy I'd noticed when I checked in. The owner's. I could hear a circular saw going in the front office, but I didn't stop in to say hi. I swiped my room key, entered, and flopped onto my back on the bed. Like in the grave, I told myself to close my eyes for a few seconds only.

Minutes or hours later, a steady 4/4 knocking at the door started to pull me out of sleep. It was the side of a fist on the maroon-painted steel door, not a maid's knock, not even a checkout-time management knock. The digital clock on my left read 10:57, still an hour to go before I had to get out of the place. Now that I'd had a chance to lie down in comfort, I could fully evaluate the damage to my body as I unkinked my limbs and slowly walked to the door, focusing on the chipped paint around the doorknob to get my eyes used to being open and in use. The drug that Ragman Frank had shot me up with still oozed around in my veins, in the cottony thickness of my tongue, the tingle in my fingers. Opening the door, I was glad for the talk I'd had with imaginary Shurn out in the woods. If not for that, I wouldn't have spoken to anyone for hours, and was worried I might have forgotten how to do it properly.

"Boss?" Gary Leung asked, when I had the door pulled open a slice. I forced myself to believe it was him there, not another hallucination, because it was. That tobacco/vanilla scent he wore wormed into the room.

"How did you find me here?"

"You texted Ellen the address, Martin. She sent me down. Your phone's on the counter in your house, the front desk here says you didn't sleep in the room—look, can I come in?" He was already pushing his way in, taking off his coat and shaking the moisture out before he came all the way in. It was raining, hard, a clean mist coming in along with Gary's cologne. Up in the mountains, the empty grave was being further erased by this water and wind. I relaxed a tiny bit.

"Is Kylie back? Did they find her?" I knew they hadn't, that my daughter was still with the Ragman and would be until I got her back myself, but I thought it would be strange not to ask.

"No change on that, no. Sorry. Did you sleep in that, boss? Got mud all over the—man, I hope you're planning on leaving a pretty huge tip." Gary leaned back against the dresser and took the room in. I saw the mud for the first time, the tracks I'd made and the dirt outline of my flopped-out body left on the bedspread.

"Yeah, I got kind of sick up there," I said. "Stomach bug."

"What were you even doing?"

"Looking for the psycho cop who took Kylie. He told me he used to have a campsite around here, off-trail, gave me a vague description."

"*That's* what you didn't want Ellen telling the cops?" Gary laughed, and I stared at him with a burning in my guts that had nothing to do with the stomach bug I'd invented.

"You shouldn't know anything about what I did or did not tell my wife, but yes, I am being wary about what I tell the police when. Who knows who's feeding information to Waring?" Keith was beyond being fed anything, of course, but as a dead man he was proving to be of more use to me than he was when he was alive.

"Makes sense, sure, sorry," Gary said. "Look, you've got to come back. Now. Ellen's freaking about something that lady cop was bugging her about, which, you'll be happy to know, she wouldn't tell me." Gary was staring at my clothes, and I started to strip down automatically, taking off boots and jacket. I was going for the sweater when I remembered that my t-shirt was crusted with dry blood and would be the color of the door I'd just let Gary through.

"It's not about Kylie?"

"My guess is it's the latest. Friday night, whoever it is out there took away someone else. Rochelle Stokes, the front-of-house girl at ReeseTech. Cute, blond? Remember her?"

"No."

"You should come by the office more. Rochelle was having a dinner party with her roommate on Friday, out-of-town guests and family coming in, and she didn't show. Just didn't turn up, after having worked the full day. Vanished somewhere between the ReeseTech lobby and her apartment. Cops got on it right away, because of Kylie. And that dead chick, the whore."

"I don't think Bella Greene was a prostitute," I said.

"She was a typical victim-type, and Rochelle wasn't, for something like this. Ellen figures they want to talk over every possible link between her sister and these two Reese-related kidnappings. They want to talk to you, and Ellen has no real good answer as to why you left your house without your cell phone on an overnight trip while your daughter's missing."

"Is it the cops who are curious, or you, Gary? Got something you want to chat about?" I said, sitting up. "I'm barely at the company, and I haven't been in for, what, two weeks. I've never talked to the girl. And I love my daughter enough that I'm going crazy every second that I'm not actively doing something to bring her back. Putting up Missing posters isn't my idea of getting proactive."

"No one thinks you've got anything to do with this, Martin. Come on." Gary's eyes told a slightly different story, but he brushed at his hairline and hid them from me with his right hand. "This lady cop just wants to follow up every angle. Doing her job." I got up and headed toward the bathroom, pulling my socks off.

"The cop asked Ellen if she knew you had a juvenile record. Ellen faked that she did."

"Fuck, she told *you* all this?" What would have been a lava bubble of panic a few weeks ago, Ellen finding out about my past, was just a ripple of annoyance now, an added pain under the agony of getting Kylie back.

"You weren't around, pal. You aren't around for a lot of stuff nowadays, Ellen says. Not me, her. Here, look at these," Gary said, fooling with

his iPhone for a second and handing it over to me at a series of texts from
Ellen.

You know anything about Martin, juvenile record?

> *What*

*What I said. Does he talk about having gone
to prison as a kid? What did he do?*

> *Cant tell if you're kidding, but no, nothing
> like that, he hasn't said anything*

"I gotta shower," I said, sniffing my left armpit and using the motion
to distract Gary from what I was doing with my right hand: slipping
his phone into my pocket, tapping and swiping at it to prevent it from
password-locking before I could have a good look at it in the bathroom.

"Sure. I'm going to get coffee from that crap-looking diner next door."
Gary pulled on his jacket and walked out.

I pulled the small duffel bag from the dresser into the bathroom
with me, and also took the tiny, complimentary hotel sewing kit in with
me. I flicked through the phone, finding nothing interesting in the texts
between Gary and Ellen, just endless clothing and business talk, followed
by that brief exchange about me. Telling Ellen about the stupid break-ins
and little thefts that had gotten me that short jail term, long erased from
my record, was something I'd tried to do a couple of times in our first
year of going out. But she was still too close to Tinsley's vanishing, to suspicion. I didn't want her picturing me, even as a kid, standing in the bed-
rooms of girls I'd gone to high school with, taking items of theirs while
they were at school, or lacrosse practice. Bracelets, souvenir coins, even
a sweater, once. Misty Laroche's forest-green sweater. I used to stare at
the back of it in English class for the whole period. Eventually I wanted

to have it, too badly to resist crawling into her room and taking it out of her closet. That was the one that got me caught—a retired city planner named Marvin Khan had spotted me, and was waiting in the yard under the window when I swung a leg over to jump down. He sat on my back until the cops came.

I set Gary's phone down and got into the shower, thinking back to the one I'd taken at ReeseTech after finding Bella Greene and the girl who wasn't Tinsley. I was much dirtier this time, each pore clogged with grave filth and my own blood, which started to flow again under the high-pressure stream from the showerhead. I stepped out of the shower with the water still running, and got to work on the next part of my normalization process. I dried my fingers and wiped steam off the mirror, sticking a hand back into the shower to turn the knob to cold, so the steam would stop. I'd learned to sew in my brief stint in juvenile, working a slack job stitching uniforms for local factories. I'd never stitched myself, though.

"It's going to keep opening up," I muttered. Not exactly in a place to explain this at an ER, either. I threaded the needle with white thread from the sewing kit, put on my best Rambo face, and put the needle into the opening the Ragman had made in me. I started to sew that long, flat grin in my chest shut with widely spaced pricks of the needle in and out of my flesh, the thread dragging through each new tiny hole I made. I stopped a quarter of the way through when the pain and stupidity got to me, looking hard in the mirror at what I was doing.

"Control," I muttered. Mastering the pain I was putting myself through wasn't bringing me any closer to controlling the Ragman, or that detective, or even Ellen. The entire world outside of that bathroom door was focused chaos, intent on disrupting my life. Pretending to be an action hero wasn't going to fix that. It'd give me an infection, at best. I snipped and pulled the thread out, then opened the bathroom door a crack, expecting to see Gary sitting or lying on one of the beds. He wasn't, so I tracked wet footprints across the carpet over to the bag I'd brought in with me. I pulled a roll of duct tape, an item I always carried with me on digs, out of the side pocket, and laid a long strip of it across the cut. I'd just have to keep my shirt on around Ellen until I could think of a decent excuse.

I went back into the bathroom to finish dressing. I heard the heavy motel door open while I was in there—Gary must have taken the key card out with him when he went out to get coffee or whatever he was doing—and called out that I'd be done in a second.

"No rush," Gary's voice came through the door, along with a metallic clanking noise.

After drying my hair with the last fresh hand towel, I checked my fingernails. Still rimmed with dirt, which I boiled out with hot water, wondering how many of Rochelle Stokes's cells were washing down the drain along with the earth. I was glad I'd never spoken to her. It would make this even worse.

I came out, ready to face Gary with my best wry grin and a comment about intestinal troubles piling up alongside life troubles as we age, a joke adapted from a sitcom Ellen constantly streamed on Netflix while I cooked and talked to Kylie. All of which seemed longer ago than it really was. It hadn't been much more than a week since I'd last cooked for the family, but the unbreakable tension of those weeks expanded the time into a geologic age.

The grin and the joke died forever when I saw what Gary had been doing while I was in the bathroom. With his gloves on, he was tossing the keys to my Jeep from hand to hand. In front of him were two things from the back of the vehicle: a shovel and a bottle of bleach. Parts of my dig kit, laid out like a corpse in a forensic lab. Or like the evidence it was, in a courtroom, except it was on the damp carpet of my shitty motel.

"We don't have to talk about this," Gary said, smiling, before he tossed the keys back to me. "But, boy is it going to cost you, boss. Cost you big."

I stared at him for a moment, then looked away as my thoughts caught up. I couldn't let Gary see me smile.

35

THE RAGMAN WAS CRYING. FRANK CONNELL, crying, clasping his steering wheel and trying not to make weepy noises, manfully swallowing phlegm and squinting whenever the road came to a curve, forcing clear vision through the prismatic glimmer of the humiliating liquid in his eyes. Like a fucking kid stood up by a prank prom date, he thought, briefly considering holding the wheel straight and piloting the truck into the next rock face he came to.

He'd held it together well enough in the mountains. Hadn't lost control when he found out what he'd done, that the girl was dead and that he had no ability to plan properly. To work, to perform his basic function. Competence. All of that was apparently as much a part of the past as the women in the ground, the ones Jason and Carl had put there. But Martin Reese figuring it out, that the Ragman had fumbled his needles, had killed when he didn't intend to—it was too much. It couldn't be fixed except by total erasure.

"You never did anything at all," Frank Connell said to the Ragman.

"You helped out before and after. You fucking janitor for the capable." He wiped his face with the side of a fist.

"Because that's where the function is. Not in drawing out a plan, or keeping it together afterwards." He twisted the cap off a bottle of ginger ale in the cupholder and guzzled for a few seconds, steering with one hand and closing his eyes in slow, stupid blinks. "No. No."

Martin was too smart to give any traction. If he stopped panicking, if he had too much time to think, to collect himself, there would be a real problem. That whole play up there, the cut on the chest, the burial, the girl covered in blood—it was just performance. That same ritual shit that was meaningless to the Ragman. Martin had his pictures, his digging, his reverence. The Ragman had his memories and his ability to *do*, to make murder happen and vanish. And now he had none of it. The girls gone, the talent vanished.

"Just another old fuckup who deserves to be behind bars." Jail wasn't for the immoral, for violators: it was for the incompetent. For failures. He'd always thought of Jason, and especially Hillstrom, fond as he could be of them sometimes, as weak. Martin wasn't like that. He was sick like those other two, but not in a way that made him a weakling. Even in that hole, blood and panic leaking out of him, the drug cocktail and adrenaline fighting it out in his bloodstream, he hadn't looked tame, beaten, like a victim. He struggled like the women did, the ones Carl and Jason took down. The ones who wanted to live at any cost. Jason and Carl hadn't minded surrender when it came. They had their run and then it ended.

"Martin gets one more run and then I kill him. Me. I do it." Properly. He'd kill Martin right, just after they killed together and the Ragman had control, dominion, again. There were never going to be any police involved in this, not on the Ragman's part, anyway. Martin could handle the cops who came for him because of the ReeseTech secretary, and if he couldn't, then he didn't deserve to kill alongside the Ragman. Rochelle Stokes and the bones of Cindy Jenkins, bagged in the Ragman's trunk, they'd go the same way as Keith and his car, tonight. The Ragman could still do that. Make dead objects vanish. Go away for good.

"Mistakes can be erased," the Ragman said, stopping his tears and clenching the steering wheel tightly. The way he'd squeeze Martin, and Kylie, and Ellen Reese, if Martin didn't properly respect him when the time came.

Pulling into his property an hour later, the Ragman checked his video bank, examined the feeds from cameras that would be tripped into life if anyone walked onto his land, investigated the home where he lived and where Kylie Reese was a temporary guest. Nothing. And Kylie was sitting placidly in her cell, on top of the freezer, of all places. She was hugging her knees and staring at the wall, probably doing some sort of mental exercise. The feed was HD from that camera, and the Ragman was able to get in close, to see the flickers of fear in the teenager's eyes. They calmed him down.

He walked through the corridors of his home, the carefully arranged stacks of newspapers and open containers of accelerant, and made his way to the slot that opened into Kylie's cell. He opened it, and waited. Inside, Kylie stirred and walked over, waiting for the food she expected to be pushed through. She waited four minutes, staring at the open slot. It didn't move, and nothing came through.

"What do you want?" Kylie asked. Silence. "Have you even talked to my parents yet? My dad? He'll give you anything, man. Sir. Whatever you want me to call you. I just want to go, okay?"

Kylie stared through the open slot. She couldn't see anything around its edges, no fingers, no edge of a tray, but as she got closer, she could see a banister in the background. A dirty red carpet on it, an untidiness of papers and garbage that had a hoarded look to it, opposite to the antiseptic cleanliness of her small prison.

Kylie came close enough to the slot for her breath to be visible against the pushed-up metal flap. This bothered her, made her feel visible. She stopped breathing. Just waited there, for another full minute. Nothing. So she reached her hand through, slowly, questing with her fingers for a knob, a button, anything.

Instead, she found hot, living fingers. Four of them, and a thumb, coming together into a fist that gripped her hand and pulled with incredible force, taking her whole arm up to the shoulder into the space on the other side of the door as she screamed and screamed and screamed. The jagged pain of a needle inserted clumsily, hard, at her inner elbow joint, made her scream more.

"Don't!" she said, and repeated, louder each time. "Don't."

The door surrounding the slot was pulled open, revealing seams in the wall that Kylie hadn't been able to see before. And there he was, the man who had her, impossibly tall, a blank mask on his face. She could feel the drug moving through her already, and knew she didn't have much time. When he bent down, she pushed herself back and delivered. A kick, with her dominant right leg, the one that had always thrown off her movement through the pool until she'd learned control and balance. Kylie didn't worry about either now as she kicked out, just about hitting what she wanted to: the round bump of flesh in the center of the man's throat below the bottom rim of the mask.

The Ragman staggered back, croaking for a few seconds until he could gasp, taking in air. Then, controlling himself, he breathed quietly and deep, and laughed. The girl on the floor, the last of the strength in her legs seeping away under the influence of the chemicals in her blood, cried. He picked up her limp body and walked toward the freezer.

He made sure Kylie was conscious when he opened the lid of the deep freeze, feeling the cold smoke lick out, and lowered her into it. He shut the lid a second before her eyes, full of panic her tongue could no longer voice, closed.

36

BEING BURIED SHOWED ME THE WAY OUT. IT'S always been like that for me. Pressure. At the company I needed impossible deadlines. With Ellen, the occasional huge fight, the threat of loss. The stakes Kylie brought into our lives. And going through the files, the mass of information, it was only when I had all that competing information in my head at the same time that I could see my way to a grave, to where a killer had left the bones I set out to find. In that motel room, Gary had thrown what he thought was a complication at me. And that was what I had to embrace to save Kylie.

I was on my way to ReeseTech, after placating Gary in a long chat in the motel room. He was on his way back to *tinsley*, ready to open up for the day, to repel the reporters who would be even more fervent after Rochelle's disappearance. The most important thing I'd left Gary with was a promise that Ellen would know nothing about our conversation. "I'll tell her what she needs to know," I'd said. By then, he hadn't cared.

"I came as soon as I heard," I said to the windshield wipers, which were batting furiously at the downpour that had been keeping me company on the ride back to ReeseTech. Nothing on the stereo, not music, not news, not Jason Shurn's voice. My scrapbook was at home in its desk drawer, the voices and images banked there and backed up in my mind. None of it was worth anything to me if I couldn't get through the next two days.

"How can I help? What can I do?" Maybe something like that. "Do we know anything yet? Is this the same guy who took Kylie?" No, not that. Mustn't seem too curious, or assume involvement. Care about the company, be concerned about the girl, but make it clear you never knew her. That you don't want to take a piece of someone else's grief. That sadness belongs to her family and friends, and you respect it.

"I'm just a guy who used to own the company she worked at." Rolling into the Elliot Bay neighborhood, I breathed deeply a few times, feeling the tape around my chest grabbing at the skin around the cut. My arms and legs were aching from my labors with the shovel, but my head was clear, purged of the drug hangover by adrenaline and chilly planning. And hate. Resenting and disliking Gary had always been something I wasn't proud of, but I could be, now. I'd been absolutely, instinctually right about what a piece of shit he was.

I parked the car well in the back of the ReeseTech lot, taking in the outside of the building for the first time, really, noticing the security cameras outside, the ones on the poles that rose out of the rain-spattered asphalt. I looked at the whole setup the way the Ragman would have when he scouted the area before picking Rochelle up, plucking her out of the universe with his hands and a needle.

Gary's smugness had been mitigated by awe, back in the motel room. "You really are a genuine over-the-moon sick fuck, boss," he said. "I knew there was something off about you, but I didn't think it went—didn't think it went here. Were you fucking Rochelle? Jumped on your own daughter's kidnapping to cover up inconvenient business? Wow. You're not supposed to have an affair with the secretary *after* you retire, Martin. You fuck her while you're still working late at the office." He prodded at what he'd laid out on the tarp for his show-and-tell blackmail act. The shovel and the sloshing bottle of bleach.

"I don't know what half that gear I saw in your Jeep is for, but I know what the package as a whole is, and don't try to tell me otherwise. They call it a 'kill kit' on TV," Gary said. He backed off from the pile, sat down on the bed. "I made very sure not to touch any of it barehanded, either." That may have been true, as far as he knew, but I was already leaping ahead of this conversation, knowing what was coming next. Most of it, anyway.

"You're not going to say anything, boss?"

"What do you want, Gary?"

"I had this slow-burning plan all worked out. You can probably think your way to what that might have been. I'm no more cut out for retail than I am for plugging away at code for a dying company until I'm sixty-five. Not that ReeseTech is going to last that long. That's why I put my selling bonus into real estate, to get as much money as I could within a couple of years."

"Recession fucked you," I said, paying attention and thinking on several tangents at the same time. Gary's phone was still on the bathroom counter behind me, which meant he hadn't taken any photos of my dig kit, hadn't emailed anything about them to himself or anyone else.

"Oh, recession and worse. Sketchy condo development—that place near the Marriot, on Waterfront, the one they stopped building about halfway through and then started up again a year and a half later? Well, that year and a half was when my money got eaten up. Panicked and sold up. I don't know money, Martin. People yes, money no. Most people, that is. I didn't know you had this in you." I waited for him to get to the point.

"All I wanted, the whole time, was exactly what you have. Not the wife and daughter, even though you may not have to worry about the daughter anymore. The forget-about-money money you've got. So much of it. Enough that I never have to check my bank balance again, worry about what's going to come next. I was going to get it from you the old-fashioned way."

"And how's that?" A different emotion was leaking into the constant fear I'd been carrying with me since taking hold of Bella Greene's wrist in her grave. Rage, a tiny thread of it, like a drop of red dye plinking into a cup of water.

"Take your wife, take your money. You know how much she complains, either silently or out loud, about you? 'If it wasn't for Kylie . . .' that's how she says it, trailing off. And shit like this, coming on an errand to find you after you were dumb enough to leave your phone behind—although I guess that was on purpose, since you were being a naughty boy with Rochelle and didn't want to be interrupted by pesky calls—generally listening to her, and running her goddamn dream business with her. Why did you think I was doing all that? Because I like nice shirts? It's because I'm edging you out, sweetie. She gets a divorce, enough of your money for her and I to enjoy two years or whatever the minimum decent interval is, and then I take a payoff to get out of her life for good. That was plan A."

I walked over to the motel blinds and pulled them up. The rain I'd be driving through in a few minutes had started up, a vicious coastal downpour that looked like bites of the ocean being dropped on the landscape by firefighting planes. Gary kept talking.

"Ellen ain't the cheating kind, even for a genuine, sweet, and understanding boy like me. And divorce courts shake a finger at adultery anyway. But love? I could do that, I could make that happen. You're only invested in Kylie. Anyone can see that. Even now that you've fucked up in the worst way."

"My wife's not an idiot. And my daughter's not dead."

"More time I spend with her, more I realize that yeah, Ellen's not at all an idiot. But you are," Gary said, in his real voice, with the play sapped out of it. I turned to him. He was standing, now, pointing at me, his face relaxed into cool, real, hate. "You're the dumbest fucking guy I've ever met, for what you're willing to piss away. Whatever you did with this Rochelle girl, and I have a pretty good idea, probably has more to do with you not having the balls to tell a few people that you're fucking on the side than it does with you following through on being the dirty bird you so clearly are. You've been disappointing your wife in every conceivable way for years."

"Get to the point."

"Never tell me what to do again. The point, Martin, is that instead of making a full pitch at taking your money and life away from you, I'm going to speed things up by not going to the cops about any of this. For the low, one-time price of three million dollars, paid to me cleverly by some untaxable way you and I think real hard of, together. In return, I ease out of the store bit by bit, and I'm living in Thailand for the rest of my comfortable days by this time next year. Hmm?"

Cheap, elementary, and effective blackmail. What he'd seen was enough to bury me. With Ellen and the law.

"Ellen never would have gone for you."

"Why not? She settled for you *and* stuck it out for way too long. She may not be dumb, but she's capable of fucking up. You're proof. Probably has a lot to do with that vanishing sis of hers. Vulnerable, and all. Did you do Tinsley, too, all those years back? Now I'm just curious. And did you steal my phone?"

I waved the iPhone at him, but didn't give it back yet. I stared at the objects between us on the carpet. The shovel, in particular. It was rimmed with dry blood, a lipstick tracery around the blade that offset the dull dustiness of the rest of the steel. Rochelle Stokes's blood, a physical testament to her death, the postmortem wound I'd given her when she fell into the grave.

"I didn't touch her," I muttered. "Not when she was alive."

"I don't know what the fuck that means, Martin, and it's something you should reserve for a trustworthy therapist. I sure don't want to hear it. Tell the prison shrink next week, if you want. Up to you."

"Did you take anything else out of the car, Gary?"

"Nope. I think my word would be more than enough for Ellen and for the cops to take a harder look at you than you can afford. And I'm not a bit afraid of you, either. You're too smart to get rid of me right after Rochelle. So let's chat about the three million."

We did talk for a little longer before my drive back. I put on gloves after he left and got to work on the dig kit with the bleach in the motel bathtub. I took special care with the shovel, which I collapsed, before prepping the whole works for selective stop-and-dumps in containers on the way back to town. The cops would have no call to search me, no matter what Sandra Whittal suspected. She had nothing but suspicion and I had to keep it that way, which started by being as forthcoming as possible. I stared at the ReeseTech building for another minute, picking out which cars out front likely belonged to cops. Picking up the leather messenger bag from the seat next to me, I slung it on and opened the driver's side door.

I ran through the slackening rain all the way to the lobby, hoping to add breathlessness to my look of concern. I didn't need to key my way in, though. A big cop with a triangular torso and black hair, a former college jock who'd gotten used to delivering his beatings in the street and precinct instead of on the field, closed a friendly but controlling hand over my shoulder as he opened the lobby door.

"Detective Chris Gabriel, Mr. Reese. I work with Detective Whittal. Assuming you've heard what happened here? My partner's come and gone, but she really, really wants to talk to you."

I'd been braced for an encounter with the woman whose incisive eyes I'd faced down and buckled in front of in the station; this gorilla represented no obstacle. I relaxed and smiled exactly as much as was appropriate.

"Could you give me ten or twenty minutes to go upstairs and check on my people? Just to show my face. It's not my company anymore but I want to, you know—"

"Reassure. Go ahead, I'll wait. Another twenty minutes on top of the three hours I've already been here won't hurt any." Gabriel took his phone out of his breast pocket and started toward the front desk, where Rochelle Stokes used to spend eight hours a day. For a moment, as I pressed the up button for the elevator, I thought he was going to examine her drawers, boot up her computer, as other cops had no doubt already done. But no, he just sat in her chair, without adjusting the height, and started clicking out a text message.

Upstairs was as busy as the lobby was empty. The ReeseTech higher-ups, the ones who were actually in the city and not overseas, had corralled every employee.

"They only talked to me for five minutes. God, you must be worried sick. Your daughter," said Bob Suchana, the first familiar face I saw up there. He was tall and shaped liked the ball-chair he used at his desk, the one Gary used to pray would explode someday, sometimes throwing darts from the games room at it while Bob was deep into code. We all watched, but nothing ever happened. Gary got his laugh one day, when Bob turned around suddenly and caught the tip of a dart in the flesh of his thigh. Just now he looked pale, calm, intrigued. He polished his glasses as he spoke to me, placidly mentioning his alibi first: he'd left for his kid's hockey game right after work on Friday, and had been doing dad duty ever since.

"I don't know why they're going all red alert on this right off the bat." I waved at a few other people as Bob talked, and slowly walked us to the part of the office where I wanted to be. "Rochelle, I didn't talk to her much, but she was pretty wild, you know? Not a reliable homebody type. She's probably off somewhere on her own, forgot her parents were coming to visit this weekend."

"What does 'wild' mean to you, Bob?"

"She doesn't have a boyfriend, and she goes to shows, punk, metal shows, every weekend. Sometimes with friends, but sometimes alone."

"Sounds like a lead," I lied, feeling a little bad for Bob when I imagined how bland his college days and life up through and including marriage had been if he looked at weekend concert-going as evidence of a dissolute, late-eighties Axl Rose life. "But she was still a nine-to-fiver, Bob. Couldn't be too unhinged."

"You didn't know her. Not really. And I told them that, when they asked. I also said they had no right to be giving you a hard time, what you're going through right now, you know?"

"Thanks, Bob. Who's they?" We were close to where I wanted to be now, the center of the warren of desks that ReeseTech had blossomed out of. In the middle of the room, the first six desks stood where they'd been the day I moved the company in, and the few of us who did all the work sat down and built up the millions we took with us. All except for Gary. That was his desk, at the end, decorated just how I remembered it. I took a look at the camera setup, remembering the day we'd installed it, when I'd made sure that the grid was as unhackable as possible and that, most important, nobody could get a look at what was on any of our screens in that middle hive section. Hyperparanoia, especially in the days before HD digital security cams, but I always liked being vigilant. Which is why I kept Bob Suchana between the nearest camera and myself as I positioned myself next to Gary's desk, popped my messenger bag onto the surface, and claimed what I'd come for. Bob didn't notice, and neither did anyone else, because Gary's original desk backed onto my own—untouched for years except by dusting—original desk. We'd kept them the way they were when we were still plugging in code every day. The new owners had insisted on it, calling it the "preserved heart of the company." Pickled.

I closed the bag just as Bob was finishing up.

"That lady detective, she was right off TV. Too pretty to be a cop, right? Have you met her?"

"Yeah. I guess she is pretty."

"A mad dog, though. She wouldn't let me finish answering questions, especially when she heard I was definitely elsewhere, and that I hadn't been around when Rochelle left work. I still think this is all stupid. She'll turn up tomorrow, hungover from some concert she went to in Portland."

I shook hands and reassured a few other staffers, letting them see me looking shook up. I recognized exactly seven people up there, and remembered about four names. One was Priya Canetti, my last personal hire, a short and efficient project manager. The back of her hand, soft but slightly dry, was like Rochelle's skin, just warmer, fresher. Rochelle, transmuted into cargo that the Ragman was now unloading in some anonymous place, spattered with my blood, waiting to be used against me.

Concerts on the weekend, no boyfriend. Even Jenny Starks, lying up in that clearing by the gravel pit, when all of this started, back when I was in college—her skin was dead skin. Gone for long enough to undergo the violations and humiliation of death. Other than that prick in her neck and the cut from being dropped on the shovel, Rochelle Stokes had been wearing her living skin, what she came to work in, what she showered in, what she listened to music in. The idea of Kylie being anywhere close to this wretched death, that her brain and her jokes and her brilliance and her ability to see through me like I was a pane of glass could be ended forever and covered in dirt if I stepped wrong just once—it didn't weaken me, not anymore. It steadied me. I wasn't allowed to make a mistake. A mistake meant the only worthwhile thing I'd ever made would die. So there would be no mistake.

I tried to forget it, on the elevator ride down to Detective Gabriel, and I managed to push it aside. Dwelling on Rochelle Stokes, on the fact that she could have continued the collection of activities and thoughts and speech that were her life if I hadn't started digging around in the Ragman's past—it wasn't useful. I shifted my bag, muttered Gary's name, and put on my best face for company as the doors opened and I walked over to the sitting detective.

37

"YOU WANT TO DRIVE YOUR OWN CAR?" THE BIG COP
asked. "You can follow me, or I can just get one of our
guys to run you back here when Whittal's done with you."

"You make her sound menacing," I said.

"You've met her," Chris Gabriel said, getting up and walking toward
the door, shortening his stride a little to let me keep pace. I'd ditched the
dig kit, so the Jeep wasn't teeming with evidence. But I didn't like the
idea of parking it in the police lot.

"I'll hitch along with you, if that's okay," I said. "I feel like you guys
think I don't want to help you. You don't think I'd be protecting Keith
Waring over my own daughter, do you?"

"I don't think that, sir. I can't say what Detective Whittal thinks, but
I'm sure it isn't that, either."

Gabriel pushed the door open and let me out first, pointing to a
sedan illegally parked near the ReeseTech entrance. Not even parallel to
the curb. I wanted to chide him, just for a second, phrasing it jokingly to

lighten things up, but his flat look and refusal to make eye contact with me killed that impulse very quickly.

"Detective Whittal probably thinks you're being less than frank. And she's not wrong too often."

"And what do you think?"

"I'm not concerned about this part of the investigation, sir. As soon as I drop you off I'm getting right back to looking for Rochelle Stokes."

"You'll find her," I said, trying to get some civic-minded confidence and hope for the future into the words.

"Yup." We got in the car and went on a completely silent drive to the cop shop. I almost forgot my bag when I got out of the car, but Gabriel whistled at me and grabbed it from the back seat as I was getting out.

"Tell Whittal I'll check in with her in an hour."

"An hour? Shouldn't she be spending this time looking for the man who has my daughter?"

"I can't answer any of your questions, buddy. Sir. That or I just don't want to, right now."

Sandra Whittal was talking to the desk sergeant when I entered.

"I was just telling Sergeant Priestley to send you right over to me whenever you rolled in, Mr. Reese."

"Here I am," I said, the words leaking out as I exhaled. I took a deep breath, feeling the duct tape on my chest again, the hot burn of the cut beneath it. I followed Whittal down into the guts of the station, past Keith's desk, her desk, and the room where we'd had our first talk. Any cops along the way who looked at Whittal quickly looked away, and none of them glanced at me. We ended up in a small, cold room, just a couple of chairs and thumbtack holes in the walls.

"All the rooms up top are taken," Whittal said. "Busy day."

"Did you talk to my wife last night?" I asked. A gentle way of starting on the offensive couldn't hurt me.

"Today, actually. Just after getting the call about Rochelle Stokes. It was my first stop."

"You treat her the way I'm being treated?"

"And how's that?"

"Not so much like the parent of a kidnapping victim as the suspect of a kidnapping."

"No, we're not treating her that way. Could I ask you why you left your phone behind when you last left your house, Mr. Reese?" Whittal pulled her own phone out of her pocket here, typing in her pass, flicking around in it. She waved her other hand at me, a motion that I should sit down. I did, but she stayed standing.

"I forgot it."

"It's genuinely unusual for a person to leave their phone behind. Unless they're drunk or something. Everything's in these little gadgets."

"I wear a watch, so I don't look at my phone as often as many. I got a little burnt out on technology in my career. And I've been preoccupied recently, Detective."

"You got out of the city the morning after a woman who works at your office vanished."

"I did. And, as I think my wife can and probably has already confirmed to you, I was at home the night Rochelle Stokes went missing, and either at my desk or in the living room with her all night. I had no idea Stokes was gone when I left to look for Keith."

"Yes, Mrs. Reese said so. Ellen. Don't worry about that. I don't think you took Rochelle, if that's really what happened to her. Could just be a runaway, right? An adult, career-woman runaway. Why not."

"I don't know if that's the right word, and knowing nothing about her, I can't say what she might have done. But I definitely hope she's just going to text her roommate from Vegas or something tomorrow."

"Phones have all sorts of annoying software in them. So many ways to track movement. We just kind of got comfortable with them attached, right? Remember when people used to be paranoid about having their credit card bills looked at, because it gave away where you were on a certain day? That worry just seems to have faded right away."

"I guess so. Different ideas of privacy, and all that." I decided to try a different tack, because I was getting scared. A version of honesty. "Look, I'll level with you. I didn't want to be tracked, yes. I was looking around for this campsite Keith Waring had described to me a few times, never too accurately, and I was scared of being tailed, in case I found it."

"Why didn't you tell us about this campsite?" Whittal asked the question as though she was asking about the plot of a movie she didn't have much interest in, looking at the wall behind me. My eyes flicked over to the closed door, the doorknob. Whittal caught the glimpse and smiled.

"Because I didn't want to alert Keith. In case he's got friends here, or listens in on a scanner, or something. I don't want to do anything that will get my daughter killed, Detective. Which, might I add, you guys seem to be getting pretty relaxed about. My wife from our fucking living room is doing more to get Kylie back than you people are."

"It may look that way to you, Mr. Reese, but we're very actively looking for Kylie," said Whittal, finally sitting down. She was wearing a boxy, not-quite-correctly fitted suit. It looked like something from the earlier seasons of *The X-Files*. But she still looked sharp, in a way that had nothing to do with fashion and everything to do with the intentness of her speech and eye movements. That voice the Ragman had used when he still had his mask on; here was a version of that, but real. The Ragman made mistakes, but Whittal didn't seem to really understand what mistakes were, at least at a personal level. She understood fucking-up as something other people did. People like me.

"Young female cops get asked for their origin story a lot," Whittal said. I knew she'd noticed that I was studying her, trying to figure her out. "Some of them actually have stories. Family-of-cops stuff, or surviving an assault at some point and getting into the force as a way of getting back control. Domineering parents, too. I almost wanted to make one up, just to have one to tell at the bar. But there's nothing. I got sick of college, but saw it through, then joined the academy right afterwards. Liked the work and did it for crazy-long hours. The end."

"That's nice. Nice to find work that you love."

"That's what I tell everyone here, anyway. Because there's no reason to know."

"Know what?"

"I had a very troubled father. A violent man, even though he never brought any of that violence to me."

"I had a bad one as well. I'm sorry to hear you had to deal with that."

"He was sorry, too, eventually. When I had enough of a brain to-gether to figure out how to get him to stop hitting my mother for good, I said the right things to the right institutions and he ended up shuttling around from jail to mental hospital to care home for the rest of his sorry, short life. Crazy's one thing, Martin, but crazy and hurting people's an-other. You agree?" Whittal watched the ceiling during her threatening version of confession, but locked eyes with me again when she asked me that last question.

"Sure."

"So what's your origin story?" Whittal asked. She didn't lean in, she leaned away, looked at the ceiling.

"I dropped out of school and started a tech company. Made money. Sold the company. That's it."

"Where along the way did you meet Keith Waring?"

"Postretirement. A few years ago, I don't know exactly."

"At the post office, right?"

"That's right."

"Keith had access to all sorts of records, you know. Stuff the press never had a look at. Serial killer records dating back years. Investigative details. Lots of material on Tinsley Schultz. Jason Shurn." Whittal was watching me. Watching for a reaction. I thought of the knife raking across my chest. I thought of Kylie. I didn't twitch.

"Yeah?"

"Yes, Mr. Reese. Waring also looked up your criminal record, did you know that?"

"I have no record."

"Well, not an active one, but these files are never properly gone, you know? You know." Whittal wasn't looking at the ceiling anymore. "So why would he do that?"

"Not sure. A blackmail plan? It was clear to me towards the end that he was getting crazier and crazier. I'd expect anything from him. Short of the kidnapping of my child. Remember that?" Keith wouldn't think of making an official request for my record as a misstep: he would have thought of it as being cautious and clever. *The research is what gets you in trouble, Keith, not what you find out.* I'd tell him that if he were still alive.

"I think your record is part of your origin story, Martin. It may even be part of why Kylie was taken away."

"It isn't a record. Not anymore. And how fucking dare you implicate me in the worst thing that has ever happened to my family."

"A record, even a sealed one, is a story of what you used to be like. It just can't legally be held against you anymore."

"I broke into a couple of houses. Dumb teenage shit. My parents didn't care about keeping an eye on me, and I was acting out. I was a shitty kid."

"Definitely not," Whittal said. It made me understand why she'd taken me to this nameless room. We were invisible down here. Our talk was only for her, and for me.

"I don't want you to be concerned, Martin," she said. "I don't think you're killing these women. Bella Greene. Rochelle Stokes."

"Are you people even bothering to investigate? Rochelle might still be alive out there. Screw 'might,' there's no reason to believe she's dead."

"Chris Gabriel is the department bloodhound. He's great at finding people. Living ones. But you know and I know that he's not going to bring Rochelle back to her family." Whittal put her phone away. She took a small envelope of photos out of the bulging pocket of her suit jacket and handed it to me. I opened it up and sorted through them as she continued to talk. The Irish cemetery. Not as I'd left it, but as the Ragman had left it. Bella's body out in the open. Muddy. Ugly.

"Not a pretty scene, Martin. Not like your usuals."

"What?"

"You make the calls, Martin Reese. I know that's you on the phone, that it's been you for years, digging up girls and calling in to tease us. I know that you bought files from Keith Waring. Pretty soon I'll have proof of that. His bank account was drained, by him, and the boys have already turned up all sorts of irregularities in his monthly income, expenses. Some months he never spent a dime out of his checking account, you know. Like he was picking up envelopes of cash from somewhere or another. But like I said, I don't think you killed Bella Greene, or took Rochelle Stokes away. Or your daughter." She reached out and touched me then, her hand chilly enough to radiate through the denim over my knee, as though she were pushing her intellect and hatred through my flesh.

"But someone is hurting all of these women, and you know who it is. Is it Keith? Maybe. Or maybe he's dead. I only know that it's got to stop. I don't think you're far enough gone to disagree with me on that. Not a single additional woman can die here, because each one devalues your already questionable existence that much more. Your own daughter, Martin. Cut the shit."

"This is completely—"

"You have a chance to talk to me. You have a chance to get Kylie back." She grabbed the photos and the envelope, very quickly. One of the photos left a whispering papercut on my right index finger, and I winced. Whittal smiled.

"That doesn't count as police brutality, sorry. We're here because I like your wife."

"Pardon me?" I wiped the little trace of blood from my finger onto my jeans, and resisted sucking the cut. I stared right at Whittal, and started to genuinely loathe the smile she was turning on me.

"Your wife. I like her. Don't you?"

"I love her. Are you implying otherwise? I love my wife and my daughter."

"Your actions imply otherwise, Reese. Your little secret life threatens everything about Ellen, and it's going to get your daughter killed. I know you think that this is all just guessing, that you're several steps ahead of the stupid cops, but you're wrong. And I'm not the stupid cops. Right now, in this room, looking at you, there's nothing stupid or official about me, do you get that?" Whittal took off her jacket, dropping it on the floor next to her chair. She dropped the smile, too. She was wearing a white shirt tucked sharply into her pants, no bulge around the waist, just a hard plane of white into gray. No badge clipped to her belt. The pictures had scattered when the jacket hit the ground, and I stared at one, a close-up of Bella's wrist, the one wearing the bracelet. The one I'd touched.

"I don't even know how to begin addressing this insane series of accusations and implications and completely unproven, untested bullshit. How you think you can say these things to me—it makes me wonder how you treat kids you pull in off the streets for actual crimes."

"No crimes are more actual than this," Detective Whittal said. "You may not push the knife or the plunger of that needle, but you glory in it. Dead girls. Women. Humans. Organized and cataloged. Under control. Tackle dummies so you don't act out against living women, girls you see on the street. Against your wife.

"Those messages you've left for us, years in—you're so focused on being better than us at investigating, it hasn't occurred to you that you're just as bad as them in every other way. Just as bad as Shurn, as Horace

Marks, as whoever the guy is out there who killed Bella Greene and took Rochelle Stokes."

"Are you finished? Are you going to arrest me now?"

"I brought you down here to tell you I know the pig you are and to give you a chance to let your wife, to let Ellen, hold on to some of her dignity and distance herself from you before there's no chance. Tell me what you've been doing, Martin. Tell me who he is, and where I can find him. So I can bring your daughter back."

I stared at Whittal and remembered to keep shaking my head, but I was thinking. Frank Connell. I could say that name and keep myself alive, keep Ellen safe, take away any power Gary thought he had over me. Frank Connell. Whittal would call upstairs and they'd have an address. That big cop, Gabriel, he'd whip in behind us in traffic, we'd speed toward the Connell house, or apartment, or compound, wherever a thing like him lived. I'd be in back of Whittal's car, lifting my shirt and peeling back the tape while I told her about what he'd done to me after he'd killed Rochelle Stokes, how he'd forced me to handle her tiny cold hours-away-from-being-alive body, how different it was from what I'd done before with the skeletons, how it wasn't exciting at all. That I was sad for Rochelle Stokes. That I hated what Frank Connell had done to her. That I knew her death was partially down to me, but no one can be blamed for a murder that they didn't commit, that they just partially motivated. I was just part of the chain of causality.

But I knew that if I uttered his name in this room, Kylie was a dead girl. The only way out of this was the way in. Secretly, in the dark. In the woods, in the ground.

I stopped shaking my head and looked at Detective Whittal squarely.

"Officer. Lady. You're fucking crazy and really pushing the limits of legality. I'm not a cop or a lawyer, but just because this isn't on tape doesn't mean it didn't happen. I won't be accused of vile—"

"Is that what you have to say?" Whittal asked me. She asked the question more deeply with her stare, a cold, drilling, disgusted one that tried to pin me to the wall.

"That's all I can say."

"Let me offer a full apology, and please do have a good day. We'll check back in with you if there's anything else, sir. If I am right, which we both know that I am, however, I should say this. It's a shame you're such an awful person, because you must be an excellent detective for us both to have ended up here. I'm going to keep looking for your daughter without your help." Whittal was up and out of the room before I could reply, leaving the door swinging behind her.

Whittal was another problem to solve on my way to getting Kylie back. She wasn't an escape from the work ahead of me. Just another task. I got up and walked up the stairs and out of the station, stopping by the desk sergeant. I figured I might as well get this step accomplished while I was here instead of calling from home.

"Excuse me. The detective—Whittal—I'd like to talk to her commanding officer. Her lieutenant, whatever it is. I'd like to speak to him or her right now, if that's possible. My name's Martin Reese, and I need to make a complaint."

38

SANDRA TOOK OUT HER ANGER AGAINST MARTIN
Reese on the accelerator pedal, flooring it as she drove to ReeseTech to meet with Chris. "Cuban Missile Crisis," she muttered. It was what had come to mind when she was laying into Reese in the tiny room, during that completely off-limits interrogation she'd been hoping to convert into a real confession in the properly miked and filmed room upstairs after she'd cracked him. Instead, she'd gotten that look.

Sandra engaged the siren so she could justify her speed, and started threading through traffic aggressively. Looking into Reese's handsome face, hoping it would get more confused and emotional, she'd only seen strategy and, finally, blankness. Sandra had flashed back to Mr. Potts's senior history class in high school, hearing him say something that had always stuck with her: "But Khrushchev had vastly underestimated John F. Kennedy." Vastly underestimated. Reese was as smooth and maybe as smart a bastard as the dead president, but she hadn't seen the steel in him until she started presenting him with her case, her guesses, her knowledge.

"Even knowing how much I knew," Whittal said to Chris, who was sitting on the hood of his ride just in front of ReeseTech, watching the recently interviewed staff stream out to their cars to return to their families with tasty stories about Mommy's or Daddy's huge role in the ongoing investigation. "Even seeing how right I was, he wasn't fazed. He just took it in, Chris."

"He was confused. Really seems like a pusscake to me, Sandra. Jumpy as hell when I had him in the car. Scared about his daughter, scared of us being suspicious."

"He's one of those, you know, grace under pressure dudes. A fumbler until he has something to focus on. I didn't think it. I thought he'd crumble once I brought up his wife, the nightmare he's about to put her through."

"Nightmare," Chris said. The last of the ReeseTech employees had streamed out, a few of them nodding at the two cops, Bob Suchana even half-finishing a salute before he thought better of it and turned the motion into a sleeve-mop of the impressive amounts of sweat dumping out of his scalp. "A nightmare, yeah. We've pulled video from every camera in the radius, Sandra, and it looks like the grab took place in a video dead zone. There's a couple-hundred square foot area that isn't covered by any lens around here, and that's where Rochelle Stokes parked every day. Like Kylie's grab, this was something that was scouted out, researched."

"We'll find him. Reese will give him to us by tonight."

"Get in the car, Sandra. Detective Whittal." Chris walked around to the driver's side, and Sandra, hesitating for a moment because she normally would have withered at least one of his ears off for speaking to her in that tone, got into the passenger seat. Chris started the car and punched the gas.

"Chris, I don't know if I locked my ride."

"No one's going to steal it. And forensics are still in the lot. Not, as you and I both know, that they're going to find anything."

"Yeah."

Chris stared straight ahead. What neighborhood he was aiming for wasn't yet clear, but he didn't look like he wanted his thoughts or steering interrupted. Sandra's phone wormed around in her pocket and she took it out. The lieutenant. She thought about picking it up, but took a sneak look at Chris's eyes in the mirror and decided that she'd wait to get whatever it was between them over with before she took on Daley.

"That's the lieutenant. Gonna ask him about putting a tail on Reese, tie it to gathering information about his kid."

"No, you're not."

"Excuse me?" Sandra said, just as Chris pulled off the road and into a Shell parking lot. He got out without speaking to her, boosting Sandra's annoyance into near fury. When he came back with a pack of cigarettes and rolled the window down, lighting one after a couple of out-of-practice flicks, she grabbed it from his fingers, considered grinding it out on his shirt, then flicked it past him out the open window.

"You think this is lover's quarrel time, Chris? Playtime? Would you tease out an argument this long with Gutierrez or any of the other schlubs out of the station?"

"Shut up. And do not make this man-woman shit. It isn't. It never has been with us, except when we're actually fucking. I've never looked down on you, joked about you, gave you shit I wouldn't give any other guy. This is about your. Pure. Fucking. Arrogance. And that dead girl." Chris wasn't talking to her in his suspect-intimidating voice; she'd never heard this one before. It was cold. Two high school girls a little older than Kylie Reese walked past the parked car on their way in. Probably trying to score a pack of cigarettes of their own. They paused for a second and the lead girl, all legs in a skirt too short for the season and an open duffel coat, gave Sandra a coded look through the windshield, an are-you-okay widening of the eyes that Sandra found both humiliating and touching. To reassure the kids outside, and herself, she grabbed

Chris's chin between her thumb and forefinger and turned his big cop's head toward her.

"In any context, you never speak to me like that. Understood? Just so we're extraclear that this is a professional discussion—"

"It is."

"Shut up. Just so we're absolutely clear on how seriously I take this case, our after-hours relationship is officially terminated, over, done."

"Fine by me," Chris said, and he looked like he meant it. He didn't blink. In her peripherals, Sandra watched the girls walk by and enter the gas station store, turning on the flirt jets with the clerk, whose face she couldn't see.

"Then say your fucking piece, Detective. With the respect due to an officer of equal rank."

"I'm mad because you're smarter than me, Sandra. You should have been way ahead of this whole case, way ahead of me, for sure, but instead you've poured your whole brain into nailing a guy you've even agreed *isn't the guy*. He's not the killer, Martin Reese, if he is anything at all. And the killer is what matters. All this Sherlock Jr. bullshit, these links you've pulled out of the ether—"

"Out of the facts, Chris. It still counts as police work even if you're not kicking in an informant's knees."

"I have zero excessive force charges in my file."

"You're smart enough to pick the right knees to flamingo. But not smart enough to keep up with my closure rate, so if you're going to criticize my methods, let's hear some specifics."

"Specifically, we have a vanished girl with a clear connection to another vanished girl, and you did absolutely no practical on-scene work to help find her. You're the best extractor of information from witness interviews in our division, and you spent the day talking to an IT jagoff and his wife. A guy who is alibied for the day and night in question."

"He left his phone at home so we wouldn't be able to back-trace him if we wanted to. He was up to something, Chris. Gave me some bullshit about using the time to hunt for Keith Waring's secret hideout."

"I don't give a shit about Martin Reese's phone or weekend drives. I give a shit about the habits, patterns, and whereabouts of the man who took, and potentially murdered, Rochelle Stokes. Who took and potentially murdered Kylie Reese. Who definitely killed Bella Greene. Who was smart enough and knows surveillance well enough to avoid turning up on a single screen or piece of digital recording. That's what I care about."

"Martin Reese is our connection to that killer."

"You have to explain yourself to Rochelle Stokes. Her family. Because the time you poured into taking down this big, glamour target, this completely unlikely nerd? We could have spent that looking for the man who kills. The man who matters. The perp. Not his cleanup crew."

"Reese has got you snowed, Chris, the way he's had his wife and everyone around him snowed for years. His juvie record screams creep, and the way he handled me at the precinct—that fucking calm curtain that came down when he started deciding how he was going to take me on—he's pure, complete psycho."

"He's a millionaire businessman, of course he's a psycho. Just not one who's of primary interest to us. Investigate the actual crime, not a target you've made your hobby."

Sandra's phone started buzzing again, but with a text, not a call. More for a break in the argument than out of any concern for what was on the screen, she took a look.

"Holy shit," she said.

"What?"

"It's the lieutenant."

"Lieutenant doesn't text," Chris said, craning to take a look at the screen.

"He does today. And you're going to love what he said." She showed him.

fuck off Martin Reese's back ASAP and call NOW

"Goes well with what I have to tell you, then," Chris said.

"You didn't bring me out strictly for the lecture?" Sandra felt around at her feet for her bag, before realizing she'd left it in her car. Never something she'd normally do. Chris was right about at least one thing: she was stretched thin, her brain working in directions that may not have been the most directly relevant or useful. But she was not going to let him criticize her police work.

"While you were interrogating Reese, I heard back from a detective I'd been trying to get through to. Rick Campion in Eugene, Oregon. He worked a case I thought might be relevant."

"What case?"

"Sarah Weaver. She was nineteen years old and five nine when she vanished in 1995. I've been going through every single possible in the files for five states and three provinces around to put a name to the bones buried with Bella Greene. The kind of thing you would have been doing if you hadn't gotten so fixated on Martin Reese. I kept going on it, and I found who the bones in that Irish cemetery belong to. Sarah Weaver. The gravesite was chosen by Jason Shurn, and he put her there, with someone helping him to do it. The same someone Shurn hunted and killed other women with, including, we've got to assume, Tinsley Schultz. I know who that someone is, now. And he's still out there, and he's taken Tinsley's niece away from her family. Her family, who we're supposed to be helping."

"Out there meaning where?"

"North end," Chris said, starting the car. "Fifteen minutes away."

39

ONCE KYLIE REESE WAS STOWED, THE RAGMAN started the big clean. The erasure of his life and every death he'd been involved with, starting with the electronics. First by wiping the drives, then by using a forensic program to perform a deeper wipe, then dumping new, pointless, random data from the internet onto all of his computers, phones, and auxiliary hard drives. He did this in the wire-and-screen-infested surveillance room in his house, the place where he'd sat as he monitored Martin Reese and Keith Waring, and where he'd tapped into the security cameras around *tinsley* and ReeseTech, measuring for blind spots, scouting for a place to grab Kylie, for the parking space where he'd waited for Rochelle Stokes. It had been her bad luck, her bad decision, to consistently park in that dead zone. Maybe she enjoyed a slightly longer walk to her vehicle from the office door. More likely, she didn't want to get entangled in any after-work conversations with the squatting tech creeps she worked with. Parking where she did had probably allowed her to dodge all sorts of casual-desperate invitations for drinks.

Stage two of the electronics wipe was the physical part. The Ragman slept, first, on a cot in the surveillance room, everything unplugged around him. For two hours of dreamless black, he shut off, opening his eyes to the early dark of autumn, and a deep chill from the windows he'd left open. He took armloads worth thousands of dollars out to the yard. In two large steel barrels, he mixed violent solvents, inhaling and coughing the smoke that emerged when he dumped the equipment in. He'd let it all marinate for a couple of hours.

The nap he'd taken had partially been a mistake. He needed the rest, but the aches of his labors over the past twenty-four hours had manifested all over his body. The knees, especially, which didn't used to creak even when he was doing squats in the prison yard, or manually loaded shipments into the back of his store. Now they made crackling sounds, like dead leaves being crushed, and a powerful line of agony ran the lower length of his spine. The dent Kylie Reese had made in his throat had added a feeling of congestion to his physical woes as well. The girl had some legs.

"Expiring," he said, smiling to the empty yard around him. He coughed again when a breeze pushed more of the noxious stink of the dissolving electronics into his nostrils. He walked into the garage and took out a steel barracks box he'd bought at the army surplus, checking on its contents. Forty-eight never-used, superabsorbent shammies. Pulling the locker over to the old Buick he kept in here, fueled up, always intending to drive it again, the Ragman unscrewed the gas cap and started siphoning fuel into the locker, saturating the cloths. He'd never drive this vehicle again, but didn't feel compelled to run a nostalgic hand over the blue paint job, or to look around the garage at any of the other tools or equipment that were soon to be out of his life.

"Martin," he muttered. Jason, Carl, Martin. Two dead, one soon to be dead. He didn't feel angry at Martin Reese for digging out his memories, anymore, for laying the bones in the air for anyone to see. Because that shovel of his, with its probing, intelligent dives into the earth, had dug into Frank Connell as well, cutting through the aging, sagging flesh of the form that had grown around the Ragman, the polite small-business owner with a strange past that had been his self for years.

The Ragman needed his memories active, something he'd learned in this game with Martin. A game he'd lost the talent, but not the taste, for. Martin had filled a need he'd felt for years without even knowing it. He'd killed Frank Connell and resurrected the Ragman, and now the Ragman could kill Martin, as soon as he finished Frank off himself, with this box of soaked cloths.

The fuses were already set, trailing through the yard, leading into key rooms of each house. He started his rounds, laying down accelerant-drenched rags in the rooms where he'd slept, studied, hunted, stared.

40

I CAME HOME TO SUITCASES. THREE OF THEM, packed in Ellen's efficient style, every gap filled by balled socks or stockings, every pant and shirt folded to emerge without a wrinkle when she reached her destination. I could hear her in the bedroom. I set down the satchel I'd been carrying with me since leaving ReeseTech. Shutting my eyes and leaning against the door behind me, I waited for Ellen to come downstairs.

What you can control is what you focus on. Everything in front and ahead of you. Rule all of that and you'll be able to control how people react to you. That's how it should work, anyway, how it had always worked for me in business, and before that. But there's always information out there, people out there, that you can't control. The trick is not to let those uncontrollables overwhelm you and distract you from doing exactly what you have to do. From looking straight ahead and taking care of the problem presented to you.

"You were in jail," Ellen said. She'd appeared at the top of the staircase, wearing a green skirt and stockings, a black sweater, and with her hair piled up in an elegant arrangement that must have taken some time. Time she'd spent staring in the mirror and coming to various conclusions, making various decisions.

"No, but I was just at the police station. Talking to that same charming pig who came and visited you at the store. I can't tell you how sorry I am about that," I said.

"You're sorry about *that*? About her visiting me? How about lying to me for twenty years, from the time we first met? Where the fuck is our daughter, Martin?"

"What could they have possibly told you that would make you believe I have anything to do with Kylie being gone? Can you hear yourself? Come down here so we can actually talk like people about this."

"No!" Ellen screamed. "You stay the fuck away from me. She'd still be here. Kylie would still be here if you—you're a fucking liar, Martin. You did this to us."

"That's ridiculous," I said, stabbed by the fact that it was true. Ellen didn't have to be scared of me, but if she knew everything I'd been up to for years, and knew what I'd brought into our lives in the form of the Ragman, she would be scared, yes she would. And I hadn't kept Kylie safe.

"Do you know what the first thing that flashed into my mind was when that detective woman told me what it is you'd done? Jason Shurn. You were a fucking peeping tom, Martin? A creep who followed girls around and stole from them?"

"No. And if she said that, Whittal's a liar as well as the string-pulling psycho she's already proven herself to be. Got that, Ellen? You're going to let some woman you don't know tell you what your husband is actually like? Or are you going to listen to him?"

"I know who my husband can pretend to be, but I don't know what kind of thing you really are, Martin." This winded me, and I think it showed on my face. Even if Ellen had been rehearsing the line in front of the mirror while she made up that elaborate Medusa bundle on top of her scalp, it cut. It worked. And I think whatever twinge she saw in my face satisfied something in her, some need to hurt me back. She kept going.

"I think you've been dealing me a PR package of an adequate husband for two decades, and if I'd been paying proper attention, if I was willing to admit what I was overlooking just so I wouldn't have to derail my entire fucking life, I would have known what you were like a long time before anyone came along and told me." Despite herself, Ellen had been moving down the stairs during this argument, pointing and approaching for emphasis, driving her words home with the increase in proximity. I was relieved. It meant that ultimately, she wasn't scared of me, not really. Anger I knew what to do with. Fear, no.

"I didn't PR being a dad, Ellen. You know Kylie. You know us. You know me. I love both of you more than anything and yes I do feel like this is my fault, her being gone. But do you believe even for a second that I haven't been working, in my way, doing every fucking thing I can, to get her back?" I stared at Ellen, coming closer to her, not menacing, just bringing as much of myself as I could into my eyes and pressing it into her.

"I think you are trying," Ellen conceded.

"And the record shit? I was ashamed, Ellen. Don't you get that? I was beyond shy as a kid, way beyond shy, and I just didn't know how to talk to anyone, guy or girl. I had no friends. My parents were interested in everything except me—they paid for my food and some clothes, but that was basically it. So I got a little obsessive and weird, but I never, ever crossed a line into violence. It wasn't even sexual, it was just weird. I mean, you've been with me—we've been having sex for years. I'm not weird in bed, or out of bed. Why anything about me, no matter what's said, should remind you of Jason fucking Shurn is absolutely beyond me."

Ellen had approached a little more, and she kicked the suitcase lids shut as she walked right up to me and planted a finger on my chest. My impulse was to bat it away, but I tamped that feeling down and let her push. She'd made a lucky choice, forcing her nail into the place where the Ragman's knife had cut me the most deeply. The duct tape pulled on the uncut skin while Ellen's finger reopened the cut, and I felt blood start to well out again. Not enough to show through my sweater, as long as I could wrap this conversation up quickly enough.

"The way we met, Martin," Ellen said. "You think I didn't notice you following me around campus? Daring yourself to get as close as you could? I'd been on high alert every day since Tinsley vanished, and you spiked my radar. I even thought about going to campus security. Not just thought about it, I was going to, that day I decided to talk to you, instead."

"And that was the right decision."

"Shut up. I went to you instead because I figured that if I kept on going to other people, to other men who would barely believe me and stare at my chest while they pretended to listen to me or take a statement or whatever, that I'd keep on being as scared as I'd been since they took my sister away. So I went up to you. And when we started talking, I laughed at myself, and figured that hey, I'd been wrong. That the campus cops and my friends would have been right to laugh it off, that you were just a harmless, sweet, shy boy working up the courage to ask me out.

"So I need to apologize to my past self, because I was right about you. A peeping tom creep, probably panty thief. Lowest kind of sicko."

"I didn't do any of that, Ellen," I said, stepping back from her finger and the flame of pain it was spreading through the Ragman's cut. My spine bumped into the knob of the front door. "I broke in and took little things. Little things, pencil cases, barrettes, not underwear. It was dorky and misplaced-romantic."

"It's fucked-up, antisocial—"

"It's twenty-five years ago."

"How do I know? How do I know what else you've been poking into for these past years? And how do I know you weren't just interested in me because of Tinsley, anyway? Because I reminded you of something you really wanted to do to a woman?"

"Is that what this is about?"

"Don't belittle me. Don't confuse what I'm saying to you with petty, stupid jealousy," Ellen said, lowering the volume and upping the rage.

"People around you are messing with your head, Ellen. That doesn't include me, unless I've been doing it accidentally. This cop. Gary, even."

"Oh, so it's Gary you're going to pick on now," Ellen said, sitting down on one of her closed suitcases. It was packed so tightly that its cloth lid barely dented under her weight.

"I made a mistake trusting him at ReeseTech. I've allowed you to make the same mistake, because I thought he'd grown up. I didn't warn you about what I thought he was like. What I know he's like. Gary's been planning to con you into some sort of compromising position, insinuate himself between you and me, and then blackmail me that he's not going to leave us alone until I pay him off to scram."

"You think I'm that dumb?"

"I know you're not. He thinks you're that dumb. And don't tell me you haven't noticed him upping the attention and concern, that he's especially ready to snap to attention when you have something bad or doubtful to say about me. He's trying to get into your head. Just like that cop tried to get in your head, except he's been taking his time. He's fucking scum, Ellen."

"I don't know if I can trust your value judgments of other people, Martin."

"I've been the same guy for you since we met, Ellen. Absent-minded, too focused on work sometimes, I get fat twice a year and then thin again, I don't listen to you enough, I go camping instead of taking you to resorts, but we built this house together and we have a perfect daughter and I love you and I'm not a scumbag or a monster. I would do anything for you and for Kylie. And I tell you the truth. What I'm telling you now is that Kylie is alive and I'm going to do everything I can to get her back." I took a breath and watched her think. Watched her turn over the last few weeks with Gary, the conversation with Detective Sandra Whittal. The couple of decades we'd had. Kylie. Tinsley.

"I'm going to go to a hotel for a few days. I need full concentration on getting Kylie back and getting the right press and people on it. I don't have time or emotional room to deal with this," she said.

I knew I'd won something major. The three suitcases she had, whether she was going to end up taking them just to preserve appearances or not, were not what you took to a hotel for a few days. Those were moving-to-a-sublet suitcases, separating and divorce-prep suitcases. Hotel for a few days, we could come back from. It was perfect, actually, to allow me to do what I had to do before I could focus on getting Ellen back entirely.

"I'm going to respect that space. And I'm going to get Kylie back."

"That would help," Ellen said, almost smiling through the delirious, unreal strain of it all. Four pairs of Kylie's sneakers were piled in a corner next to the door, and we both looked at them at the same time.

"Why is that police officer so convinced something's wrong here, Mart?"

"She has a hard-on for me, Ellen. A nonsexual abuse-of-power cop hard-on, where she's going to use any little fact or coincidence she can find to support her weird imagined scenario where I'm wrapped up in acts too disgusting for either of us to be thinking about. Okay? So just stick to not telling her shit, because there's nothing to say. I used to have coffee and beer with a depressed cop out of pity. It was a mistake and I sure regret it now, but it had nothing to do with murder or stalking or anything like that, and I don't want it to be the foundation of a charge that would land us both in the newspapers for months." If Whittal had already thought to use the potential wreck of Ellen's reputation against me, Ellen had already factored it into her thinking about this whole thing. Didn't hurt to remind her.

"I told her you were with me all Friday night," Ellen said, standing up and beginning to zip all the suitcases.

"I was, Ellen."

"I know. That's how I know you didn't do this. That you didn't take that girl Rochelle away from her life. Don't you understand how awful that is, Mart? That the only way I can be absolutely, dead sure you had nothing to do with what happened to that girl is that I know you have an alibi?"

She stood the suitcases up while I thought about what to say, then told me she had to take a nap in the living room before she left. I stopped her for a moment, holding her face gently, but not risking an attempt at a kiss.

"I mean it, Ellen. I'm going to get Kylie back. You'll see. You'll know the kind of person I am, the way you've always known."

She didn't answer.

"WON'T BE THIS WARM OUTSIDE FOR QUITE A FEW months," Chris said. "Enjoy it. October and it's t-shirt weather," he went on, taking off his blazer and unbuttoning his shirt to prove it. His shoulder holster and undershirt visible, he leaned back against the car and watched Sandra frantically dialing her phone. The flames from Frank Connell's house—the houses on his property, if they were indeed all his—fought with the sunset for lighting rights of the darkening sky, orange and white taking on the familiar pinks and purples over North Seattle.

"Shut up, Chris," Sandra said, giving up on dialing the lieutenant. The fire department was already here, in deep force, three trucks hosing the structures down, no firemen inside any of the buildings. A couple of squad cars had shown up and Sandra had immediately sent them knocking on doors, to ask if anyone had seen Frank Connell, occupant of this soon-to-be-carbonized evidence treasure trove. Half the houses on this street were sitting empty, and the drive up had been a study in bleakness.

They'd taken the ride to Frank Connell's in silence, and by the time the sirens had started sounding behind them and the smoke became their beacon, they were deep in a neighborhood Sandra had barely ever been to. A few motels were clues to how close they really were to downtown, but they were the beaten-down highway ones that charge patrons by the month and occasionally book an unsuspecting family for a weekend, during which the kids learn all about bedbugs and the quotidian lives of prostitutes. A lit-up sign, the brightness of its surviving bulbs competing with the setting sun, indicated that a place called the Sunflower Motel was a left turn and a half-block away from Connell's houses. The fire trucks had taken a different route, and the structures were being doused by the time Sandra and Chris showed up.

"Was I right or was I right?" Chris said, without any triumph in his voice. "We can effectively call this proof of suspicious behavior."

Sandra turned to him, slowly, and he shut his mouth. He looked to be reaching for his gun, but he was starting to do up the buttons of his dress shirt. The flames created the illusion of heat, but it was still cool outside, and waiting to get colder when the sun disappeared. The flames were too hot, inferno hot, to risk setting foot into any of the buildings.

"Can I remind you there's every chance that, if you're right about this Connell guy, Kylie Reese is trapped in one of those flaming houses? Chris. Detective Gabriel. If you think this represents a victory over me, an investigative edge—it doesn't. If you look at it as a failing that you didn't share this information, this alternate path you'd taken on my fucking cue, as you'll recall—then you'd be right. I was focusing on Martin Reese because he was our bird in hand. The Shurn angle turned out to be a good one, too, obviously."

"Putting the link between that weird graveyard and Shurn was easy enough, with the bodies and the timing already there for me," Chris said. "I called everyone who worked on him in juvie, finally got the shrink who did his interviews. Some prompting was all it took to make him remember that Shurn's stepdad was obsessed with the place. Shrink, twitchy, lonely retired guy out in Spokane, now, he remembers those interviews well, thanks to the murders that came afterward. And yeah, you did do the groundwork on it, and got me gunning towards this guy, with the Tinsley Schultz link, with Waring's files, all this digging," Chris said.

"She's not in there," Sandra said. "I know Kylie's not in there."

"She can't be," Chris agreed. They didn't look at each other. Two more patrol units had showed up, and Sandra gave them orders to drive the perimeter, to look out for a guy matching Frank Connell's description. For the description itself, she turned to Chris.

"Connell's a big guy," he said. "We have no recent pictures, but he's six three, used to have a bunch of jail-yard muscle, but that was decades ago. About fifty years old, probably scary looking, white. Look for that paired with weird behavior, but I'm seriously guessing he's far away from here, boys." Chris shrugged and the patrol units took off to their cars.

"When we're investigating together, Chris, you talk to me. You're working a different angle, you tell me, keep me up to date. This helps no one. Don't try to teach me a lesson with dead bodies. Don't fucking scold me." Sandra didn't let Chris off the staring hook while she told him off, even as he started looking down, preparing to apologize. "What's the Shurn link?"

"There's nothing in the Shurn file on him, but the prison shrink remembered them hanging out, a mention or two Shurn made of his 'friend' that didn't make it onto tape. And Shurn, the one year he lived with his mother in early high school, it was in Eugene, Oregon. Same class as Sarah Weaver. My guess is that Shurn and Connell used to talk about girls in juvie, and they decided on going for Sarah together."

"I'm impressed you sewed this all up."

"I found Connell because I checked on any other juvie records Keith Waring requested. He asked for Connell's a few months ago."

"Goddammit." Sandra spat the word out and pounded the hood of the car with her fist. It was definitely a mistake on her part not to have done that. A true fuckup. Here and only here, Chris was right. She'd been too focused on the link between Keith Waring and Martin Reese to ask the next few obvious questions.

"Jason Shurn and Frank Connell. He drew both files at the same time, which is weird, because there's a copy of Shurn's juvie record in the main file. I guess he was too lazy to pick it out himself. There's a note in the Connell file that he and Shurn were pally in the yard. Connell's never been in trouble after the first conviction—he beat the shit out of his mother—and he runs a surveillance, spy store downtown. He's been invisible to cops for decades. Keeping clean. But I think you're right about the partner-killers thing, Sandra. This has to prove it," Chris said, gesturing at the flames.

"Shurn and Frank Connell met in prison and worked together killing women after they got out," Sandra said. "Shurn never ratted out his pal, so there'd always be a living piece of what they'd done together, outside the walls of the prison. And Connell was kept from killing because he had a dead record of what he and Shurn had done. The buried girls. The ones Martin Reese couldn't help himself from digging up, with Keith Waring's files and help."

"If it was Reese."

"Who the fuck else could it have been, Chris, with Kylie and a ReeseTech employee missing and this connect back to Keith Waring? Get in the car."

"To go where?"

"Reese's house."

"Lieutenant told us to lay off him."

"We're not going there to arrest him. We're going there to protect him from Frank Connell."

42

WITH ELLEN SLEEPING ON THE COUCH, I COULDN'T
do the work at my desk. So I took the bag down to
the basement and set it on the never-used workshop surface down there,
a picnic-table length of wood. Getting a tarp out, along with some gloves,
I went upstairs for my scrapbook, along with a notebook I'd filled with
the details of the procedure I was about to get into. Ellen was snoring
lightly, which meant she'd probably had a couple glasses of wine today.
She never snored during sober sleep.

In the basement, I put a skullcap on and a shower cap over it. I
gloved up, even put on a makeshift paper mask. I set the scrapbook down
on the clean surface, next to my satchel, and got to work. Getting this
right, and doing it clean, meant everything, because I could be sure that
the wrong eyes were on me, waiting for my mistake.

I don't know how long I was in that state, total focus, but by the
time I was finished checking and rechecking everything, and the satchel
was closed up again, ready to go, I realized I hadn't heard Ellen leave.

Hadn't heard her move, even, not across the creaky board at the base of the stairs, not in the kitchen. I put the satchel on crosswise and walked back upstairs.

The needle was visible before I saw him. Sticking out of Ellen's neck, with her facedown on the couch. A little runnel of blood coming down from where the needle had penetrated. I ran toward her, and right into the iron cylinder of the Ragman's arm.

"Speeding things up a little, Martin. I'd hate to give someone as clever as you a big head start on planning." I pushed against his arm, which was wrapped around my chest, holding me against him, and he responded by straightening up and lifting me into the air.

"Don't kick me in the shins or knees, I'll be annoyed. Stop. Stop it."

I did. My living room looked different from this vantage, a few inches higher off the ground. The two wooden turtles I'd picked up at that gigantic flea market in Maine were on the mantel, and Ellen had unsuccessfully tried to conceal them with vases that were usually empty. One of them, the dark blue one, had some half-dead peonies in it. The fireplace would be lit soon, in a month or so, if I ever made it back into this room. If Ellen woke up. If she wasn't dead already.

"Don't worry about her yet," the Ragman said. "She was sleeping when I came in, and she's just going to sleep for a little longer now, then wake up headachy. If things go bad tonight, if you're not obedient, I'll come back and do her in a proper, painful way. Break bones. Shoot her up with something much less tame. Watch her have seizures with those shattered legs and arms bucking out of control. That's a lot of pain, Martin. Worse even than anything Kylie's gone through under my watch."

"Stop it," I said. Unexpectedly, the Ragman let me go, and I ran to Ellen. Pulled the needle out without thinking, taking her pulse. It was there. I pushed my nose into her hair and smelled her, past the shampoo and into the sweat, the traces of breath leaking in and out of her mouth. I clenched the syringe, hard, and turned to face the Ragman. No mask this time. Frank Connell laughed at me.

"You going to stick me with that? It won't do you much good."

"You didn't have to do this. I've already chosen someone for us to go for. Someone to kill."

The Ragman leaned in, that civilian mask dropping off. I put the needle in my back pocket. "Who is she?"

"I don't want that. I don't want a typical kill, not for us. I want a man."

"Why?"

"Because there's no sex to it for me," I said. "That was never what I wanted when I went digging. That's coarse, and it leads to mistakes, to fuckups like the ones Jason Shurn and Carl Hillstrom made. It's over for me now: you too. There's no getting out of this, going back to normal.

"So if we're going to kill someone, if that keeps Ellen and Kylie safe, I want to kill someone I really want dead. Someone I hate. And I don't want to do the same thing you did with Shurn or Carl. I want our thing to be unique. Powerful, perfect. Then finished."

I used a bit of spit to clean the thread of blood off Ellen's neck. I rolled her onto her side, and she napped on, chemically aided, but still just napping. I really loved her then, and always had. I'd just never actually thought about it when I said the words. I took my phone out of my jeans pocket and set it on the coffee table in front of her. Wiping the blood off her skin was more meaningful than a verbal goodbye, so I left her with that.

"You've got to tell me one thing," I said to him. "Please."

"I don't have to do anything for you, but maybe I will, Martin. What?"

"Kylie. You didn't hurt her, did you? You didn't. I need her back as soon as we're finished tonight. I need her. If not, you might as well kill me and Ellen now."

"You'll see Kylie soon, Martin."

Frank and I left through the garage, walking to his big Ford on an invisible path he led me along, between the limits of the neighbor's driveway cams. As we walked toward it I saw the covered bed of the pickup. When we climbed in, I looked over my shoulder to the digging gear in the back seat. At that point, it was just hope, but it felt like knowledge: Kylie was under that cover. Alive or dead, she was there. The agony of waiting, of not tearing it off to see, was almost more than I could take. But I took it, because I knew the Ragman now. He wouldn't want to lose the chance to have me see her alive before he killed her, and then killed me.

43

I ASKED THE RAGMAN TO STOP AT A STORE SO I could pick up a throwaway phone, and he reached past me and popped open the glove compartment. Inside were the registration, the gun he'd pointed at me outside the Pemberton, and a still-packaged TracFone. I hesitated for a second.

"The gun's not a toy, but it is useless. No firing pin, no bullets. Nothing to it. Never been a gun guy, Martin."

"Me neither," I said, wishing that weren't true. Even if the gun had been usable, I wasn't Lee Marvin. Couldn't have pulled it out of the glove box and put a bullet in Frank before he had pulped my skull with that big fist of his. I took the TracFone out instead, attending to the difficult task of opening an already unopenable plastic package with gloves on. When it was done, I dialed Gary. It took three calls before he picked up. Like everyone else, he wasn't exactly up for answering a phone call from an unknown phone number, unless taking it would end the annoyance of a constantly vibrating phone.

"I have what you want. Two-thirds of it, anyway," I said, right after his wary "hello."

"Martin?"

"Yep. Two of the three. I have it. Will get you the rest once you're securely out of the country, in Thailand or wherever the fuck you want to end up. But we need to work some of the details out in person before I can give this to you."

"You want me to meet you somewhere?"

"Like you said, I can't hurt you. It's impossible. The cops would tie Rochelle to you, then to me, and that's that. And, by the way, the cops are all over me today. So don't make a single weird move, tell anyone what's up, or they're going to have questions as to what you and I are up to together, okay?" The truck had slowed down a little: the Ragman was still headed where I told him I wanted to end up, but he was tuned in for warnings, code words. Or just interested, I guess.

"Can't we just wait?" Gary asked. "I don't need the cash today."

"I need to get it to you today, or not at all. I can't explain on the phone. But I've got a lot more to lose than just some fucking money. If you're scared of me, I don't know what to tell you."

"Why didn't you call from your phone?"

"We've got to keep this as secret as possible. You have to realize that. Ellen can't know, my accountant can't know, there can be no trail on this cash. You leave me to worry about the paperwork pain-in-the-ass side of that. But if there's any trace, any at all, of me handing you a vast sum of money and then you leaving the country, we're both fucked. You for blackmail and me when you inevitably rat me out. So that's why I used this phone, and that's why I want to keep this call as short as possible." I could tell that Gary was in his apartment, from the relative lack of background noise. Some music—a John Carpenter score, maybe—was behind him, but no voices.

"Where do we meet?"

"Bring your car to the alley across from the store. Plenty of traffic around so you can feel nice and safe, but dark and quiet enough that we can talk before I give you the cash."

"Let's meet at a bar. Somewhere public." We were turning into the alley I'd just mentioned to Gary. The Ragman killed the lights, and we hunkered in the large vehicle as it went dark, looking at the cars darting briefly across the alley's mouth. The *tinsley* logo was visible, tiny, across the road. I wouldn't have been able to read it if I hadn't already known what it said.

"We meet in public, we have to deal with security cameras, with witnesses, with people saying that they saw that dot-com guy whose daughter got kidnapped hand a huge suitcase of cash to some Asian guy. We meet in an alley, that doesn't happen." I waited for the inevitable result. The mention of the suitcase had done it. Gary said okay, and hung up.

The Ragman opened the driver's door and checked out the laneway, a place I assume he already knew well, from watching Ellen and me over the weeks, the months. When he walked back, he came up to my window and started talking. The window fogged up with his words, hiding the lower half of his face for a second. I fumbled for the control. When he inhaled, he sucked that cloud off the window.

"What'd you say?" I asked.

"Nothing important. Maybe I didn't want you to hear," he said. There was a new, abstracted intensity in his face. He looked like a guy concentrating on not orgasming too quickly during sex, both focused and distracted at the same time.

"You going to wait out there?"

"Depends. How long will it take?"

"You know where Gary lives, don't you?" I said.

"I do. Just making conversation."

The Ragman got back in. I considered switching the battery on, burbling the radio to life, but the Ragman hadn't told me to, and he hadn't offered. He said nothing, but I could sense him sinking deeper into that strike zone he clearly had. I was counting on that focus narrowing to a pinpoint when it came time for us to do the thing, the killing business. I needed all of his attention on that.

"Give me a dose," I said. "A needle, for Gary."

"What if you just turn around and stick me with it? And what if I don't have one strong enough? Or only one that's too strong?"

"I'm not trying to outsmart you anymore, Ragman," I said. "I want this guy gone. I don't want a mess here, across from my wife's store. I want another kill the way we do it."

He'd twitched a little when I called him "Ragman." I could tell he liked it. He opened his jacket and dug into an inside pocket, drawing out two needles, one with an orange sticker on it, one with a blue. He put the orange one back.

"Gary's what, 150?"

"About that, maybe a little less."

"There's your dart, then." The Ragman handed the needle to me by its sheathed tip. We were both gloved. I put it into my own inner pocket, conjuring a little reverence to go along with my fake cool as I did so.

"When's Ellen going to wake up?"

"An hour or so."

The car was beginning to smell like man, like breath and enclosed perspiration. Ten minutes into the wait I hazarded a question, a relevant one.

"What did you do before you came to my place?" The Ragman cocked his head, like a feeding dog who's heard a distant call.

"Thought of a good kill site. You'll like it. Your friend is going to show up alone? He won't tell anyone, won't leave a note?"

"No. He can't imagine he's lost control. And he's not scared of me. To him I'm a guy who had an affair and tried to cover it up. To him, I'm the scared one."

"You are scared," the Ragman said.

"Of you. Not him."

That was it, until Gary rolled into the inviting space right in front of *tinsley*, just under the fifteen minutes he'd predicted. I waited to see if he'd stay parked there, if he was going to try to walk over to us. That would ruin everything, or at least complicate it. But he couldn't give up the false armor of the car around him, so he started it up again. I asked the Ragman to duck down, but he'd beaten me to it, reclining his seat and sliding down into a coiled crouch. Gary's car began edging into the mouth of the alley, the lights picking me out in the passenger seat of a vehicle he'd never seen me in.

I moved out of the truck before Gary could think too much, and waved him forward. I held up my satchel, trying to position my arms in a way that suggested the bag was heavy. I had no idea what two million dollars would have looked or felt like, in any denomination, but figured Gary's greed wouldn't be up to doing the spatial math.

I walked toward Gary's slowly advancing car, then stood right next to the driver's side door, so he wouldn't have space to open it. When he rolled down the window, I had the needle out. I fumbled with the cap for a second before pulling it off with my teeth. Gary wasn't quick enough with his window control—I had the thing in his neck and was pulling the door open as he pressed the up button. I shot the venom in, then pulled the needle out and pounded my fist into the back of his head, just once, for luck. His forehead bounced off the wheel. There wasn't a drip of blood, not a trace. I checked, before bundling him out into the alley. The Ragman was edging out of his truck, which made the next second crucial: I opened my satchel and lunged into Gary's car in one motion.

"What the fuck are you doing in there?" the Ragman asked when I came back up to face him.

"I tripped. His leg kicked out at me."

"Ah. They do that, you know."

"I do now."

We quickly loaded Gary into the Ragman's truck, nestling him into the same fatal berth that Rochelle Stokes had occupied a couple of days prior. Before taking off, I asked the Ragman if I could lock Gary's car up. I wanted to make sure it got towed at worst, not stolen, but I didn't tell him that. Just that it would look odd for Gary to leave his BMW unlocked when he left it, and that might eat into what little time we had, right?

"Right," Frank Connell told me. I was starting to get a grip on how distracted he was. How done. How sure he was that he was going to kill me and himself as soon as we finished with Gary.

44

"I CAN'T WAKE HER UP," CHRIS SAID. "YOU STILL REALLY
shouldn't have broken that glass, Sandra, Christ."

"That's two phones on the table. His and hers. Reese fucking took off
again, or Connell took him."

"Or he's scared of you and sick of being hounded. You've got him
paranoid as fuck." Ellen Reese stirred while Chris was talking. Sandra
pushed him aside and tapped her on the cheek with two fingers.

"Get water," she said to Chris.

"I took a pill, but just—it's just herbal stuff in it. I don't usually feel
like this."

"We're going to get you to a hospital."

"No." Even with a fat-tongued slur, Ellen was sharp, the eyes below the
cloud zeroing in on Sandra with increasing focus. "You don't wanna take
care of me. You want proof of something that just didn't, never happen."

"You're confusing words, Mrs. Reese. I'm concerned. This isn't a natural wake-up."

"Two cops coming into my house and shaking me isn't natural, no."

"You look like you've been drugged," Chris said.

"You look like you're still in my house, Officer. Officers. Please get out."

"Can we have your permission to secure the house? Make sure there's no one in here?"

"I'm on my way to a hotel." Ellen Reese sat all the way up, opened her eyes a little wider as if to clear the murk in her head. "Just leave me alone."

Chris and Sandra left. "Should we tell her about the busted window in the door?" Chris asked, on the front step.

"No," said Sandra. "She'll see it in a minute. I'll pay out of pocket for it if I have to. I had a legitimate concern for her welfare, willing to explain that to the lieutenant, to a judge, to whoever the fuck."

"What do we do now?"

"You stay here," Sandra said. "If she isn't out of the house and on her way to that hotel in fifteen minutes, you go in again, no matter what she says. Then you follow her to the hotel and make sure she gets to her room safely. Let her notice you, it doesn't matter. I'm getting back to my car out at ReeseTech, and I'm going to look for our boy."

"Which one?"

"Both. They're together. Frank Connell and Martin Reese are together, right now. Maybe one of them's dead, but I know Connell made his way here the second after he lit that match. I'm not going to let these animals beat me."

45

I WASN'T SUPPOSED TO BE SURPRISED BY THE KILL
site, especially after that "You'll like it" comment the
Ragman had made. We drove into deepening darkness, the streetlights
and headlights getting more intermittent as we branched from the highway to a small turnoff road. Traffic was thin, but I could hear it while the
Ragman and I drove Gary up through the woods behind Torland's gravel
factory. The area had been developed since I'd found Jenny Starks here.
Instead of the brush and spruce I'd pushed through, there was dead grass
and dirt between thick Douglas fir trunks, and a good many of those had
been cut to stumps. We got within fifteen feet of where Jenny Starks had
been lying back when this started, twenty years ago, the Ragman's headlights picking out the rise ahead where I'd first seen her.

I gloved up and mummied Gary's legs with duct tape when we
pulled over. When he tried to struggle on the way out, he moved like a
mermaid being hauled ashore.

"Decent technique," the Ragman said. "We'll have to take off the tape wrapped around his face when we get into the forest. It'll have your cells all over it."

"Yes," I said. It was dark, real outdoors dark. I grabbed Gary's bound ankles.

"No dragging," the Ragman reminded me. He picked Gary up by the head, using the tape as a handle, and we carried him over to the site. "You must be excited to be back. Martin Reese's ground zero. Jason had this spot all picked out for Jenny Starks, way ahead of time. Told me about it. Then he went and did her on his own, starting to get antsy because he knew he was about to get caught. I can't blame him for wanting one last go, but I was ashamed at how he left the site. Total mess.

"I didn't expect to see you here, though. I watched you circling Jenny on the ground, making your plan. I thought you were going to touch her. I even thought of helping Jason out at that moment, getting everything pinned on you somehow. Didn't know much about DNA way back then, though. I would have had to hope you fingerprinted her eyeballs or did something dirty to her."

"I get it. Stop," I said, surprised to find myself embarrassed at the idea of Gary overhearing this.

There were a few flattened areas of greenery surrounding the site. Places where tents had been pitched in years past. Then we came to the right spot in that slight rise in the hillside, the incline where Shurn had hastily buried Jenny Starks. We set our human bundle down again. Gary's terror made him look less than human, all bugging eyes and trails of saliva escaping from the tape. I was glad the dark made only the palest parts of him visible.

"Jason didn't want or need my help by then. He wanted posterity, wanted recognition. I didn't want to get in the way, but I didn't want the last kill to be stumbled on by some idiot. Which is what I thought I was seeing when you came up here and had yourself a good stare. If you were a few minutes later, I would have killed you right there."

"Where's the shovel?" I asked. I looked down. Gary was trying to master his panic in order to look at me, imploring, confused. I looked right back at him for a second.

"Don't you want the kill first?" the Ragman asked.

"No. I want to kill him in the hole."

"That's fair," said the Ragman. "And a good idea. We'll leave less scatter up here."

Digging was, of course, my job. The Ragman started back toward his truck, but I stopped him.

"The backseat, right?"

"That's right, Martin." I started walking, gauging the darkness as I went, the distance between the Ragman and myself. I could jump in the truck and drive off if Kylie was in the back. I could do that. But it wouldn't finish what was happening up here. It wouldn't allow me to be sure.

I came up to the back passenger door and quickly dodged a hand under a loosened corner of the pickup bed cover, feeling around.

"Please. Please," I muttered. And I heard it. A sound, a whimper. Then I felt her, her hair, her face. I couldn't risk jumping up to peer into the back, but I knew it was her. Kylie. I opened the back passenger door and grabbed the shovel handle, whispering as loudly as I dared.

"Kylie, it's Dad. It's me. You're going to be fine. Just, you have to be quiet. Be quiet and don't listen to anything until I come back for you, okay?"

There was no sound from the bed. I took that as a good sign. I had to. While I was reaching for the gear in the backseat I checked to see if the keys were in the ignition. They were. I came back with the shovel and the large, flimsy plastic bag full of liquid-filled jugs that had been on the backseat. Cleanup materials. The Home Depot price tag was still on the shovel's handle. I stepped over Gary and pointed out a spot in the shallowest slope of the hillside. The Ragman pointed four feet to the right. I drew an outline with the tip of my shovel. He nodded.

"This is where I remember her being," I said.

"That's right," the Ragman said. "There was a spread of paw marks around—I don't know if you noticed them—coyote, had to be. Jason was in a rush, yes, but to leave your kills in coyote-digging range is odious. I mean, he wasn't hiding them for his own freedom at that point, he was hiding them to give me something to come back to. A small gesture, sure, but it had the bigger effect of making me sure he wasn't going to rat on me. That he intended me to be out here, celebrating what we'd done. Damn sloppy digging job, though."

I pushed the blade into the soon-to-be grave, and it went in more easily than I hoped. I tossed the earth into a circumscribed area behind me and to the left. Once I heard some bucking sounds of protest, and saw that I'd caught Gary with a stray cast of pebbles and dirt. I went over to him and wiped his face off, so he could watch what I was doing. The more scared he was, the calmer I became. That time-flattening excitement that came with me on hunts arrived, and the shovel entered and left the expanding hole with a hypnotic regularity. The Ragman stayed quiet the whole time, sometimes breathing more heavily, always with his eyes on my back. I looked back once to see him kneeling next to Gary, his big palm overlaying my old assistant's chest, feeling the heartbeat. He nodded at me, and I continued. The pit spread below and around me, and I stopped only when it was up to my shoulders.

"Now?" I asked the Ragman.

"First you kill, and then we clean."

The Ragman wasn't next to Gary anymore. He was a few feet away, waiting to see exactly how I'd do it. The front of his pants bulged, and his eyes were absent, glossy, far away.

I went over to Gary. He screamed as well as he could, using the give he'd created with the saliva and lip movement eating into the duct tape glue. It still came out as a sad, muffled bleat, but there was enough real terror in it to make the Ragman make a small puffing sound of contentment. With the tip of my boot, I started to roll Gary toward the pit. He was little, so small and light, and it was easy work until I reached the incline. At that point, I grabbed him by the shoulders and pulled him upright. I pulled him a foot off the ground, though my exhausted arms screamed, before I dropped him into the hole.

The Ragman ran up behind me, but his footfalls didn't have any scare left for me. The beam of a flashlight filled the grave, where Gary lay on his back, up-angling from the pain of falling five feet and having the wind knocked out of him. I could hear it wheezing through his nose as I lowered myself in there with him. The flashlight beam danced around to the upper part of the grave, illuminating the back of my neck, reflecting light off Gary's eyes.

I read in those eyes, for a moment, a collaborator's hope: Gary thought maybe I was going to pull a last-minute switch, pretend to leave him for dead, deal with this huge stranger behind us through trickery that I'd explain to Gary on our backslapping, triumphant ride back to town. Fantasies built from the movies we'd all seen, the books we'd all read.

But Gary should have felt what was coming even before my fingers started pressing into his neck. Once you start something, it has to be finished. I pressed harder.

I stopped for a moment and hope flooded into his eyes again. I tore the tape off his mouth. His voice, when it came, was quiet. The work I'd already done on his throat had squeezed the volume out, even the tone.

"Please. You can't. I left a note, I texted—people know I'm with you."

"I already figured out that angle, Gary. Don't worry about that. And you didn't leave a note or text anyone, did you? Just like you couldn't wait to get your phone back from me in the motel so you could take some pictures of what I had in the Jeep. You just couldn't wait to show me how much better you were than me, how much smarter, how much more deserving of my money."

"Speak up," the Ragman said. He was at the rim of the grave, crouching. "I want to hear all of this." I obliged.

"You're not better, Gary. That's why you're here, without my money, without any part of my life. And you're going to stay here forever." For a moment, a moment that made me feel both disappointed and relieved, I did feel sorry for what I was going to do. Not sorry enough to save him, but sorry.

"I have to, Gary. For Kylie, for Ellen." And for myself. I pressed down on the soft parts of his flesh, on the cartilage structure of his windpipe, which gave in the rubbery way the undesirable parts of a fried chicken thigh do. His neck was slender enough for my fingertips to meet at his spine when I used all my strength. I pressed and leaned down, time fading out altogether, the reflected beam in Gary's eyes jumping and darting as blood vessels burst and threaded complicated rivulets around his irises. His arms and legs spasmed, the bones and tendons themselves seeming to scream. I kept the pressure on until he was dead, and then for a few minutes more.

"That's good," the Ragman said, his voice quiet, strained. He was craned over the hole with the flashlight, and startled back when I looked up at him and the beam caught whatever the expression on my face was. He dropped the heavy, old, nickel-plated thing into the grave, and I handed it back up to him. He wouldn't grab it.

"Leave it in there, douse it with the body." The Ragman's tone was almost back to normal, assuming some authority as he swatted the flashlight out of my hand. He walked back toward the truck. I stepped on Gary's chest and boosted my way out of the grave. One of his ribs gave under my boot.

The Ragman flicked on his headlights, outlining the scene around us.

"Don't worry about anyone noticing the lights. We'll be quick." He walked toward the bag of jugs, each full of a different corrosive fluid, and set them on his side of the grave. "It's not a matter of being delicate. We spill all of this stuff over him, over everything we touched, and we should be fine. They'll be able to find traces of us, maybe, but the samples will be too contaminated. If they find him at all, we're done for anyway." He passed me over one of the jugs, pure white with a blue label, a knockoff of the Clorox logo.

"Usually I cut the tops off them so they pour more easily," he said. "Give me that back. I forgot. Got kind of charged up watching you do the kill." He reached for the jug, almost bashfully, and took it out of my hand. He poured out a cup's worth of bleach into the grave, where it dropped onto Gary's pants and began turning the black cloth orange. The Ragman took a Leatherman knife out of his back pocket and carved off the top of the jug. He handed it toward me, and I backed a pace or two away. He came to the lip of the grave and offered me the jug again, a little closer. The knife was closer, too.

"Is she here, Ragman?" I asked.

"What? Oh, your daughter. Yes, she's in the truck. The bed. I gave her a real scare today, I'll tell you, popping her in my freezer for a second." The Ragman laughed like a little kid, an enthusiastic honk. "She still hasn't seen my face, don't worry. We'll come up with a great story."

"You and me," I said.

"I didn't think I would, but I want to do this again, with you," said the Ragman. I took the bottle of solvent from him. "Rochelle's hidden very well, now. I can show you later tonight, just so you know how well. Then we can start talking about what's next."

"Yeah." I didn't go on, not moving until he spoke again. It took a moment. He folded the Leatherman up and pocketed it, and when he spoke again, I understood something had changed. Without aiming for it, I'd made him trust me. He really did see another kill for us, together. He didn't want to stop.

"You shouldn't call me Ragman," he said. "That was Jason's thing. Let's go with just Frank," he said, reaching out with his right hand in the beginning of a gesture. I'd never find out if it was going to be a handshake or an arm squeeze. I steadied the bottom of the jug on my left palm and juddered the container toward his face with my right hand on the handle, pulling back when it was closest to the Ragman's eyes, so the maximum amount of liquid would spill into them. He screamed and I dropped the jug into the grave, then grabbed his shoulders and pulled him toward me. He stumbled, clutching his searing face, falling over the grave without going all the way in. I had to jump on his back, making him scream again, differently, making him fall in under me. I hauled myself out, evading the wild hand that whipped out for me, and ran for the truck. His huge bulk wasn't a factor as long as he was in that hole, not with the pain from the burns.

I covered the fifteen feet to the vehicle and got in, twisting the key and hoping for exactly the sight I saw. Frank Connell, strong again in his anger, had levered himself upright, his head and massive chest poking out of the grave. The engine came to life and I floored the accelerator, taking it full speed toward the Ragman, smashing into him with crushing, beautiful force, continuing up the sloping ground as I felt his ruined skull slide under the pickup, bumping along the metal until it struck the muffler with a wet clang. I reversed and looked out at what I'd done.

It was a big mess.

46

THROUGH THE BURNING, THROUGH THE AGONY OF
his melting eyes, the Ragman took in the ending, accepted it as perfect and his due. He tried to get proper words out, to let Martin know this was okay, he'd gotten exactly what he wanted, this was perfect. He couldn't get his tongue to work. All he could do, all he did, was position himself when he heard the motor start and knew what Martin was about to do. His brain was still working, in fits and starts, until the muffler punched the largest shattered piece of his skull right through it. All that was left before that point, the pain being so great that it had crested and stopped, was happiness.

SANDRA HAD BEEN CRUISING FOR FIVE HOURS, trying to shake leads out of Frank Connell's business connections, from the crew going through the burnt hulk of his house, when the call came in from Chris.

"Reese. He made contact with Ellen. She came down to the Sheraton lobby for me, yelling, not herself at all."

"Where is he?"

"At her store. Reese said all he could think to do was go back there and set the alarm off. He's got the kid, Ellen says. He has Kylie."

Sandra gunned the engine and made it to *tinsley* in ten minutes. Martin Reese was sitting in front of the store, barefoot, a pickup truck parked halfway on the curb in front of him. Kylie Reese, intact, part of the green dress she'd vanished in visible under the swaddling of wool blankets that cocooned her, was next to him. They were holding onto each other very tightly.

"Mr. Reese. Kylie. Kylie, are you okay?"

"She's alive. He didn't hurt her. You were right," Reese said, tilting his head up at her. "It was—the digging up, all of that. They explained it to me. The whole thing."

"Who did?"

"The big guy. The one with that truck," Reese said, pointing. "The one who took Kylie. He had—Gary told me to come meet him here, he told me to turn up without Ellen, that the cops had been threatening him too. I came here, and that truck—Gary was in that truck, with a huge, just a fucking insane looking man. He told me Kylie was in the back, and if I didn't do what they said, if I didn't do it—"

"It's okay, sir, slow down," said Chris. Sandra couldn't help flicking a betrayed look at him. Convinced so quickly. Chris stooped to pull the blanket more tightly around Kylie Reese.

"You okay?" Chris asked her.

"I'm okay," she said. "He's dead. My dad killed him. I told him my dad would help me. I told him."

"Shhhh," said Sandra, putting a hand on the girl's hair. The chattering speech stopped, and Martin Reese started talking again.

"They made me get in. They grabbed me, they didn't ask. Blindfolded me, took me to the woods. Forty minutes of driving, but I don't know—I couldn't tell in what direction, at first, but they pulled off the blindfold a little before we got up into the place, up to the big hole. God. It was behind Torland's, the old plant. I thought they were going to kill me. I thought I was dead. The whole ride up, Gary was telling me the same things you told me. Except it was him, not me. When I tried to scream he put a piece of tape on my mouth. That he'd been obsessed with Ellen since he started working at ReeseTech. He took the job because he knew I was married to Tinsley Schultz's sister. He digs up bodies, I mean, he dug up bodies, bought files from Keith Waring. They killed Keith last week, him and the big guy. That big guy and him, they started killing women together. Rochelle. That other one. They were going to keep doing it. The cop, he was part of it, spying on me.

The big guy said Keith's body was gone for good, and I don't even know what that means.

"When I got up there, when they took the blindfold off, that was it. I was going in the hole. But the big guy put Gary in it instead. He got in there with him and started strangling him, making these awful noises, both of them. I wasn't tied up or anything, and he must have forgotten, or just been too—he wasn't paying attention to me, so I got into the truck. I just meant to reverse, to get out of there, but my brain wasn't working right. I drove forward."

Martin Reese pointed at the truck, and started to cry. Sandra walked around to the front of the pickup, where it had nosed up onto the curb. A great dent in the front fender. She bent down a little and saw the marks of gore beneath it.

"Jesus," she said.

"I can take you there," Reese said. "I can take you to them. Once Kylie is safe at home with Ellen." Sandra told Chris to take Kylie into the squad car, get her warm. Reese let her go, making encouraging sounds, and Sandra faced him, leaning down, whispering almost.

"Are you bullshitting me? I mean, I know you're bullshitting me, but are you going to admit it?" Sandra stooped, looked into Reese's shaking face, the tears in his eyes. He was shaken up, for real, but that didn't mean the version he'd just given her had anything to do with what happened.

"I'm telling you the truth. I'll show you the bodies."

"I'm sure you can. That's not the part I don't believe."

For a moment, Reese stopped shaking, staring at her dead-on, a different expression than she'd ever seen in his eyes before. Something cold and white hot at the same time.

"My daughter's back. I brought her back alive. There's nothing you can do to me that will hurt."

48

THE HARDEST PART WAS NOT TELLING SANDRA

Whittal that Gary's car was in the alley across from the store. I couldn't point it out without making her even more suspicious, so I kept my mouth shut. When Ellen's car pulled up, nudging over the curb just before she careened out of the driver's seat, running over to pull Kylie out of the back of the squad car and hold her in a heap on the pavement as uniform officers got gawkers out of the area, no one was paying attention to me anyway. But it was Ellen who spotted it, as we were all heading inside *tinsley*.

"That's Gary's car, isn't it?" The yellow boot clamped on it picked up the streetlight.

I didn't indulge an impulse to look over my shoulder as Detective Gabriel jogged across the street to look at the vehicle. Ellen let me hug her, even hugged me back. I was doing a good job of looking like a wreck. I heard Gabriel call out as he shone a flashlight in. It was almost dawn, but not quite—still dark. "It's locked up. Laptop half-under the passenger seat."

"Call it in. Don't let them tow it or touch anything unless I'm there," Whittal said, eyeing me. "Now let's get more units out and check out your little spot at Torland's, Mr. Reese."

"You're going to take him?" Ellen said. "We just got our daughter back, and you're taking him back out to god knows where." She looked at me, half-fear and half-hardness, knowing that she had to let what I'd done, whatever it was, come to an end. Kylie knew, too.

"It's okay, Dad, go." I'd talked to her in the truck when we drove down, speeding through the dark streets, away from the carnage I'd left in the hills. "I never saw his face, Dad. I love that I never saw his face," she'd said, and then somehow fell asleep. The way she was looking at me now, just before walking into *tinsley* with her mother, I wondered if Kylie had heard something when we were up on the hill. If she had figured too much of this out.

We left Kylie and Ellen behind and went up to the hill behind Torland's, squad cars and forensics flanking us. It was the parade I'd wanted to lead twenty years ago, when I found Jenny Starks. And there was the scene, laid out as I'd told them, with Frank and Gary in the grave, a generous sloshing of bleach around. I'd filled in that part of the story on the way up, how Gary had been telling me they were going to make the site spick-and-span after I was dead and buried, how he'd taken the bleach out just before the big man had seized and pushed him, that I'd heard a scream from the guy before I got in the truck, which must have been Gary trying to fight him off by throwing the bleach at him. Whittal never believed me, but she started to look just suspicious, instead of absolutely sure.

49

SANDRA WHITTAL WALKED INTO *TINSLEY* A WEEK
after it reopened, in early December. She saw Martin
Reese going into the back, but not because he'd noticed her. He was carrying a stack of gray coats and muttering something. His wife was at the
till, ringing up a purchase for two college boys with extremely frustrat-
ing haircuts. They paid—Sandra heard the number and wondered who
paid that credit card bill—and were gone by the time Sandra got to the
counter. Ellen's smile dented a bit at the right corner, but didn't entirely
vanish.

"Hello again," Sandra said. "Business good?"

"It has been. Probably thanks to some of that other kind of press, but
money's money, Detective."

"Not detective," Sandra said. "Not for a little while, anyway. I got a
pretty hard time for harassing your husband—and no, I know that wasn't
either of your doing—but it was more the way I snapped back that got

me a temp suspension. I snapped back at that, too, so the force and I have both decided it's best that I take some time off."

"I am sorry to hear that," Ellen said. "You're clearly passionate about the work. And I know—I of all people know—that it's easy to get fooled by people, to focus on the wrong thing."

"What?"

"With Gary. Gary fooled me."

"Oh," Sandra said. "I'm sorry about your front door, too. I appreciate you not making a deal about that. I still wish you'd let me pay to replace the glass." She was eyeing the door to the stockroom.

"Do you want to talk to Martin?" Ellen said.

"Was hoping. I want to apologize, you know."

Reese was sitting on the pile of coats Sandra had seen him carrying, scrolling through his iPhone. He got up immediately when she entered.

"Sorry," he said, like a kid who'd been caught slacking behind the counter at McDonald's.

"I'm not your boss, she is," Sandra said, pointing back at Ellen before gently shutting the door. "And I won't tell."

"What brings you here?"

"I was just telling your wife that I came here to apologize."

"No need," Reese said, pocketing the phone and waving an open hand.

"I was lying to her. I came to tell you to never do anything like this ever again."

"Like what?"

"You know what I mean," Sandra said. "You know."

Reese stared at her for quite a few seconds. Looking for words that would do exactly what he needed them to do, without doing anything he didn't want them to do. She'd seen dumber people do the same thing before, but she had a feeling Reese was going to succeed. He did.

"You don't have to worry about me, Detective Whittal."

Sandra left the stockroom, with the door open, and said goodbye to Ellen. Because the store was still empty, she added, sincerely, "I'm so sorry about your sister. I hope you get resolution on it one day. This is a beautiful thing you've done for her." For good measure, and with a thrill of adrenaline that compared with entering a building with gun drawn, Whittal bought an incredibly expensive scarf. She wore it out of the place, and got into Chris Gabriel's waiting car.

"What did you say?" Chris asked when she sat down. "And why did we come here, again?"

"Told her I left the force, told him to be a good boy. And I came up here because the last thing I picked up on my work voicemail was a four-minute weeping message from Bella Greene's mother, thanking me for making things right for her daughter, for getting her killers what they deserved."

"Did you pass the message on to Martin?" Chris asked.

"I didn't. I had to take a look at him again, see how he'd come out of his game. If he looked any weaker, different. See if he thinks about those victims for even a minute a day."

"You able to pick any of that up from looking at him?"

"I got nothing from him, just like before," Sandra said. "Can we go to your place? Mine's a mess." Chris obediently did an illegal u-turn.

"You aren't really, really leaving, are you?"

"I'll stick to the temporary leave, probably. Gives us a chance to date without the department scolding, or you pathetically trying to one-up me in the field."

"I'm sorry about that. I said I'm sorry."

"I have to come back at some point, if they'll let me. What the hell else am I going to do, hang out with your kid?" Sandra smiled at Chris, and he laughed, then stopped laughing.

"You want to meet Mike?"

"It's not that I want to, it's that it's getting weird that I haven't yet. And I know it will make you happy, which has the bonus of also shutting you up."

Chris started making enthusiastic plans out loud as he drove, forgetting what they'd just been talking about. Forgetting that he was about to ask Sandra if she was going to quit watching Martin. Which was good, because Sandra didn't want to lie. She wanted to find Rochelle Stokes's body, to find out who exactly killed her. As long as that body was out there, hidden, she wouldn't be sure if she was right or wrong about Martin Reese.

Sandra didn't think she was wrong.

50

IT WAS THE SCRAPBOOK THAT CLINCHED MY STORY about Gary, once they opened it up.

Bob Suchana at ReeseTech told the cops that Gary was meticulous about his desk, particularly the row of old laptops he had arranged like books on a shelf above his workspace. Including the PowerBook they'd found in his car, the one I'd taken off the shelf when I went to ReeseTech after our talk at the motel.

"No one was allowed to touch them," Bob had said, repeating the words in an interview with KOMO-TV. "He was more than protective of them. They were—like, forbidden territory. Maybe especially that one."

The hardware and software transfer I'd done in my basement between my scrapbook and Gary's old laptop had been difficult. Precision work. Altering dates on files, blanking out data. I'd anonymized all the information on my scrapbook from the beginning, so there was no chance of any file carrying my name. Swapping hardware into the shell of Gary's laptop was where I was most careful, because our desks had been next to each other—hey, I even recall using Gary's computer a few times in 2005, I could say, we all swapped or just used the nearest terminal in late-night programming sessions—but it had to be mostly his matter or none in that machine, especially with Whittal leaning on forensics to tie it to me.

But they didn't. All the photos of my digs, which I'd been careful to leave any of my limbs out of, and trace of my identity or possessions—they were in Gary's computer. No one could pinpoint where he was on the days any of the calls had been made, thanks to ReeseTech's slack record-keeping when it came to workplace attendance, and Gary's genuinely depressing lack of a social life outside of casual sex dates.

So Gary was the "Finder," which is apparently what a couple of the cops had been calling me. Forensics dug around a little more up there, too, and yes—they found Jenny Starks. The Ragman hadn't moved her far at all, back when I came to look for her again and found her vanished. He'd just put her underground. I'm taking a partial credit for that find, even if Seattle PD publicly claims it.

I've always been comfortable not getting notice for my accomplishments, and I still am. I made the papers as the unlucky tech guy who'd ended the Ragman's killing spree, saved his daughter, and been witness to the bizarre ending of the Finder's bizarre career. If I'd been at all famous, instead of just middling rich, it might have been in the news for more than a couple of days. But the story vanished, quick.

After I was sure that Ellen believed me, that she was at least able to believe in order to keep her life, her past and present, the way it was, I swore to never mention any of this again. Whenever we talk about the store, about *tinsley*, I do think about our real Tinsley, her bones lying in a grave I can't go looking for. And I think I can let them lie there.

Kylie and I don't talk much about those few days. We got her a therapist, of course, one who even had her go out to the burned-out hulk of the Ragman's properties, so she could see where she'd been kept, what she'd escaped. She digested the trauma, somehow, came through it with knowledge, a little more fear, and more courage. That's a nice gloss; something has still been taken from Kylie that I can't put back, that the doctor can't help her with. And that's my fault.

On her fifteenth birthday, after Ellen had gone to bed and I'd let Kylie have a glass of wine for a toast, she did ask me one question about it. I didn't have to lie.

"Dad."

"Yeah."

"Did you do anything wrong? That night up there when you brought me back. Did you do anything wrong?"

"I did exactly what I had to do to bring you back, kid. How could it have been wrong?"

ACKNOWLEDGMENTS

THANKS TO RUDRAPRIYA RATHORE, WHO MADE THIS BOOK POSSIBLE.
Thanks also to my family: Kay, Sam, Mandy, Paul, Rouba, Seamus, Samson.

To my agents Samantha Haywood and Stephanie Sinclair, and everyone at Transatlantic. To Rakesh Satyal, Laurie Grassi, and everyone at Atria, Simon & Schuster Canada, and Text Publishing.

For reading drafts of this over the years: Andrew Sullivan, David Bertrand, Graeme Desrosiers, Kris Bertin, Julie Chapple. Thanks to Simon McNabb for telling me the idea was worth following through.

And: Emily Keeler, Sarah Weinman, Saelan Twerdy, Rob Inch, Bess Lovejoy, Kirby Kim, Craig Davidson, Andrew Pyper, Troy Fullerton, Sam Wiebe, Michael Haldane, Chris Ferguson, Marlaina Mah, Christian Cantamessa, Jeff Lee Petry, Buddy, Jack Illingworth, The Writer's Trust and the Journey Prize team.

ABOUT THE AUTHOR

© IAN PATTERSON

NATHAN RIPLEY is the pseudonym of Toronto resident and Journey Prize winner Naben Ruthnum. *Find You in the Dark*, Ripley's first thriller, was an instant bestseller. As Naben Ruthnum, he is the author of *Curry: Eating, Reading, and Race*. Follow him on Twitter @NabenRuthnum.

Turn the page for a sneak peek at

YOUR LIFE IS MINE

Coming to bookstores soon.

e a shooter is a shooter, he's just a man in a room.

It's what follows that brings the background to the scene, to the way we remember it. The domestic dispute reports, the spotty employment record, the legal and illegal firearms history, the I-always-knew neighbors. Before all of that, he comes into the room with his gun, hidden or not, and he is just a man, and not the kind that anyone is used to noticing. Not remarkably handsome, and remarkably ugly only in retrospect. After what he's done.

On August 17, 1996, Chuck Varner walked into the Harlow Mall in Stilford, California, with a Beretta 92FS in his waistband holster. I was there, too.

Chuck owned an AR-10 with an expensive, post-manufacture scope, and had used it on the highway earlier that afternoon, but it wasn't suited to this final step. The radio—it was just the radio and television then, no digital feeds to warn us or lull us with repetitive news of imminent mass death—had said that there was a shooter, that death had come to some already and was likely headed to others soon. But the radio hadn't been able to say anything useful, anything actionable. The shooter was a man in a truck with a rifle. He'd shot from an overpass, and people had died. It wasn't the radio's job to guess what would happen when he parked the truck, when he set the rifle down and picked up a different gun. When he picked a building to use it in.

Chuck Varner chose the Harlow Mall months, even years before, seeing this panorama of waiting bodies and vivid lights in his fantasies and behind the paper targets in his practice drills. It was 2:30 p.m.—no one with a day job would be there, unless they were taking a too-late lunch, or a lazily long break. The adults were mostly stay-at-home parents or the unemployed, Chuck told me. As always, I listened, absorbed, knowing I would be tested later. And because it never occurred to me that he could be anything but absolutely right. The mall was also full of kids, retirees. Night workers like Chuck himself, but ones who drank heavily as part of their bat-hanging flipped schedules and therefore looked worn. Chuck collected conversations, speculated about potential future disciples, and made ambitious plans for his followers, until he realized that he didn't especially care to carry any of them out. He cared about killing.

Chuck never turned up anywhere in public looking strung out, haggard, anything but the upright leader of men that he aimed to be. He slept six hours every morning. Drank two cocktails max, no beer. Calisthenics, runs. At home, his family nurtured his routine with the full knowledge that it was the best way they could love him. That and listening to his gospel, following his drills and instilling his philosophy into the essence of their daily lives. Chuck could always count on his family. If Chuck read, or even if he watched documentaries about people like himself, he would know this made him an outlier, remarkable in a certain way: he was happy at home.

But that day, he didn't let happiness distract him from his purpose. From what he was there in the mall to do, looking tidy if casual in a black T-shirt with an unreadable band name overtop a skull logo, a costume that news outlets discussed in depth in the following weeks and months.

Even I wasn't a distraction for him: he'd brought me as a witness. It was my reward.

Because it was such a common sight in this mall, in any mall, it wasn't reported that the man who later held only a gun had come in holding a girl by the hand. Me. No one noted that Chuck Varner, before he became the shooter, had patted her on the shoulder, and gone up the escalator with her.

When I sat on one of the food court chairs that ran the length of the atrium railing, he left me and descended. When the first shot came, when the running, ducking, and panicking came a thick few seconds of disbelief and processing later, I didn't move. I didn't exactly watch, but I didn't look away. I knew that I was the only person in that building who had nothing to fear from Chuck Varner.

Chuck Varner was holding his daughter's hand when he walked into the mall. My hand. He took me up that escalator and told me that he loved me. He told me to walk away from the mall and go back to my mom once he was done. That everyone would be screaming and running, that no one would get in my way. He also said that if I didn't do just as Dad said, he would be very disappointed. That I should listen to him and trust that he was about to become everything that we'd ever talked about. He nodded at me as he went down the escalator, smiling and trying to do something with his eyes, achieving a look I'd never seen from him before. Then he got distracted and started touching the holstered Beretta through the thin fabric of his T-shirt, and by the time he reached the killing floor, I knew he'd forgotten about me absolutely.

I was seven years old. And I thought that Chuck won, that he did exactly what he said, that he updated the Bible in cordite and blood, and that no one would ever be the same. For my mother and me, that was true. Nothing was ever the same.

The night I left her forever, my mother, Crissy Varner, stayed in the trailer while I left with Chuck's AR-10, promising to return. After Harlow Mall, we'd kept it hidden. The cops had the Beretta, but we had this—he'd dropped it off at home before his last run, and Crissy had buried it at the base of a hollow tree trunk. I'd shown the tree to Crissy myself: it was where I hid my little toys, the dolls that I'd pulled the hair out of and given waterproof clothing of my own devising, working mainly in ziplock and candy-wrapper fabrics. She hadn't taken the rifle out again until she, until both of us, thought we were ready to use it again as Chuck intended.

Almost ten years after Harlow Mall, I took the rifle from Crissy and hid it in pieces, each of them scraped and scrubbed clean. I was sixteen and doing what I thought I had always had to do: my duty, for my parents, the living one and the dead one. Crissy, alive. Chuck in the ground except for his words and his Great Act, the shooting that had ruled our lives—mine and Crissy's—until I buried the sections of the rifle in deep, widely spaced miniature graves across Stilford, each burial another step away from the trailer I'd shared with Crissy and Chuck's ghost in the vacuum that was my entire life. Until Crissy finally made me realize that I never wanted to kill, or control, anyone. Ever.

Maybe Crissy hadn't known that I wasn't going to come back to her when I left with the rifle in a battered Benetton bag. But she wasn't stupid. That's part of what made Chuck's hold over us so compelling— I knew that I wasn't stupid, and I knew that Crissy wasn't stupid, so it wasn't possible that Chuck's construction of the universe could be entirely wrong. We believed it. We chose his world every day that he was gone, every day that we didn't have to: we followed his code. The code he called Your Life Is Mine.